PENGUIN BOOKS

REMEMBER ME

Remember Me is Lesley Pearse's twelfth book. A number-one bestseller, she is greatly loved around the world, and her novels have sold over 2 million copies in the UK alone. Her seven most recent books, including *Till We Meet Again*, *Father Unknown* and *Trust Me*, are published by Penguin. Lesley lives near Bristol, has three daughters and one grandson.

Remember Me

LESLEY PEARSE

PENGUIN BOOKS

PENGUIN BOOKS

Published by the Penguin Group
Penguin Books Ltd, 80 Strand, London WC2R ORL, England
Penguin Putnam Inc., 375 Hudson Street, New York, New York 10014, USA
Penguin Books Australia Ltd, 250 Camberwell Road,
Camberwell, Victoria 3124, Australia
Penguin Books Canada Ltd, 10 Alcorn Avenue, Toronto, Ontario, Canada M4V 3B2
Penguin Books India (P) Ltd, 11 Community Centre,
Panchsheel Park, New Delhi – 110 017, India
Penguin Books (NZ) Ltd, Cnr Rosedale and Airborne Roads,
Albany, Auckland, New Zealand
Penguin Books (South Africa) (Pty) Ltd, 24 Sturdee Avenue,
Rosebank 2196, South Africa

Penguin Books Ltd, Registered Offices: 80 Strand, London WC2R ORL, England

www.penguin.com

First published by Michael Joseph 2003
Published in Penguin Books 2004

10

Copyright © Lesley Pearse, 2003
All rights reserved

The moral right of the author has been asserted

Typeset by Rowland Phototypesetting Ltd, Bury St Edmunds, Suffolk
Printed in England by Clays Ltd, St Ives plc

To John Roberts, my very own Boswell.
Mere words cannot fully convey my gratitude to you.

Acknowledgements

To Pam Quick in Sydney, New South Wales, not only for all the information, books and pictures you passed on to me about the First Fleet, but for being there for me too. Without your keen interest, generosity with your time, unflagging help and support I could never have finished this book. When I come back to Sydney I owe you a slap-up dinner at least. Bless you.

I read dozens of books in my research for *Remember Me*, but these are the most outstanding ones.

To Brave Every Danger by Judith Cook. Truth is often stranger and more heroic than fiction, and Judith Cook's meticulously researched book on Mary Bryant of Fowey is truly inspiring and a must for anyone with a passion for history.

Fatal Shore by Robert Hughes. A fascinating, fabulous book on Australia's early years.

The First Twelve Years by Peter Taylor. Amazingly informative without being dry or dull. Good pictures too.

Orphans of History by Robert Holden. An often tear-jerking story of the forgotten children of the First Fleet.

The Floating Brothel by Sîan Rees. The story of the transported women who sailed on the *Juliana*. Shockingly informative.

Boswell's Presumptuous Task by Adam Sisman. A wonderful work on James Boswell.

Dr Johnson's London by Liza Picard. Wonderfully readable, an incredibly vivid image of London in the eighteenth century.

English Society in the Eighteenth Century by Roy Porter.

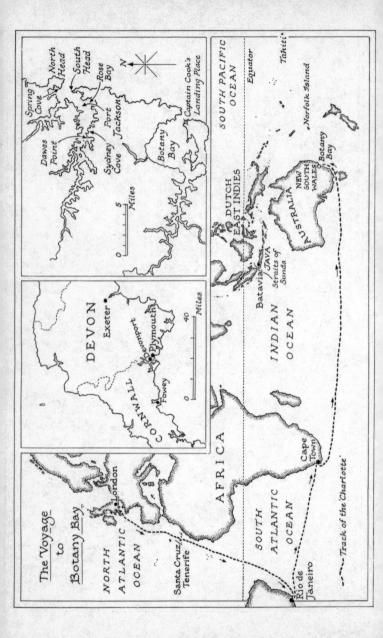

The Voyage to Botany Bay.

NORTH ATLANTIC OCEAN

Santa Cruz, Tenerife

London

DEVON

Exeter

CORNWALL

Fowey

Plymouth

Devonport

40 Miles

AFRICA

SOUTH ATLANTIC OCEAN

Rio de Janeiro

Cape Town

INDIAN OCEAN

Track of the 'Charlotte'

SOUTH PACIFIC OCEAN

Equator

Tahiti

DUTCH EAST INDIES

Batavia

JAVA

Straits of Sunda

AUSTRALIA

NEW SOUTH WALES

Botany Bay

Norfolk Island

N

Spring Cove

North Head

South Head

Rose Bay

Dawes Point

Port Jackson

Sydney Cove

Botany Bay

Captain Cook's Landing Place

5 Miles

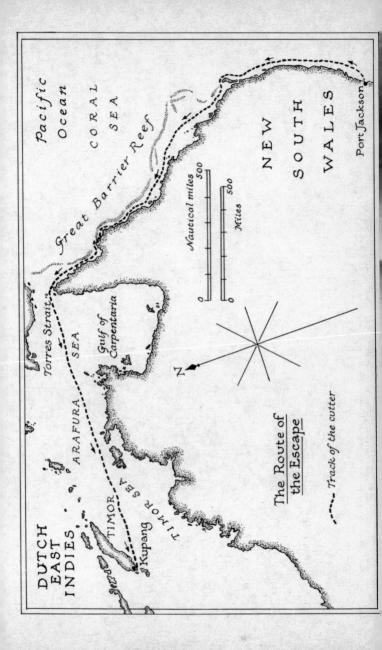

DUTCH
EAST
INDIES

*Pacific
Ocean*

CORAL
SEA

Great Barrier Reef

NEW

SOUTH

WALES

Port Jackson

Torres Strait

ARAFURA
SEA

Gulf of
Carpentaria

TIMOR
SEA

TIMOR

Kupang

Nautical miles
500

Miles
500

N

The Route of
the Escape

— — Track of the cutter

Chapter one

1786

Mary gripped the rail of the dock tightly as the judge came back into the courtroom. The windows were small and dirty, letting in only a meagre light, but there was no mistaking the black cap over his yellowish wig, or the expectant hush from the gallery.

'Mary Broad. You will be taken from this place, back to whence you came, and there you will be hanged by the neck until dead,' he intoned, not even looking directly at her. 'May God have mercy on your soul.'

Mary's stomach lurched and her legs buckled under her. She knew only too well that hanging was the usual punishment for highway robbery, but a small part of her had clung to the belief that the judge would be merciful because she was such a young woman. She should have known better.

It was 20 March 1786, and Mary Broad was just a few weeks short of twenty. She was an average girl in every way, neither particularly tall nor short, not outstandingly pretty but not plain either. The only thing which set her apart from the other people on trial that day in the Lenten

Assizes was her country girl appearance. She had a clear complexion, which even after weeks of incarceration in Exeter Castle still had a faint glow. Her dark curly hair was tied neatly back with a ribbon and her grey worsted dress, though soiled from the gaol, was a plain, serviceable one.

A babble of noise broke out all around her, for the courtroom in Exeter was packed to capacity. Some of those present were friends and relatives of other prisoners to be tried that day, but the majority were mere spectators.

Yet the noise was not one of sympathy, nor outrage at such a severe sentence. Mary hadn't one friend in the whole room. A sea of grimy faces turned towards her, eyes alight with malicious glee, the slight movement wafting up the smell of their unwashed bodies to her nostrils. They wanted a reaction from her, be it tears, anger or a plea for mercy.

She wanted to cry out, to plead for her life, but the defiant streak in her which had led her to rob someone in the first place urged her to hold fast to her dignity if nothing else.

A guard's hand clamped down on her shoulder. It was too late now for anything but prayers.

Mary was barely aware of the ride on the cart back to Exeter Castle, the gaol she'd been held in since she was brought up from Plymouth following her arrest. She hardly noticed the rasp of the iron shackles on her ankles which connected to another heavy band around her waist, her seven fellow prisoners in the cart, or the jeering from the crowds in the streets. All she could think of was that the next time she saw the sky above her would be the day when she was taken to the gallows.

She lifted her face up to the weak afternoon sun. This morning, as she was brought out to go to the Assizes, the spring sunshine had almost blinded her after the darkness of the cells. She had looked about her eagerly, seen new leaves unfurling on the trees, heard pigeons cooing in a mating display, and foolishly taken all that as a good omen.

How wrong she was. She would never see her beloved Cornwall again. Never see her parents or sister Dolly either. All she could hope for was that they would never find out what she'd done. It was better that they should think she'd abandoned them for a new life in Plymouth, or even London, than endure the disgrace of hearing her life had been ended by a hangman's noose.

The sound of sobbing made Mary look at the woman sitting on her left. Her age was impossible to ascertain for her face was ravaged by pock-marks and she clutched a tattered brown cloak around her head to try to conceal it.

'Crying won't do no good,' Mary said, assuming the woman was to hang too. 'At least we know now what's coming to us.'

'I didn't steal anything,' the woman gasped out. 'I swear I didn't. It was someone else and they got away and left me to be blamed.'

Mary had heard that same story over and over again from other prisoners since her arrest in January. She had believed most of them at first, but she was harder now.

'Did you tell them that today?' she asked.

The woman nodded, her tears flowing even faster. 'But they said they had a witness to it.'

Mary had no heart to ask for the full story. She wanted to fill her lungs with clean air, fill her mind with the sights and sounds of the bustling town of Exeter, so that when she got back to the filthy, dark cell she would have some memories to draw on. Hearing this woman's tale of woe would only bring her down even further. Yet her natural sympathy wouldn't let her ignore the poor creature.

'Are you to be hanged too?' she asked.

The woman's head jerked round to look at Mary, surprise registering on her ravaged face. 'No. It was only a mutton pie they said I took.'

'Then you're luckier than me,' Mary sighed.

Once back in the Castle, thrust into a cell with around twenty other prisoners of both sexes, Mary silently found herself a space against the wall, sat down, adjusted the chains from her shackles so she could pull up her knees, wrapped her cloak around her tightly and leaned back to take stock of her situation.

It was a different cell to the one she'd been taken from this morning, better in as much as fresh air was coming in through a very high grille on the wall, the straw on the floor looked marginally cleaner, and the buckets weren't yet overflowing. But it still stank, with an all-pervading stench of dirt, body fluids, vomit, mould and human suffering which she inhaled with every breath.

There was an ominous hush. No one was talking loudly,

4

swearing or screaming abuse at their gaolers, as they had in the previous cell. In fact they were all sitting much as she was, submerged in thought or despair. Mary guessed that meant they were all sentenced to death, and as stunned by it as she was.

She couldn't see Catherine Fryer or Mary Haydon, the girls she'd been caught with, although they'd all been taken together to the Assizes that morning. She had no idea whether they were still back there waiting to be tried, or if they'd escaped with a lighter punishment than her.

Whatever the reason, she was glad they weren't there. She didn't want to remember that but for them she would never have considered robbing anyone.

It was too gloomy to see her other cellmates clearly, the only light coming from a lantern in the corridor the other side of the grilled door. But at a cursory glance, aside from the fact that there were men there too (her previous cell had been all women), they didn't appear very different from those she'd been imprisoned with for the last couple of months.

The age range was wide, from a girl of about sixteen, who was sobbing on an older woman's shoulder, to a man of perhaps fifty or even older. Three of the women might have been whores, judging by their colourful and even quite elegant gowns, but the remainder were very ragged, women with hard faces, bad teeth and stringy hair, and gaunt-faced men staring silently into space.

There were two women from her previous cell. Bridie, in a red gown with a tattered lace collar, had confided in Mary that she'd robbed a sailor while he slept. Peg was much older, one of the very ragged women, but she had steadfastly refused to say anything about her crime.

Mary guessed from the experiences in that cell that however subdued they all were now, within a few hours the naturally dominant types, like Bridie, would rally themselves to take charge. Much of this was bravado – it was necessary to appear strong if you were to survive prison. Fighting, shouting and demanding food or water from the gaolers was one way of sending out a message to your cellmates that you weren't to be pushed around.

Mary wondered if there would be any point in anyone asserting themselves now. She certainly didn't feel inclined to do so herself; all she wanted was to know how many days she had left to live.

Seeing Mary, Bridie hitched up her chains and hobbled across the cell towards her. 'Hanging?' she asked.

Mary nodded. 'You too?'

Bridie squatted down on the straw, her woebegone expression confirming it. 'That bastard of a judge,' she spat. ''E don't know what it's like for us. What good will hanging me do? Who'll look after the old folks now?'

Bridie had told Mary soon after she was brought to Exeter that she'd taken up whoring to keep her old parents from the parish. But there was something about her colourful clothes and even more colourful nature that suggested she hadn't had much of a moral struggle. Yet ever since Mary's first night in prison, Bridie had been kind and protective towards her, and Mary felt she was at heart a good woman.

'I thought you'd get off though, what with yer innocent

face an' all,' Bridie said, reaching out her dirty hand to caress Mary's cheek lightly. 'What happened?'

'The lady we robbed was in court,' Mary said sadly. 'She pointed me out.'

Bridie sighed in sympathy. 'Well, let's hope they get it over quick. There ain't nothin' worse than waiting to get a body down.'

Much later that night, Mary lay on the filthy straw-strewn floor among her fellow prisoners, who all appeared to be sleeping soundly, and found her thoughts slip back to her home and family at Fowey in Cornwall. She knew now that she had been born more fortunate than many of the women she'd met since leaving there.

Her father, William Broad, was a mariner, and although there had been hard times when he had no work, somehow he'd always managed to make sure his family never went hungry or lacked a fire. Mary could remember being cuddled up in bed with her sister Dolly, hearing the sea crashing against the harbour walls, yet feeling safe and secure, for however long her father was away at sea, he always left enough money to tide them over until he returned again.

Just thinking of Fowey with its tiny cottages and cobbled streets made a lump come up in her throat. The bustling harbour and town were never dull, for she knew everyone, and the Broads were a well-respected family. Grace, Mary's mother, set great store by respectability; she kept the tiny cottage spotlessly clean, and tried to instil in her daughters her high standards in cooking, housekeeping and sewing. Dolly, Mary's older sister, was the dutiful, obedient one, happy to follow her mother's example, and her dreams were only of finding a husband and having children and a home of her own.

Mary did not share Dolly's dreams. It was often said by friends and neighbours that she should have been a boy. She was clumsy with a needle and household tasks bored her. She was happiest when her father took her out sailing and fishing, for she felt at one with the sea and could handle a boat almost as well as he. She preferred male company too, for men and boys talked of exciting things, of lands overseas, of war, smuggling, and their work in the tin mines. She had no time for giggling, simpering girls who cared for nothing but gossip and the price of hair ribbon.

It was a thirst for adventure which made her want to leave Fowey, and she fully believed she could make her mark upon the world if she was just somewhere else. At the time Mary left, Dolly had said somewhat unkindly that it was just because she'd never had a sweetheart, and she was afraid no one would ever want her.

That wasn't true. Mary had no real desire for marriage. In fact she felt pity rather than envy for the girls she'd grown up with who were already saddled with two or three children. She knew that their lives grew tougher with each new mouth to feed, that they lived in fear of losing their husbands through drowning at sea or in an accident in the mines. But then life was hard for everyone in Cornwall, unless you were gentry. Work was either fishing, mining or going into service.

Dolly was in service with the Treffrys of Fowey as an under-housemaid, but Mary had stubbornly refused to follow her example. She didn't want to spend her days emptying slop pails and laying fires, at the beck and call of a hard-faced housekeeper. She'd seen no future in that. But the alternative was gutting and salting fish, and although she'd done that since childhood, and enjoyed the freedom to chatter as she worked, and the camaraderie of her workmates, no one ever got rich gutting fish. You smelt disgusting, and it was freezing in the winter. Mary would look at the bowed backs and gnarled fingers of the women who'd spent their whole life doing it, and knew it meant early death.

She had heard about Plymouth from the sailors. They said there were fine shops and big houses there, and opportunities for anyone with determination. She thought she might get work in one of the shops, for even if she couldn't read and write, she could add up quicker than her father.

Her parents had mixed feelings about her leaving. On the one hand they wanted to keep her at home in Fowey, but times were hard and they were struggling to support her. Perhaps, too, they hoped that a couple of years away from them in a respectable trade would settle her down, that she'd find a sweetheart and eventually marry.

Mary couldn't wait to get away, yet now as she lay on the hard cold floor of the prison cell and recalled the day when she left her home, she was filled with remorse.

It was very early in the morning, a beautiful July day without a cloud in the azure sky, and the sun was already warm. Her father had sailed off for France just a few days earlier, and Mary had insisted that only Dolly should come down to the harbour to see her off. She didn't want any further lectures from her mother about behaving like a lady on the boat, or being wary of strangers.

Her mother had never been given to displays of emotion, so it was a little unnerving as Mary went to kiss her cheek at the door to find herself suddenly being hugged tightly.

'Be a good girl,' her mother said, her voice cracking. 'Say your prayers and don't get into any mischief.'

Mary remembered how she hurried away with Dolly, giggling with excitement. It was only as she got to the end of the narrow street and glanced back that she saw her mother was still standing in the doorway, watching them. She looked so old, small and oddly vulnerable, for she hadn't yet braided her hair up for the day. It was as grey as her dress, making her almost disappear into the stone of the cottage. Even without being able to see her face clearly, Mary knew she was crying. Yet Grace still managed to wave a cheerful goodbye.

'I don't know why you think Plymouth will be better than here,' Dolly said waspishly as they got down to the harbour and saw the boat waiting. 'I bet you could go right round the world and never find anywhere so pretty.'

'Don't be like that,' Mary retorted, thinking Dolly was jealous. Her sister was far prettier than her, her eyes as blue as the sky above, her complexion clear and pink, and she had a dear little upturned nose. But Mary had a feeling that Dolly often wished she was more daring, and perhaps resented that her life was already mapped out for her.

'I can't help it,' Dolly replied in a small voice. 'I'm going to miss you so much. Don't stay away too long.'

Mary remembered how she'd hugged her sister then, and said something about how she would make her fortune and send for Dolly to join her. If she had known that was going to be the last time she'd see her, she would have told her how much she loved her. Yet that sunny morning she couldn't get on the boat fast enough. It didn't even cross her mind that she might fail in Plymouth.

What Mary hadn't anticipated was that hundreds of girls came off the boats in Plymouth every week looking for work, and it was the literate, the prettiest and the ones with good references who got the best positions. All she landed was a job in a seamen's ale house, washing the pots and scrubbing the floors. Her bed consisted of a few sacks in the cellar.

It was around Michaelmas when the landlord threw her out. He said she'd stolen some money, but that wasn't true. All she'd done was refuse to let him have his way with her. Without a reference she couldn't get another job, and she was too proud to go home to Fowey to hear 'I told you so'.

The moment she met Thomas Coogan down by the harbour, she knew that she was on the way to hell in a handcart. Surely no decent young woman would allow a complete stranger to buy her a dinner, let him hold her hand, and not run a mile when he suggested she stayed with him until she found another job? But there was something about his lean, bony face, the sparkle in his blue eyes, and the stories he told her of voyages to France and Spain that captivated her.

Thomas wasn't bound by any of the rules Mary had been brought up with. He cared nothing for the King, Church, or indeed any authority. He had a gentlemanly manner and was fastidious about his appearance, and he was more fun to be with than anyone she'd ever met before.

Maybe it was partly because he seemed to desire her so much, to hold her and kiss her. No man had ever wanted her that way before, they saw her just as a friend. Thomas said she was beautiful, that her grey eyes were like a brewing storm and her lips made to be kissed.

That first day with him was utterly magical. It rained hard and he took her into a tavern by the harbour and dried her cloak in front of the fire. He introduced her to rum too. She didn't like the taste, or the way it burned her throat, but she did like the way he leaned forward and licked her lips lightly with the point of his tongue. 'It tastes like nectar on you,' he whispered. 'Drink up, my lovely, it will warm you all over.'

He made her feel so wanton, her whole body seemed to glow, and it wasn't just the rum. It was his wit, the feel of his hand in hers, the suggestion that she was on the brink of something dangerous yet wonderful too.

With hindsight she ought to have suspected there was something amiss when he never attempted to bed her. He kissed her passionately and told her he loved her, but it never went any further than that. At the time Mary had foolishly believed his caution was out of love and respect for her, but it was only later she discovered the truth.

Thomas Coogan cared for no one but himself. He was a pick-pocket, and when he'd spotted her crying down by the harbour, he knew her well-scrubbed, innocent country girl appearance would make her an ideal accomplice. All it took was a few sympathetic words to win her trust.

It never crossed Mary's mind in the first few weeks after meeting him that as they stood arm in arm looking in shop windows or strolled around the market, he was often engaged in helping himself to someone's pocket-book, fob-watch or other valuable with his spare hand. She was too enamoured with his charm, excited by his interesting friends and acquaintances, and bowled over by his generosity to her to study him closely.

By the time she did become aware of it, she was so entrenched in his easy, fun way of life that he could have told her he was a grave robber and she wouldn't have turned a hair. When he disappeared just after Christmas, leaving her in the dwelling-house he'd taken her to, she was inconsolable.

The chances were that he'd been caught by the constables, and that was what made her fall in with Mary Haydon and Catherine Fryer. She didn't want to lose face with these two cut-purses, whom Thomas had held in such high esteem. They appeared so worldly, so very daring, and she needed money to pay the rent on Thomas's room for when he came back.

At first she was just a lookout while the other two

snipped off purses in the crowded streets and markets. Sometimes she caused a diversion by pretending to faint or claiming that she'd had her own purse snatched. But the day came when Catherine said it was time she took on some of the danger herself, and when they saw the small, neatly dressed woman walking home through the main street with her arms full of parcels, it appeared to be the perfect initiation.

Maybe if Mary hadn't been so anxious to prove her courage, she would merely have tripped the woman up and sped off with just one of her parcels. But instead she grabbed the woman's pretty silk hat with one hand, and scooped up everything she dropped in alarm, throwing the parcels to the other Mary and Catherine before running for it. Unluckily for them, people gave chase, cornered them in an alley and called for the constables.

Most of the details of Mary's arrest and imprisonment in Plymouth were hazy to her now, for the journey to Exeter later on eclipsed everything else. It took four days in an open-topped cart where she was shackled to three other women, two of whom were her supposed friends but berated her most of the way for getting them caught too. It was January, and the icy wind swept across the bleak moors, almost cutting them in half with its ferocity. If they wanted to relieve themselves, all the women had to get down together, with the guard leering at them. Every step was torture, for the shackles dug into their tender skin and they weren't yet practised at moving together. At nights they were thrown into a stable at an inn, with bread and water the only nourishment they received.

Mary thought she would die of the cold, in fact she hoped fervently that she would, if only to shut out the scorn and ridicule of her companions and the knowledge that her crime, highway robbery, was a hanging offence.

On her first night at Exeter Castle it was Bridie who had comforted her and assured her she would become accustomed to the rats, lice, dirt, stale bread and using a slop pail in front of everyone. Mary supposed that she had now, in as much as she accepted that was all part and parcel of prison life and she deserved punishment for what she'd done. But she couldn't accept that she was to die in a few days' time, and would never be free to walk country lanes, to watch the sea breaking on the shore, and see the sun set again.

She wept then, for failing her parents and bringing shame to the family, and for not listening to her conscience when she knew that stealing was wrong.

It was a well-known fact that as many as half of those sentenced to death would get some sort of reprieve. In the next three days Mary's fellow prisoners talked of nothing else, everyone hoping they would be among the lucky ones.

But Mary was no fool. She knew you needed friends on the outside, a concerned and kindly master or mistress, a member of the clergy, or even a friend with money to plead for you. As the hours and days ticked slowly by, it became clear which of her companions were that fortunate. They were the ones who got food, drink, money and even clean clothes sent in.

Mary looked enviously at the young girl and the woman she knew now to be her aunt, as they ate hot meat pies brought in by one of the gaolers. They had been charged with theft from a lodging-house, but had been protesting their innocence ever since their arrest. Now, judging by the pies and the blankets they'd been given, maybe they had been telling the truth, for someone on the outside was obviously working for their release.

Yet some of the prisoners, even those without any hope of reprieve, had become quite jovial in the last couple of days. Maybe it was because in their eyes a quick death was preferable to the misery of a long prison sentence, or a lingering death through gaol fever. There was also a certain amount of status in being hanged, for huge crowds gathered to watch. If they could go to their death with dignity and courage and get the admiration of the watching rabble, they might become heroic figures, maybe even a legend.

Dick Sullion was one man who felt this way, and he had cheered Mary considerably with his humour and his philosophy of life. Like her, he had been charged with High Toby, the common name for highway robbery. But Dick's crime fitted the description more accurately than Mary's did, for he'd lain in wait on isolated roads for unwary travellers, taking not only their valuables but their horses too.

He was a big man, close to six feet, with a ruddy face, wide shoulders and an irrepressible sense of humour. The first morning after her trial, Mary had woken to hear him singing some bawdy ale-house song about going to the scaffold drunk. She had of course assumed he was drunk then, for those who had money or goods to bribe their gaolers could be inebriated all day and night. But as she sat up, he smiled at her, and his blue eyes were clear and bright.

'No sense in lying around moping,' he said as if to explain himself. 'I've had a good life, and I reckon it's better to hang than lose my wits and looks in a place like this.'

'Some of us would rather sleep than think on that,' she retorted.

Mary had learned in her first few days of imprisonment back in January that it was advisable to befriend someone tough and wily as a protector, and as Dick appeared to fit the bill in every way, she allowed him to move closer to her, and talked to him.

She soon discovered that Dick had no money left to buy drink or extra food. He told her he'd blown all he had in the first few weeks before his trial. But even if he couldn't make her last few days more comfortable in a physical sense, he was strong, tough and knew the ropes, and his chatter and laughter cheered her.

Dick was Cornish too. It was good to be able to talk about home with him, and it wasn't long before she told him how she felt about her crime and letting her family down.

'Ain't no good worrying about that,' he said, his local dialect as thick and reassuring as her father's. 'We all do what we gotta do to survive. It's the government's fault we've come to this. The high taxes, the Enclosures Acts, they rob us blind at every turn and live in palaces while us lot starve. I took from those who could afford it, so did you. Serves 'em right, I say.'

Mary, who had been brought up to be honest and God-fearing, didn't entirely agree with him about that, but she wasn't going to say so. 'Aren't you afraid of dying though?' she asked instead.

He shrugged. 'Been too close to it so many times, it don't have no meaning any more. What's hanging compared with a naval flogging? I had my first when I was only sixteen, now that's summat to be scared of, pain so bad you cry out to death. Hanging's quick. Don't you worry, little one, I'll hold your hand right up to the end.'

Mary took some comfort in Dick's words. She made up her mind that if she was to die, she'd do so bravely.

Four days after her trial, around ten in the morning, the gaoler came to the cell door and called out for Nancy and Anne Brown. They were the aunt and niece accused of robbing a dwelling-house. He said they had been acquitted due to new evidence and were free to leave.

Despite her own predicament, Mary was delighted for them, and got up to hug and kiss them goodbye. She'd talked to the two women at some length in the previous couple of days and was sure they were as innocent as they claimed to be. They had barely left the cell when the gaoler called out a further four names, three men's and Mary's.

'You lot come with me,' he said curtly.

Mary turned to Dick in dismay, thinking she was to be led to the gallows then and there.

Dick put one big hand on her shoulder and squeezed it. 'Don't reckon it's that,' he said confidently. 'At the end of each quarter session they go through the list and pick out likely folk for transportation. My guess is that's what they want you for.'

The gaoler roared at them to follow him, giving Mary no time to say a proper goodbye to either Dick or Bridie.

As she shuffled along the dark passage behind William, Able and John, her fellow cellmates, their shackles clanking against the rough stone floor, she heard Dick's voice boom out behind her. 'Seven years, that's all it is till you're free, my little one. Be brave and strong and you'll see the end of it.'

Able, a sickly-looking man in his thirties, glanced back at Mary. 'What does he know?' he said dourly. 'I heard tell they ain't sending no more felons to the Americas now the war's over.'

Mary had heard the same thing too while she was in Plymouth. If it was true, it would be a relief, for she'd been brought up with horror stories passed on by sailors of the terrors that lay in store in that far-off land. Convicts there were treated the same as the black slaves, starved, beaten, made to work on the land till they dropped dead from exhaustion. Yet if not to America, where would they be sent, and would it be any better?

Once out in the yard, Mary saw other prisoners lined up, including Mary Haydon and Catherine Fryer, her old partners in crime. There were five women in all, and some fifteen or sixteen men. Mary Haydon tossed her head and looked the other way when she saw Mary, but Catherine glowered at her, so clearly they still held her responsible for their plight.

A judge, or at least Mary assumed that's what he was, by his wig and gown, came down the few steps into the yard, flanked by a couple of other men, then read aloud from a piece of parchment.

Mary could make no sense of what he was reading. She heard 'At Assizes and general delivery of the gaol of our Lord the King,' then what sounded like a string of 'Sirs' who were all unknown to her. It wasn't until she heard her own name mentioned that she began to listen more intently. At the words, 'His Majesty has been graciously pleased to extend the royal mercy on them,' Mary's heart leaped. But as the judge read on, her heart sank again, for it was as Dick had said, mercy on condition they be transported for seven years.

After the judge had left the prison yard, leaving the prisoners there alone with the guards, they turned to one another, their delight that they weren't to be hanged mingling with an acute fear of what transportation would mean.

'I never met anyone who ever came back from it,' one man said gloomily. 'They must have all died.'

'I know a man that did come back,' another man retorted loudly. 'He had money in his pockets too.'

Mary tried to make sense of the babble of conflicting opinions around her. While she personally felt that a seven-year sentence, however hard, had to be better than hanging, every single person in the yard appeared to be more knowledgeable on the subject than she was, so there was no point in her volunteering that opinion. But as the woman standing next to her began to cry, she put her arm around her to comfort her.

'It's got to be better than dying,' she said softly. 'We'll be out in the fresh air, we might even be able to escape.'

Able, who was standing in front of her, must have heard what she said for he turned to her, a scornful expression on his face. 'That's if we don't die on the voyage,' he said.

Mary thought privately that he wasn't long for this world anyway. He had a hacking cough, he was very thin and the only one of them in the cell who showed no eagerness when the daily mouldy bread was dished out.

'As long as I'm still breathing, then I'll still hope,' she retorted staunchly.

Less than an hour later, doors in the prison yard opened and two large horse-drawn carts were led in.

The prisoners had all pondered on why they had been left out in the yard, but no one had anticipated they would be moved from Exeter Castle that same day. But that was what was planned, and without any further delay, they were chained together into groups of five and ordered up on to the carts. Once again, Mary found herself alongside Catherine and Mary. On the other side of her was the woman she'd comforted earlier, whose name was Elizabeth Cole, and another called Elizabeth Baker. Behind their bench were five men, one of them Able.

For the first hour, as the cart slowly trundled its way out through Exeter, Catherine Fryer and Mary Haydon kept up a volley of abuse towards Mary.

'It's all your fault,' Catherine repeated again and again. 'You brought us to this.'

Elizabeth Cole, who went by the name of Bessie, squeezed Mary's hand in sympathy, and finally called a halt to it.

'Shut yer mouths, you two,' she snapped at them. 'We're all in this together now, whether we like it or not. There ain't no sense in blaming Mary, you'd have been caught before long anyway. Besides, none of the rest of us wants to hear all that stuff.'

Mary was touched by Bessie's intervention. She was an odd-looking woman, red-haired and fat, with a cast in one eye and several teeth missing, but the fact she'd been brave enough to speak out suggested she wasn't as downtrodden as she looked.

There was an echo of agreement from the men sitting behind them, and perhaps that finally persuaded the two women to stop, for they lapsed into silence.

After a little while one of the men in the back prodded Mary. 'Sweet-talk the guards into telling you where we're heading,' he whispered.

'Why me?' she whispered back.

'You're the bonniest,' he replied.

Up until that moment Mary had fully believed she had absolutely no assets – no money or property she could bribe anyone with, no influential friends. All she had was the clothes she was wearing and they were worn and soiled. But as she glanced at the row of women, she saw she was younger, healthier and stronger than all of them.

Mary and Catherine had been living by theft for years before she met them. Back then she'd been fooled by their gaudy clothes into thinking they were superior to her in every way. But cheap silk didn't wear well, not in prison, and their pinched features and grey skin, the hollow look in their eyes and their gutter language showed up what they really were. As for Bessie and Elizabeth, while she didn't yet know what crimes they had committed, or anything of their family background, they both had that worn-out appearance she had observed so often among the very poorest back home in Fowey.

All at once she saw a chance for herself. She was young and strong, no man had spoiled her, she knew she had a quicker mind than most, and she had determination.

She waited until Bessie asked to relieve herself, and once all the women had climbed down from the cart, Mary positioned herself so that she shielded her squatting friend from the guard with her skirt, and smiled warmly at him.

'Where are you taking us?' she asked. 'Is it back to the prison in Plymouth, or straight to a boat for the Americas?'

He was a hard-looking man, with brown, broken teeth and a battered hat pulled down over his slanty eyes.

'You're bound for the prison hulks at Devonport,' he said with an evil grin. 'Don't reckon you'll get much beyond there.'

Mary gasped involuntarily. She might not have seen a

prison hulk but she knew their evil reputation. They were old warships, moored in estuaries and creeks, the government's answer to overcrowding in prisons. The responsibility for running them was passed over to private individuals whose only interest was making as much money as possible from each prisoner. It was said that the unlucky felons who got sent to them would die either of starvation or of overwork within the first year. For the sideline of these notorious hell-holes was that the prisoners were forced to do slave labour on land, usually building 'hards' along the river bank.

'I didn't think they sent women there,' she said, her voice trembling.

'Times are a'changing,' he grinned. 'You'd better pretty yourself up if you want to make it off there alive.'

Mary gulped and looked him in the eye. She knew gaolers and guards were punished too harshly to dare let anyone escape, however 'nice' a prisoner was to them. But he probably thought she was stupid enough to be ignorant of this and hoped she might make up to him imagining he would help her in return.

'But the judge said it was transportation.' She forced herself to squeeze out a few tears.

'They mean it to be,' he said, his voice softening. 'But they can't send no one to the Americas since the war. They tried Africa, but that didn't work. There's talk of a place called Botany Bay, but that's on the other side of the world.'

Mary vaguely remembered the sailors in the ale house she'd once worked in talking about a man called Captain

Cook who had claimed for England a country that was on the other side of the world. She wished now she'd listened properly, but at the time it held as little importance for her as whether King George was really mad, or what grand ladies wore to balls in London.

'Do you think that's where we're bound then?' she asked.

He shrugged and scowled at the other women who were crowding around Mary to hear what he was saying. 'Get back on the cart,' he said curtly. 'We've got a fair few miles to cover before dark.'

Once back on the cart, Mary decided there was no point in thinking upon anything more than the present. It might be uncomfortable in the cart, but it was better to be out in the spring sunshine than in a stinking gaol. She would keep herself poised for an opportunity for escape.

She doubted there was any hope of that before Devonport. If the guards on this journey kept to the same routine as those on the way from Plymouth to Exeter, she and her companions would remain shackled together constantly.

But there was a faint possibility that the chains would be removed when they had to get into the small boat to be rowed out to the hulks. If so, she could jump out and swim for it. She smiled inwardly. It was a very faint hope, for surely any guard worth his salt would anticipate such an attempt, but then few people knew how to swim, even sailors like her father couldn't. The thought of swimming was pleasing, to be able to wash off the prison stink and make for a stretch of coastline she knew well. It was worth any risk, and even if she couldn't do it then, maybe she could jump from the side of the hulk at night.

But as the afternoon shadows lengthened and it grew colder, Mary's spirits began to sink again. Even if she could escape, where would she make for? She couldn't go back to Cornwall, she'd be caught again in no time. And how would she get anywhere else with no money, wearing filthy clothes and boots with holes in them?

By dusk Mary was in too much pain to think beyond lying down. Even the slightest movement from herself or one of her companions made the iron shackles bite into her ankles. She had torn a strip off her petticoat to act as a bandage beneath the iron, but the cotton was stiff with dried blood now, and it rasped against the wounds rather than protecting them. She had hunger pains in her stomach, her back was so stiff she doubted she could walk, and she was shivering with cold.

Four days later, when the cart eventually reached Devonport, Mary's companions were too deeply demoralized even to react to their first sight of the prison ship moored out in the river. It had been raining solidly for the past two days, and they were all soaked through to the skin. Many of them were feverish and everyone was exhausted through lack of sleep due to the cold in the barns and sheds they'd been locked into overnight.

There had been no conversation on the cart today. The only sounds were groans, sneezing, coughing, sniffing and the clank of chains as they vainly attempted to get more comfortable. Able was now seriously ill, unable to sit upright, and with each strained cough he brought up blood.

'That's yer new home, the *Dunkirk*,' the guard said, turning in his seat to grin maliciously as he pointed at the old hulk moored out in the river. 'She ain't a very pretty ship, that's for sure, but then you lot ain't so pretty either.'

Mary had suffered as much as her companions, but whether it was because she was the youngest and the most healthy at the outset, or just because she had kept her mind active by thinking about escape, she appeared to be the only one affected by the sight of the hulk.

With its masts cut down to mere stumps and surrounded by wispy sea mist, it had the eerie look of an ancient wreck waiting for one good storm to dismember it. But worse still than its appearance was the putrid stench wafting from it on the wind.

Mary was already shivering so violently that her teeth were chattering, but she felt an even icier chill run down her spine, and her empty stomach lurched with nausea. This, she sensed, was going to be real hell, a hundred times worse than Exeter Castle.

She thought she'd been in hell there, and was glad when they'd first left, delighting in the fresh air and sunshine. But all too soon she'd found herself wishing she was back in the Castle. Late the previous night, cold, wet and hungry, every bone in her body screaming in pain, she would even have accepted a noose being put round her neck to end it all. Now it seemed there was even more horror in store for her.

'Ain't no use looking like that,' the guard said, and leaned back in his seat to give Mary a poke with the stick. He'd already struck several of them when they took too long getting off and on the cart. 'That's the wages of sin out there. You lot deserve it.'

A few days earlier Mary would have cursed him, spat in his face or even lashed out at him, but she had no fight left in her.

'Are we to be taken out there now?' she asked instead, her quick mind telling her she'd better keep on the right side of him.

'No, it's too late,' he said, touching the horses with the whip to get them to move. 'You got another night in a warehouse first.'

It wasn't just the occupants of the two carts from Exeter who spent the night in the warehouse. They had hardly got inside and slumped down on to the dirt floor when the doors opened again and another couple of dozen people joined them.

They were in an even worse state than Mary's party, having come all the way from Bristol. Their clothes were mere rags, they all looked feverish, and gangrene had clearly taken a hold of a gaping wound in one of the men's legs, for the smell was unmistakable.

There was a feeble attempt at conversation, questions asked about friends who had been incarcerated in Exeter Castle and Bristol's Bridewell, but the main thing everyone was concerned about was how long they would be kept in the prison ship before being transported.

'I heard a party escaped from Gravesend,' one fierce-looking man from Bristol claimed. 'The guards opened fire on them and killed a couple, but the rest got away. Since then they've kept everyone in chains.'

Bessie, sitting next to Mary, began to cry. 'We might just as well been hanged,' she sobbed out. 'I can't take no more.'

The same thought was in Mary's head too, but faced with Bessie's utter dejection she swept it away. 'We will be all right,' she insisted, putting her arms around the woman and hugging her tightly. 'We're just cold, wet and hungry now, we can't think straight. In a day or two everything will look different.'

'You're so brave,' Bessie whispered. 'Aren't you scared too?'

'No,' Mary replied without a second thought. 'Not now I know I'm not going to be hanged.'

Later that night as Mary lay in a huddle with the other women, desperately trying to draw some warmth from their bodies, she realized she really wasn't scared. She was angry that people could treat others so cruelly, ashamed of the crime that had brought her to this, apprehensive about what would come next, but not scared. In fact, when she thought about it, she'd never been fearful of anything. She had taught herself to swim at six by just plunging into the sea. After she'd discovered she could keep afloat, the sea held no terrors for her. Nor did anything else. She was the one who always took dares, found risk exciting. Even when she first found out how

Thomas made a living she wasn't horrified – it just seemed daring, a bit of a lark.

She remembered then how her father had always remarked on how sharp she was. She had always been much smarter than Dolly and her friends of a similar age. She grasped things quickly, was curious about how things worked, and retained the information. She could almost hear her father boasting to the neighbours that Fowey was too dull for Mary, and that he had no doubt she'd come home one day having made her fortune.

How was he going to hold his head up when her recorded crime and punishment was seen in the *Western Flyer*? He couldn't read himself, but there were plenty of people in Fowey who could and would be only too glad to pass on such a shocking piece of news.

Knowing she was only about forty miles from home brought on an unbearable pang of homesickness. She could imagine her mother sitting on a stool in front of the fire, some mending in her hands. Mary took after her in looks, the same thick curly hair, which she braided tightly round her head, and the same grey eyes. When Mary was small she could remember her mother undoing the braids at night, running her fingers through them till her hair fell in a dark shiny storm on her shoulders. It transformed her from being just an ordinary woman into a beauty, and Mary and Dolly often asked why she didn't leave it loose for everyone to admire.

'Vanity is a deadly sin,' she'd reply, yet she always smiled as if it pleased her to have a beautiful secret, unseen by anyone but her own family. She kept her feelings secret too, and the girls had learned from a very early age to gauge them purely by her actions. When she was angry she banged pots and poked the fire vigorously; when worried she was silent. Her way of showing affection was no more than a tender stroke of the face or a squeeze of the shoulder. Yet now that Mary knew she would never see her again, those little gestures seemed so precious and important.

She remembered how her mother had hugged her as she left home that last morning in Fowey. She hadn't really hugged her back, for she was impatient to leave. The last memory her mother would have of her was that. A daughter who went off giggling carelessly. Never to be seen again.

Chapter two

Thankfully the rain had stopped when the prisoners were ordered out of the warehouse the following morning. But the sky was still grey, with a keen wind blowing off the river which made them all huddle together for warmth.

Breakfast had been nothing more than water and a lump of stale bread, and as Mary looked across at the prison ship *Dunkirk*, and saw it really was as decrepit as it had appeared at dusk yesterday, she guessed the provisions there would be no better.

Yet her spirits were a little higher than on the previous day. Despite her wet clothes, she had slept quite well, and at least there was no further travelling today. She thought escape was out of the question for the time being. Apart from her shackles, which she now doubted would be removed, the quay was busy with watchful Marines, all carrying muskets.

Dozens of boats of all sizes were bobbing around on the water, ferrying passengers across the river and carrying goods to the bigger ships anchored at deep water. Mary couldn't smell the prison ship today, but whether that was because the wind had changed, or she had imagined the smell last night, she couldn't guess. It was good to breathe in the salty air, and if she ignored her fellow prisoners and her hunger, and just drank in the sights, sounds and smells, it was almost like being back in Fowey.

At midday Mary was still waiting on the quay, still chained to her four companions. So far several small groups of male prisoners had been rowed out to the *Dunkirk*, and they had watched them climb up the ladder to the deck, then disappear from view. But the women's interest in this procedure had long since waned. Most were trying to improve their appearance, combing or plaiting their hair, attending to wounds on their ankles from the chains, and any who were carrying belongings were sifting through them, sorting out another dress or petticoat.

Mary had no belongings beyond a comb, and that had been given to her by another prisoner at Exeter, so her grooming could go no further than trying to remove as many lice as possible from her hair. They had been provided with a bucket of water to wash their faces and hands that morning, but she longed to be able to strip off her dirty clothes and wash herself completely. She hadn't done that since before her arrest, and she felt she must stink.

None of the other women seemed that concerned about their filthy state, but then Mary had discovered almost as soon as she left home that the high standard of cleanliness her mother had instilled in her was rare. When she confided in Bessie about how she felt, the other woman looked at her askance. 'We can't look that bad,' she said. 'Those Marines over there are giving us the glad eye.'

Mary glanced at the group of men surreptitiously and observed that she was being singled out for particular attention from them. She thought that red jackets, well-fitting white breeches and highly polished boots gave almost any man, however homely-looking, an unfair advantage over civilians. But she wasn't going to delude herself that they were looking at her because she was outstandingly attractive.

Mary had been around seamen all her life, and she knew the first thing they did when they got off a ship was look for a woman. Mostly they landed up with whores, and with that came the near certainty of disease.

These Marines were in a slightly different position to seamen. They would be guarding the prisoners, both male and female, here and on the transport ship later. Mary guessed they knew they'd get little if any shore leave. It stood to reason they were all hoping that amongst this ragged, demoralized bunch of women, there would be some eager to meet their sexual needs. A young, fresh-faced and disease-free country girl would be their ideal. Mary thought she'd sooner throw herself off the *Dunkirk* in her chains than be used that way.

It was mid-afternoon before Mary's group were rowed over to the hulk. The chains linking them together had been removed, but they were still shackled from their ankles to their waists. As they drew closer to the prison ship, Mary saw the sides were green and slimy with weed, and the smell of human effluent gradually increased until the women were gagging.

Once up the slippery ladder, they were lined up to be examined and measured, and their crime recorded.

'Mary Broad,' a young Marine called out, and ordered her to stand in front of a rule marked on the broken-off mast. 'Five feet four,' he called out to another man who was recording it. 'Grey eyes, black hair, no visible scars. Crime highway robbery. Seven years' transportation.'

As soon as the whole group had been similarly dealt with, and each of them been handed a worn, stinking blanket, a hatch was opened and seamen pushed them roughly through it, down a steep companionway. Bessie tripped on her shackles and fell the last few feet, letting out a cry of pain. They were in a narrow area which appeared to lead on to the guards' quarters, then another hatch was opened.

The stench that burst out hit the women like walking into a brick wall, and they all moved back involuntarily, horror on every face. Each one of them had grown used to filth in all its forms in the past few weeks, but this was something far beyond anything they'd experienced previously.

'Get in there,' the guard shouted, hitting at them with a stick to make them climb down the stairs. 'You'll soon get used to it. We have.'

Mary resisted, but the guard hit her on the shoulder and forced her down through the hatch into what must have been the hold when the vessel was still sailing. The first thing she glimpsed was a sea of ghostly white faces, and when her eyes grew more used to the gloom, she saw a series of wooden shelves which were to be their beds, four women to each. There was some air and light though, coming from open hatches on the seaward side of the ship and a further grille at the far end through which Mary could just make out the male prisoners' quarters. The evil smell came from the floor, which was awash with the contents of overflowing slop buckets. Clearly this was one place which was never cleaned.

Mary realized this meant that rats, bugs and lice would be living here in their hundreds with the women. Just to look at their haggard grey faces, stringy hair and bony bodies was proof that the diet was one of starvation. Fever could sweep round in one night and under these conditions would claim them all.

She thought she would be lucky if she survived long enough to be transported.

An hour or two later Mary was as despairing as everyone else. All around her was moaning, groaning, crying and the occasional demented scream from a woman who appeared to have lost her wits. One woman was suckling a newborn baby, and Mary was told it had been delivered down here by the other women.

The beams were too low for them to stand up, so there was no alternative but to sit or lie on the wooden shelves. When the evening meal, a thin floury soup and stale bread, was brought in, the women fought to get it, and by the time Mary managed to reach the pot, everything was gone. The rats didn't even wait for total darkness to fall, they scuttled along the beams and under the bed shelves, and even jumped across bodies.

But to Mary, the most terrifying prospect was that she could expect nothing better. She had learned they were never allowed up on deck, their quarters were never cleaned, they couldn't wash their clothes, and the slop buckets were emptied only once a day.

She fell asleep eventually, tucked between Bessie on the inside, closest to the ship's hull, and a girl called Nancy who was only fourteen. Taking up the outside position on their shelf was Anne, a woman of over fifty.

Mary's last thought before sleep overcame her was that there had to be some way to escape. The other women had insisted there wasn't, but from what she'd observed of them, they were all dull-witted.

She would find a way.

Over the next few days Mary watched and listened to her fellow prisoners. While her whole being wanted to hammer on the door, scream for release, even to insist that she'd rather be hanged than endure this, she knew she had to control herself. By staying quiet, learning about the running of the hulk and observing the other women, she would arm herself with knowledge.

She noted that many of the women were so deeply immersed in their misery that they barely moved from their sleeping places and hardly spoke at all, and she guessed they hoped that death would come speedily to release them.

At first Mary had every sympathy with them, but as she began slowly to accept her imprisonment and get to know those women who still had a spark of life and hope in them, so her feelings for the remainder turned to scorn and irritation.

Almost all of the women who talked and even found something to laugh about now and then had been convicted of theft. Nancy, the fourteen-year-old, had taken some food home to her family from the house in Bodmin where she was a scullery maid. Anne had taken a dress from the laundry where she worked in Truro. There was a woman who had acted as a look-out for a cut-purse, and another had helped herself to a blanket left out on a washing-line to air. Yet another had stolen a couple of silver teaspoons. None of the women were hardened criminals, they had all committed opportunist crimes, out of need.

When Mary admitted she was convicted of High Toby, she saw awe on the faces of her audience. Back in Exeter Castle, she had learned the hierarchy of crime, and a highway robber was at the top of the pile. To Mary it seemed a little absurd that snatching a hat and parcels should be considered in the same light as waylaying a stage-coach. But she supposed she had technically robbed on the highway, as opposed to stealing from a shop or dwelling-house.

While she knew that in reality she was exactly the same as most of these women, just another country girl who had fallen by the wayside, she saw immediately that it would be smarter to keep that to herself. Status was as crucial to survival as food and drink. She would make it work for her.

Another thing she observed was that not all the women were filthy and in rags. Four of them had fairly decent clothes, their hair looked as if it had been washed recently, and they were plumper, less strained and hollow-eyed. Because of their appearance, and the fact that some of the prisoners gave them the cold shoulder, it didn't take long for Mary to realize these women had friends among the guards and Marines. Clearly they were trading their bodies for extra comforts.

'They ought to be ashamed of themselves,' one old biddy exclaimed, pursing her lips in disgust. By the way she coughed she had to be in the grip of consumption. 'Dirty whores!'

Mary had always believed that any woman who sold her body was beyond redemption. In Plymouth she had seen whores grappling with seamen in alleys, and heard about the terrible diseases they passed on, and she felt almost faint with disgust.

Yet as the days slowly passed on the *Dunkirk*, and the horrors seemed to grow greater rather than diminish, she found herself looking at the whole question a little differently. While she still thought that offering her body in return for food and a clean dress would be the surest way to hell and damnation, surely she was in hell already? She intended to survive at all costs, and if sacrificing her chastity would prevent a slow death from starvation, she was prepared to do it.

It wasn't just the desire for more food and the chance

to get out of this stinking hold into fresh air once in a while. Escape was most prevalent in Mary's mind, and for that she needed her chains to be removed. While there was no certainty that a lover would do this for her, she hoped she could persuade him to. Maybe if he grew to like her enough he'd even help her escape.

Sadly, she had no idea how to go about getting a 'friend' on the upper decks. The ugly brutes who came to collect the slop bucket or bring the rations had to be the lowliest of the crew, and they were the only ones she had any contact with, and that only briefly.

At the end of her third week she was growing desperate. Her twentieth birthday had passed at the end of April, and May Day, with all its happy memories of village celebrations, had made her spirits plummet even further. She would stand all day at the open hatch, looking out seawards, watching the sunshine glint on the water, aching so badly to be out in it that she thought she would lose her reason.

She knew all forty women's names, where they came from, their crimes and about their families. She had even seen a change in Catherine Fryer and Mary Haydon's attitude towards her, perhaps because they saw she was stronger and quicker-witted than anyone else, and it was better to be on a winning side than a losing one.

Mary had spoken to some of the men prisoners too, at least shouted to them through the barred grille. Because they were often taken out to work ashore, she'd learned from them the names of the few humane officers on board.

Lieutenant Captain Watkin Tench was the one who had captured Mary's interest. The men said he was young, and that they found him fair and reasonable, an intelligent man, who had been held prisoner himself during the American war. He sounded perfect for Mary's plan, but as yet she had no idea how to get his attention.

She had gone out of her way to befriend all the women who were labelled as whores. It wasn't difficult as they were only too glad of someone taking an interest in them, and Mary discovered that in the main they were very like her, a bit daring, more amusing than the other women, and warm-hearted.

But although they often gave her titbits of food or a new ribbon for her hair, and passed on rags when she was menstruating, they were all tight-mouthed about their men and how they got themselves picked in the first place. Mary could understand why. They weren't going to take the risk of losing their lovers and the comforts that came with them to another prisoner.

She had thought of picking a fight with another woman, to create such a big disturbance that she would be hauled out of the hold. But it was likely she'd be flogged for that, and even if she got to meet Tench, under those circumstances it was hardly likely to endear her to him.

One evening, the pot of soup and bread were brought in as usual, and as always, the strongest pushed their way forward to grab the lion's share. It was only the fear of dying of starvation that made the women fight to get to the soup. It was invariably cold and watery, mainly barley with a few bits of vegetable and strands of rank

41

meat. It had taken Mary several days to overcome her nausea before she felt able to elbow her way in to get her share.

That evening, she was up by the door talking to Lucy Perkins, a girl from St Austell, when the men unlocked it to come in. For once she was in a strong position to get a better helping, but as she took her place, and the women behind her began to push and shove, she glanced backwards.

It was a shock to see the plaintive faces of those who were too sick and weak to get off their beds to collect their share. Some were holding out their bowls, their feeble cries for help drowned by the clamour, and their distress unnoticed by anyone but herself.

Mary hated injustice. Even as a small child she had despised bigger children who bullied younger and weaker ones. Knowing that healthy women capable of fighting their way forward were sentencing the sick ones to death by depriving them of food, she suddenly saw red.

Turning in the queue, she held her arms out wide, blocking the way to the soup pot. 'Let the sick ones have their share first,' she commanded.

There was a hush, surprise on every grimy face. 'We should take care of the sick,' she said in a loud, clear voice. 'They might treat us like animals down here, but we are women, not savages.' Seeing Bessie at the back of the queue, she shouted to her, 'Get their bowls and bring them here, Bessie. When they are served everyone else can have theirs.'

Mary heard the rumble of dissent, and it frightened

her. But she had no intention of backing down. She was aware that the guards were watching from the grille on the door, and she hoped that if the stronger women rushed her, they would step in.

'Who d'you think you are? Fuckin' royalty?' Aggie Crew, one of the most ragged and dirty of the women, shouted out.

Mary had crossed swords with this woman on several previous occasions. In Mary's opinion she was totally brutalized. She stole from others, she didn't even attempt to wash her face and hands when the morning washing bucket was brought down. She belittled anyone with a shred of decency left. She had sneered at Mary for washing out the rags she used when she had her menses, and for her attempts to rally some of the other women to join her in asking for buckets of water and mops to clean the floor. Now Aggie's thin face was alight with malice, and she was clearly spoiling for a fight.

'I don't think I'm anyone other than a woman who doesn't want to behave like an animal,' Mary said, looking hard at her. 'It isn't right to act like this. The food should be shared equally, and I'm going to see it is.'

Bessie squeezed through the crowd with the sick women's bowls. 'Fill them, Jane,' Mary ordered the very young pregnant girl who was standing right by the soup pot, her hand on the ladle. Mary had talked to Jane a great deal, for as if it wasn't enough to be transported for stealing a candlestick, the parson who had made the complaint to the constables had also raped her.

Jane dutifully began to ladle soup into the bowls, and

43

Mary ordered those standing nearest to take them over to the sick ones. 'You'll get your share next,' she said by way of an inducement.

For a while it seemed as if Mary had won the day. The sick got their rations, and the other women were queuing properly for theirs, but as Mary turned to look at the soup pot, to make sure there was enough to go round, she was suddenly hit over the head with a bowl. She fell forward, knocking another woman off her feet, and all at once Aggie Crew was screaming blue murder, trying to entice the other women into hitting Mary.

The door flew open and in came the guards, lashing out with their sticks. They hauled Mary to her feet and unceremoniously dragged her out.

She knew they must have watched the whole proceedings through the grille on the door, but she also knew better than to hope they'd be on her side. Back in Exeter Castle, Dick Sullion had explained to her that the whole business of running prisons was put out to private tender to save the government money. As he pointed out, it was a good business for those who had no scruples; they hired the most brutish men as gaolers, ones who weren't above cutting corners with the rations. And in turn the owners turned a blind eye to their men taking bribes and treating their charges with the utmost brutality.

The two who held her by the arms now were typical of their breed, with their ugly, foxy faces and broken teeth. There was no light in their eyes.

'Why me?' she asked them when she'd caught her breath. 'It wasn't me who hit anyone.'

'You were inciting riot,' one said. 'Bloody trouble-maker.'

'Take me to Lieutenant Captain Tench,' she said boldly. 'I'll explain it to him.'

They didn't reply, just dragged her on along the passage and up the companionway, out on to the deck. Mary was sure she was going to be tied up somewhere for a flogging but at that moment, as her lungs filled with the sweet, fresh air after breathing effluent for so long, she didn't care.

She saw the night sky, sprinkled with a million stars, and the moon cutting a silver path across the dark waters of the river to the shore, and it seemed to be a sign that this was her moment, the opportunity she'd hoped for.

'I want to see Tench,' she screamed out at the top of her lungs. 'Get him now.'

One of the guards struck her, knocking her down on to the deck. 'Shut up,' he hissed at her, and added a stream of profanities.

All at once Mary saw what they were about. They hadn't dragged her out of the cell for formal punishment. They were intending to have their way with her, then shove her back later, with no one the wiser.

Determination was one of Mary's strongest attributes. While she might be prepared to be bedded by someone who would feed her, allow her to wash and perhaps show her some affection, she wasn't going to let herself be taken by a couple of rutting animals. She guessed too by the way they'd tried to silence her that there were men on the *Dunkirk* who didn't approve of prisoners being

45

raped. So she yelled again and again, and when one of them tried to cover her mouth, she bit his hand and punched him, screaming still louder for Tench.

'What's going on?' a voice boomed out, and as the two men let go of her, she saw a slim male figure silhouetted in an open doorway to one of the many sheds that were built on the deck.

'Mr Tench?' Mary yelled out. 'They dragged me out, I've done nothing wrong. Help me, please.'

'Stop that yelling and come in here,' he said. 'And you too,' he added to the men.

The shed was part ward room, part office. At the centre of it was a table littered with papers and lit by a couple of candles. It looked to Mary as though this man had been writing, for there was an open notebook and an inkwell in front of the stool he'd obviously just vacated.

Mary had no way of knowing if this was Watkin Tench. But the gold braid on his well-fitting red jacket and his spotless white breeches proved he was an officer, and he spoke like a gentleman. He was of slender build, with dark crinkly hair and brown eyes, and she thought he was around twenty-four or -five. His face was unremarkable, with small, neat features and clear and glowing skin. While he looked irritated at being disturbed, he certainly didn't give the impression of being bad-tempered by nature.

'Your name?' he asked curtly.

'Mary Broad, sir,' she said. 'I was trying to make the women let the sick ones have some soup,' she added quickly. 'Some of them didn't like it, and one hit me, then these two dragged me out.'

'She was trying to start a fight,' one of the guards claimed. 'We had to separate her.'

'Wait outside, you two,' the young officer said.

They left, one muttering something under his breath. Once the door was closed, the officer perched on his stool and looked hard at Mary.

'Why were you calling out my name?' he asked.

Mary felt a sense of relief that she had found the right man. 'I'd been told you were fair,' she said.

Tench nodded noncommittally, and asked Mary to explain what had happened.

Now that she had a platform to air her complaints, she spared him nothing. She said how the strongest women got the food while the weakest were starving, and that in her opinion there wasn't enough food to keep so many women alive.

'Our punishment is supposed to be transportation,' she said heatedly. 'Surely it's wrong to try and kill us before we ever get put on a ship?'

Tench had been surprised enough to hear his name being called out, and even more so by this woman's obvious intelligence. But most of all he was touched that she had the courage to speak up for her weaker fellow prisoners.

He had been a prisoner of war himself in America and had feared he would die from the terrible conditions there. When he arrived at this posting on the *Dunkirk*, he was horrified to find his fellow countrymen were capable of even worse barbarities. To his distress he found there was nothing a Marine officer could do to prevent it. The

47

hulks were run by private companies, and the Marines were merely there to keep order, without any control over the management.

When he had voiced his strong feelings on the matter he'd been severely reprimanded, and as he was only a junior officer without anyone higher up in agreement with him, there was nothing more he could do, and in truth he had become apathetic. When he took men to work outside, he was kindly to them; he tried to make certain the guards were giving the full quota of rations to the prisoners, and when someone was brought to him for punishment he was always fair. But he knew that wasn't enough.

Mary's Cornish dialect sliced through his apathy. He had spent his childhood in Penzance and had a store of happy memories of its natives. He felt compelled to find out a little more about this woman before dismissing her. Realizing she must have foregone her own supper during this skirmish, he put his head outside the door and ordered one of the men to bring something from the galley.

'Am I to be flogged?' Mary asked, once he'd shut the door again. She didn't hear what he had said to the men, and assumed he'd sent one of them to fetch someone of a higher rank than himself.

'No,' he said. 'And in future I shall order the guards to make sure the rations are shared out equally.'

'While you are about it, could we have more?' she asked cheekily.

Tench had an overwhelming desire to laugh. The

woman reminded him poignantly of many Cornish miners he'd known, dogged, tough and fearless. He remembered from the records that she had assaulted the woman she'd robbed, yet her calm grey eyes and gentle manner belied a vicious nature. Likewise, the innocence in her face sat uneasily with her impudent demands. A woman to be watched, he thought. But a rather admirable one for all that.

The guard brought in a plate of bread, cheese and pilchards. Tench pulled up another stool at the table and told Mary to eat.

It was so long since she had tasted either cheese or pilchards that it was all she could do not to cry. She wolfed down the food, holding on to the plate with one hand, afraid Tench might snatch it before she'd finished.

He poured her a little rum too, and topped it up with water, taking a glass neat himself. As he watched her bent over the plate, he noted that although her hair was alive with lice, her neck was very clean, an extremely unusual sight in a prisoner.

'I'll get someone to take you back now,' he said when she'd finished.

Mary had always found it easy to talk to men, but she had no idea how to flirt with them, nor would she know if a man found her attractive. As she looked into his soft brown eyes she thought she read curiosity in them, and she wished wholeheartedly she was in a clean dress with her hair newly washed, at least to give herself some sort of chance.

'Can't I stay a while longer?' she blurted out impulsively.

He smiled, and his eyes twinkled. 'No, you can't, Mary,' he said. 'I have work to do. But why do you want to stay? I've given you food, you aren't to be flogged.'

'Because . . .' she began, but to her horror she felt tears welling up in her eyes. She couldn't find the words to explain what it meant to be out of that stinking hold, or how it felt to have a full belly. And she certainly couldn't say it had been her intention to offer him her virginity in the hope she would get some privileges.

Perhaps he understood at least some of it, for he put his hand on her shoulder. 'You have to go back,' he said gently. 'But we'll talk again.'

Watkin Tench's kindness comforted Mary that night. As she lay between Bessie and Nancy, she wasn't so aware of the moans and groans, the coughing and the sobbing from the other women. Nor was she so aware of the stench or the rats scuttling around. Instead she was able to immerse herself in the thought of the amusement in his eyes, the shininess of his hair, and his gentle manner. For just a few brief minutes she'd felt clean, forgotten she was a felon. It was a form of escape, and a very welcome one.

Mary didn't know whether it was as the result of Tench's influence or not, but a couple of days later she, Bessie and two other women, Sarah Giles and Hannah Brown, were called out of the hold for work. There had already been a marked improvement in the food sharing, as the guards stayed in the hold to check everyone got fair shares, whether sick or not. To Mary that was enough. And to be called out for work was an unexpected bonus.

The job they were given was washing clothes, mainly shirts. It wasn't an easy task as they had to carry the four heavy wooden tubs out on to the deck from a store-room, which was difficult wearing chains, then lower buckets on a rope to the river to fill them with water. But it was good to be out in the sunshine, to be able to look over to the shore and see the lush green of fields and woods, and even if the guards did watch their every move, at times leering at them in a frightening manner, it was a million times better than being cooped up in the hold.

'Do you think we could wash ourselves when we've finished all these?' Mary whispered to Sarah as they scrubbed at the dirty shirts with blocks of hard soap.

Sarah was one of the women the others called whores. Small and pretty, with red-gold hair, she was twenty-five, a widow with two small children. Her fisherman husband had been lost at sea when his ship went down in a storm, and Sarah had left the children with her mother in St Ives and gone to Plymouth. Her story was very like Mary's – she'd turned to stealing because she couldn't get work – and she'd already been on the *Dunkirk* for eight months.

'You can if you want,' Sarah said, and laughed as if it was funny. 'But I hope you ain't intending to do it with nothing on.'

'Of course not.' Mary coloured up. 'I'll just get in the tub with my dress on and wash that too while I'm about it.'

'Chains and all?' Sarah raised one eyebrow.

'Well, I can't get those off,' Mary said offhandedly, and looked round at Bessie. 'What about you? Fancy a bath?'

Bessie began to giggle, and it infected them all. Sarah rubbed soap into her hands and blew bubbles, Hannah splashed Mary with water, and Mary retaliated by slapping her with a wet shirt. If the guards noticed they didn't intervene or stop them, and all at once it was as if they were just girls at a Sunday school picnic. They giggled, chatted and sang. Bessie even did a little dance, rattling her chains in time with her feet.

Once the washed shirts were hanging up on lines to dry, the women were completely hidden from the guards' view. 'Go on then if you're going to,' Sarah urged Mary. 'Before we empty the tubs.'

While Bessie and Hannah looked on, tempted to join her, but afraid of being caught at it, Mary stepped into the tub, gasping at the cold. Elated by the almost sensual touch of water on her skin, she began to laugh. 'It feels wonderful,' she gasped out, crouching down so that the water came up to her middle and looking to the others to join her in their tubs. 'Do it quickly if you're going to, before we get caught.'

Bessie and Hannah got into theirs without any hesitation; only Sarah held back, claiming she was keeping watch. The three women scrubbed themselves and their clothes eagerly, aware they hadn't long to finish the task, yet smiling with delight as they saw the dirt floating away from them.

After soaping her hair, Mary dunked herself right under

the water several times. As she came up for the last time, to her horror she saw the two guards and an officer staring down at her. A quick glance revealed that Bessie and Hannah were already out of their tubs, trying vainly to wring the water from their dresses. Sarah was white-faced and agitated.

'We weren't doing no harm, sir,' Mary said, addressing the officer. He was a portly man with a big nose and he looked astonished. 'Just using up the water before we threw it overboard. We've done all the washing.'

Mary could see no good reason why bathing should be considered something punishable. But one glance at her two wet friends alarmed her. Their dresses were clinging to their bodies, showing clearly the curve of their breasts and hips, and the guards were looking at them with naked lust. Aware that her own body must be similarly displayed, she was stricken with embarrassment.

'I'm sorry, sir,' she said as she struggled to get out of the tub. 'But you can't blame us, we're never given enough water to wash properly.'

'Why is it that you women always take advantage of any situation?' the officer asked.

Mary glanced at her companions and guessed they were tongue-tied with fear. The officer was older than Tench, perhaps thirty or more, his voice high-pitched and clipped. Yet she could see no cruelty in his eyes, only puzzlement.

'Wouldn't you?' she retorted. 'What else are we to do? That hold you keep us in wouldn't stink so much if we were allowed to bathe and come up here for exercise, and if it was scrubbed out now and then. If you kept animals in such a place there'd be a riot.'

One of the guards sniggered, and the officer silenced him with a stern look. 'Take those three back,' he said, pointing to Bessie, Sarah and Hannah. 'I'll deal with this one.'

The other women were pushed away through the lines of washing by the guards, leaving Mary alone with the officer. She vainly tried to wring out her skirt as she waited for him to speak.

'Your name?' he asked.

'Mary Broad, sir,' she said. 'Am I allowed to know yours?'

She thought she saw a glimmer of a smile, and she ran her fingers through her hair and smiled back defiantly. Her mother and sister had often remarked how pretty her hair was wet, as it sprang into ringlets, and she hoped that was true because the wind felt chill now she was wet, and she wouldn't look anything more than pathetic if she began shivering.

'Lieutenant Graham,' he said. 'It seems to me, Mary, that you haven't quite grasped the gravity of your situation.'

Graham was a name she'd also heard from the men prisoners. He was reputed to be dangerous when crossed, but decent enough most of the time.

'Oh, I have, sir,' she said boldly. 'I can see that I won't be alive to be transported, not unless I get a lucky break and a chance to have a bath and some extra food from time to time.'

He gave her a long, appraising stare which seemed to go right through her clothes, and she knew in that moment that he wanted her.

She had set her heart on Tench as a prospective saviour, and Lieutenant Graham would be an extremely poor substitute. His face was fat and flabby and she suspected he had little hair under his very well-cared-for wig. But there was no harm in having someone in reserve in case Tench couldn't be tempted. And Graham wasn't entirely repulsive as his teeth and skin were good. Besides, she wasn't looking for true love, only to survive long enough to escape.

'Are you trying to suggest something?' he said, his eyes narrowing. They were a muddy brown, not the kind which could keep her awake as Tench's did.

'It's not for me to suggest anything, sir,' she said, making a bob of a curtsy and grinning impudently. 'I was just saying how it is for me.'

He ordered her back to the hold at that, but as the guard roughly pushed her down through the companion-way, she felt Graham was watching her with interest.

Down in the hold, the afternoon's bath was being discussed by all those women still strong enough to be interested in the others. As Mary was pushed inside, they broke off their chatter to look up at her.

'What happened to you?' Bessie asked, wringing her hands with anxiety. 'We were afraid you'd be punished, or . . .' She broke off, not wanting to add the word 'raped'.

'I told him we need more food, fresh air, and this hovel cleaned out,' Mary said. She didn't feel inclined to discuss it any further as her wet clothes were making her cold and she wanted to talk in private to Sarah.

Her chance didn't come till much later that evening. She took off her wet clothes, hung them from a nail on the beam to dry and huddled in her blanket, but each time she looked across the hold, Sarah was talking to Hannah.

It was almost pitch dark when Mary saw Sarah move towards the bucket. By then most of the women were lying down ready to sleep. Mary got up and shuffled over to her, holding her blanket round her.

'When you've finished, can we talk?' she whispered.

In the gloom she saw Sarah nod her head.

The bucket was the best place to stay, furthest away from any of the women, but without room to stand up. When Sarah had finished, they perched on a beam. 'What is it?' Sarah asked.

'Who is your lover?' Mary asked. She saw no point in being more subtle.

Sarah hesitated. It was too dark for Mary to see if she was angry at being asked.

'Is it Tench or Graham?' Mary persisted.

'No, neither of those,' Sarah whispered. 'But you shouldn't ask such things, Mary.'

'Why not? I have to, if only so I know who not to make up to,' Mary whispered back.

'Tench can't be drawn into such things,' Sarah said with a sigh. 'Most of us have tried. And I wish you luck if you're going to try Graham, he's a hard man.'

'How do I go about it?' Mary asked.

She felt rather than saw Sarah's shrug. 'Give him the

glad eye whenever you see him, that's usually enough for them to call you out on a pretext. But don't hope for much. You'll only be disappointed.'

'Does your man remove your chains?'

'Sometimes, not often,' she said wearily. 'Now, go to bed, Mary, I don't want to tell you these things, it's not good.'

Mary heard the sadness in Sarah's voice, and knew instinctively it was only desperation that had driven her to such an arrangement and she wanted no part in seeing another girl follow her lead.

'We have to do what we can to survive,' Mary said, taking Sarah's hand and squeezing it. 'That's all it is, Sarah, nothing more. I don't see any shame in that.'

'You will when the others turn their backs on you,' Sarah said, her voice breaking.

'Better a turned back than dying of hunger,' Mary insisted.

For over a week Mary waited, each day hoping she would be called out again for work. The weather had turned really warm and the hold was stifling. A woman called Elizabeth Soames died one night and was only discovered dead at daybreak, but what shocked Mary most was that no one had anything to say about her. She'd been locked in here for months, yet she hadn't made one real friend and no one seemed to know anything about her.

'She was already here when I came,' Sarah said when Mary pointed this out. 'She was sick then, she barely spoke. She was old anyway, don't fret about it.'

Mary did fret about it. She wondered where the guards took Elizabeth's body for burial, whether the woman had any relatives and if they'd be told. It also made her own desire to escape even stronger.

The only comfort she could find was reliving memories of home. She found that if she sank into them far enough she could forget the heat, hunger, smells and the other women. Sometimes she would imagine herself walking down the path to Bodinnick with Dolly and their mother to catch the boat up to Lostwithiel. Mary could only recall going there twice, the last time when she was about twelve and Dolly fourteen, but both occasions were hot, sunny days, and she remembered sitting in the boat trailing her hand in the cool, clear water.

For much of the boat journey the river ran through steep, thickly wooded banks where the trees grew right down to the water's edge, their roots reaching out into the water like gnarled fishermen's fingers. It was a journey of enchantment, dragonflies hovering over the water, herons standing patiently in the shallows, and often timid deer peeping out from the trees. Kingfishers perched on the tree roots, waiting for an unwary fish to swim by, and then they would swoop, a glorious flash of turquoise, and come back up with their silver prize in their beaks.

Lostwithiel was the farthest Mary had ever been from home until she went to Plymouth. It might have been no bigger than Fowey, but to her it was thrilling because coaches thundered in from as far away as Bristol and London. She watched bug-eyed as the passengers alighted, marvelling at the women's beautiful clothes and pretty hats, and wondering why, if they were rich and important enough to travel so far, they didn't look happier.

Last time they'd gone there, Father had given her and Dolly tuppence each to spend. While Mother was buying material for new clothes, they looked in every single shop and examined each and every market stall before they decided what they would spend their money on. Dolly bought some artificial daisies to put on her Sunday bonnet, and Mary bought a kite. Dolly said she was stupid wasting tuppence on something she could make at home for nothing, and anyway girls didn't fly kites.

Mary didn't care about being the only girl to fly a kite, and she thought Dolly was foolish wanting daisies on her bonnet. Besides, kites made at home were too heavy to fly well; hers was made of red paper, with yellow streamers, and the string was waxed so it slid through her hands smoothly.

The very next day after church, Mary took the kite up on the hill above the town to fly it. Dolly came with her, but only because she wanted to show off her newly trimmed bonnet. As always on a fine day with a strong breeze there were many boys flying kites, and they all looked enviously at Mary's when it took off effortlessly, soaring up into the sky way beyond all their homemade ones.

Dolly overcame her prejudice about it being a boy's game, mostly because there were several boys she liked up there, among them Albert Mowles whom she was sweet on. Mary might have known she shouldn't have allowed Dolly to persuade her to let her hold the kite. She only wanted to do it so she could attract Albert's attention.

A gust of stronger wind came, and to Mary's horror, Dolly didn't hold the string tighter, but let it run right through her fingers. The kite was off, swept along on the wind in the direction of the beach at Menabilly.

Everyone gave chase, some abandoning their own kites to rescue the superior one. Mary remembered how she ran like the wind, determined to beat all the boys, and they were all whooping and shouting at the unexpected excitement.

The kite came down suddenly and dramatically as the wind dropped, landing on some rocks to the side of the little beach. The tide was out and Mary didn't stop to think about her Sunday clothes and shoes, but ran full tilt across the seaweed, sand and mud, her mind only on rescuing her kite.

She tripped on a half-submerged rock and fell face down. It was Albert who reached the kite, then turned back to help her up.

'You can run faster than most boys,' he said in admiration.

Now, as Mary lay sweating in the stinking hold, she thought she ought to remember the wallop she got from Mother when she returned home soaking wet and smeared with mud. Perhaps too she should remember Dolly's baleful look when Mary was the recipient of Albert's praise. Maybe she would have been wiser to have taken note of her father's lecture that girls who acted like boys came to a sticky end.

Yet none of those things were important to her then, or now. Nothing could detract from the thrill of seeing the red kite soar up into the sky, feeling the warm sun on her face and the soft grass beneath her feet, experiencing the joy of running wild and free, the beauty of that little beach where she so often caught crabs and mussels. It was even more important now to hold on to those memories, to think of herself as that kite, straining to be free. For hadn't she been told at Sunday school that if you prayed hard enough for something, it would come to you?

But it was hard to believe God listened to her prayers. Did He know or care that she was terrified she'd never see Fowey again? Was it too much to ask to go back to stand on the hill and look down at the pretty little town as the sun was setting? To watch the fishing boats come in, laden with their quivering silver pilchards, or hear the men singing in the tavern by the harbour?

Tears came into her eyes as she reminded herself that she had lost the chance to make her mother and father proud of her. That she'd never be able to dance at Dolly's wedding. Mary knew they despaired of her for being a hoyden, but she had always known they loved her. What would it do to them when she didn't come home again?

Just as Mary was beginning to believe that the hot weather would never break and she was going to be stuck in the hold for all eternity, she was called out for work again. This time it was just herself and Sarah.

It struck Mary that Sarah must have had some hand in it, as she'd spent two nights out of the hold since the wash day, but if she had, she didn't let on. Once again they were instructed to wash shirts, and as they were lowering buckets over the side they saw a group of male prisoners being brought up for work too.

Although Mary often spoke to the men through the grille and could put names to the different voices, she had no idea what any of them looked like. But the moment she saw a big man, well over six feet tall with wiry, fair hair, a thick beard and pale blue eyes, she knew with certainty that was Will Bryant, the man most of the other women liked best.

Mary liked him too, mainly because he was Cornish and knew Fowey well. They had talked on several occasions, but once the initial delight of finding someone to share her memories of her home town had worn thin, she'd found him to be something of a braggart. He boasted he was one of the few men to be convicted of smuggling.

This seemed odd to her, for it was a crime that was usually ignored because everyone in Cornwall, from the poorest people to the gentry, were involved in it to some extent. As he was a fisherman by trade, with a boat of his own, he would know the rugged coastline well, and certainly have all the necessary skills for bringing contraband ashore, but Mary didn't believe that was all he'd done. Nor did she like the way he considered himself to be the cleverest, toughest prisoner on the *Dunkirk*.

But seeing him in the flesh, she had to admit he was handsome. Even grime couldn't spoil his strong features, or the loose shirt hide his muscular body. His fair hair shone in the sunshine, there was a sparkle in his blue eyes, and his skin was golden-brown from working outside. He was probably only a couple of years older than her, still fit and healthy despite having been on the hulk for over a year. Clearly he'd found a way to get extra rations, which proved he was resourceful.

'Who are you two?' he shouted, as if they were at the market place, not prisoners in chains.

'I'm Sarah, this is Mary Broad,' Sarah called back. 'A good day for working outside!'

'It's worth breaking my back to see you two beauties,' he replied impudently, making the other men with him laugh. 'If you can get away later, I'll meet you at the tavern and buy you both a drink.'

Mary had to smile. A man who could still make jokes when he was about to start a ten-hour stint of shifting rocks was someone to be admired.

'I'll buy you two each, me darlin's,' another man called out. He had an Irish accent and Mary knew right away he had to be James Martin, the man who made all the women laugh with his florid and often suggestive compliments. But whereas Will was better in the flesh, James was disappointing. His large nose dominated his gaunt face, his brown hair was stringy, and his ears stuck out. His shoulders were stooped and his teeth were very brown.

'I thought a horse thief would look more dashing,' Mary remarked to Sarah as the men climbed down the ladder into the waiting boat.

Sarah laughed. 'That one's got more cheek than an elephant's behind,' she said. 'I don't think he needs looks too to attract women.'

'Who were the other two with Will?' Mary asked. One had bright red hair and freckles and looked about the same age as herself. The other was younger still, perhaps only sixteen. He was very small and nervous looking, with sharp, bird-like features. 'The young one had a nice smile.'

'They arrived about the same time I did. The one with the ginger hair is Samuel Bird. He's a bit gloomy, not one to brighten up a girl's day like Will and James,' Sarah said with a grin. 'The little one is Jamie Cox. He don't say much, too shy I guess. He's lucky Will and James Martin keep an eye on him, it don't bear thinking of what some of the brutes in that hold would do to him otherwise.'

Mary asked what she meant.

Sarah shook her head. 'If you don't know, then I'm not going to be the one to tell you,' she said. 'There's some things men do that are better not mentioned.'

It was quiet up on deck after the male prisoners were rowed ashore. The sun was hot on the women's arms and heads, and a heat haze shimmered on the water. They scrubbed at the clothes in companionable silence, and there seemed no need for conversation as both of them savoured the light breeze, the sound of the seagulls and the gentle movement of the hulk in the water.

Later, once they'd rinsed the first load of shirts with fresh water, both women bathed in the water, giggling delightedly as they helped each other to wash their hair. The two guards, who were lounging on crates further back on the deck, smoking pipes, made no comment. Perhaps the hot sun had mellowed them too.

The women's clothes dried quickly as they hauled up fresh water for the second load of washing, but Mary was horrified to see how faded and flimsy her dress was becoming – another couple of washes and it would fall apart.

'What will we do when these clothes are just rags?' she asked Sarah. Many of the other women were already semi-naked, clutching the last vestiges of their rags around them to hide their bodies.

'My man gave me this dress,' Sarah said, her eyes downcast. 'Hold out for clothes and food, Mary, don't let him have you for nothing.'

Mary looked thoughtfully at her friend for a moment. Her dress was blue cotton, nothing fancy, and it was too big for her slight shape. But it was by far the best one down in the hold. She guessed that Sarah had been quite a head-turner back in Penzance, for her red-gold hair was pretty and her dark eyes smouldered.

'Is it terrible?' she whispered. 'I've never done it.'

Sarah sighed. 'I thought lying with my husband was wonderful,' she said, her voice cracking. 'It hurt a bit the first time, but he was so gentle and I loved him. It won't be like that for you, I fear, the men here that want a woman won't care about your feelings. You are nothing but a warm body to use any way they like.'

'Is there any way I can make it better?' Mary asked nervously.

'Don't struggle, try to pretend you like it.' Sarah sighed. 'But don't think he'll love you, we're only convicts after all.'

Chapter three

Around noon Watkin Tench came back to the hulk in a small boat. Mary's heart leaped as she heard his voice calling out from below. But she continued bailing out the wash tub over the side, waiting for him to appear.

As he clambered on to the deck, she smiled. He was wearing a white shirt and breeches and his face was shiny with perspiration. He looked hot and tired, but to Mary that only made him more desirable.

He nodded when he saw the two women. 'Good day, Sarah, Mary. I hope you are behaving yourselves today?'

It was clear by his light tone and the hint of amusement in his voice that he'd heard about the bathing in the wash tubs. Mary wondered what he'd have to say if he knew they'd repeated it today. But their clothes were nearly dry now, and they were spinning out the remaining washing to delay the moment when they had to go back to the hold.

'We'd behave still better with something to eat,' Mary called out cheekily. 'Any chance?'

She saw Sarah turn away and guessed her friend thought she was being too forward.

'Isn't it enough you've got out of the hold for a few

hours?' Tench asked, taking a few steps closer to them. There was no real irritation in his voice, and Mary decided she had to charm him now or lose the chance for good.

'Oh yes, sir, we really appreciate the chance to come up here, to look at the woods and fields, hear the birds singing, and feel the sun on our faces,' she said, trying not to laugh because she was aware she sounded insincere. 'I wouldn't complain about anything ever again if we had work like this every day.'

He smiled then, his teeth very white against his tanned face. 'Tell me about yourself, Mary,' he asked, then added, 'And you too, Sarah.'

It seemed to Mary that Fate was smiling on her for once, for Tench sat down on a crate and looked relaxed as he talked to them both. No guards came near and there were no distractions of any kind; they could have been two ordinary girls chatting to a friend after work.

Mary let Sarah talk first. She spoke of her husband's death and the children she was afraid she'd never see again. She went on to explain that her parents were past the age when they should be bringing up children, and if they should die, the children would go to the workhouse.

Tench really listened. Mary saw him clench his lips as if he was incensed that Sarah's family circumstances hadn't been taken into consideration when she was sentenced.

Mary's own story was very short. She told him about her family in Fowey and how she'd left for Plymouth to get work.

'I wish to God I'd stayed at home now,' she said

ruefully, as Sarah tactfully moved away to check the drying washing. 'It pains me to think that I'll never set foot in Cornwall, or see my family ever again in this life.'

She half expected Tench to insist she would, that seven years weren't so long, but she knew by his grave expression he could hold out no hope for her.

'It is more difficult for women convicts to return,' he said. 'Men can sign on a ship coming home when their time is up.'

He didn't have to add that there was no such opportunity for women, and therefore they were forced to stay. Mary heard it in his voice.

'I'll get back,' she said with determination. 'Somehow. But do you know where we are to be sent?'

He shrugged his shoulders. 'There's talk of Botany Bay, in New South Wales, the country Captain Cook discovered. But no one else has been there to confirm or deny it's a viable proposition. America is out of the question now since she gained her independence. They tried Africa and that failed.'

'If we stay here on the *Dunkirk* we shall all die,' Mary said dolefully.

Tench sighed. 'I agree it's bad, but what can the government do? Every gaol is overcrowded.'

Mary was tempted to comment that if they didn't send people to prison for petty crimes like stealing a pie, there would be no overcrowding. But she wanted to keep Tench's interest, not have him scuttling away in haste.

'Tell me about you yourself, sir,' she asked instead. 'I heard you were in the war in the Americas?'

'I was,' he grinned ruefully. 'Taken prisoner of war too. Maybe that's why I'm a little more sympathetic to prisoners here than the average Marine. I grew up in Penzance too, so I also know how hard life is in Cornwall for most people.'

Mary sat on the deck by the wash tub entranced as Tench told her of his happy childhood memories of Penzance. He had of course come from an entirely different world to her – a big house with servants, a boarding school in Wales, a family with a good name and money. But there was common ground, their love of Cornwall, his interest and affection for ordinary people. He could paint vivid pictures with just a few words of his life with the Marines, of America and of London.

'I have to go now,' he said suddenly, perhaps aware he'd stayed talking to her for far too long. 'You empty that tub and clear away. I'll bring you up a little something to eat.'

'He's not the kind to take a woman,' Sarah said sharply as soon as Tench had walked away. She had remained silent all the time Mary was talking to him, only nodding and smiling from time to time. 'You won't get what you want from him, Mary.'

'How do you know?' Mary asked, hurt because she thought the older woman was ridiculing her.

'I know about men,' Sarah said simply. 'He's the kind who will save himself for the woman he'll marry. A rare breed.'

Mary thought Sarah was mistaken when Tench came back to give them a lump of bread, some cheese and an orange. But as he hurriedly walked away, urging them to finish up and go back to the hold, Sarah looked at his slender figure retreating down the deck and sighed.

'He's a kind, good man,' she said. 'No doubt if you can keep his interest he'll always help you, Mary. But don't hope for love, or even sharing his bed. His kind don't fall for convict women.'

The bread and cheese were both a little mouldy but that didn't matter, it was solid food after all. It was the orange which thrilled them even more, for such fruit had always been a rare treat even before imprisonment. They ate it all greedily, even the peel, licking every last drop of juice from their chins and laughing at each other.

They had just emptied the last of the washing water over the side when Lieutenant Graham appeared. He was in full uniform and looked very hot and tetchy.

'Time you were back in the hold,' he said curtly.

'We were just going to take down the dry washing and fold it,' Mary said.

She had caught the sun on her face and arms, she could feel the familiar sting and knew it would be tender for days. But up here she felt free and even happy and she didn't want to go back down to the hold just yet.

'My men will do that,' he said, giving her a piercing look. 'I know what you women are like, you probably aim to steal a shirt or two.'

'You are mistaken, sir,' Mary said indignantly. 'We just wanted to finish the job properly.'

He leaned back against the sawn-off mast and sneered.

'Is that so? I think it's more likely you'd sell your souls for a new dress, food or a drop of rum.'

Mary glanced at Sarah, saw her anxious expression and guessed she had already passed a message that Mary could be tempted into becoming a bed partner. After talking to Tench, Mary had no real interest in Graham any longer, but her common sense told her she mustn't wipe him right out of the picture.

'I wouldn't sell my soul,' she said pointedly. 'And I haven't considered selling my body either, not yet.'

'You women are all whores,' Graham said nastily. 'Now finish up and get back.'

His words stung, but as they lifted the tub to empty it completely, Mary felt Graham's eyes on her legs. She had tucked the sides of her dress up into the chain around her waist and forgotten she'd left it like that.

She looked round at him and winked cheekily. She had no doubt he could be lured, even if Tench couldn't.

Over the next few weeks, Mary was called out for work regularly. Sometimes it was just with Sarah, often with other women. But she wasn't slow to notice she was always picked, whether it was for washing, mending or peeling vegetables. Sadly, she had no way of knowing whether it was Tench or Graham who was putting her on the list.

She saw both men on nearly every occasion, and although Tench didn't stop to speak again for as long as he had before, he almost always slipped her something to eat. Graham on the other hand lingered longer each time, often calling Mary away from the other women under a pretence of chastising her for something.

The man puzzled her. He could be so curt and even nasty, but now and again he showed a touch of real kindness, like the occasion when she got a splinter in her foot from the deck planking. Several of the women had attempted to get it out for her without success. By the end of the day she could barely stand on it, and when Graham saw her limping, he called her over.

'What's wrong with your foot?' he asked.

She explained, and he asked her to let him see it. She turned her back on him and with some difficulty because of the chains, lifted her foot up by bending her knee.

'It's embedded,' he said. 'I'll get a needle to dig it out.' He then ordered the other women back to the hold and told Mary to stay where she was.

'Sit down,' he said sharply as he came back with a needle and a small bottle of liquid.

Mary did as she was told, and Graham squatted down on a crate before her and lifted her foot on to his knee. It hurt as he prodded the needle in, but he eventually got the splinter, then rubbed a dab of the contents of the bottle on to it, making it sting. Mary squealed with pain.

'That's to kill any infection,' he said. 'Now, put something round it, and don't walk around in any muck until it's healed.'

'Difficult down in the hold,' she retorted.

'Don't you ever give up on complaining?' he asked, but he was still holding her foot in his hand.

In that moment Mary knew for certain he did have a

real interest in her. 'If you think that's complaining, just let me get into my stride,' she said with a wide grin. 'What would you like to hear about? The filth, the stink or the lack of decent food?' She laughed then, to soften her words. 'But I don't want to put you off your supper tonight. It was very kind of you to see to my foot.'

He said nothing, but his hand strayed on to her leg, just above the shackle, smoothing the skin. 'You keep yourself cleaner than the others,' he said, his voice suddenly lower and more intimate. 'I like that about you. I wouldn't want to see you get a poisonous wound.'

'Keeping clean is one way to survive this hulk,' she retorted. 'That's my aim, to survive it, whatever I have to do.'

He smiled then, a warmth coming into his plump face, and for a brief second he looked almost handsome. 'Whatever you have to do?' he asked, raising one eyebrow.

Mary couldn't look at him. She sensed he wanted her to spell out to him that she was available. Knowing that he could, if he wished, take her by force made her feel a little tender towards him.

'I've never been with a man,' she said softly, keeping her eyes down. 'I always intended to wait till I was wed. But that's not going to happen now. I could easily die of starvation before I see the country they plan to send me to. So if a man was to offer me food and a new dress, I think I would do what he wanted in return, as long as he was kind.'

'You don't mind if it's not love?'

That seemed a strangely sensitive question to Mary.

Not what she would have expected of a man of his class.

'Love doesn't come to women like me,' she said. 'I'll settle for kindness.'

He ordered her back to the hold then, but as she got up he gave her a strip of cotton to bandage her foot. 'Keep it clean,' was his only comment, but his eyes said a great deal more.

That night Mary was in a quandary. It was Watkin Tench she wanted: for him she could feel very much more than mere gratitude. But she felt Sarah was right in saying he wouldn't ever take a woman he wasn't married to. Yet if she allowed Graham to have his way with her, and Tench found out, he'd be bound to despise her for it.

All the following week she could think of nothing else, agonizing over whether it was nobler to allow herself to starve to death than lose her self-respect, or fight with the only weapons she had for survival.

The long hot spell broke with a fearsome storm. The old hulk bucked and shuddered, the timbers groaned as if it was about to break up. The hatches had to be closed, and remained that way day after day as heavy rain continued to bucket down. As the women lay on their benches in complete darkness, listening to the cries of those who had become sick, the already fetid air was so thick and heavy it was difficult even to breathe.

Baby Rose, who had been sickly from birth, died first, followed a day later by her mother and the woman who shared the same bed. Within twenty-four hours a further eight women were running a fever, and a dozen more, including Mary, were vomiting and had diarrhoea. Most were so weak they couldn't even make it to the buckets and just lay in their own mess.

Mary saw for herself then that the only women who weren't suffering so badly were the so-called whores. They were the ones still healthy enough to be able to wipe another woman's fevered brow, to offer a few words of comfort. Even Mary, who had considered herself so strong, barely had the strength to crawl to the bucket.

She made up her mind then that survival was far more important than morality.

Eventually the rain abated, and the hatches were opened again, to reveal a foot of bilge water beneath the sleeping shelves, vomit and excrement floating on it. The sickness among the prisoners persisted, claiming yet another two souls. The men called through the grille to the women, but they were suffering just as badly. Mary heard that Able, her cellmate in Exeter, had died, as well as a young boy, barely fifteen years of age, and two of the older men.

Mary spoke to Will Bryant one morning. Even he didn't sound as brash and full of confidence as previously.

'If it's gaol fever that's come amongst us, we'll all die,' he said gloomily. 'We've got to find a way to make them swill out these holds. There's more rats than ever and I fear for us all.'

'I'll try and do something,' she said.

'What can a little thing like you do?' he retorted arrogantly.

'I can try pleading for us,' she said, more determined because he doubted her.

'You can try, but it won't get you anywhere,' he said. 'They want us all to die, then they'll fill the hulk with new 'uns who'll die too. Save 'em a fortune it will.'

'You bring shame to Cornishmen,' she shouted at him. 'Talk like that won't help anyone.'

'I'll marry you if you get the holds swilled out,' he called back, and gave a raucous laugh.

'Be careful I don't hold you to that,' Mary yelled at him.

Sarah smiled weakly as Mary told her what she intended to do.

'The guards won't get Tench or Graham down here,' she said. 'They'll just ignore you.'

'I've got to try,' Mary insisted.

There was no point in banging on the door, no one ever answered. So Mary waited until the guard came down to order two of the women to bring out the slop buckets, and as soon as he unlocked the door she pounced on him.

'I've got to see Lieutenant Captain Tench or Lieutenant Graham,' she insisted.

'Bugger off,' he said, pushing her away with his stick. 'You'll see no one.'

'I will,' she said, grabbing him by the arm. 'If you don't take a message to one of them from me, I'll see you punished.'

'*You* get *me* punished?' His narrow eyes became even

narrower. 'D'you think anyone up there would take the word of a bloody felon?'

'Ignore me at your peril,' Mary replied menacingly. 'I'm telling you, give them the message, or take what will come to you.'

'Bugger off,' he repeated, but this time with less conviction. He ordered two women to take the buckets, holding Mary back with his stick.

'Tell them,' she yelled out as he slammed the door and locked it. 'Tell them or be damned – it's important.'

Mary tried again when the women came back with the buckets, but with the same response. As the hours crept by and still no one came, she stared out through the hatch at the dark grey sky above and cried. More women were going down with the fever, and she feared that if they were left like this they would all be dead within a week.

'You did your best,' Sarah said in an attempt to comfort her. 'It's just like Will said, they don't care if we die.'

'That may be true of most of them but I can't believe it of Tench or Graham,' Mary said. 'I won't believe it.'

She had no idea what time of day it was, as there was no sun to tell her, but it felt like late afternoon when a guard came in and called her name.

'Up there with you,' he said.

It wasn't the same man she'd threatened earlier, but she felt he knew of it because for once he didn't whack her with his stick. As Mary reached the top of the companionway she took a deep breath of clean air, and it made her giddy.

Lieutenant Graham was standing on deck. 'You wanted to see me?' he asked.

Mary poured out what was wrong. 'The holds must be scrubbed out,' she pleaded. 'We'll all go down with fever if they aren't.'

He remained impassive, and it infuriated her. 'If we all get fever it will spread to all of you too,' she said heatedly. 'In God's name do something, you don't want the death of a whole ship's company on your conscience.'

He gave her one of his long, penetrating stares. 'And what will you do for me, if I do what you say?'

Mary gulped. She hadn't expected him to bargain with her.

'Whatever you want, sir,' she replied.

'I don't want you unwillingly,' he said, and for the first time ever Mary saw a trace of nervousness in his face.

'I don't want you to help those down in the hold unwillingly either,' she said.

He looked away from her, over towards the sea, and Mary could see he was struggling with his conscience. Not so much whether it was right to let prisoners die for want of clean air, but whether it was right to bow to Mary's demands because he wanted her.

After what seemed an interminable silence he turned back to her. 'I'll pass the order that the holds are to be cleaned,' he said sternly. 'You will come to me as the other women are sent back.'

It was dark by the time the scrubbing of the women's hold was completed. The women had been brought up on deck, and the evening soup and bread were dished out there while the guards went down to do their task. For some of the women who had never been out of the hold since they were originally put there, it was almost too much. They crouched on the deck fearfully, shivering in the brisk breeze, their eyes dull as if they were partially blinded by the daylight.

Mary was shocked by the condition of some of them. In the gloom of the hold she hadn't been able to see the full horror of it. Some were nothing but skin and bone, and all were pale, gaunt and listless, dirt so deeply embedded in their skin and hair that it would take more than one bath to clean them. She saw ulcerating sores where their leg irons rubbed, the lice crawling on them, the bites on skinny arms and legs which could only have come from rats. Sadly, she sensed that the cleaning of the hold wouldn't help them unless they were given better food. She doubted that all of their number would survive to be transported.

As the guards returned on deck, sweating profusely from their efforts, the smell of vinegar sharp in the evening air, Mary began to tremble with fright at the thought of what was coming to her.

She knew what love-making entailed. In the tiny cottage at Fowey there was no privacy, and she had heard her parents at it in the darkness. During her time in Plymouth she had seen it going on all around her too, so the act itself wasn't frightening. Thomas used to kiss her passionately, and she would have gladly let him go further if he had pressed her. But there was a great deal of difference between being seduced and being compelled to submit to it.

Apart from her fear of being taken by a man she scarcely knew, there was the information Sarah had passed on. She said that although the officers turned a blind eye to one of their number taking a convict woman, that didn't always stop them from banding together to flog a woman afterwards if they had some grievance against her. Mary guessed she would be a marked woman now for daring to complain about the holds.

Lieutenant Graham appeared just as the guards were ordering the women back below. He gestured for her to follow him to the stern of the ship, and disappeared into one of the shed-like structures up there.

He closed the door and locked it as soon as Mary was inside. It was very like the room Tench had taken her into before, tiny, with a bunk, a desk and a couple of stools. Graham lit a candle on the desk, and it was then that Mary saw the small bath of water on the floor.

'For me?' she asked.

'Yes. You stink,' he said, looking faintly embarrassed. 'Wash yourself all over, including your hair. I'll come back later.'

'Will you take these off?' Mary indicated her chains.

He hesitated for a moment, which suggested to her he hadn't done this before, then taking a key from his pocket released both her ankles and drew the chain from around her waist. He left her without another word.

For a moment Mary could think of nothing but the sheer joy of being released from her chains. To be able to move easily and not to hear the hated clank she'd lived with for so long was bliss. But she regained her wits within minutes and sprang to the door to try it. It was locked of course, just as she'd expected, and the two porthole windows were far too small for her to get through, so she peeled off her clothes and got into the bath.

To her delight it was warm, and the soap he'd left wasn't the rough stuff they used for washing clothes. The bath was too small to do anything more than squat in it, but it felt so good, especially without the hated chains weighing her down.

She was drying herself with the towel he'd left when she spotted a looking-glass on the wall and took a look at herself, almost falling back with shock at what she saw. Hollows had taken the place of her plump red cheeks and her eyes seemed to be bulging out of her head. When she looked down at her body she saw that was emaciated too, her ribs sticking out below her breasts. Stranger still were her brown face and forearms when the rest of her was ghostly white.

But her newly washed hair did look pretty, hanging in dark shiny ringlets to her shoulders. She rubbed at it hard with the towel, and combed it through with Graham's comb to remove the lice, then washed that too in the bath water and put it back where she'd found it.

As she heard the sound of Graham's feet coming back she dived into the bunk, quickly covering herself with the blanket.

Graham came in slowly. He was carrying a small tray

which he put down while he locked the door again. Mary felt too shy to speak, but at the smell of the food, she couldn't resist sitting up.

'Is that for me?' she exclaimed, hardly able to believe her luck, for it was some kind of pie, the pastry all golden the way her mother used to make it, with a rich gravy poured over it.

'I guessed you were still hungry,' he said gruffly, without looking at her, as if embarrassed.

'That was kind of you, sir,' she said.

'You don't have to call me sir in here,' he said, passing her the tray and sitting down on the edge of the bunk. 'My name is Spencer, now eat it up before it gets cold.'

Mary didn't need to be told twice, and fell upon it with glee. It was rabbit and vegetable pie, the best she had eaten since she left Fowey, and even though the food meant more than the man who brought it to her, she couldn't help but notice he seemed to be enjoying her obvious delight.

The Lieutenant was surprised by his own emotions as he watched Mary eat. He had expected either to feel guilt that he was betraying his wife's trust in him, or so lustful once he got back to his cabin that he wouldn't be able to give Mary time to eat the dinner. But instead he felt able to put aside both his guilt and his lust, because the way she ate the food made him feel good. She hadn't noticed as she was eating that her breasts had become exposed, two small perfect little mounds with pale pink nipples. A little gravy had run on to one of them, and it was all he could do not to lean forward and lick it off.

He had married Alicia, his second cousin, at twenty, ten years ago now. They had played together as children, learned to dance and ride together back home in a village near Portsmouth, and there had always been an understanding that they would eventually marry. Alicia had come to live in his parents' home, and she was very much the daughter of the house. She painted, sewed and played the piano, was gracious to all their guests, never complained when he was away for long periods. She even produced first a son, then a daughter, without losing her shapely figure.

Graham considered it a very successful marriage. They were in harmony with each other, and he knew that other men envied him such a pretty and vivacious wife. He didn't understand why he sometimes felt disappointed.

Yet as he watched Mary eating, he realized why. Alicia was like biting into fruit, delicious and good for him, but not satisfying in the same way as a meat pie could be. Alicia never argued with him, everything he said was right. She always looked lovely when she welcomed him home on leave, but there was never any passion, no real emotion.

Mary was not even close to being as pretty as Alicia. Even if she were dressed in the most expensive silk gown, her hair arranged in an elegant coiffure, she would still look what she was, a simple country girl with no social graces.

Yet she was so very desirable, especially now, scrubbed clean and her dark hair flowing on her shoulders. She had a defiance he'd never seen in Alicia; she was proud, daring, wilful and outspoken. It would be a challenge to make this convict woman love him, and he felt that if he succeeded he'd discover something marvellous and sustaining. It even thrilled him that he was risking his career in the Marines by bringing her to his cabin. He'd never done anything so daring in his life before.

'That was wonderful,' Mary said, surprising him that she could be so grateful. 'And the bath, that was wonderful too.'

She felt she was up to sharing his bed now. Warm and clean after the bath, with a belly full of food, she was ready for almost anything. Somehow she didn't think he'd be very rough with her, not if he thought to bring her such good food.

'Would you like some rum?' Graham asked.

'Just a little,' she said. She didn't really like the taste, but she enjoyed the warming effect it had on her. Besides, Sarah had warned her to drink whatever she was offered, saying it would help to numb her.

Graham handed her some rum in a glass and began to strip himself of his clothes. Mary gulped down her drink as she saw his white, hairy legs, suddenly afraid she couldn't go through with this. The fear grew greater still as he threw aside his shirt: he had a pigeon chest and a fat white belly which quivered as he moved.

All her life she had been used to seeing semi-clothed male bodies. Fishermen and sailors were often stripped to the waist in the hot weather and they had hard, lean bodies rippling with muscle. That was how she thought all men were, and Graham's unexpected white, flabby flesh made her feel suddenly queasy. But there was no backing down now, so she wriggled down under the blanket, leaving room for him beside her, and averted her gaze.

He was on to her within a second of getting into the bunk, pressing her into the mattress under his weight, his hands moving wildly all over her body and his lips clamped to hers like a limpet. Mary had no idea how to respond; her only experience had been with Thomas, and he'd given her gentle, sensual kisses that left her aching for more.

Graham's mouth moved from her lips to her breasts, sucking at them so hard it hurt, and his breath came hard and heavy like a horse's after a long gallop. She could feel his penis against her belly, hard and hot, but mercifully it appeared to be small. Within seconds, with his face buried in her neck, he was prising her thighs apart and forcing his way into her.

It didn't hurt, but it wasn't pleasant either, just the sensation of a pole being shoved into a dry tube which was barely large enough to accommodate it. She didn't like the way he gripped her buttocks, grunting like a pig.

But thankfully it didn't last long. The grunting grew gradually louder, his body grew hotter and more sweaty, then all at once he sighed deeply and was still, his face buried in her neck.

It was only then that she felt a slight tenderness towards him. After all she had been through in the past six or seven months, it was good to be held, and to lie in a warm and comfortable bed. She lifted one hand and caressed his neck and shoulders, wondering if she should say something.

But what could she say? Not that she loved him or that he thrilled her. Nor could she ask if he intended to do it again to her, tonight or any other night. That was another reminder of her status, a wretched convict woman who had no rights and was considered to be without feelings or needs. She was pretty certain that most people imagined such women were incapable even of thought.

He moved down the bunk a little, cradled his head against her breasts and almost instantly fell asleep, his arm tightly round her.

Mary lay there for some time. The air coming through the porthole was clean and fresh, only Graham's gentle breathing breaking the total silence. It was good to know that no rats were likely to run across her in the night as she slept, and no hunger pains would wake her. Yet she couldn't sleep, for it suddenly occurred to her that she might be able to escape.

Graham had locked the door when he came in, and she was sure he'd put the key in his jacket pocket. Could she possibly get out of the bunk and find her clothes and his keys without waking him? Would there be a guard posted outside?

The last question was answered when she heard the tread of heavy boots pass by the door. She listened closely for some time, mentally seeing the route the guard was taking around the deck. As he approached the cabin door for a second time, she counted out the seconds before he made a complete circuit. Ninety seconds, but on the third circuit he stopped somewhere, perhaps to smoke a pipe, or rest.

She realized then that there were too many unknown quantities to deal with to try to escape tonight. She didn't know how heavy a sleeper Graham was, she wasn't certain where the key was, nor had she checked the sides of the hulk to find the best place to climb down to the water. Jumping over the side would be foolhardy; she'd alert the guard in a second with the splash. All she could hope for was that Graham would want her again, that she could build up his trust in her, and meanwhile take careful note of the deck layout and best escape routes.

Mary dreamed she was at home in bed with her sister Dolly, waking to find that the hand caressing her belly was Graham's, not her sister's. She feigned sleep, hoping he would drop off again too, but to her surprise she heard him lighting a candle.

It was so tempting to open her eyes to see what he was doing, but if she did he might send her back to the hold, and she was too warm and snug to relish that. She felt him move the blanket back, and felt the slight heat from the candle coming nearer her.

All at once she became aware he was sitting up, the candlestick in his hand, studying her body. It was unnerving, but still she didn't open her eyes. He gently probed at her private parts with one finger, parting the hair, then with two fingers held the lips apart.

It was even harder to pretend sleep, knowing he was looking at a part of her no one but herself had ever seen. She wondered why he wanted to look at it. Had he never seen one before? Or was he checking her for a disease?

But as his finger slid over her there, the strangest sensations washed over her. It felt good, the way Thomas's kisses had, and involuntarily she opened her legs a little wider. The hesitant rubbing became a little stronger, and she knew he was looking at that part of her, not at her face, because she could feel the warmth of his breath on her belly. She half opened her eyes and saw that he wasn't holding the candlestick as she supposed; that was resting on the side of the bunk. He was rubbing his penis with one hand while stroking her intimately with the other.

She shut her eyes tightly. She didn't want the image of his fat belly to spoil the pleasure he was giving her. While it seemed peculiar that a man would prefer to do such things to her while she was asleep, rather than awake and responding, she had no real idea what lovers did to one another anyway.

Again and again his finger slid into her, and it was all she could do to lie quietly and not call out. She could hear his breath becoming more laboured, his hand moving faster and faster on his penis, and then just as she was about to reach for him, urge him to put it inside her, he made a grunting sound and was still.

He got back into bed beside her a few seconds later, and again fell soundly asleep. Once more Mary lay awake, disturbed by the feelings he'd aroused in her, and even more puzzled by his actions. Was he being caring by not waking her for what he wanted to do? Or was it some deviation of normal male behaviour?

She must have fallen asleep eventually, for the next thing she knew he was shaking her. 'Wake up, Mary,' he said. 'It's time for you to go back.'

It was barely dawn, just a faint pink glow in the east, as she walked across the deck, the chains back on her. Graham was in front of her, and as he reached the first of the two doors to the hold, he turned back to her.

'Do not speak of this to anyone,' he said, his face tight with tension. 'If you are asked to explain your absence tell them you were locked up on deck as a punishment. Next time I will try to have a dress for you.'

He said nothing more, just unlocked the first door, then went down to the next and unlocked that, gently nudging her in without a word of farewell.

If anyone heard or saw her come in, they said nothing. Mary made her way to her bench, nudged Anne over as she had taken up her space, and lay down. After the warmth and softness of Graham's bunk, the planks seemed very hard and cold. But she noticed it smelt far more pleasant in the hold, and that pleased her. Yet Graham's last words had made her feel uneasy, for it was obvious he didn't know how the other women would react to one of their number going missing for a night. They wouldn't ask where she'd been, they'd just ignore her.

To Mary's utmost surprise there was no animosity towards her when she woke again later. In fact her status appeared to have been raised to one of heroine. 'Did they flog you?' Anne asked first, and with that every single woman, even the sick ones, raised themselves to thank Mary for her courage in demanding to see Graham. Only Sarah gave her a knowing look, and she grinned when Mary told the story that she'd been chained up on the deck until dawn.

All the women seemed much less apathetic now the hold was cleaner, and throughout the day Mary was unable to get to speak to Sarah for them complimenting her, asking questions, and remarking on how no one else had ever dared do such a thing. The men were cleared out of their hold that morning too, for cleaning, and later, as they came back, Mary was subjected to shouted praise from them too.

Will Bryant called her over to the grille. 'You're a plucky little lass,' he called out. 'Bless you for it.'

'You got to marry her now,' James Martin shouted, and Mary laughed along with the men, amused as much by their ribald remarks as their praise for her.

'I won't be holding you to it, Will Bryant,' she called back. 'I know you're all talk, and besides, I've got no wedding finery in here with me.'

While it felt good to receive so much admiration, Mary felt guilty too. The next time Graham called her out, not only would she lose all this respect, but they'd hate her for deceiving them.

After dark she managed to slip on to Sarah's bench to talk to her. 'I was with Graham,' she whispered. 'What do I do now about all this?'

'But for you there would be many more deaths,' Sarah whispered back. 'Besides, they'd all be offering their fannies if they thought there was anyone up there wanting them. But never mind that, what was it like?'

'Not so bad,' Mary replied. Much as she would have liked to share her experiences with her friend, she couldn't out of loyalty to Graham. He had after all been kind to her.

Four days later Mary was called again by Lieutenant Graham. This time she had been set to work cleaning the galley alone, and when she finished the filthy job, Graham appeared and ordered her into his cabin. It was late afternoon, and seconds after the door was locked behind her, she heard the male convicts arriving back from their outside work.

Again he removed her shackles, and again there was water for her to bathe in. But he didn't stop to undress, and took her swiftly, before she was even dry, and when he had finished thrust a clean dress and petticoat at her.

'You can't stay up here,' he said. 'It would be noted. Put these on and be gone.'

'Can I have something to eat?' she asked as she put the petticoat on. It was very worn, but soft and clean. The grey dress was equally worn, but it looked wonderful to her as her old one was in shreds.

'I thought you'd steal food while you were in the galley,' he said with a sneer.

'Our arrangement wasn't for me to steal what I need,' she said sharply. One of the guards had watched her most of the time she was in the galley, and to her disappointment all she'd managed to get her hands on was a bit of cheese. 'I've kept my part of the bargain, so you keep yours.'

As she put the new dress on he turned away and opened a tin box. 'Very well,' he said, his back turned to her. 'But keep your mouth shut about this. If word gets out I'll have you flogged.'

He handed her a cold pasty and an apple.

'Thank you, sir,' she said, and made an insolent curtsy. 'I won't be boasting about it. I'm not proud to stoop this low either.'

As he bent to lock her chains, she felt his hurt. She might have added something kinder, but she was too busy eating the pasty.

The weeks and months passed very slowly into autumn and finally to winter, bringing with it the prospect of freezing to death. With only one blanket apiece, the women huddled even closer together at night. There were several more deaths among the older ones, but a new influx took their places, and still there was no news of the transportation.

Will Bryant had been on the *Dunkirk* for two years already and he often joked to Mary through the grille that his seven-year sentence would be up before they set sail.

Mary was still every bit as desperate to escape. She knew the layout of the upper decks intimately: who patrolled at any given time of the day; the times when there were fewer guards on duty. But no feasible opportunity to escape had presented itself yet, however vigilant she was. She certainly wasn't going to attempt it in a foolhardy way, for if she was caught she could expect a hundred lashes at least.

So, like Will, she had learned to bear her imprisonment, concentrating her energies on finding ways to alleviate the misery and stay alive and healthy. Whilst her continuing good health and her work up on deck, and nights away, did create some jealousy among the other women, she still commanded their respect for being their spokeswoman when required. She also helped herself to anything useful which came her way – rags for the women's menses, soap and small amounts of food when she could get it – and gave it away to those who needed it most.

Mary Haydon and Catherine Fryer, along with Aggie as their vociferous mouthpiece, did their best to make the other women turn against Mary, but the only real charge that stuck against her was that she was aloof and proud. Mary didn't mind them saying that of her – pride to her wasn't a fault – and as for being aloof, she supposed she was, in as much as she kept her own counsel and tried to rise above the petty squabbling some of the others went in for. But no one ever called her a whore, though she was well aware that was in fact what she'd become, even if it was only with Lieutenant Graham.

Once, sometimes twice, a week she slept in his cabin. He slipped her extra food, gave her clean clothes now and then, and showed her a certain amount of affection. But she was still nowhere nearer understanding the man.

At times it seemed as if he was in love with her, at others he appeared to loathe her. She now knew he was married with two children, and when he did speak of his wife Alicia it was almost with awe. Yet he persisted in bedding Mary, and seemed desperate for her to say she loved him. At times he gave her some pleasure, but more often his love-making was like the first night, fast, furious and without any feeling.

Mary's feelings for Graham were based on pity more than anything else, for she sensed he was a complicated man, who didn't appear to have any true friends. He had no real love for the Marines and had told her many times he wished he could resign his commission. Mary sensed he was a coward, and that he lived in fear of being given new orders to go somewhere dangerous. Yet he liked the power he had as an officer and knew there was no place for him in civilian life.

Mary suspected that even the marriage he claimed was such a happy one survived because husband and wife were apart so much. Lieutenant Captain Watkin Tench, whom Graham belittled at every opportunity, was a far happier man.

Tench was Mary's other problem, for she felt she had fallen in love with him. While she doubted she would ever have looked his way if she'd met him when she was free, right from the first night they talked, she'd been smitten. It wasn't for his looks, which weren't that remarkable, nor because he could be relied on to give her extra food. It was because he cared about people, even convicts. He could command without brutality, and had a sense of humour too.

She loved his ready smile, a certain eagerness for life,

his generosity of spirit and his lack of prejudice. She had long since given up any hope of him as a lover, but she counted him as a friend.

She knew now that it was he rather than Graham who put her on the list for work up on deck. He always spoke to her kindly, and listened sympathetically when she went to him with complaints. While mostly he couldn't reduce the hardships the prisoners had to bear, for decisions were made much further up the hierarchy, he did what he could.

Tench was well aware of Mary's arrangement with Graham, but he did not appear to despise her for it. He was an intelligent and adventurous man, who had already seen more of the world than anyone else Mary had known. He liked order and calm, but he was courageous too, loyal and dutiful to his King and Country. Mary doubted he would ever lie or take a bribe, yet he had compassion for those who did.

He loved books, and had told Mary that he kept a meticulous diary which he hoped might be published one day. Mary often wondered if he mentioned her in his writings, for she felt he was fond of her. He had said once that he wrote a great deal about his view of the penal system, because it would be of interest in the future to historians.

One day just before Christmas, Mary was called out for washing duties with Bessie. It was a bitterly cold day, and for once Mary would have been glad not to have been chosen. Bending over a tub of washing, up to her armpits in icy water and exposed to the elements, was not something to be desired. Only the prospect of possibly seeing Tench made it bearable.

It was even worse than she feared. The wind from the sea cut through the poorly clad women like a knife. Bessie began to cry within minutes of putting her hands in the cold water, and however much Mary tried to take her mind off it, she couldn't be cheered.

They didn't wash the clothes as thoroughly as they had during the summer and by noon the job was completed, the whole deck festooned with wet shirts which would freeze on the lines.

As they made their way back to the hold, Tench appeared. 'I want a word with Mary Broad,' he said to the guard. 'I'll take her back myself in a few minutes.'

To Mary's surprise and delight, he ushered her into his cabin on the deck and gave her a cup of tea to drink. She clasped the cup with her two hands to warm them.

'Bless you,' she said gratefully. 'I'm so cold I thought I might die in a few more minutes.'

'I didn't just bring you in here to let you get warm,' he said. 'I have some news for you. Your transportation has been arranged.'

'When and where to?' she asked, hoping it was to be soon, to somewhere warmer than here.

'We are bound for New South Wales,' he said.

Mary could only stare at him for a moment. He had told her what he knew of this country on the other side of the world in a previous conversation. Captain Cook had reported on a place there he had named Botany Bay, which it was thought might be suitable for a penal colony.

But at the time Tench told her this, he considered New South Wales was unlikely to be the final destination of the convicts on the *Dunkirk*.

'"We" are to go?' she said. 'You mean you too?' She didn't think she'd mind being sent to hell if Tench was to be there along with her.

He smiled. 'Me too, they need Marines to keep you all in order. I am excited at the prospect. It's a new country, one I very much want to see. England needs a presence in that part of the world, and if this country is all that has been reported, it could become an important place for us.'

Tench's enthusiasm warmed Mary even more than the hot tea. As he went on to speak of the fleet of eleven ships being sent, of convicts building towns, of farming and being given free land when their sentences were up, she shared some of his excitement. She had always wanted to travel, a long voyage by sea didn't daunt her, and if they were to be the first people to land at Botany Bay there could possibly be good opportunities for someone as quick-witted as herself.

'Swear you won't tell the other women,' he warned her. 'I'm only telling you because I hoped it might cheer you. I watched you earlier out there in the cold and my heart went out to you.'

He went on to tell her that Botany Bay had some native people with black skin, that the government believed there was flax and timber there, and the climate was good, far warmer than in England. He said Captain Cook had reported many strange animals and birds, including a large furry beast that bounded along on its back legs, and a huge flightless bird. But though Mary was interested to know more about this new country so far away, it was Tench's words, 'my heart went out to you', that resonated in her mind.

'When will we sail?' was all she could ask.

Tench sighed. 'We have orders to take you to the ships on the 7th of January, but I suspect it will be some time before we set sail. Captain Phillip, who is commanding this operation, is not yet satisfied with the supplies of goods and food to be taken with us.'

'Will I be on the same ship as you?' Mary asked.

'Would you like to be?' he asked, his dark eyes looking hard at her.

'I would,' she said bluntly, seeing no point in being bashful.

'I think I could arrange that,' he said, and smiled. 'Now, not a word to anyone, especially Lieutenant Graham.'

'Is he going too?' she asked.

Tench shook his head. 'Does that sadden you?'

Mary smiled. 'No, not at all. I don't think he's a man for an adventure.'

Tench chuckled, and Mary wondered if that meant Graham had in fact refused to go. 'No, he's not one for adventure, Mary. But you and I are, and perhaps we'll see things we never dreamed of.'

Chapter four

The prisoners were not informed of the date of their transportation until the morning of 7 January, the day they were to be moved to the *Charlotte*.

Ever since Tench had told Mary when it would be, she'd been in a state of agitation, made far worse because she was unable to share it with anyone else. One moment she was hugging herself with glee that her days on the *Dunkirk* were numbered, the next she was terrified that the sea voyage and the land at the end of it would be even worse.

As the days slowly passed and she'd still heard nothing official, she began to think Tench might be mistaken. She couldn't even ask Graham to verify it, for he would undoubtedly take Tench to task for telling her.

Lieutenant Graham was behaving very strangely though. More and more, he fluctuated wildly between tenderness and malice. This in itself seemed to confirm Mary really was leaving.

'You are just a whore,' he said with venom one night. 'You might think you are different from the rest of the women in the hold, but you aren't, just a damned whore like all the rest.'

Yet on another occasion as she was getting dressed to go back down to the hold, he fell down on his knees before her and clung to her with his face buried in her breast. 'Oh, Mary,' he gasped out. 'I should have done more for you, not used you the way I have.'

On Christmas night he was very drunk and he told her he loved her. That night his love-making was gentle and very tender; he kissed the marks on her ankles made by the shackles and with tears in his eyes, begged her to forgive him for his moments of cruelty to her.

'There's nothing to forgive,' she said. His previous insults hadn't really hurt her, at least not if she stacked them up against the good things he'd done for her.

'Then tell me you love me,' he begged her. 'Let me believe you came to me for something more than food and clean clothes.'

'Of course I did,' she lied, feeling sorry that he wasn't able to accept their arrangement as she did. 'But you aren't free to love me, Spencer, so please don't give me false hope by saying such things.'

She didn't love him, she wasn't sure that she even liked him, yet that night he had moved her, touched some inner part of her. As she made her way back to the hold the following morning, with another, newer grey dress, she wondered whether if they'd met under different circumstances it could have been different.

On the night of 6 January he called her out again, and she expected it was to tell her about the move the following day. But he said nothing about it, offered no endearments, further apologies or good wishes for her future.

He just took her roughly, and curtly ordered her back to the hold. If she hadn't known better, she might have thought he didn't know what was coming for her.

It was barely light when the guards opened the door of the hold and read out the names of the women who were to go up on deck. Mary wasn't surprised by the brusque order, but she was startled to hear just twenty names called, and some of those the old and infirm.

The reaction of the women called up on to the deck in a sleet storm was understandable. They were suspicious, puzzled and dismayed, clutching their ragged clothes about them and huddling together for warmth. Mary had to act just like them, for if anyone was to guess she knew where they were going, she'd be in trouble for not telling them. Yet as she stood there shivering on the deck, she was at least glad that Sarah and Bessie had been called, and Aggie, her old adversary, left behind.

Mary Haydon and Catherine Fryer were on the list as well, something Mary viewed with mixed feelings. They made a show of friendship now and then, but she sensed they would always be waiting for her downfall. Among forty women Mary had been able to keep her distance from them, but now the number was down to twenty it would be harder.

Thirty men were called out too, six of whom looked so sick and frail that they could barely be expected to stand, let alone survive a long voyage. But Mary was cheered to see Will Bryant and Jamie Cox among them, though disappointed that James Martin and Samuel Bird were not. Mary had grown to like all four men during her chats with them through the grille: Will and James both made her laugh, and Jamie had become like a younger brother. His crime had been stealing some lace valued at only five shillings, and he worried about how his widowed mother was managing without him. He was so mild and gentle that she was very relieved he could stay under the mantle of big Will's protection. She hoped James and Samuel would look out for each other when their other friends had gone.

The news that they were to be moved immediately to the *Charlotte* came from a man Mary had never seen before. He wore civilian clothes covered by a thick cloak, and a three-cornered hat trimmed with gold braid, and seemed ill at ease addressing felons. Perhaps his nervousness was because he expected his announcement would be met with anger. And it was: the majority of the prisoners let out a wail of outrage, for many had already served over half their original sentence and had husbands, wives or children they now feared they would never see again.

As always, protestations were ignored, and the guards moved menacingly closer. Only Mary dared to raise her voice with a question.

'Sir, are we to receive clothes for this voyage? Some of our number have little more than rags to wear, and I fear they will die of cold before we reach warmer climates.'

The man lowered his spectacles and peered over them at her.

'Your name?' he asked.

'Mary Broad, sir,' she called back. 'And some of the

women are already sick. Will there be a doctor to see them before we leave?'

'Everyone will be checked,' he said, but there was no certainty in his voice. He made no reply to the request for clothes.

It was dusk before all the prisoners from the *Dunkirk* were ferried out to the *Charlotte* in Plymouth Sound. Mary's only thought as she saw the ship was surprise that it was so small, just a three-masted barque perhaps a hundred feet long. But it looked sturdy, and she was so perished with cold that she was incapable of taking anything else in.

The belief they were to set sail within a few days was soon dashed. It seemed the rest of the fleet wasn't ready and there was a problem with the seamen's wages. The conditions on the *Charlotte* were superior to the *Dunkirk*'s in as much as rations were larger, and the twenty women were not joined by any other prisoners, so they had more space. The men were not so lucky, for they had been joined by prisoners from elsewhere in England, making a total of eighty-eight. But as the *Charlotte* was anchored out in the Sound, and the hatches to the holds were closed because of bad weather, many of the women suffered from sea sickness immediately. Within days the conditions were almost as foul as those on the *Dunkirk*.

Week after week passed with no news of sailing. As they were still chained and kept in darkness for most of the day, with the ship wallowing in the waves, any optimism the women had felt at first was soon replaced by despair. Many of them took to their bunks and sought refuge in sleep. Those who found themselves unable to do this squabbled among themselves.

There were times when Mary fervently wished she was still on the *Dunkirk*. She desperately missed her conversations with Tench and the male prisoners, and even her visits to Graham. Tench was on leave, and on the rare occasions the women were allowed up on deck, the few Marines and sailors on board ignored them.

The brief periods on deck were a torment to Mary. While it was wonderful to breathe clean, salty air, to be able to stand upright and walk, the sight of Cornwall on the horizon was almost too painful to bear. And it was worse still to be forced to return to the stinking hold, never knowing when she'd get out again.

She found herself recalling the most inconsequential things about her home and family as she lay shivering on her bunk. The way Dolly and she used to brush each other's hair at night, laughing at how it crackled and sparked. Father chopping up wood for the fire, shouting through the window that he should have had boys so they could do it. Mother straining her eyes threading a needle by candlelight. She wouldn't sew and mend by day when the light was good because she felt it was sinful to spend daylight hours doing something she enjoyed.

Mostly these memories were tender ones, but now and again Mary would be stricken by a bitter one too. Like the time her mother beat both her and Dolly because they'd gone into the sea naked.

On the day it happened Mary hadn't understood why their mother was so angry. It seemed totally illogical to her. It was after all a very hot day, and surely if she and Dolly had spoiled their new clothes with salt water, that would have been much more serious.

Of course it wasn't Dolly's idea: she couldn't swim, and a paddle was all she wanted. Mary made her do it.

Mary could see them both now. Dolly was about sixteen, and had the Sunday afternoon off from her job in service, so they'd gone for a walk to the beach at Menabilly. Both girls were wearing new pink dresses. Their uncle Peter Broad, who was a mariner and rumoured in the family to be making a lot of money, had brought back the silky material from one of his voyages overseas, and Mother had spent weeks making them.

Dolly was absolutely thrilled with her new dress. She adored the colour pink and the style was a very fashionable one, with a nipped-in waist and a small bustle. Mary wasn't struck on pink, nor did she want to be dressed identically to her sister. It was bad enough that Dolly always managed to look perfect, whatever she wore, for she was naturally neat, but when they were dressed the same, Mary thought her own defects showed up more. They were very alike in as much as they both had the same dark curly hair, but Dolly was much daintier, with a tiny waist, a graceful way of walking, and big blue eyes that enchanted everyone. Next to her Mary felt plain and awkward.

By the time they got to the beach they were very hot,

and Dolly was disappointed that there was no one there to see her in her new finery.

'It was silly to come here,' she said peevishly. 'Now we've got to walk all the way back in the heat.'

'Let's cool down in the sea then,' Mary suggested.

Dolly was worried about their dresses of course, but after some persuasion Mary convinced her that they could go beyond the beach and through the woods, then come out again at the water's edge, take their dresses off and paddle.

One thing led to another. Once they were in a place where they couldn't be seen, Dolly saw no point in getting her petticoat or shift wet either, for she was sure Mary would splash her. Maybe for that one time she wanted to be as daring as her younger sister, and when Mary took off every stitch of clothing and went in for a dip, Dolly followed her willingly.

It was the most fun they'd ever had together. Mary held Dolly under her stomach and tried to teach her to swim. She couldn't get the hang of it, so Mary pulled her along in the water by her hands. They were so engrossed in playing that they forgot to keep an eye out for anyone watching.

Later, dressed again, they giggled all the way home, and Dolly told Mary funny stories about some of the other maids where she worked.

Their mother was standing outside the house when they got home, and even from a distance they knew she was very angry. Her mouth was set in a straight line and she had her arms folded across her chest.

'You little hussies,' she shrieked at them as she came closer. 'Get inside at once and explain yourselves.'

It seemed a fisherman in his boat had seen them bathing, and passed on the information to someone else, who hastily reported back to their mother.

'The shame of it,' she kept saying over and over again as she clouted them up the stairs and ordered them to remove their clothes.

She beat them with a stick across their bottoms and backs, drawing blood on Dolly. Then she banished Mary to bed without any supper, and Dolly back to her employers.

Mary had thought then that her mother was a cruel kill-joy. She couldn't see what harm there had been in swimming naked. And she continued to blame her mother when Dolly never seemed to want to go anywhere with her again.

Mary sighed as she remembered that day. She had been so innocent then, barely aware of her own budding breasts, let alone of how desirable Dolly was. She certainly didn't have any idea that her mother was afraid of what might have happened if her daughters had been spotted by a couple of sailors.

But she knew now, and understood what animals men could be. It seemed to her that almost everything her mother had tried to warn her about had happened. Even the absence of the menses.

Mother had always been vague about what happened between men and women, but she had warned them about what she called 'funny business', and said when the menses didn't arrive it meant a girl was having a baby.

Mary tried to convince herself this couldn't be so, that perhaps it was only the result of the anxiety of waiting for the ship to sail. But by March she was forced to face the possibility that she was expecting Graham's child, and she consulted Sarah.

'I reckon you are,' she said, looking at Mary thoughtfully. 'You poor cow, I'd throw myself overboard in the chains if I thought I was. I've heard tell you can get a reprieve from hanging because of your belly, but I never heard of anyone getting off transportation because of it.'

Mary's heart sank even further then, for she had expected Sarah to pooh-pooh her fears. 'Well, if I am to have it, I'd rather have it here than on the *Dunkirk*,' she said defiantly. She had witnessed Lucy Perkins giving birth there and the horror of it hadn't left her. Lucy was not released from her chains, and after some twenty hours of labour her baby was stillborn. Lucy died a few days later. No doctor was called, the only help she'd had was from the other women. Sarah had been one of them. 'Besides, you'll help me, won't you?'

'Of course I will,' Sarah said quickly, perhaps remembering that birth too. 'You're strong and healthy, you'll be all right.'

Mary lay awake all that night worrying. Not so much about the birth, but what Tench would think of her when he found out. She would never stand a chance with him now.

*

It was the start of May, just after Mary's twenty-first birthday, when they finally heard they were to sail on Sunday the 13th to join the rest of the fleet. There would be eleven ships in all, four of them carrying nearly 600 convicts and a full company of Marines, some with their wives and children, and the rest carrying stores and provisions for the first two years.

During the long wait, most of the other prisoners had written home, or if they couldn't write, had others write letters for them. One day back in April while Mary and the other women were allowed up on deck for exercise, Tench had suggested writing one for Mary, but she refused his offer.

'It's better they don't know where I'm bound,' she said, looking sadly towards Cornwall across the choppy sea. A green haze of spring had suddenly appeared on the land in the last few days, and she thought nostalgically of primroses on grassy banks, birds nesting, and newborn lambs out on the moors. It seemed unbelievable that she was to be torn away from the land she loved so well. 'Better for them to think I don't care about them any more than to imagine me in chains.'

Tench glanced down at her chains and sighed. 'Maybe you're right. But I think my mother would sooner know I was alive and thinking of her, even if I was on a prison ship.'

Mary felt even sadder at his words. Before long her belly would be swollen and he'd see she was having a baby. She doubted he would want to continue to be her friend then. She could just about cope with never seeing her family again, but she didn't think she could stand to be rejected by Tench too.

As the *Charlotte* finally weighed anchor and slipped out of Plymouth Sound, many of the women were crying and saying their goodbyes to England forever.

'I shall come back,' Mary said firmly. 'I swear it.'

While many of the women grumbled even more about sea sickness, the sound of the wind in the sails, and the cuts and bruises they got from falls in bad weather, Mary found herself exhilarated once the ship got underway. The sound of wind in canvas was like music to her and she delighted in watching the bows cleave through the clear water.

The captain of the ship, a Royal Naval officer called Gilbert, was a humane man and he ordered the prisoners' chains to be removed, and only put back on as punishment for bad behaviour, or when they reached port. And as the ship sailed down the coast of France and the weather improved, the hatches were opened up again and the stink in the holds gradually dispersed.

Mary had always loved sailing, but she had never been in anything bigger than a fishing boat, and then only for a few hours at a time. It was very different on a big ship, for you could move about and even find quiet hideaways between coiled copes and lockers to get away from everyone else.

All at once she understood why her father had always eagerly anticipated his next voyage. It was exciting to feel the deck roll beneath her feet, and there was a kind of awe in seeing the wind harnessed to drive the ship along and the way everyone from the lowest sailor to the captain worked as one to maintain her speed and direction. The *Charlotte* was one of the slowest ships in the fleet, and the men had to work hard to keep up. Yet striving to hold their position was a challenge, and Mary could see the pride in their faces each time they managed to outrun the *Scarborough* or the *Lady Penryn*.

But it was the freedom to be up on deck for long periods which Mary appreciated above all else. She could cope with the hold at night, lying wrapped in a blanket between Bessie and Sarah; it wasn't so terrible if she'd been outside nearly all day.

Up on deck she was free from the carping and squabbling of the other women. She could feel the wind in her hair, the sun on her face, and she forgot the filth and smells below. Her fears for the future vanished like a feather tossed up into the wind. She felt as free as the seabirds who followed in the ship's wake.

The sounds on deck were almost as clamorous as those below: the roar of the sea, shouts from sailors, the rasps of pulled ropes and the creaking of sails. But they were good sounds, and the wind and sea spray were so clean and pure that she felt intoxicated.

She was glad most of the women found the sea frightening and the wind too cold to stay up there for long. Alone, gripping the deck rail, she could pretend to herself that she was an heiress taking a trip to Spain or even America. She could tell herself truthfully that she was doing what she'd always wanted to do, travelling the world.

Once they were underway, Mary found the sailors very much like the men back in Fowey, strong, wiry, friendly souls who grinned at her cheerfully. Without other women around she sometimes got opportunities to talk to them and ask them questions about the route to Botany Bay. Some of them were only too happy to tell her about the ports along the way they had visited before, and explained that they had to go right across the Atlantic Ocean to Rio, instead of down the African coast, to take advantage of the Trade Winds. Mary wondered how many of them had originally been press-ganged into the Navy, for they seemed to have some sympathy for the prisoners, and resentment towards most of the Marines who had precious little to do on the voyage.

Many of the Marines had brought their wives and children along too. The women looked fearful whenever they took a walk along the decks, and Mary felt sorry for them even if they were too snooty to smile. They were as much prisoners as she was, but while she knew just how harmless most of the real prisoners were, these women probably imagined they were all desperadoes, waiting for an opportunity to take over the ship and kill every soul on board.

Mary was glad that she seldom saw Tench on deck, for she could feel her body changing, even if it wasn't apparent to anyone else. Her breasts were fuller, her belly had a curve to it. She was dismayed that her liaison with Graham had led to this predicament, something she'd never really considered could happen to her, but she was becoming resigned to it. Part of this acceptance was because she'd been brought up to believe that all babies were a gift from God and therefore must be welcomed wholeheartedly. Whilst she had some fears about the delivery, and her own ability to be a good mother, she felt strangely warmed by the prospect of having someone all her own to love and nurture. In good weather she would find a sheltered place to sit up on deck, and lapse into day-dreams about her child. She hoped for a boy, and imagined him a little like Luke, a son of one of the Marines.

Luke was seven, a sturdy boy with dark hair and blue eyes, who smiled at her when his mother wasn't looking. Mary liked to watch him trying to help the sailors – he was clearly as keen on sailing as she had been as a girl. As the ship sailed down the coast of France to Spain and the weather became warmer, Luke's mother often sat with him on deck, helping him to read and write. Mary wished then that she had such skills to pass on to her child.

It was fear for her baby's safety that finally made her approach Surgeon White. Her father had always said that ships' surgeons were either butchers or drunks, but she had never seen White drunk. His jovial face, and his gentle manner when he checked her health just before sailing, didn't appear to belong to a butcher, either.

She hadn't told anyone but Sarah of her predicament, and she was certain no one, especially not Tench, had guessed. But however embarrassing it was to admit it to the doctor, she realized she must face up to it.

'I think I'm with child,' she blurted out, after first asking him if he could give her something for a cut on her foot which wouldn't heal.

He raised one bushy grey eyebrow, then asked her a few questions and got her to lie down so he could feel her belly.

'Will I be all right?' she asked when he made no comment.

'Of course you will, a birth at sea is no different to one anywhere else,' he said a little sharply. 'I'd say it is due in early September, so we'll be somewhere warmer and more congenial by then. You are strong and healthy, Mary, you'll be fine.'

Mary realized then that she had probably conceived at Christmas, the night Spencer Graham had been his most loving.

'Who is the father?' the surgeon asked, his sharp dark eyes boring into her as if he'd read her thoughts. 'You must say, Mary, for the father must be made responsible. If it is another convict you can be married, and a Marine can be made to give the child his name.'

It was surprising to Mary that anyone should care who'd got her pregnant, and even more so that they would take any man to task for it. But she wasn't prepared to name Graham. Without him she wouldn't have survived the *Dunkirk*, and then there were his wife and children who didn't deserve the hurt of knowing he'd been unfaithful.

'His name, Mary?' White said more firmly.

'I don't know who the father is,' she said, folding her arms in a gesture of defiance.

'I don't believe that of you,' he said reprovingly. 'Some of the other women I might, but not you. Now tell me and leave me to deal with it.'

'I won't,' she said stubbornly.

White tutted. 'Your loyalty is admirable but misplaced, Mary. Do you want your child to have "bastard" on his record of birth?'

'It's no worse than having a convict for a mother,' she retorted.

White shook his head, then dismissed her, with only the parting shot that she must think on it and come back to him if she changed her mind.

The day following her visit to the surgeon, a storm broke out, and once more the hatches were battened down and Mary was forced to stay in the hold. After the freedom of the deck it was hideous to be trapped again in darkness with the women, most of whom were in the throes of sea sickness. The ship rolled and pitched, the slop buckets overturned, and icy sea water rushed in, soaking them all. All Mary could do was clutch her blanket more tightly round her, cover her nose against the smells, and pray for the storm to pass quickly.

It took three weeks to reach Santa Cruz in Tenerife, the ship's first port of call, by which time Mary had got to know a couple of the Devonshire sailors quite well. It was from them she learned that on one of the other transport ships the male convicts had broken through the bulkheads to get at the females, even before they sailed. They said too that the women who had been brought down from the London prisons were vicious, hardened criminals, always fighting among themselves, ready to sell themselves to anyone for a tot of rum.

This was frightening to Mary, for she had imagined the prisoners on the other ships to be no different to those on the *Charlotte*. Some of those were bad enough, she knew they'd happily steal pennies from a dead person's eyes. But at least she knew which ones to watch, and she felt secure in the knowledge that Captain Gilbert would never allow the male prisoners on his ship to threaten the women.

Although a humane man, he was very strict. On the few occasions when male prisoners were on deck at the same time as women, they were watched carefully by the Marines for any misbehaviour. And the threat of being put back in chains or receiving a flogging was enough to deter both male and female from taking any risks.

Yet like on the *Dunkirk*, there were illicit relationships, formed not with the officers, but the Marines and sailors. Mary Haydon and Catherine Fryer were two of the worst offenders, going with any man who would have them. Neither Mary nor Sarah chose to go down this route; they laughed together about it, and said if they couldn't have an officer then they didn't want anyone. The truth of the matter was that they didn't have to fight for survival any more. They had enough to eat now, water to wash with, and after a day on the deck in the sunshine it was preferable to go back to the hold at night than be humiliated and mauled by a rum-soaked sailor.

The only male prisoner that Mary saw often was Will

Bryant, and occasionally Jamie Cox was with him too. The rest of the men weren't allowed up on deck for long. Whether this was because they outnumbered the crew, or that Captain Gilbert felt the women prisoners and the Marines' families needed fresh air more, Mary didn't know, but Will got special privileges. It seemed he had talked his way into being allowed to do some fishing to supplement the ship's rations, so he spent a good part of every day on deck. Mary admired his resourcefulness, and thought they had a lot in common.

When the ship dropped anchor in Santa Cruz to take on fresh water and more provisions, the ship's company were free to go ashore, and once again the prisoners were chained and the hatches closed. It was June and the heat was suffocating, and to be forced to lie sweltering in the darkness after the comparative freedom they'd enjoyed before was intolerable. For Mary it was even more unbearable as now that her belly was swelling she found it impossible to get comfortable on the hard bench, and the lack of fresh air made her nauseous.

But as they set sail again to Rio in South America, the chains were removed and they were allowed on deck again. One afternoon, Mary was sitting dozing in the sunshine when she heard Will Bryant swearing because his fishing net was torn. She got up and made her way back to the stern where he was sitting and offered to mend it for him.

He had become even more attractive during the voyage. The increased rations had put flesh back on his body, his eyes were as blue as the sky above, his fair hair and beard bleached by the sun and his skin a golden-brown. He also had an impudent grin and a great deal of cheek.

'You know how to mend a net?' he asked, looking surprised.

'Would any girl from Fowey not know how to?' she laughed.

Mary thought that it was because she was usefully employed mending the net that no one came over and ordered them apart. She and Will spent the whole afternoon chatting together, mostly about Cornwall.

'You're looking very bonny,' Will said suddenly. 'When's the little 'un due?'

Mary was stricken with sudden embarrassment. She hadn't realized anyone other than Surgeon White and Sarah knew. If Will had guessed, maybe Tench knew too!

'September,' she murmured, blushing to the roots of her hair. 'How did you know?'

'I've got eyes,' Will laughed. 'It ain't something you can hide forever, not when the wind blows your dress close to you.'

Mary felt a little queasy. 'Does everyone know?'

Will shrugged. 'Dunno. Why? Are you scared?'

'A bit,' she admitted. 'I don't want folk to think badly of me, and I don't know much about babies.'

'Don't you trouble yourself about what folk think,' he said with a grin. 'There'll be plenty of other women having a babby afore we get there. As for not knowing about babbies, reckon that comes natural like. The other women will help you too, so don't you fret about nothing.'

Mary was touched that he could be sensitive, she'd

always thought of him as being something of a hard man. A little later he told her he'd heard that a convict on the *Alexander*, another ship in the fleet, had hidden on the deck in Tenerife and lowered himself into the sea later when it was dark and stolen the rowing boat tied to the stern.

'Damn great lummox gave himself away by going to a Dutch ship and asking to be taken aboard,' Will laughed. 'I'd have made for the town and hidden up till the fleet was gone.'

'I used to think about escape all the time on the *Dunkirk*,' Mary admitted. 'There's no point in thinking on it now, not in my condition. But as soon as the baby's born, I'll be watching for an opportunity again.'

'I'll wait to see what Botany Bay's like first,' Will said. 'If I can fish, build a decent place to live, grow a few vegetables, it might not be so bad.'

'But we don't know what the prisoners on the other transports are like,' Mary pointed out. 'All us lot are from Devon and Cornwall. None of us are real bad 'uns. But I've heard tell the women on the *Friendship* are a tough lot, mostly from London. They got put in irons for fighting among themselves. Once we go ashore in Botany Bay we'll have them to put up with.'

'Reckon you can handle most kinds of folk,' Will said. 'I can too. We'll get by.'

It was only a few days later that Tench spoke to Mary up on deck. He asked if she was enjoying the voyage, and explained that he hadn't had much opportunity to be on deck as he had many duties elsewhere. 'Are you feeling well?' he asked, looking at her intently. 'The surgeon told me you were expecting a child.'

Mary could only nod. While to some extent she was relieved it was out in the open, she was afraid that he would question her as White had done.

'I don't pass judgement on others,' he said gently, as if guessing what she was thinking. 'I'm just concerned about you. You are lucky White is aboard this ship, he's a good surgeon. Are you getting enough to eat?'

Mary nodded again. She didn't trust herself to speak.

'If you need anything, come to me,' he said, patting her on the shoulder. 'I'll try and get you some fruit in Rio. Scurvy is a menace on these long voyages. But Captain Gilbert appears to be more aware of all our needs than most sea captains.'

He walked away then, and as Mary watched his slim back, the neatness of his dark hair and the cleanliness of his white breeches, she wished it could have been his child she was carrying.

There were some terrible storms on the way to Rio. The ship pitched and rolled in the heavy seas, and water rushed into the holds, sweeping the women off their bunks. Again and again they thought they would all perish – every crack of the ship's timbers appeared to be evidence she was breaking up. Even Mary, who hadn't suffered from sea sickness before, fell prey to it, retching until she had nothing more to bring up, so weak she could barely move.

But the storms passed and then there were periods of

calm when the ship barely moved at all. It was on one of those days, as Mary stood at the deck rail watching the rest of the fleet, and keeping an eye out for dolphins and porpoises, that Tench suggested she looked among the male prisoners for a husband.

He didn't often get the opportunity to speak to her, and even when he did it was never for more than a few minutes, but since the day when he'd told her he knew of her pregnancy, he usually slipped her something when he saw her. Sometimes it was a piece of hard cheese, or a couple of ship's biscuits; on two occasions it had been a hard-boiled egg. That he cared about her health was enough for Mary. She didn't want him getting a reprimand from the captain.

'Have you considered how it will be when we get to Botany Bay?' Tench began, looking not at her but out to sea and the rest of the fleet marooned in the calm. 'I mean, have you considered how many more men there will be than women?'

She shook her head.

'There will be three to every woman,' he went on, frowning as if deeply concerned by this. 'I suspect it may prove difficult for you women.'

Mary realized with some shock that he was alluding to the likelihood of rape. 'Won't you Marines look after us?' she asked.

'We'll do our best,' he said seriously. 'But even with the best will in the world we won't be able to be every-where, all of the time.'

Mary shuddered. She knew from Will that many of the

122

men were very desperate characters, but then so were many of the women. Theft of food and belongings was the main thing she'd thought about, but now Tench had made her aware that stealing wasn't going to be the only problem.

'You'd do well to consider getting wed,' he said.

For one brief second she thought it was a proposal, and her heart leaped.

'Wed?' she repeated.

'To one of the prisoners, of course,' he said quickly. 'Your baby will need a father.'

Mary knew she was blushing and she hoped he didn't know why. 'I hardly know any of them,' she said indignantly.

Tench looked over his shoulder, checking to see who was watching them. 'I must go now,' he said. 'But think about what I've said, will you?'

He walked away before Mary could say anything more.

Mary did think hard about what Tench had said. The more she thought about it, the more sense his words made. Men who had been locked away from women for so long were likely to be dangerous, and so were some of the women too.

It was Tench she wanted, she felt she would love him forever and no other man could make her feel that way. But she was a realist; he might like her, maybe even have some romantic feelings for her, but it would take more time than she'd got to make him love her enough to step over the line and take a convict woman. Besides, he was due to go back to England after three years, and she'd still have another four years of her sentence to complete.

There was only one convict she'd seen that she could admire, and that was Will Bryant. He was strong and capable, and he could read and write, he had a real trade in fishing, and he shared her love of boats and the sea. He was also handsome, and he was a natural leader.

The more she thought about Will, the more certain she became that he would be the ideal husband. Of course he wasn't going to see her as much of a catch, she'd have a child which wasn't his for a start. Nor was she that pretty. But there had to be some way to make him see she'd be an asset to him.

All through the eight weeks to Rio, Mary thought of little else but how she was going to persuade Will to become her husband. Because of her condition, Surgeon White gave her permission to stay on deck all day in good weather and have a larger share of rations. This meant she saw Will almost every day, and she mended his nets, gutted the fish for him, often gave him some of her extra food, and flattered him.

Almost daily she found some new facet in Will. His bragging could be wearing, he thought he could do almost anything better than another man, but he was strong, practical and knowledgeable. Yet he had a gentle side too. He always inquired how she was feeling, and once he'd asked if he could put his hand on her belly to feel the baby kick, and looked astounded when he felt it. He was protective of those weaker than himself, and he was a jolly man, rarely down in the mouth about anything.

When the ship had docked in Rio, the chains went on again, hatches were locked, and the crew went ashore. From time to time the prisoners were allowed up on deck for short periods and those who had money could buy produce from the swarthy men who came alongside the ship in little boats to barter with them.

Some of the more fortunate convicts had relatives close enough to Devonport to bring new clothing, food, money and other items for them before the ship sailed. A few had money they'd managed to hang on to throughout their time in prison and the hulk. Will was one of these – he told Mary he'd kept it in a pouch hidden beneath his shirt. He bought oranges and gave half of them to Mary. He also bought a length of white cotton and handed it to her. 'To make some baby clothes,' he said with a strangely shy smile.

When Tench came back on board, a little fragile from all the drinking and carousing he'd done with the other men ashore, he too had a present for her. A blanket for the baby.

'Will bought me cotton to make some clothes,' she added after she'd thanked him, biting back tears of gratitude. 'I'm lucky to have two such good friends.'

'Will's the man you should marry,' Tench said abruptly, taking her completely by surprise.

'Marry me!' she exclaimed, as if such a thing had never crossed her mind. 'Why would he want me when there's prettier women without a child on the way?'

'Because you're clever, good company and steadfast,'

he said, his brown eyes twinkling. 'Those are the attributes I'd look for in a wife.'

'What about love?' she asked, wishing she knew how to flirt the way she'd seen other women do to lure the man they wanted.

'I believe love comes when two people are completely in tune with one another,' he said earnestly. 'I think many people mistake lust for love. The two are very different.'

'But don't they go together?' she asked.

'Sometimes, if you are very fortunate,' he smiled. 'Sadly most of us get one or the other, not both. Or worse still, feel all that for someone who just isn't suitable.'

Mary had a feeling he was trying to tell her that was how he felt about her.

'But surely if you feel that way they can become suitable?' she said wildly.

'Maybe.' He shrugged his shoulders and looked across the harbour to Rio. 'If you could take that person to some new place where your backgrounds didn't matter.'

Their conversation was halted abruptly by Captain Gilbert coming aboard. Tench had to go and greet him, and Mary slipped back to the stern of the ship to gaze at Rio across the bay and wonder if Tench had wished he could take her there.

But if he had, why was he encouraging her to think of Will? Surely that wasn't what men did? But Mary had long ago realized that Tench wasn't like other men.

They sailed out of Rio harbour on 4 September, and three days later, in the evening, Mary went into labour.

It wasn't so bad at first. She lay quietly next to Bessie and even managed to doze. But by the early hours of the morning she was in real pain, and she had to get up and hold on to one of the ship's beams to alleviate it. Surgeon White was called at mid-morning, but he pronounced everything to be normal and said first babies always took a long time. His only preparations were to order two women, who just happened to be Mary Haydon and Catherine Fryer, to collect some straw for Mary to lie on.

The ship was rolling in a heavy swell, and Mary and Catherine were entirely unsympathetic towards Mary. To make matters worse, the hatches were closed because of high winds, so the hold was dark and stuffy.

'You 'ad the pleasure,' Mary Haydon said spitefully. 'Now you got to suffer the pain.'

Mary had always been aware that these two women had continued to hold her responsible for their plight, however much they had insisted in the past that it was done and forgotten. Every time Mary had received gratitude or praise from the other women, she had sensed their jealousy. She guessed they saw her labour as a chance to get even, hoping she'd make an exhibition of herself and lose some of the admiration the others had for her.

But Mary wasn't going to give them the satisfaction of that. When the next pain came she gritted her teeth and bore it silently.

On and on it went, each pain a little stronger until she was forced to lie down and cling to the knotted rope one of the older women had thoughtfully tied around a beam for her to pull on. Sarah sat beside her, bathing her head, and making her take sips of the brackish water.

'It won't be long now,' she whispered encouragingly. 'And if you want to scream, you do it, don't pay no mind to those two witches.'

Mary thought she might die of the agony, and wondered in a brief moment between pains how women could bring themselves to have more than one child. But then, just as she felt unable to bear any more, there was a new sensation, one of wanting to bear down.

She had heard other women, including her mother, speak of this part, and knew it meant the baby was fighting its way out. Suddenly she felt a wave of tenderness for the child within her, and a determination to expel him or her as quickly as possible.

'It's coming now,' she whispered to Sarah, and as the next pain came she clenched her teeth together, brought her legs up, pulled on the rope and bore down hard.

She was vaguely aware that the other women were having their evening meal beyond the blanket Sarah had thoughtfully hung up to give her some privacy – she could smell the stew and hear them chewing. The rolling and the bucking of the ship seemed to echo what was going on with her body, and she was glad of the darkness hiding what she knew must be a very ungainly sight.

She heard Sarah order someone to go and get the surgeon, but it was some time before he came, and he left almost immediately after giving Sarah some curt instructions and a lantern to see by.

'Don't leave me,' Mary screamed as he walked away.

'The women will deal with it,' he said sharply. 'I can't stand upright in here.'

'Bastard,' Sarah spat at his retreating back. But she leaned over to wipe Mary's face tenderly. 'You still got me,' she said soothingly. 'I know what to do, love, you'll be all right.'

The pain was red-hot, and it seemed to Mary she could almost see it glowing through her skin as Sarah washed her bottom and thighs with cool water. As she gave one long huge push she felt the baby coming, and heard Sarah's cry that she could see its head.

Mary had the sensation that a big slippery fish was being drawn out of her. The pain had ceased, and she could hear voices from behind the blanket curtain.

'You've got a little girl,' Sarah crowed delightedly. 'A fine big one too.'

The light from the lantern was dim, but Mary could see Sarah holding up what looked like a skinned rabbit. Then all at once its cry burst out, an angry, defiant yell as if dismayed to find itself in a dark ship's hold.

'She'll make it,' Sarah said with relief in her voice, and put the baby in Mary's arms. 'Now, what are you going to call her?'

Mary couldn't reply for a moment. She could only stare down in awe at her baby. She had a shock of black hair, she looked purple in the dim light, and her little fists were pummelling the air. It seemed unbelievable that this angry little scrap was something which had grown within her.

'I'll call her Charlotte,' she said eventually. 'After the

ship.' Then, as she got a flash of Graham's face looking tenderly at her the night their baby was probably conceived, she added, 'Charlotte Spence.'

'Spence?' Sarah asked. 'What sort of name is that?'

Mary didn't trust herself to answer that one. 'Could I have a drink now? I'm parched.'

It was very late at night when Charles White got back to his cabin, having returned to the hold to find that Mary's baby had arrived safely. He poured himself a glass of whisky, then sat down to write up his diary.

'8 September,' he began. 'Mary Broad. Delivered of a fine girl.'

He sat for a moment, unable to think of anything else that had happened during the day. Mary, lying cradling her baby in that filthy, stinking hold, filled his mind to the exclusion of all else. He had been called to many births over the years, from women of quality in fine houses to peasant women in hovels, and he'd helped them all and been touched by the wonder of new life. He felt some shame that he'd left Mary to fend for herself, for she was clearly a good woman, a cut above her companions with her intelligence and her calm, reserved manner.

Perhaps it was because he knew it was unlikely the infant would survive more than a few weeks. Infant mortality was high enough on dry land, but on a ship with rats, lice, foul water and every kind of disease lurking, waiting to find some weakened recipient, a newborn baby stood little chance. There had been surprisingly few deaths so far, most of those attributed to sickness brought with the convicts from the prison hulks. But there was still a long way to go before they reached Botany Bay.

And when they arrived, things would get far tougher. There were houses to be built, land to be tilled and planted. The natives might be hostile, the weather inclement. It was hardly an ideal environment in which to rear young children.

But he thought Mary would make an excellent mother, she had so many remarkable qualities. He wondered again who the baby's father was, and considered Tench, for he had been on the *Dunkirk* with Mary. He had obviously been waiting for news of her, and his eyes had lit up when White told him about the new arrival. He'd been eager to hear the sex and name of the baby and whether Mary was well.

Yet for all that, he couldn't see Tench as the kind to take a convict woman. He was an upright, honest young man, with a great deal of natural dignity, more interested in putting the world to rights than philandering. But he did have some feelings for Mary Broad, that much was evident. Understandable really, when even a crusty old surgeon like himself found her intriguing.

Charles sighed deeply. There were so many unknown factors in this grand idea of emptying out the prison ships and sending all the undesirables to the other side of the world. No one really knew about the country's climate and its native people, or whether the land could be cultivated. It was a huge gamble, not just with the prisoners' lives, for precious few people back in England cared a jot about them, but with those who were sent to keep them in line.

Captain Arthur Phillip, the commanding officer of the whole fleet, had himself expressed concern that there weren't sufficient provisions, tools and clothing in the supply ships, and that the quality of them all was poor. Nor were there many skilled craftsmen among the prisoners.

Charles stared gloomily at his unwritten diary. If all the prisoners had been like Mary Broad and Will Bryant, intelligent, resourceful people, then the project might have a chance of success. Sadly, a huge proportion of them were complete scoundrels, the slime at the bottom of England's barrel. In truth, the idea was doomed before it had even started.

As the ship sailed towards the port of Cape Town five weeks later, Mary stood at the rails with Charlotte in her arms and marvelled at the beauty of the scene before her.

The sun was setting, the sky pink and mauve, and all eleven ships were close to one another now, their sails billowing in the wind. The sea was turquoise, and a school of dolphins were leaping and diving around them, as if putting on a special show. They had been seeing dolphins and whales too for some days now, a sight Mary never tired of.

'And you aren't even watching,' she said tenderly to Charlotte, who was fast asleep, wrapped in the blanket Tench had given her.

The horrors of her daughter's birth were quite forgotten now. Mary had ample milk and Charlotte was thriving. But then Mary devoted her entire attention to her child.

She never would have believed that she could feel so much for her baby. She rarely put her down, for she didn't trust the other women not to stick their dirty fingers in her mouth, or drop her if they picked her up. One of the sailors had made a little crib for her to sleep in, but though Mary would put her in it up on deck during the day, with a cloth hung over it to keep the sun off, at night she was too worried about the rats, and kept Charlotte firmly in her own arms.

Captain Gilbert had said she could be baptized when they got to Cape Town, as the clergyman for the fleet would be coming on board there. That had touched Mary: she had expected that a prisoner's child would be treated with disdain, as if it wasn't quite human.

'We'll be able to see Table Mountain by tomorrow morning, I expect,' Tench said suddenly by her elbow. Mary hadn't seen or heard him coming towards her. 'It looks just like a table too,' he went on. 'Flat on the top, and when there's mist hanging around it makes a tablecloth, at least so I'm told. I haven't been to Cape Town before.'

'You'll be able to explore it,' Mary said wistfully. 'See all those wild animals and things.'

She knew Tench liked exploring and writing in his diary about where he had been and what he'd seen. She had never met a man with so much enthusiasm for new places and strange things.

'You won't always be a prisoner, Mary,' he said, his

133

voice soft with sympathy. 'Once the settlement in Botany Bay is thriving, and your sentence is up, there will be opportunities for a woman like you to make good.'

'You'll have gone home by then,' she said, trying to keep her tone light.

'I expect so,' he said. 'But you'll be part of a new community, and I've no doubt you will be married too. Perhaps little Charlotte will have a brother or sister.' He bent his head closer to the baby in Mary's arms and kissed her forehead. 'Go for Will Bryant, Mary, he's the best man for you.'

Tench had said nothing more about Will since long before Charlotte was born, but the fact that he'd obviously kept it in his mind proved to Mary he was completely serious about it.

'How would I go about it, just supposing I thought that was a good plan?' she asked.

Tench thought for a moment. 'I'd lay my cards on the table. Point out the advantages for him having a wife. Especially one like you.'

Mary half smiled. 'Back home I would've been thought of as the worst possible choice for a man. I'm not good at cooking and sewing or womanly things.'

'There won't be much call for domestic talents in Botany Bay,' Tench said with a wry smile. 'It will be the toughest, the most adaptable that do well there. You've got backbone, Mary, and plenty of determination. Will knows that, he admires you. I don't think he'll take much persuading.'

'How would you feel if a woman asked you to marry

her?' she asked him, smiling as she asked, as if it was only banter.

'Now, that would depend who asked me,' he laughed. 'If she was rich and beautiful I'd be flattered.'

'So a poor, plain convict girl would have no chance?' she said, trying to sound as if she was joking, but she could hear a plaintive note in her own voice.

He didn't answer and Mary was shamed.

'I'm sorry, I've embarrassed you,' she said.

To her surprise he turned to face her and laid the palm of his hand gently against her cheek. 'I said I'd be flattered by someone rich and beautiful asking me. I'd also be just as flattered if it was a convict girl I really liked. But I wouldn't agree to either,' he said, looking right into her eyes. 'Not because I didn't care enough for her, or thought she was too lowly for me, but because I'm not the marrying kind, Mary. There's too many places I want to see to settle down with anyone.'

'You might end up a lonely old man,' Mary said, swallowing down a lump in her throat and fighting back tears.

'Yes, that's true, but at least I wouldn't have left a wife lonely without me while I explored the world,' he said, and smiled. 'Or children without a real father.'

Charlotte's baptism took place after they had been anchored at Cape Town for three days. The Reverend Richard Johnson came aboard on Sunday morning during a service for the entire ship's company and the prisoners.

Mary was the only prisoner not in chains. Hers had been removed for the duration of the service, but would be put back on immediately afterwards. She had made an effort with her appearance, washing her hair till it shone, and wearing the grey cotton dress given to her by Graham on the *Dunkirk*. She wished it wasn't so crumpled as she'd had to conceal it in the hold when given a 'slop', the shapeless, rough dresses doled out to the women prisoners.

The Reverend Johnson directed his sermon to the prisoners, saying that Botany Bay was a golden opportunity for them all, if they turned away from the wickedness which had caused them to be sent there. He urged the men to choose a wife, for only in matrimony would they find true happiness and contentment.

Mary became aware of Will's eyes on her as she stepped forward holding Charlotte in her arms for the christening ceremony. As the Reverend Johnson poured some water on the baby's head and she began to howl lustily, drowning his words, Mary offered up a silent prayer, not just for Charlotte's safety, but that Will would want her for his wife.

It was a week before Mary had any opportunity to speak to Will as they had run into some rough weather and had had to stay below deck. It was still a little precarious climbing up the companionway with a baby in her arms as the steps were slippery, but she was desperate to get out into the fresh air.

Will was on deck fishing again. Hearing footsteps behind him, he looked round and grinned. 'Good to be out of there, eh!'

'I couldn't stand another minute of it down there,' Mary said with a laugh. 'It's like breathing week-old soup.'

'You and I are made of the same stuff,' Will said, looking at her in approval. 'How's the little 'un?'

'Doing fine,' Mary said, looking down at the sleeping baby she had tied across her in a shawl for safety. 'I wonder if there's any babies on the other ships?'

'Several, I heard,' Will said. 'So at least Charlotte will have some playmates when she's bigger.'

'And if folk get married like the Reverend suggested, there'll soon be more,' Mary added.

Will laughed. 'A lot won't wait for a wedding service. Reckon we'll be overrun with babbies afore the first year's over.'

'But there's three men to every woman,' Mary said pointedly. 'I reckon wives will be in great demand.'

She felt nervous now, sure this was the moment, but afraid to say what was on her mind.

'I'll do all right,' Will said. 'I'll have them lining up for me.'

Mary felt a stab of irritation at his arrogance. 'You'd better choose carefully then,' she said sharply. 'From what I've seen below these decks few of the women have any common sense, and the ones on the other ships may be even more stupid.'

'You wouldn't be a bad prospect for any man,' Will said unexpectedly. 'You've got a good head on you, and you ain't a slattern like most.'

Mary took a deep breath to steady herself. 'I'd be a good prospect for you,' she blurted out. 'I know boats and fishing. We come from the same place, the officers like us both.'

Will seemed staggered at such a suggestion. He stared at her open-mouthed.

'Are you wanting me to wed you?' he said at length, his voice a little strained.

'You could do a lot worse,' she said, blushing furiously. 'I'm healthy and strong, I can work hard for what I want. I know I've got Charlotte and maybe a man doesn't want another's around . . .' She stopped suddenly, unable to think of any other good reason why he should choose her, and ashamed she had to beg.

'Well I never,' Will exclaimed, but he grinned broadly. 'I thought you was too proud to bend to anyone.'

'I'm not bending,' she said quickly. 'I like you, and it's practical.'

'I'd want a wife who does more than just like me,' he said. 'I want her to be hot for me.'

Mary was prepared to go to some lengths to get Will to agree to her proposition, but she didn't feel able to pretend a great passion for him. Faced with his smug grin, she felt foolish and inadequate.

'We've been good friends for over a year,' she said after a few minutes' thought. 'Would you want a friend to lie to you?'

'Of course not,' he said, though he was still grinning smugly. 'But I'd still like a wife who was hot for me.'

'Maybe I could be, in time,' she said wildly, blushing scarlet because she was sure he'd rush off to the other men and tell them what had passed between them. 'We haven't had a chance to get to know each other like that yet.' But before she could say anything further, a sudden shout of warning came from one of the Marines — clearly they were too close together for the man's comfort.

'I've got to go,' Mary said quickly. 'Think on it.'

The weeks that followed were hard, with violent storms and squalls, contrasting with periods of calm when the ship barely moved. The fresh-water ration was cut to conserve it, the food was becoming rotten. Mary had times of extreme anxiety when her milk looked as if it might fail, and she was frightened too of what lay ahead.

Most of the other women were so empty-headed they appeared to imagine they were going to a place that would be ready for them. Mary knew they would be living in tents, and that it was likely some of the foodstuffs taken with them would have perished on the voyage, the same way as many of the animals had. Before Charlotte's birth she had never dwelt on the possibility of the ship being wrecked, but now the fear was with her in every storm. The waters they were sailing in were barely charted, none of the crew had been there before. For all anyone knew, the natives in Botany Bay could be cannibals, there could be wild animals that would tear them apart.

But even worse in one respect was that Will hadn't said another word to her about her proposition. She didn't know if that meant he was still thinking about it, or if he found it too ludicrous to contemplate.

Chapter five

1788

Mary was just coming up the companionway with Charlotte in her arms when she heard the cry 'Land ahoy'. A surge of wild excitement grabbed her and she rushed up the last few steps and across the deck, to join crew members and other prisoners at the rail.

It didn't look much like land to her, just a slightly darker line on the far horizon which could easily be cloud, but she knew the sailor up in the rigging who had spotted it was unlikely to be wrong.

It was January, a whole year since Mary had been transferred to the *Charlotte* from the *Dunkirk*, eight months of that time spent at sea. Charlotte was now five months old. Five male prisoners and a Marine's wife on the *Charlotte* had died, but their deaths were attributed to diseases they carried with them from England, rather than lack of care on the voyage. In the main the prisoners were healthier than when they'd boarded the ship, thanks to fresh air and better rations. Few people had escaped some kind of accident, however, whether a broken limb or mere cuts and bruises, for the ship's deck and steps were dangerously slippery during foul weather.

On the whole, Mary had found the voyage an enjoyable experience. While she was often terrified in the worst of the storms, and despaired at the spite and depravity of some of her fellow prisoners, this had been balanced by the happiness Charlotte had given her. Contrary to all the gloomy predictions, she was thriving. She seemed to charm everyone, from the officers, Marines and sailors right down to the other prisoners, with her ready smiles and placid gurgling. She had given Mary real hope for the future, but now they were nearly at their destination, Mary's natural excitement was also tinged with anxiety.

Tench had told her back in Cape Town that the fleet would be split, the fastest ships going on ahead to prepare the settlement, but she knew that hadn't happened. Bad weather and unfavourable winds had slowed the first ships down, and the others, which included the *Charlotte*, had caught up with them. Mary could see all the ships now, and it was daunting to know there would be nothing ready for them, and that for all they knew the natives could be hostile.

Will Bryant and little Jamie Cox were at the rails, and Mary joined them. ''Tis a grand sight,' Will said with enthusiasm, making an expansive gesture with his hands at the other ships. 'I feared we might lose at least one of them, but they've all made it.'

The prospect of shipwreck had been in everyone's minds during the bad storms, and doubly so for Mary with Charlotte to protect. She had always found it comforting after a bad night to see at least one of the other ships close by in the morning. Will's remark suggested he felt this too.

'Aren't you scared of what's to come?' she asked.

He shrugged. 'Only that there won't be enough food to support us till we've grown some,' he admitted somewhat reluctantly.

'And you, Jamie?' Mary asked.

He smiled shyly. 'The natives mostly. What if they're cannibals?'

'You won't make much of a meal for them,' Mary laughed, and prodded him in the side. Jamie had put on a little more flesh during the voyage, but he still looked like a skinny child to her.

'So what are you scared of?' Will asked Mary.

'The other prisoners we don't know, mostly,' she said. 'And whether I'll be able to keep Charlotte safe and well.'

'I'll be looking out for you,' he said, patting her on the arm with one great paw.

Mary wondered exactly what that remark meant. Although she had gradually picked up the old friendship she'd had with him before her proposal, she'd never mentioned it again, and neither had he. She had to assume he didn't want her as a wife, and that silence was his way of not embarrassing her further.

'I hope you mean that,' she said with a smile. 'But I expect you'll be kept busy taking your pick of all the women. So I won't count on it.'

*

It was another three days before the *Charlotte* sailed into Botany Bay, for the wind had been against them. But there were no cheers, smiles or laughter from the seamen, Marines, officers or prisoners as they got their first view of the new land they'd come so far to populate. For once they all reacted in the same way, shocked into silence.

It looked utterly desolate, and parched by the burning sun. There was none of the expected green pasture, the few trees were scrubby and stunted. Yet even more daunting was the sight of the very black, stark naked natives who brandished spears menacingly at the ships. It was quite clear they weren't pleased to see white strangers invading their territory.

Most of the fleet had got there before the *Charlotte*, and a party of officers and Marines had already gone ashore to try to find a suitable site for their camp. But the prisoners were not allowed to stay on deck to watch the proceedings; once again they were made to return to the holds where they were locked in.

It was weeks later that Mary heard what had happened during the long days when she and her companions were incarcerated below decks in the suffocating heat. One story that would have amused them was that the natives hadn't known which gender the white officers were, and one of the group was asked to drop his breeches to show them.

It seemed that Captain Arthur Phillip had managed to divert the natives' hostility with gifts of beads and trinkets, but he'd been alarmed to find Botany Bay could not support over a thousand people and all the animals. The soil wasn't fertile, and the water supply was in the wrong place. So, with a small party, he set out in the ship's boats to try to find a more agreeable place further down the coast, leaving the rest of the company to clear trees in case he couldn't find anywhere better.

He came to a place called Port Jackson which he understood from Captain Cook's report to be a mere cove. As it was late afternoon he ordered his men to row in through the two giant headlands to check it, and once inside discovered it was not a cove at all, but a huge natural harbour, the best he'd ever seen anywhere in the world.

Delighted to find such a jewel with many sheltered bays, trees and fresh water, he pressed on and came to a place where the water was deep enough for the ships to come close to shore. He named it Sydney Cove after Lord Sydney, Secretary of State, to whom he sent his despatches. It even appeared that the natives were more friendly there too. So Sydney Cove was where the first settlement in New South Wales would be.

Mary and the other prisoners knew nothing of all this. Sweating and gasping in the heat of the holds, all they knew was that they'd been landed in a hellish, barren place peopled by fearsome savages. It was no wonder that many of them believed their long voyage had been for nothing and now they were going to die.

It was only on 26 January, when the prisoners heard the weighing of the anchor and the sound of sails being hoisted, that they felt a renewal of hope for their future.

By the time the *Charlotte* reached Sydney Cove it was night-time and too dark to see anything. The prisoners were not told that the flag-ship *Sirius* had arrived much earlier in the day, and that its officers had gone ashore, raised the English flag and held a simple ceremony where they fired a volley and toasted the royal family and the success of the new colony. But it was obvious to all the prisoners from the joyous shouts coming from the ships' companies anchored out in the bay, that this was where they would be settling.

Down in the steamy, fetid darkness of the holds they couldn't share in the excitement. They felt relief that they would soon be walking on solid ground and sleeping in tents, but they were fearful too, for this new prison which they had yet to build was so remote that they knew it was unlikely they would see England and their loved ones there again.

At first light the following morning the sound of axes felling trees filled the air and the women rushed to the hatches to look out.

'Looks better than that other place,' Bessie said cheerfully.

'It does too,' Mary agreed. The early-morning sun was glinting on the turquoise sea, and on land there were many trees, some quite large ones growing on the hills behind the bay. While there wasn't what could be called pasture anywhere that she could see, this place certainly didn't have the same desolate appearance as Botany Bay.

As they watched, they saw boats being lowered from the other ships, and male prisoners on the *Friendship* climbing down to them.

'I wonder when we'll go ashore,' Bessie said longingly.

'I hope it's soon,' Mary sighed. 'It's far too hot for Charlotte down here.'

It was over a week later that the women left the ships. They were allowed up on deck during that time as the men put up tents, cut trees and built store-sheds and a saw-mill, but they were told they had to stay on board until there was more order ashore.

Excitement grew with each day. It reminded Mary keenly of the sense of expectation before May Day back home. Women who had other clothes stored got them out and went through them to find something more fetching to wear, but most of them, like Mary, had arrived on the *Charlotte* with only the clothes they stood up in.

A new generosity bloomed, however, and ribbons, pieces of lace and small trinkets were offered to others who had nothing. They helped one another wash and curl their hair, and those who could sew were eager to assist those who couldn't.

They could hear the women on the *Lady Penryn* engaged in much the same way. Their laughter and ribald comments wafted across to the *Charlotte*, and the rigging was festooned with drying clothes in every colour of the rainbow.

Although Mary felt every bit as excited as the other women, she was nervous too. Just a glance across to the

Lady Penryn was to know that all those London women were going to be more worldly than her, and undoubtedly more attractive. On board the *Charlotte* she had a sort of distinction, admired for her ability to speak up for the women and her sense of fair play, and for being a mother. Her friendship with Will would almost certainly protect her from any harm amongst his large group of friends. She was also respected by most of the officers and Marines. She'd even gained the trust of their wives and children.

But on shore she would have to start all over again. She would need to be on her guard all the time. She was afraid that Mary Haydon and Catherine Fryer might seek to malign her to anyone who would listen, and enjoy seeing her humiliated. Officers from other ships wouldn't give her the trust and freedom she'd grown used to. She would be just a very small fish in a big pond, with no one to protect her and Charlotte.

On Sunday, 3 February a church service was held for the men by the Reverend Richard Johnson, under the shade of a big tree. Like all the women, Mary watched from the ship's deck, a little awed to see around 700 men, prisoners, officers, Marines and sailors gathered together in prayer. Will stood taller and broader than most of the men, his fair hair bleached almost white in the sun. Jamie Cox stood next to him, so small he looked like a child compared to Will.

A mop of red hair in the crowd made Mary look more intently and to her surprise she saw it was Samuel Bird.

Looking again, she saw James Martin beside him, his stooped shoulders and big nose unmistakable.

She was thrilled, for it was almost like seeing family members again, and she had to assume they'd been put on one of the other transport ships, maybe even separated from Will purposely to prevent them from inciting any kind of rebellion together.

Tench stood with the other officers, his hat tucked under his arm, and just the distance between prisoners and officers was a further reminder to Mary that the friendship between herself and Tench was unlikely to continue now the voyage was over.

Three days later the women went ashore. The excitement had been building up gradually over the last week, and as they were rowed to shore, Mary felt as giddy and giggly as her companions. It was wonderful to see everyone so happy, after the hardships on the voyage, with flushed cheeks and bright eyes, just like a bunch of bridesmaids at a wedding party.

For Mary, the prospect of walking on dry land again, to be rid of the smell of slop buckets, and to escape the nightly menace of rats was enough to start her heart pounding. But she was aware that for the other women it was mostly the men waiting on the shore that had them fired up.

As the boat got closer to the shore and Mary could clearly see the men waiting for them, she felt suddenly afraid, and hugged Charlotte closer to her breast. The expression on the men's faces reminded her of when a ship came into Fowey harbour after weeks at sea. She had observed that same hungry look then, and although she hadn't understood at the time why her mother always called her and Dolly indoors, she did now.

Sailors had a kind of rough charm, they were fit and strong, scrubbed up to look their best for shore leave. But these men waiting for the women prisoners were ragged and dirty, more like a vast pack of wild dogs than human beings.

Some of the women began to shout crude things to them, pulling their neck-lines lower and blowing kisses. In another boat coming from the *Lady Penryn*, one woman actually stood up and lifted her dress to show her private parts.

Marines pushed the men back as the boats were grounded on the beach and the women climbed out, but it seemed to Mary that the Marines were almost as bad as the convicts. They were laughing, winking, grabbing at the women's hands, and there was certainly no sense of them being there to protect the fairer sex.

Mary elbowed her way through the crowd, Charlotte's small crib under one arm, the other defensively round her child, almost deafened by the cat-calls, crude remarks and appeals for a kiss. It was exhilarating, like all the fairs and festivals she'd ever been to rolled into one, but frightening at the same time. It seemed odd to her that the officers were just standing by watching after all their stringent efforts to keep the men and women apart during the voyage.

Other boats came in, depositing more and more women on the beach, and the hubbub grew louder, the pushing and shoving more aggressive. But it was as much on the women's part as the men's – some of them were even running over to the men to kiss and embrace them.

Mary wanted so much to take off her boots, to run barefoot along the sand, to look at the strange birds watching them from the trees, to revel in her new-found freedom. But she could see this wasn't an option right now, she had to stay in the safety of a group.

Seeing a small bunch of women with children, standing apart, Mary ran over to them.

'Lawd have mercy on us,' she gasped out. 'It's getting out of hand!'

A tall woman in a plain dark brown dress and bonnet, holding a small child in her arms, responded. 'We asked to be taken to a place of safety some time ago,' she said. 'But our husbands seem distracted.'

Mary realized then that these women were Marines' wives and families, and as she'd been treated with some kindness by those who travelled on the *Charlotte*, she assumed this group would be the same.

'May I stay with you?' she asked. 'I'm afraid for my baby.'

The woman's expression stiffened. 'Join the other women from your ship,' she said curtly. 'That's where you belong.'

Shamed, Mary turned and walked away, realizing that brief encounter had shown how things were going to be here.

A little more order came later when the Marines fired a warning volley over the prisoners' heads, and the women were led to the tents allocated to them. But even as they were marched along, Mary overheard comments and giggles that suggested most of the women were too excited by the eager men to be kept under control for long.

Mary, Bessie and Sarah managed to stay together, but the other three women they were to share the tent with were strangers. The leader of the three, who announced herself as Cheapside Poll, was a tall, skinny woman with hard blue eyes, wearing a striped dress and a battered red hat. She deposited a carpet bag by the tent pole and glowered at Mary and her friends.

'Any of you so much as think of digging in there and I'll slit yer nostrils,' she said. She looked round at her companions and urged them to tell what she was capable of.

'She done it to a woman in Newgate,' a fat one with a pock-marked face said gleefully. 'Never 'eard screams like it afore.'

'We aren't thieves,' Mary said, even though technically she supposed they were. She was frightened now; all three women had harsh voices and a way of speaking which was very different to her own. As she knew Newgate was the infamous prison in London, she supposed that was where they came from.

'Keep that brat well away from me,' Poll said viciously, pointing to Charlotte. 'I can't be doing with a screamer.'

It was perhaps fortunate that the three Londoners were anxious to get out of the tent as quickly as possible. After laying their blankets down, they disappeared.

Mary sat down to feed Charlotte, but it was clear from the way Sarah and Bessie were fidgeting that they were anxious to get out too. Both her friends looked much better now than they had back in England. Sarah was plumper, with pink cheeks and shining hair, while Bessie, who had been fat when they arrived at the *Dunkirk*, was a couple of stones lighter, and her once grey complexion peachy with health.

'We'll just look around,' Bessie said, primping up her hair. 'We'll be back when we've found out where we get our rations from.'

Mary had been looking forward to going ashore as much as anyone, but now she felt close to tears. It was so hot, sweat was already soaking her dress, she needed to find water, both for a drink for herself and to cool Charlotte down. All around her she could hear strident, coarse voices, but the language they spoke wasn't English as she knew it. She guessed it was the Newgate prison cant she'd heard about in Exeter, for odd words had a familiar ring to them. She hadn't expected that she would have to learn a new language on top of everything else.

On the ship she had known exactly what was expected of her, a daily routine that seldom varied. She was one of only twenty women, an individual with a name and a character. Now she was to be one of some 200 women, thrown in together without any clear-cut rules of behaviour. If Cheapside Poll was an example of what she could expect of the rest of the women, she knew she would need to find new strengths for survival.

Tears dripped down her cheeks as she held Charlotte

to her breast, and the words she'd so often heard in church at Easter-time came to her: 'Lord, why hast Thou forsaken me?'

Darkness came suddenly, taking Mary by surprise. There appeared to be no twilight period like back in England. The noise which had grown louder and louder throughout the afternoon reached fever pitch.

Mary had plucked up courage to explore the row of women's tents to seek out her old companions and get food and water. She had spotted James Martin with Samuel Bird, but though they waved and shouted out greetings, Mary didn't go and talk to them as they were with other more desperate-looking men. She did try to join in the revelry for a while, but the underlying menace in it drove her to join some of the older women who were as nervous as she was.

Again and again the Marines had tried to separate the men from the women, with little success, but as darkness fell all attempts to control the prisoners broke down, and couples were seen scurrying off into the bushes.

Mary was just laying Charlotte down in her crib in the tent, when a flash of lightning lit up the entire bay. Thunder followed it, so loud it was like a cannon, making Charlotte scream out. More thunder and lightning followed, and then came rain, heavier than Mary had ever seen in her life. Within minutes the hard ground was awash, water running through the tent like a river.

Mary expected that the storm would at least dampen the spirits of the revellers as it put out the many fires burning along the beach. Yet as she crouched in the shelter of the tent looking out, to her horror she saw that the storm was only inflaming people more. Each flash of lightning lit up acts of obscenity, women pulling off their clothes, men rushing to grab them and taking them there in the mud. But if such acts were horrifying, they were at least mutual; elsewhere she saw men rushing like ravaging beasts, pulling down women who were running for their lives, their screams reverberating around the camp. It wasn't only the convicts either, some of the men were Marines, and as she stood with her hands clamped over her mouth in horror, she saw old women, too frail and bent to run, being knocked to the ground and raped.

It was like a scene from hell she'd once seen a picture of at Sunday school in Fowey, the men demonic in their lust, some women spurring them on with gleeful shouts, others screaming in terror. She saw one woman get up unsteadily from the ground as her rapist left her, so thickly coated with mud she had no features, only to be leapt upon by a second man, while another stood waiting for his turn.

Mary didn't know what to do. To run from the tent would be folly for she would surely be caught by someone, and if she took Charlotte with her she might be dashed from her arms and killed. Yet the tent offered no protection. Even as she hesitated, another flash of lightning revealed a band of men coming along the rows of tents looking in each for new prey.

Grabbing Charlotte from her crib, she wriggled under

the back of the tent and cowered there for a moment, considering which direction would be the safest. Going inland appeared to be the best choice, with luck there might be bushes to hide under, so hitching Charlotte under one arm and holding up her dress with the other, she ran for her life into the shelter of the trees.

She stubbed her bare feet against stumps of felled trees and tripped over dead branches, but somehow she managed to hold on to her baby. Just as she thought she was well away from the mayhem on the beach, however, she saw two men in front of her.

'Lookee here,' one of them shouted. 'Fresh meat.'

'Don't hurt me,' Mary screamed out in terror, for she knew whichever way she ran, one of them would catch her. 'I've got a baby with me.'

'We ain't after hurting a baby,' one of them said. 'Just put it down and be nice to us.'

Mary screamed and clutched Charlotte even tighter to her. But one of the men grabbed her shoulder and pushed her down to the ground.

Flat on her back, still holding Charlotte who was now screaming too, Mary fought with the only weapons she had, her legs and feet. It was too dark to see, but she felt the heel of her foot land in a soft place and the yell that followed it suggested she'd struck his belly.

'Get off me, you brutes,' she yelled. 'There's plenty of willing women back there.'

One man pinned her down by the shoulders, the second one grabbed her by the knees and forced them apart. She could smell their sweat and rancid breath.

'Damn you to hell,' she screamed out, still bucking frantically. 'Help me, someone!'

The man who held her legs apart was pulling her on to him as he knelt in front of her, the other one was still holding her shoulders in a grip of steel. She heard someone crashing through the bushes even over Charlotte's screams, but that increased her terror further as she thought it would be another man wanting to join in.

'Let her go,' a male voice bellowed out, and to her shock she recognized the voice as Will's. She saw nothing more than a dark shadow, then heard a crack, and the man about to rape her toppled back on to the ground.

There was another loud crack and the hands on her shoulders fell away. 'That's my woman,' Will roared out, and all at once he was pulling her up and holding her in his arms.

'There, there,' he said gently, disengaging himself slightly so Charlotte wouldn't be crushed. 'You're safe now.'

Taking her arm, he led her away. Mary had to suppose he had knocked the two men out with some kind of cudgel, but she didn't turn to look.

'Did they do it?' he asked breathlessly.

'No,' she gasped out. 'You were just in time.'

Will took her much further into the trees, and when they came to one that offered some real shelter from the heavy rain, he stopped and made her sit down.

'Are you or the babby hurt?' he asked, sitting down beside her and putting his arm around her.

'I don't think so,' she replied, rocking Charlotte in her arms to soothe her.

All at once she was crying as she had never cried since her trial. All the hardships, deprivations, the cruelty and humiliations she had endured for so long seemed to come to the surface, just because one man cared enough to comfort her.

'You're safe now,' he whispered, holding her tight and rocking her. 'I won't let anyone touch you again.'

A little later it stopped raining as suddenly as it had begun, and the moon came out from behind the clouds. Will continued to hold Mary as she offered Charlotte her breast to calm her. They were soaking wet and covered in mud, but at least it wasn't cold.

'I came looking for you when it all got nasty,' Will explained. 'I'd seen Sarah and Bessie earlier and they said you was back in the tent putting Charlotte down. I should have come to you then.'

'I was scared almost as soon as we came ashore,' Mary admitted. 'Everyone was so wild.'

'It was like a madness caught them all,' Will said, his tone hushed and shocked. 'I've never seen the like afore.'

'How did you find me?'

He was silent for a moment, and she guessed his conscience wasn't entirely clear either.

'I saw a gang going through all the women's tents,' he said eventually. 'I guessed if you were in there you'd get out the back and run for it. So I went that way, and I heard a babby crying.'

'Will it always be this way?' Mary whispered. She was

shivering with shock, the vivid pictures of what she'd seen down on the beach still dancing before her eyes.

'I don't reckon so,' he sighed. 'Tomorrow the officers will take control, there'll be floggings for some, chains for others, it will settle down.'

'I hope you're right,' she said. 'But I don't like the thought of living with those London women, they scare me to death.'

'You scared?' he teased. 'A girl who is brave enough to ask a man to marry her?'

'I wish I hadn't now,' she admitted. 'It must have seemed so forward. It was just that we appeared to have so much in common, I really like you and as tonight proved, women do need some protection here.'

'They do indeed,' he said thoughtfully. 'But I think us men will need a good woman beside us too. So we will get married.'

'You want to marry me?' She was so surprised it dried up her tears instantly.

'Well, I don't want one of those London harpies full of pox,' he said with a chuckle. 'You were right, Mary. We'll make a good team, you and me. They'll need someone to fish, a lot of the food they brought with us is rotten. I think I can bargain for us to get a house of our own, my mind's a bit sharper than most of the others.'

Mary was very aware he wasn't saying he loved her, only that he thought she was clean and useful to him. Yet he had fought off those men for her, he'd comforted her just when she needed it. This place was going to be a living hell, and she doubted she could survive it alone.

She didn't expect or need romantic love, she'd settle for protection.

Four days after that terrible night, Will and Mary were married by the Reverend Johnson under the shade of the big tree where he'd held his first service. They weren't alone, other couples married too, perhaps for the same reasons as Mary and Will.

Mary had no finery to wear, just the same shabby old grey dress freshly washed, and an artificial flower in her hair, lent to her in an unusually generous gesture by Cheapside Poll.

Mary had no real expectations, either of her marriage or of this new country. In the four days since coming ashore she had observed that the vast majority of the convicts were bone idle and devious. They would steal anything, cared nothing for the idea of working for the common good, and many were already bartering rations or belongings with the Marines for drink. The Marines were every bit as bad, and there was a lack of organization on the part of the officers and the powers that be who had sent them out from England.

Will had been right in saying some of the food was rotten. Mary had had to eat rice crawling with maggots and the salted beef was almost inedible. Tools were of inferior quality, there were too few women's clothes, and a complete lack of skilled men.

She wondered how they could farm this desolate place when there were but two men out of hundreds who knew anything about farming or animal husbandry. How could a town be built without skilled carpenters or brick-makers? Captain Arthur Phillip had his house erected, a superior canvas one, a store-house had been built to lock away the provisions, and a few tents had been put in isolation as a hospital.

But the animals brought with them were in poor health, and dysentery had already broken out among those weakened by the voyage. Captain Phillip might be proud that only forty-eight people overall had died on the way here, but how many more would perish before the year was out?

An eighty-year-old woman hanged herself from a tree on that first night ashore. Many women still had black eyes and a hunted look. There were snakes, spiders and many flies and other insects, any of which could be dangerous. As for the natives, the officers seemed intent on getting their cooperation, when even an illiterate girl like herself could sense they bitterly resented this swarm of white people who'd taken it upon themselves to oust them from their land. Mary wondered how long it would be before their curiosity turned to real anger and they began killing.

But Will had been as good as his word. Not only had he pledged to marry her, he'd already made a deal that put him in charge of fishing and allowed him to build a hut for himself.

Mary glanced at him standing next to her, and smiled. He looked so handsome in a clean shirt and breeches; he'd even shaved off his bushy beard, and his blond hair was as bright as ripe corn. She knew most of the women envied her, for he was without doubt the most attractive and capable of all the male convicts. She might have her work cut out keeping him faithful to her, and perhaps his bragging would be wearing, but she did like and trust him. That was enough.

As the wedding ceremonies ended and everyone drifted back to their tents or the huts they were building, Lieutenant Tench stood for a little while watching Mary and Will walk away up the beach.

He was in a state of confusion about everything. Nothing was as he'd expected – not the country, nor the organization, nor the officers from the other ships. Even the stores they'd brought with them were inadequate. It was a shambles, in fact. And from what he'd seen of the convicts so far, it was going to be an uphill struggle to get any of them to work.

As far as he could see, only a handful of officers shared his will to make this place work. As for his men, most of them were behaving appallingly, every bit as devious and idle as the convicts.

He had thought he would feel more positive after the weddings today. They were, after all, one way of injecting a little joy into a new community, a show of hope for the future. Yet he had felt no joy at seeing those couples married. What he felt was utter sadness.

His mother always cried at weddings. She believed the more she cried, the happier the couple would be. But he knew his mother's tears weren't sad ones, they were pure emotion at a public declaration of love between two people.

Perhaps that was the cause of his sadness, knowing the couples married today were not in love. The women wanted protection and security, the men wanted sex.

He had thought he'd be happy to see Mary under Will's protection. But he hadn't considered till now that meant she would be her husband's in every way.

He turned sharply and walked away towards the store-sheds. Maybe if he found something constructive to do he'd overcome these ridiculous feelings milling around inside him. Mary looked pretty and happy. Will was a decent enough man. They were right for each other.

'It will be a nice little place once I've finished it,' Will said later that same night, as he laid their blankets on the hard-packed dirt beside Charlotte's crib.

They were in their new hut, which at present was nothing more than a few poles hammered together and the walls interwoven branches, with a piece of sacking tacked on a stick for a door. The roof was not yet on, and when Mary sat down on the blankets and looked up, the night sky strewn with a myriad stars looked very beautiful. Their bellies were full, as extra rations had been dished out to honour the weddings today, and Will had managed to get hold of some rum to celebrate.

Rules had been made since that first night ashore. Male convicts were banned from the women's area, and guards were on duty to make sure no one slipped in. There was also a dusk curfew when everyone was supposed to be back in their own quarters. It didn't actually work, men did get in with the women, but at least it was covert, and the women willing.

'Plenty of fresh air,' Will said, and laughed. 'I can stand upright too. Beats that stinking ship anyways, or a tent with the men. Now, come here and give your husband a kiss.'

Mary needed no urging; since Will had announced their wedding plans she'd found she had status, and for that she was extremely grateful. Even Poll and her two cronies, three of the most foul-minded women Mary had ever met, were awed that she was wanted by the most desirable convict in the colony.

There were good things here. It was hot, the sand on the beach soft and white, the sea so blue and clean, and there were hundreds of beautiful birds. Even the trees had a lovely smell that cleared your nose. It beat a prison back in England any day.

Now Mary had a home, well away from everyone else, and even if it hadn't got a roof yet, nor a stick of furniture, and the first storm would knock it down, it was theirs. Will had managed to get her a cooking pot, a bucket for carrying water, and a few other essential pieces of household equipment from the stores to start married life.

He'd already kissed her several times today, and he did so tenderly. She hadn't expected to want him, but she found she did; in fact for the first time in over a year she was really happy to be where she was.

'You're such a little thing,' he said gruffly as he helped her out of her dress. He cupped his big hands round her breasts and squeezed them, then sliding his hands down to her buttocks squeezed them too. 'A bit skinny, but I never was one for fat women.'

He lifted her up in his arms then and laid her down on the blankets. Mary expected nothing more than for him to pull off his clothes, a quick coupling, then for him to fall asleep. But to her surprise Will made no attempt to undress himself, only to caress her. She had once heard him bragging to a sailor on the *Charlotte* that once he'd bedded a woman they always came back begging him for more. She believed it now, for she was afraid that any moment he might stop. His touch was so sure and slow, his fingers found exquisitely sensitive places to touch that until now she hadn't even known existed.

The hard ground beneath the rough blanket, the crudeness of their unfinished house, even the hardship she'd been through were forgotten as Mary gave herself up to the bliss of his love-making. When she opened her eyes and saw the stars above, she could have been lying on a feather bed in a royal bedchamber, the stars just a decoration on the ceiling. Will made her forget she wasn't pretty, or that there were lice in her hair; for once she was beautiful, desirable and loved.

She never could have believed she could behave like a wanton, begging for more, asking him to show her what pleased him, and doing it all too eagerly. At the peak of it all the thought crossed her mind that it was worth crossing the world in a prison ship to feel like this. She didn't care about the future, she just wanted this night to last forever.

'Are you glad you married me?' Will whispered later, after he'd covered them with the blanket to keep off the insects.

'The happiest woman alive,' she whispered back, her cheeks wet with tears of joy.

'We'll make something of our life here,' he murmured. 'We'll plant ourselves a little garden and grow some vegetables. We'll never go hungry while I can fish, and we'll have other children for Charlotte to play with.'

'Will we go back to England when our time is up?' she asked.

'Sure, if you want to,' he said, and laughed. 'Or we might stay as free men and take some land for ourselves. Anything's possible.'

Chapter six

1789

Mary was standing waist-deep in the sea, holding tightly to the fishing net, looking as all the other helpers were towards Will in the small boat, waiting for his signal to pull the net tight.

She was very hungry, but hunger pains and the dizzy spells which went with them were just a fact of life now. After a whole year here at Port Jackson she couldn't even remember what it was like to be without them.

She was much thinner than she'd been back on the *Dunkirk*, her skin leathery and brown from constant exposure to the sun and wind, her hands hardened like the women's who gutted fish back in Fowey. But her looks weren't something she ever thought about; just keeping herself and Charlotte alive was of far greater importance.

Will gave the signal and everyone holding the net began pulling and moving back to the shore. Mary's heart leaped when she saw the abundance of fish squirming in the net. It wasn't often they were that lucky.

The colony was close to dying of starvation. The rations

had been cut again and again because no further supplies had arrived from England yet. A great many of the provisions brought out with them were spoiled, and the original hope that within a year they would be producing home-grown food was shattered. Had draught animals and ploughs been sent out, along with men from a farming background, maybe the ground could have been tilled and cultivated quickly. But all this had been overlooked. The weather and the lack of fodder for the animals soon decimated their numbers, cereals withered in the ground and vegetables didn't thrive.

Building work had been the priority at the start, houses for the officers, Marines, and then the convicts. But along with the lack of carpenters, an outbreak of scurvy, together with dozens of other diseases, kept the men from work, and so the building was painfully slow.

As the rations were cut, more people risked stealing food. Flogging was the punishment for this crime, but 100 lashes failed to be a deterrent, and Captain Phillip increased it to 500, and eventually to 1,000. When that didn't work either, he finally resorted to hanging. Just the previous week Mary and Will had watched as Thomas Barrett, who was only seventeen, was hanged from the newly erected gallows for stealing some butter, dried peas and salt pork from the stores. Mary couldn't even weep for the boy, for he'd been imprisoned for theft at the age of eleven, and she thought that death was preferable to the kind of life he'd had.

'Come on, Mary, put your back into it,' Will yelled at her from the little boat.

Mary laughed, for Will didn't really mean she wasn't pulling her weight – that shout was their secret code for 'We'll be eating well tonight.'

'I don't know what you've got to laugh at,' the woman next to her said sharply as they hauled the net back on to the shore. 'If I was in your shoes I'd be crying.'

'Why's that?' Mary asked.

She didn't trust Sadie Green an inch. She knew the only reason the woman had come down to the nets to help was in the hope of stealing a couple of fish for herself. She was one of the Londoners, foul-mouthed, cunning and lazy. And she bitterly resented that Mary appeared to have a better time of it than her.

'Will's gonna leave you soon,' Sadie said, her mud-coloured eyes sparkling with malice. 'He keeps telling the other men he isn't legally wed to you.'

'Is that so?' Mary retorted with heavy sarcasm. Will had told her he didn't believe their marriage was valid, not like a church wedding at home, but all the same she was hurt he'd bandied it about among the other men to reach the ears of people like Sadie. She wasn't going to show that hurt though.

'Just don't wait around for him, Sadie, you might be waiting a long time,' she said with a forced chuckle.

She saw the woman's face tighten with anger. Sadie could only attract the most desperate of the male convicts. Although only about twenty-four, she had the grey look of gone-off meat, and smelled much the same. She never combed her wispy straw-coloured hair, much less washed it, and dirt was ingrained in her skin. There were no beauties in this colony, the sun and starvation saw to that. But Sadie was probably born plain, and a life of prostitution had done the rest.

'Why, you stuck-up cow!' she snarled, showing the blackened stumps of her teeth. 'What makes you think you're better than the rest of us? You've got a bastard kid that ain't Will's.'

Mary hesitated. She was very tempted to hit Sadie, but that was just what the woman wanted, so she could say Mary started the fight and get her punished.

'Leave me alone, if you know what's good for you,' Mary replied wearily. 'This place is bad enough without picking fights.'

'But it ain't bad for you, is it?' Sadie put her hands on her hips and glowered at Mary. 'You've got a nice little hut, Will's got the best job, and I bet he gets extra rations too. Lieutenant Tench is always sniffing round you too. I bet he's the bastard's father.'

Mary was saved from answering by an officer coming along the beach to check the catch. Sadie gave Mary a menacing look and smirked at him, then left her place on the net and flounced off.

An hour later Mary was back at her hut, having collected Charlotte from Anne Tomkin, her neighbour, who minded her while Mary was helping with the nets.

The hut was now much improved. Because of Will's status they had been allowed planks from the saw-mill for both roof and walls. The furniture was of the most basic kind: a rough-hewn bed, with rope tied across it like a hammock, a small table made from a tree trunk with a board nailed to its top, and two stools fashioned out of wooden crates. The floor was still hard-pressed dirt, though Will intended to put some planks down soon, and the only decoration some pretty sea shells on a shelf. Another held the few cooking pots, plates, mugs and a tin bowl to wash in. Yet however primitive, it was Mary's haven, a place of comparative safety and peace for both herself and Charlotte.

At seventeen months Charlotte was a bonny child, with pink cheeks, black curly hair and well-rounded limbs. Her wide, joyous smile was worth a king's ransom to Mary, and she gave shape and reason to her life. Yet at the same time, keeping Charlotte safe and well under such appalling conditions was slow torture.

While she was still a babe in arms, feeding from her mother's breast, it was relatively easy, but once she began crawling and then walking, Mary saw danger everywhere. Aside from the most obvious things – insects, snakes, the sea and fires – there were the hidden hazards. Who knew what was buried in the sand Charlotte played on, which she could pick up and swallow. Other mothers here were very casual about their offspring, allowing them to wander and showing no anxiety if they got sunburnt, fell over, or ate something that made them sick. But Mary couldn't be that way, she had to have Charlotte near her at all times. She tied a piece of rope around her waist to keep her close when she was mending nets, and gave Anne some fish or part of their rations to mind her when she was helping to haul them in. Even in the evening when Charlotte had fallen asleep in the bed all three shared, Mary wouldn't go beyond her own door, even though other mothers went out to visit friends.

While waiting for Will to come home with their rations and hopefully some fish, Mary filled the bowl with water, peeled off Charlotte's dress and began washing her. She didn't like to dwell on the fact that the dress was merely rags now, held together by a few threads. Or that it would have to be washed tonight and put on again tomorrow because it was the only one. Nor did she want any reminders that she hadn't any friends to visit.

She couldn't win in this place.

Marrying Will had been a wise choice. He had protected her from the other men, built them this hut, and had come to love Charlotte as if she were his own. But Mary hadn't anticipated that his fishing skills would make him so important in the colony, and it was that which had brought her problems.

When they first landed, the convicts from London and other cities were suspicious of fish and refused to eat it. This was understandable, considering that where they came from it was probably at least a week old and stinking. But by the time the rations had been severely cut and starvation was a real possibility, they quickly overcame their objections. Will was elevated to hero status because he was the man who not only introduced them to something tasty and filling, but also supplied it.

Yet as Will basked in the warm glow of admiration and gratitude, Mary had lost the strong position she'd once held with the other women from the *Charlotte*. With Mary

Haydon and Catherine Fryer dripping poison in the ears of the trouble-making women from other ships, it wasn't long before most of the women were suspicious of her. Even Bessie and Sarah, whom she thought she could count on forever, had turned against her. They called her a 'dark one', as if she was guilty of some treachery, when the plain fact was that they were jealous of her.

Mary understood why. They were mostly sleeping six to a hut, while she was tucked up in a strong, weatherproof one, well away from the noise and trouble in the main camp. She ate better in those early days because Will was allowed some of each catch for himself. Nor did she have to work as a servant for one of the officers as the other women did. Added to this, the women saw Mary as a 'nark', because officers talked to her.

Tench often came to see how she and Will were getting on, and he liked to help with the fishing at night. It was reported that even Captain Phillip had remarked that the Bryants were the model family, industrious, sober and clean.

In the early days in the colony, Mary had made a good friend of Jane Randall, who sailed on the *Lady Penryn*. She too had a baby en route, though it was born while they were berthed in Cape Town. Initially it was because Charlotte and Henrietta were so close in age that Mary and Jane became friends; they had the same anxieties for their babies, and they minded each other's to help out. Jane was sweet-natured and fun to be with, and like-minded too about making the best of it here.

Then Captain Phillip decided to start a new settlement

on Norfolk Island, 1,000 miles away. It appeared to have a better climate, and the ground was more fertile, so some of the convicts, Jane among them, were sent there to alleviate the food shortages. Mary still missed her badly. Jane had never been jealous of her, she was always glad fortune seemed to shine on her friend.

Mary took the view that many of her former friends could be just as fortunate as her if they only used their brains. In the early days, Mary had tried to make them at least see the logic of appearing to be industrious. It was so easy to do, the officers only poked their noses in if there was any trouble, and to her mind the majority of the Marines were half-wits. Likewise, keeping yourself clean and tidy, and not running around hunting for men and drink, got you privileges and respect.

But sadly, one by one her old friends had fallen into apathy and allowed themselves to be influenced by a few forceful characters who thought they were proving their toughness by fighting and stealing. Nothing was safe from these women, and they recruited new members into their band by offering the drink they acquired through theft or prostitution.

Mary understood why Sarah had gone that way. She'd been raped on that first night, and found herself pregnant afterwards. Her baby was stillborn, and that brought back all the pain of the two children left behind in England. Drink was the only thing which made her life a little more bearable.

But most of the women hadn't got such a good excuse. They had become filthy slatterns who neglected their children, preyed on those weaker than themselves, and went with any man for a shot of rum.

Mary was like a pricking conscience. They sneered at her because she bathed in the sea every day, cleaned her hut and kept Charlotte constantly beside her. But Mary knew that most of their spite and scorn was purely because she had the man they all wanted.

Will was attractive in every way. His looks, height and muscular body were almost enough on their own, but added to this he was a kind man with a jovial, cheeky nature that endeared him to everyone. He was also strong and clever with his hands, so it wasn't surprising that everyone, from Captain Phillip right down to the lowest of the prisoners, held him in high esteem.

But what they didn't know, and Mary would never divulge, was that Will was in fact quite weak. He might be able to read and write, but he didn't use his brain and was unimaginative. Left to his own devices, he would be much like all the other men, living in squalor, getting drunk as often as he could, and bemoaning his bad luck.

Mary was the strong-willed and wily one. It was she who realized the importance of fish for their survival, and she talked Will into seeing his skill as the trump card to improve their life here. Will's bargaining for a hut in a good position, the use of the only small boat, and a portion of each catch for himself, was all her doing. In return, Mary made their hut more homely so that he would want to be there, and pandered to his vanity so that he felt important.

If only he had listened to her when a new rule ordering

that the entire catch should go into the stores was made. Mary had wanted him to go straight to Captain Phillip, not only to dig his heels in and insist on keeping his original rights, but also to discuss her plan with the captain. This was to build a bigger boat which would then be able to go further out into the sea and get catches big enough to feed everyone well. She also suggested they used surplus fish as a fertilizer for the soil, something she'd seen done back home in Cornwall.

But Will wouldn't do that. He might brag to his friends that Mary's ideas were his, as it made him look cleverer than them, but in reality he was too scared of losing his popularity with the officers to speak out. So instead he resorted to stealing what fish he needed.

Mary sighed deeply as Charlotte began groping for her breast under her dress. She had little milk left now, and each time the rations were cut further she was fearful Charlotte would become sick as so many others had.

It was the very young and the very old who were dying in ever-increasing numbers each week. The hospital building was always full now, the path to the cemetery so well used that a new funeral wasn't remarked on any longer.

Shouting and chatter outside made Mary start. Through the window they had plaited with twigs in place of glass, she could see the sun was very low, and Will should have been home by now. She stood up, and holding Charlotte in her arms, went to the door.

The commotion was coming from further along the beach closer to the main camp. Mary thought she saw a glimpse of Will's blond hair, so wrapping a piece of cloth around Charlotte, she went to look.

She had gone no more than two hundred yards when she saw Sarah.

Her once pretty face was gaunt. Her strawberry-blond hair was matted and filthy, her blue eyes were dulled by drink and she'd lost her two front teeth in a fight. Her slop dress still had bloodstains from the birth of her child and it was split on one side, showing her scrawny thigh.

'Your Will's been caught stealing,' she called out. 'He'll be for it now.'

Mary's heart quickened. She had of course eagerly eaten the fish Will brought home, and to help him remain undetected she had made the sacking bag to put them in. He hung this on a hook on the boat's side below the water-line to retrieve later after the rest of the catch had been weighed and taken to the stores.

It had appeared to be a foolproof plan, but Mary guessed that Will had been stealing more than he told her, selling the surplus off to others or exchanging it for goods.

'My Will's no thief,' Mary said sharply. She couldn't look upon it as theft – after all, fish were free to anyone who could catch them.

'I don't think Captain Phillip will see it that way,' Sarah said, her grin a touch malicious. 'He'll say you've been robbing the rest of us.'

Mary looked at her former friend coolly. 'Will's one of the few men here who provide anything for us to eat,' she said. 'But for him most of us would be too weak to be nasty.'

It hurt that Sarah had turned against her. Mary could not forget how close they'd been on the *Dunkirk*, and that Sarah had helped her with Charlotte's birth on the voyage. But it had never been a one-sided friendship. Mary had always made sure she saved food for Sarah, comforted her in the aftermath of the rape, and even gave her some of the fish Will got. But perhaps the horror of the rape had killed off something inside Sarah.

All the way into the town, people called out to Mary. A few, like James Martin, Jamie Cox and Samuel Bird, Will's closest friends, offered help and words of sympathy, but from the others it was mostly spiteful remarks. Mary remembered how back in the early days everyone would have stuck together if something like this had happened. But hunger and deprivation had changed them all. There was no sense of honour any more, people would peach on almost anyone in return for drink or extra food. And they took pleasure in seeing anyone they considered favoured brought down.

Mary kept her head up and ignored them all, but her insides were turning over with a combination of fear and hunger. The town didn't consist of much, just two rows of squalid little huts for the convicts, slightly larger ones set further back for the Marines and their families, and the guarded store-sheds. But Mary's eyes were drawn to the gallows. She remembered only too well the warning that anyone found stealing food would receive no mercy.

Watkin Tench came out from behind one of the store-sheds, surprising Mary for she'd thought he was away at Rose Hill, a new settlement inland where the soil was more fertile. Tench had been put in charge of it, and they were building a new Government House here too.

'Mary!' he exclaimed, his tanned lean face etched in concern. 'I assume you've been told?'

Even he, who had always been so elegant and spruce, was looking worn. His boots were rarely highly polished any more, his red jacket was threadbare and his breeches stained. But the compassion was still there in his dark eyes.

Mary nodded. 'Is it true?' she asked.

'Caught red-handed,' he shrugged. 'I'm afraid there's little I can do to help him, however much I wish I could. The Governor will have to treat him just like anyone else caught stealing food.'

'They won't hang him, will they?' Mary felt faint now, and her voice was little more than a whisper.

Tench glanced round to check who was watching, then moved closer to her. 'I certainly hope not,' he said. 'It would be folly to lose any of the skilled men.'

His first reaction to the news as he rode in from Rose Hill had been anger at Will. Will was more fortunate than any other prisoner, he did a job he enjoyed, he had privileges and a decent hut. And he had Mary for a wife. Tench knew in his heart that Will hadn't taken fish just for himself and his family, he'd been taking a great deal and trading it for rum. This incensed him, for it was not only breaking down the very fabric of the community,

178

but cheating Mary too; no doubt she was oblivious to how much her husband needed drink.

'Could I speak to Captain Phillip?' Mary asked in desperation.

Tench hardly knew what to say. He certainly couldn't bring himself to hammer home what kind of man Will really was. 'Captain Phillip has probably already made his decision,' he said after a couple of moments. Then, seeing the terror in Mary's eyes, he weakened. 'But perhaps if he saw you with Charlotte in your arms, he might be persuaded to change it.'

'Please take me to him,' Mary pleaded, and she reached out and clutched at his arm. 'Will doesn't deserve to die just for feeding his family. Surely any man would do the same?'

Tench looked at her for a moment. There had been so many times when he wished he had never suggested Will as a husband for her, for he knew now that Will was weak, easily led and very boastful. He guessed Mary felt mortified each time it got back to her that Will had claimed they weren't legally married. Or that he intended to be on the next ship home when his time was up.

He wished too that he could get Mary out of his mind. He had hoped that being sent to Rose Hill would help. But now, faced with her distress, he knew the feelings he had for her hadn't abated at all. 'Any man would do the same for you,' he said, putting his hand over hers briefly.

Captain Phillip's house was some distance away from the town, up on a hill. With its two floors and veranda along the front, it stood out as being the residence of the most important man in the new colony, but this was not because it was grand, only that it had an appearance of sturdy permanence in comparison to all the other building work.

Mostly everything else was made of clay and wood, for even though there was plenty of stone around, and a brick-making kiln too, no lime to make mortar could be found anywhere. Mary, like many of the women, had been set to collect sea shells, then grind them up and burn them to make lime. She supposed all those many hundreds of bucketfuls she'd collected had barely made enough for the foundations of Phillip's house, so it would be years and years before the real town he envisaged, complete with a church, shops and paved streets, could be built.

As Mary followed Tench up the hill, she held her head high and ignored the coarse remarks and stares. Will had always claimed that no one would ever peach on him, but that was yet another of his failings, a stupidly vain belief that he was special. He'd probably bragged about the fish to someone, and it hadn't occurred to him that when jealousy reared its head, friendship and loyalty vanished.

Mary had to wait out on the veranda while Tench went inside the house to get permission for her to speak to Phillip. Charlotte was wailing with hunger now, and Mary jogged her soothingly in her arms as she looked back down the hill towards the town.

Darkness had fallen on the way there, and for once the town looked pretty, lit only by the many campfires. Mary could see the silhouettes of women cooking on them, and the flames highlighted trees and cast a twinkling orange glow on to the sea beyond.

She sighed, for although she always told anyone who asked that she would be on the next ship back to England when her sentence was up, she had grown to quite like this strange new land. Of course she hated what it stood for, a place where all the degenerate, desperate and wicked people from England were dumped. But it had some good points. The heat of the summer was sometimes too much, but there was always the warm sea to take a dip in. She loved the sandy beaches. Winter was nothing like as severe as at home, and however peculiar-looking most of the trees were, she liked their pungent aroma. Then there were the wonderful birds. To see flocks of the grey ones with pink bellies flying brought tears to her eyes. There were also the sulphur-coloured cockatoos that sat up in the trees squawking out what sounded like insults. Birds here were every colour of the rainbow, so vivid she could hardly believe they were real. She still hadn't seen the animal Tench called a kangaroo, or the big flightless bird; perhaps they were too timid to come close to people and she'd need to go further inland.

But whether or not she much preferred the land to which she belonged, Mary was a realist. Hunger back in England was exactly the same as hunger here, except it was better to be hungry and warm than hungry and cold. Unless a miracle happened, she would never amount to anything more than a servant in England. Here she stood a chance. When she was free she could claim land of her own, and the challenge to build something out of nothing appealed to her.

Often at night she thought about having a few animals, growing vegetables and fruit, and sitting on a porch in the evenings with Charlotte and Will, gazing at their land. Will had always pooh-poohed such ideas, he wanted to live in a fishing village with a tavern at the centre of it. But as she'd often retorted, he could build his own tavern here.

'You can come in now, Mary,' Tench said softly behind her. 'I have to warn you, Captain Phillip is very angry and disappointed. I don't think you can sway him from hanging Will.'

Mary knew Tench would have done his best for her and Will, for even the hardships here, which were almost as bad for the officers as for the convicts, hadn't changed his caring nature. Mary still had that same yearning for him, which marrying Will hadn't made go away. In a year here she had seen many officers who were once above taking convict women into their beds, succumb to the temptation. And in her heart she knew that if Tench was to weaken, she would go all out to be with him, regardless of her marriage.

But she knew somehow that Tench never would. He cared for her, she saw it in his eyes every time he stopped off at her hut or looked for her amongst a group of women, and in the tender way he petted Charlotte. Just knowing he cared for her helped. It was something good to dream about at night, a reason to keep herself clean and neat, another reason to stay alive.

It also gave her the courage to face Captain Phillip, and the same defiant streak which had prevented her from crying out when she heard her own death sentence, rose in her as she marched into the house. She didn't intend to watch Will hang while she still had breath in her body.

Captain Arthur Phillip was seated at his desk, a pen in his hand, as Mary came into the room.

'Thank you for agreeing to see me, sir,' she began, and bobbed a little curtsy.

Rumours went around the town that Phillip's house was very impressive inside, stuffed with fine furniture and silver plate. But to Mary's surprise it wasn't even as grand as the rector's house in Fowey. He had his desk, the chair he was sitting on, and there were a couple of armchairs by the fireplace, but apart from a silver-framed picture of a lady who was almost certainly his wife, there was little else, not even a rug on the bare boards.

Captain Phillip wasn't much to look at either, fifty, slender and small, all the hair on the top of his head gone. But he did have lovely dark eyes, and Mary thought he wore his naval uniform well.

'I suppose you've come to plead for your husband?' he said coldly.

'No, I've come to plead for everyone in this colony,' Mary said without any hesitation. 'For if you hang Will, they will surely all die, yourself included.'

He looked startled by such a claim, his dark eyes widening.

'Without the fish he brings in we will starve,' Mary continued, hitching Charlotte higher into her arms and willing her not to cry. 'There is no one else as skilful as Will. If you hadn't taken away his rights to take a few fish home for us, this would never have happened.'

'That couldn't be helped, it was an emergency situation,' Phillip said tersely, irritated that she had the audacity to question his orders. 'And your husband hadn't just taken a couple of fish. He had a great deal. He has been bartering them for provisions stolen from the stores. Each time someone steals from there, it leaves even less for the rest of the colony. It is an extremely grave offence.'

'Wouldn't you do the same if your wife and family were facing death?' Mary said, glancing at the picture of his wife.

'No, I would not,' he said firmly. 'The provisions are rationed fairly. I only have the same as you.'

Mary doubted that, but didn't dare say so.

'So what good will hanging Will do?' she asked. 'I'll be left to bring up this child alone, the people who steal from the stores will still do it, and every one of us will be even hungrier.'

Phillip looked at Mary, noting that she was every bit as ragged as the other convict women, but that she was clean. Even her bare feet were only dusty, not filthy as he'd observed many of the other women's were.

Lieutenant Tench had often spoken of this woman, whom he considered intelligent and forthright, and claimed had been a good influence on the other women on the *Charlotte*. There hadn't been any complaints about her behaviour, in fact he had himself commented on the Bryants being model prisoners.

184

'Go home now,' he said. 'He will be tried tomorrow. Tonight he stays in the guard-house.'

Mary moved towards the door, but turned before leaving and gave Phillip a penetrating stare. He saw deep fear and desperation in her eyes as she held the child out to him.

'Please, sir,' she pleaded. 'Look at my child. She is bonny and healthy now, but without Will she may not stay that way. I'll make sure Will never goes wrong again. Please, for the love of God and this child, spare him!'

She left then, slinking off into the night like a cat.

Phillip sat for a while deep in thought. The woman was right. Hanging Bryant would bring the spectre of starvation even closer.

'Damn those fools in England,' he muttered. 'Where are the provisions asked for? How can I be expected to make this colony self-sufficient when I haven't been given even the most basic equipment or men with the right skills?'

He had deep anxieties about almost every facet of this experiment: the infertile soil, the fast-dwindling stores, the behaviour of the felons, and the natives. It was predictable that the felons wouldn't pitch in and help themselves. They were townsfolk in the main, and they were more familiar with a jug of ale than a plough. They had no morals – dozens of the women had given birth or were expecting a child, and they moved from one partner to another without a qualm. They'd rather stand about chatting than work, would rather steal vegetables than grow them. Phillip could understand them, they had after all been sent here for good reason. But he was very disappointed in the natives.

Phillip had believed that if they were treated with kindness and friendliness, they would reciprocate. Sadly, this didn't seem to be the case – over the last few months several convicts working away from the camp had been brutally murdered. He still wanted to find a way to communicate with these people, to discover where the big rivers and fertile land lay, to learn about the native animals and birds, but all his efforts had come to nothing.

In truth, by the first anniversary of the colony, Phillip was a very worried man. He had the settlement at Sydney Cove, the one in Norfolk Island, and now Rose Hill too, but the convicts showed little inclination to reform, the Marines grumbled constantly, and the situation with the natives appeared to be getting worse rather than better. Without more food and medicine, the death toll would rise even more steeply. He found it hard to sleep at night for anxiety, and he couldn't see an end to it.

Mary bit into her knuckles as Judge Collins stood up in the guard-house to tell Will what his punishment was to be. As she had expected, someone had informed on Will, and she guessed it to be Joseph Pagett, a man who had been on both the *Dunkirk* and the *Charlotte*. He had shown signs of jealousy during the voyage, and she could recall him giving Will a baleful look the day they were married.

Charles White, the surgeon from the *Charlotte*, had spoken up for Will, but even so Mary was sure he was to be hanged. She knew Will thought so too, for his face was drained of all colour, and he was biting his lip and trying very hard not to tremble.

'I sentence you to a hundred lashes,' Collins said. 'And to be deprived of the direction of fishing and the boat. Also to be turned out of the hut you are now in, along with your wife and family.'

Will shot a glance at Mary, his face registering some relief, but anxiety at how she would take the loss of the hut.

Mary couldn't think about that now. While she was relieved Will wasn't to be hanged, and 100 lashes was a light punishment compared to some she'd witnessed, any flogging was still terrible, and she felt her stomach heave with nausea.

'Take him away for punishment,' Collins said.

All the prisoners were rounded up to watch Will's flogging, even the children. They took their places in a semi-circle before the big wooden triangle, which was manned on either side by a Marine drummer. In front of the triangle stood the Marine who was to administer the flogging. He had stripped down to his shirt and was already wiping sweat from his brow with the back of his hand, for it was yet another very hot day. In his other hand he held the cat-o'-nine-tails, each strand tarred and knotted.

The Marines began to drum, and Will was brought into the circle. His guards removed his shirt, then tied his hands to the upper parts of the triangle. There wasn't a sound for a moment, not a whisper from a concerned friend, nor a cry from a child. Everyone was entirely focused on the hideousness of what they were to witness.

Will's punishment was announced again, and one of the Marines who had brought him out of the guard-house gave the signal count of one.

Mary had witnessed some thirty or more floggings, of women as well as men, and it had always appalled her, even when she thought the victim deserved punishment. Some were given 1,000 lashes, 500 one day, the rest saved for when their backs healed up. Some people died before they got even half-way, and those who survived would bear the scars for the rest of their lives. Mary felt sick even before the Marine lifted his arm for the first lash. She had caressed that broad brown back, knew every knob in Will's spine as intimately as she knew her own hands.

Will didn't flinch at the first lash, he even tried to smile at Mary as if to prove it didn't hurt. But just that one stroke had left a red weal, and his smile, however brave, didn't fool her.

The counting was slow, half a minute between each lash, and by the eighth blood was drawn. Will couldn't smile any longer, his body jerked with each lash and he was biting his lips as he tried not to cry out.

On and on it went, flies homing in on the fresh blood which spurted out all over his back like water through a sieve. By the twenty-fifth lash, Will was clinging to the triangle, his handsome face contorted with agony. Mary held Charlotte's face close to her chest, and shut her eyes each time the drum was beaten. But she could still hear the whip whistling through the still air, and the sound of the Marine's boots on the ground as he spun round to give each stroke more impact. She could also smell Will's blood and hear the buzzing of the flies gorging on it.

It took over an hour in all, many of the crowd almost passing out from standing beneath the hot sun. By fifty lashes Will was insensible, the sinews on his back showing white through the lacerated skin. He hung by the ropes around his wrists, his legs sagging like a drunk's.

Mary was crying now, hating the system which ordered such brutal punishment and despising those Marines who had often talked and joked with Will and were now his torturers.

The drum and the count finally stopped. Will was released from the triangle and he slid down it to the floor. His breeches and boots were soaked with blood, and ants were already carrying off small pieces of his flesh on their backs.

Mary ran to him, imploring someone to get cloths and salt water to bathe his back. Will was unconscious, his face still contorted with pain, and she crouched down beside him, Charlotte still in her arms.

'Let me take Charlotte?' a familiar voice asked.

Mary looked up and was surprised to see it was Sarah with a bucket of water and cloths. She had streaks from tears down her dirty face and it seemed that Will's suffering and Mary's distress had reminded her of their old friendship.

'Bless you, Sarah,' Mary said gratefully as she handed

her child over. She washed Will's face first, then looked up at Sarah again. 'I ought to get him out of the sun but I haven't got anywhere to take him now that they've confiscated our hut.'

'We'll take him to mine,' Sarah said, leaning down and patting Mary's shoulder. 'Hold on, I'll get some men to help.'

As Sarah walked away with Charlotte in her arms, Mary leaned over and put her lips close to her husband's ear. 'Can you hear me, Will?' she whispered.

He didn't reply, but his eyelids flickered. 'I swear to you we'll escape from here,' she whispered, hate for Captain Phillip and everyone else responsible welling up inside her. 'We'll find a way, you'll see. I'll never let this happen again.'

It was later that day, as Mary crouched by Will's side in the small hut, gently bathing his back, that she considered her old vow to escape. She hadn't thought of it once since her arrival, and now it seemed incredible to her that she had begun to accept this terrible place, even to like it. But she couldn't bear it any longer. Somehow she was going to get Will and Charlotte and herself away from here and do so as fast as was humanly possible.

Chapter seven

'Move over, Mary,' Sarah hissed in the dark. 'You aren't in bed with Will now.'

Mary half smiled, wishing she was in bed with Will, back in their own hut. But however cramped it was sharing this hut with five other women, plus Charlotte, she was very grateful to Sarah and her friends for letting them stay. In cynical moments she put their kindness down to her being back on their level. But mostly she preferred to believe that Sarah, at least, had had such a shock at seeing Will's flogging that she had regained her old standards of compassion and generosity.

Will was in a hut with James, Samuel and Jamie, and Mary hadn't had many chances to see him since the day of the flogging, as he'd been sent to work on the brick kilns the day after. His back still wasn't healed. Mary was incensed at the further cruelty of forcing a man to do hard physical work when his back was torn to shreds. She had gone to meet him after that first day, and she'd cried at the sight of him. He was dragging himself along, his shirt soaked in blood, his face contorted with the pain. He went into the sea for a swim, hoping that would heal it faster, but he could barely move his arms, and his face went so pale that Mary thought he was going to pass out again. The wounds didn't heal with all the bending and lifting, and dirt and dust had got into them and caused infections. Will was scarred for life now, both physically and mentally.

It seemed to Mary that she was in a dark tunnel without even a chink of light at the end of it. She'd been separated from her husband and lost her hut; rations had been cut again, even more people were getting sick and each week the death toll increased.

It had once been the custom that all work stopped for a funeral and everyone attended, but not any more, otherwise no work would ever get done. Death was commonplace now, no more remarkable than a reported theft or accident. Word would go round that Jack, Bill or Kate had gone, but the only real interest was in who would get their personal effects. That was, if they hadn't already been stolen even before the man or woman passed away. Children's deaths had even less impact; to everyone but the mother it was just one mouth less to feed.

Mary had been pressed into laundry work the day after Will's flogging. Although washing the officers' and Marines' clothes wasn't particularly hard work, the vigilance required was exhausting. Shirts were at a premium and if left to dry unguarded, would be stolen by other women. But it was always the laundress who was punished if a shirt went missing, even if she wasn't found with one in her possession.

Only the thought of escape kept Mary going now. It filled her mind from dawn till dusk, distracting her from hunger, the funerals and the depravity all around her. Four women had run off into the bush, but they were soon recaptured; others who escaped were either killed by natives or died unable to find food and water; sometimes their bodies were found later. Many more just returned with their tails between their legs, only to be put back in chains.

Mary knew from Tench, who had done a lot of exploring inland, that there was nothing there to run to, just mile after mile of barren bush land. Some men had stolen a boat a while ago, but they weren't sailors and capsized it and were soon picked up.

But Mary was familiar with boats and sailing. She knew she'd need a sextant, a great deal of provisions, and charts of the waters around here. Above all, she needed to know where the nearest civilization was, and find a boat suitable for rough seas.

She had said all this to Will a few days ago, but he'd just laughed at her. 'A boat, a sextant and some charts! Why don't you ask for the moon too, my lover?' he said.

Mary was well aware of the difficulties involved, but she didn't agree that it was impossible just because no one else had dared to do it. She knew that Captain Phillip and his officers had tried to communicate with the natives and got nowhere, but she had made inroads in that direction herself and been successful.

She attributed this to Charlotte. While the natives might be intimidated by men in uniforms, they weren't frightened of a small child almost as naked as one of their own. While walking along the beach and around to the next cove, collecting wood for a fire, Mary had become aware she was being watched by a group of women natives and their children. She sat down with Charlotte on her lap and sang some songs to her, and to her delight she heard a voice joining in. It was that of another small girl, and when Mary turned and smiled at her, the child came closer.

Mary did the same again for three consecutive days, and on the fourth the little girl came and sat beside her, the mother standing a little way back, watching. It wasn't long before other children joined them, and after only a few more days, they all knew some of the words to Mary's songs.

She showed the native women some leaves of 'sweet tea', the vine-like plant the convicts used as a drink. This was the closest thing they had to a cure-all. It seemed to alleviate hunger pains, it comforted and revitalized, and it was believed to ward off diseases as those who drank nothing else seemed to suffer less from dysentery. The convicts had exhausted all the sources of the plant close to the camp, and Mary hoped the natives would show her where there was more. They did, taking her there so fast she had to run to keep up with them, and they even picked it for her.

In general the convicts hated the natives. This was partly because these people were so free, while they had to work, but more because they felt they were inferior beings. Convicts were used to being looked down on as the lowest of the low, and to their minds the natives were lowlier still. They bitterly resented the way the officers

194

gave these savages presents and insisted they were to be treated with deference, while the convicts were subjected to cruelty, with no allowances made for their needs.

Mary had never felt this way, although she didn't see the natives as beautiful people. To her mind the stink of the fish oil on them, their splayed noses and the ever-present bubbles of snot nestling above their thick lips made all but the children ugly as sin. But she was intelligent enough to realize that they probably thought white people just as ugly, and furthermore this was their land, and they were perfectly adapted to it. Her interest in them had been furthered by Tench's enthusiasm. He believed that the way truly to settle this new country was to learn to understand its people. Mary, however, didn't want to understand them in order to settle here; she was hoping for their help in her escape.

She persisted in making friends with them. And with a warm smile, and showing interest in their children, it wasn't hard. She told them her name, they reciprocated. They touched her hair and skin, laughingly holding their own black arms against hers to show the difference. Mary drew crude pictures of native animals in the sand and they told her their names. She drew a picture of one of the boats, then a very long wavy line to show them how far the white people had come to get here. She wished she could illustrate how different her homeland was from theirs, but that was too difficult. She wondered too if they had any conception at all of the nature of the white man's colony, and what the word 'convict' meant.

As Tench had pointed out, until the white man came

these natives wouldn't even have understood the notion of theft. They weren't acquisitive people, and they left their tools, canoes and other items lying around. Much of their hostility was due to white men taking their belongings, and who could blame them for retaliating with violence?

Mary continued to cultivate this little group of natives, day after day. They appeared healthy and well fed, and although she knew much of their diet was fish, which they caught from their canoes, she guessed they supplemented this with other things. She wanted to know what, for they didn't grow or rear anything. She thought such knowledge would help in her escape.

To her shock, the women showed her grubs and insects which they dug out of rotting tree stumps. Although Mary's empty stomach heaved at the very thought of it, she bravely tried some and found they weren't as bad as she expected.

Heavy rain prevented her from going to talk to the natives for almost a week, and when she did eventually venture back into the next cove, she couldn't see anyone. This disturbed her, for although she knew that these people didn't stay in permanent camps, wandering about as the mood took them, she was aware that this was a favourite fishing spot.

She walked farther than she normally did, until a buzzing of insects and a wheeling of birds overhead halted her. Ahead, she could see something lying up by the bushes above the beach, and to her horror she realized it was a dead native, covered in a swarm of ants. Snatching

Charlotte up in her arms, she ran as fast as she could back to the camp.

She was still running when she saw Tench. He must have come back from Rose Hill the previous night. He smiled at her warmly. 'You're in quite a hurry,' he said. 'Something wrong?'

'There's a body around in the next cove,' she blurted out.

'Anyone you know?' he joked.

Mary couldn't laugh, for she was afraid the body belonged to one of the group she had befriended. 'I think it's one of the natives,' she said. 'I didn't go close enough to be sure. Surely they don't leave their dead lying around unburied?'

'I wouldn't think so,' he said, looking concerned. 'I hope it is a natural death, not an attack by one of our people, we've got enough trouble without that. But I'll go and check it out now.'

After advising Mary not to stray so far from the camp again, he walked off.

It was several days before Mary had a chance to speak to Tench again. She'd seen him sailing off down the harbour with a group of Marines the day after she told him about the body, but he could have been going to the lookout on the Heads at the end of the bay.

She was just coming out of the stores with the rations for herself and Charlotte, when she saw Tench coming down the hill from Captain Phillip's house. She thought he looked very worried and upset.

'What's the matter?' she asked as he drew near to her. 'Didn't you have a present for him?'

This was a long-standing joke between them. In the early days Tench usually brought a gift of food when he dropped in to see her and Will. It was never anything much, maybe an egg for Charlotte, or some vegetables, but when times got harder and he didn't bring anything he always apologized and looked embarrassed. Mary would tease him then and say he couldn't expect a welcome without a present.

This time Tench gave her only a ghost of a smile. 'The captain's not happy with my news,' he said. 'There's dozens of dead and dying natives around the bay. Just like the one you saw.'

Mary instinctively clutched Charlotte tighter.

Tench saw her fear and put one hand on her shoulder. 'Don't worry, Surgeon White hasn't got any similar cases here. It must be something that only affects them. But keep away, just to be safe. Captain Phillip is sending someone down there to see what he can do or find out.'

Telling Mary not to worry was like asking the sun not to shine. She was terrified that this disease would spread to the camp and kill Charlotte, so her whole being urged her to flee now, any way she could.

Just a few days earlier, the *Supply*, the smallest ship of the original fleet, had returned from Norfolk Island with news that twenty-six of the twenty-nine convicts there had devised a plan to lure the crew away from the ship and sail off in her. By all accounts this plan was a first-class one and would have succeeded but for someone informing on them. While this meant on the one hand that Mary's idea was feasible, it also meant that all security would be tightened still further now, and punishments for any misdemeanour would be harsher than ever.

This was borne out just a few days later when six Marines were hanged for stealing from the stores. It seemed they had been doing it for months, having made keys for the locks, and when one of them was on guard duty he let his friends get in to plunder.

Most of the convicts were delighted that Captain Phillip was coming down on his men just as hard as on the convicts. But to Mary it suggested that Phillip was panicking because he knew the stored food wasn't going to last until more came from England.

As usual when a punishment took place, everyone had to be there. As Mary watched the rope put round each man's neck, and heard the sound of the gallows floor pulled away beneath him, leaving him dangling in space, she had never felt so desperate and afraid.

To her there was nothing good about this place – corrupt guards, women getting thirty lashes just for fighting, and all the time they were slowly being starved to death. It seemed to Mary that she was trapped in hell with several hundred lunatics.

In April, however, things looked up slightly for Mary and Will, as Captain Phillip was forced by food shortages to let Will go back to the fishing, under supervision. Mary smiled grimly to herself for she had been right, they couldn't manage without him. The catches had been tiny without his skill, and although Will very much resented being watched over, at least he had proved he was indispensable, and they got their old hut back.

Whatever the epidemic was which killed half the native population around the bay, it didn't spread to the new colony. Only one white man died, a sailor on the *Supply*. Surgeon White seemed to be of the opinion it was small-pox, but how it had come was a mystery. If they had brought it with them on the ships, it would have shown up far earlier.

Then in early May the gloom in the whole colony was lifted for a while by the arrival of the *Sirius* from Cape Town. Although she was mainly carrying flour, not sub-stantial provisions like meat, she brought good news that other ships were on their way, and long-awaited mail for those lucky enough to have friends and family who could write.

Yet the sight of the ship anchored out in the bay seemed to have a bad effect on Will. Mary found him on the shore on many an afternoon before he went out fishing, just staring out at the *Sirius*. When she tried to speak of it he snapped at her, and when he wasn't working he didn't come looking for her and Charlotte as he once did.

One day, early in the afternoon, Mary was taking the clean washing back to the barracks, having left Charlotte playing with another child, when she heard Will's loud voice coming from James Martin's hut. Mary guessed they'd managed to get some rum from somewhere.

Mary had conflicting opinions about James, the Irish horse thief. She had been delighted to see him again, and Sam Bird too, for the friendships formed on the *Dunkirk* were the basis of a kind of family here. James was a very amusing and charming man, intelligent and articulate, and able to read and write. But he was a devil for the drink, and women.

Mary recognized him as the sort who led others into trouble but usually managed to wriggle or charm his way out of any blame. He wasn't bound by loyalty; James Martin looked after himself first and foremost. She felt he was a bad influence on Will.

Mary wasn't by nature a snoop, but Will worried her when he drank, as he became boastful and often quite belligerent. She also wanted to find out how he and James had acquired the drink; if he was stealing fish to get it she wanted to know in advance.

There wasn't anyone else around, so Mary crept round the back of James's hut. If anyone came by she would make out she had just come out of the bushes after relieving herself.

James was talking about some of the men going after the native women. He took the view that a man wasn't right in the head to do such a thing.

'I reckons you'd at least be safer than with some of the pox-carrying hags here,' Will said, and laughed heartily. 'That's why I picked Mary, I knew she were clean.'

Mary wasn't sure whether to take that as a compliment or not. It had a kind of double edge to it.

'She's a good woman,' James said almost reprovingly. 'You're a lucky man, Will, in more ways than one.'

'I'll be luckier still once I get out of this accursed place,' Will retorted. 'And I'll be off on the first ship when my time's up.'

'Won't you wait for Mary?' James asked, his tone

slightly arch, making Mary suspect they weren't drinking together after all. Maybe Will had come visiting after getting some spirits elsewhere.

'No, I bloody won't,' Will burst out. 'Firstly no ship will take me on with a woman and a child, secondly I can do better than her.'

Mary felt as if someone had punched her in the belly. It was one thing for Will to tell others he didn't consider himself legally married, quite another to say he could do better than her. She turned and fled, trying very hard not to cry.

Will didn't come back to their hut before going fishing that evening, so Mary cooked up some rice on the fire, for once barely noticing the maggots that floated up to the surface as the water got hot. She had nothing more to add to it, as they had already eaten their tiny ration of salted pork earlier in the week. But Mary had no appetite, she was only cooking for Charlotte's sake. She felt weak with misery that Will intended to abandon her.

Charlotte sat right by the fire, as she always did when food was cooking, her dark eyes never leaving the cooking pot. That distressed Mary still further, for a small portion of rice wasn't anywhere near enough to keep a child growing and healthy. She could already see in her daughter the tell-tale signs of under-nourishment that she'd observed in children from desperately poor families back in Cornwall: the distended belly, sunken cheeks and lack-lustre eyes and hair.

If Will left her and went home, escape would be well-nigh impossible. She might be able to plan it, get her hands on all the necessary equipment and handle a boat well, but it was Will who had the navigation skills. There wasn't another man in the whole convoy likely to take his place.

The prospect of being left alone here terrified her. She'd lose the hut, the women would jeer at her, the men would pester her. She wouldn't be able to protect Charlotte from the depravity that was all around. The best she could hope for was to become a 'lag wife', the mistress of one of the Marines or officers. But that would only last until he too went back to England.

Mary's emotions ranged through despair, fear and then anger that evening, but by the time Charlotte had devoured the rice and turned sleepily to her mother's breast, she had a plan. Just as she'd coolly planned finding an officer lover on the *Dunkirk* in order to survive, she was now going to use the few assets she had again.

As Will made his way back to his hut it was almost dawn. He was chilled to the bone and wet through for it had started raining and turned very cold around ten o'clock the previous evening. He was also exhausted and aching with hunger, for they'd fished all night and all they had to show for the hard work was around a dozen fish. He had experienced all that a thousand times before, both here and back in Cornwall, but what had really got him down tonight was the attitude of the two Marines sent out to watch him.

'Bastards,' he muttered, and spat noisily on the sand. But for the fear of another flogging he would have knocked them over the side. How dare they suggest the lack of fish was because he didn't know as much about fishing as he claimed! And that he was drunk when he came aboard. He had had a few tots of rum, but that didn't impair his judgement. There just weren't any fish in the bay. If they'd been prepared to sail through the Heads like he wanted to do, they would have caught thousands.

As he drew nearer the hut, he was very surprised to see a fire and Mary bending over it.

'Why the fire? Is Charlotte sick?' he asked as he got nearer.

'No, she's asleep,' Mary said. 'I thought you'd be cold and hungry so I made some breakfast for you.'

Will's spirits lifted. He had expected Mary to be sullen because he'd gone off fishing without seeing her first. If she had found out he'd bought some rum instead of something they could all eat, she'd have been even madder.

'Breakfast?' he said incredulously.

Mary touched his wet shirt. 'Take that off and hang it up to dry,' she said, her face soft with concern. 'Wrap the blanket round you to warm you up. I could only fry a bit of bread for you, it was all I could get.'

Five minutes later, sitting on a stool in the doorway of the hut, with a cup of sweet tea in one hand and a big piece of fried bread in the other, Will felt much better. The first rays of light were coming into the sky and the bay looked beautiful with a cloud of mist just above the water. It was his favourite time of day, the birds just waking to sing, the ugliness of the camp not yet visible. It might be winter here, but it was as warm as a spring morning back home. In fact, looking across at the *Sirius* wreathed in mist, with the grey-green of the other side of the bay behind her, he could almost fool himself he was in Falmouth harbour looking out to St Mawes.

He missed Cornwall so much – the little winding cobbled streets, the houses huddled together, that blinding clear light in summer, the big fires in the tavern on a winter's night. When he thought of the risks the Cornish took with smuggling, it made him smile. Straining at the oars against waves as tall as houses, watching for the warning lanterns on the cliffs that said the excise men were coming – it was a game with high stakes, and only those with speed, nerve and strength dared play. But the winners tossed back glasses of French brandy, fishermen, miners and farm labourers equals with the country squire if they had played their part well.

The lasses there were pretty as well – rosy cheeks, big breasts and sweet shy smiles. The first time he saw Mary, through the grille on the *Dunkirk*, she was like that too. Now she was rake-thin, with hollowed cheeks, and she rarely smiled.

But she'd got up to make a fire and fry him some bread. She kept herself clean, and she didn't go after other men.

'Penny for them?' Mary startled him by coming up behind him and putting her arms around his neck.

'They aren't worth a penny!' he chuckled. 'I'll tell

you them for free. I was thinking about Cornwall, the smuggling and the taverns.'

'Want to know what I'm thinking?' she asked, kissing his neck.

'Go on,' he said.

'That we get into bed,' she said. 'And I warm you proper like.'

Will smiled, and it went right down inside him. Even before the flogging there hadn't been much love-making, hunger and exhaustion saw to that. But since then it had gone completely; his lacerated back, working on the brick kiln, and further cuts in rations had knocked all the passion out of him.

'Now that's a real good idea, my lover,' he said, turning to grab her for a kiss. 'It's been far too long.'

Mary smiled to herself later that day as she washed clothes down at the water's edge. She'd almost forgotten how special Will could make her feel. It was worth getting up so early, she'd even managed to forget how hungry she was.

In early September Mary knew she was definitely pregnant again. She was thrilled, not just because she'd reached her objective and found a way to prevent Will from leaving her here alone, but because he was genuinely delighted at becoming a father. Yet as always in the colony, any happy moment seemed to be erased by something bad. This time it was a soldier raping a girl of eight. To Mary it brought Charlotte's vulnerability sharply into focus. Up until then she'd hardly considered what the future for her child would be – keeping her alive was enough to concern herself with. But when the soldier wasn't even hanged, but sent off to Norfolk Island, she found herself sobbing with rage.

'Don't take on so, Mary,' Will said, trying to comfort her. 'He'll be out of the way there.'

'But there's children there too,' she reminded him. 'Including little Henrietta, Jane's baby. You explain to me why you can be flogged just for insolence, but hurting a little girl isn't thought a real crime.'

'I don't know,' Will said, shaking his head. 'Any more than I don't know why they still keep sending a couple of men out to watch me fish. If they weren't there, I'd sail right out the bay and get a better catch.'

'We have to think again about escape,' Mary said fiercely.

'How can we do that with a little 'un on the way?' he replied, tenderly patting her belly.

'Because of this little 'un,' she retorted. 'Don't you want something better for him?'

In November the whole colony buzzed with the news that Lieutenant Bradley and Captain Keltie of the *Sirius* had captured two natives on Captain Phillip's instructions.

The captured men were called Bennelong and Colbee, and it was discovered they had no wives or children. Lieutenant Bradley, the officer responsible for their capture, got an orphaned native boy who had been taken in by Surgeon White to explain to the men that they weren't going to be harmed.

Mary watched the whole proceeding with amazement. She had always thought that abducting anyone against their will amounted to harm. She was also sure that the two natives would be even more alarmed when they were subjected to being washed, shaved, dressed in clothes and shackled to prevent their escape.

Just a few days later, news got round that both men had managed to free themselves from their shackles. Colbee got clean away, but Bennelong was caught. The majority of the prisoners found all this highly amusing. They didn't consider Bennelong to be a person with feelings, more an animal which had to be caged. But Mary was sickened by it – there was something about the tall, well-built black man that touched her. She could imagine his confusion at the peculiar world he'd been dragged into. His people weren't confined in any way. Home was the temporary shelter of a cave or a mud and bark 'humpie'. They didn't have kings or princes in their tribes, every man was equal to the next, so how could he possibly understand the white man's class distinctions, or his lust for wealth, power and possessions?

Mary saw Bennelong as being in a very similar position to herself, and as such they could be allies. It struck her that if she could show him ways to use his captivity to his advantage, in return he might be persuaded to help her and Will escape.

The weeks went slowly by, and with each one Mary felt more desperate. There were no extra rations here for pregnant women as on the *Charlotte*, and she was so hungry that she often went searching for the grubs and insects the natives had shown her. During December and January it was blazing hot, she would be wakened at dawn by the sun beating down on the hut's roof, and there was no respite all day until sunset.

Only the relationship she was forming with Benne-long gave her a little hope. With words of his language she learned from the children she had befriended, she was able to suggest to him that if he played along with Captain Phillip his leg irons would be removed and he could become important to the white man. Bennelong seemed to understand what she meant; on one occasion he showed her half a bottle of rum he'd been given and grinned broadly. He appeared to be happy to stay in the settlement as long as more of it was forthcoming.

Mary knew it was too soon to attempt to enrol his help in any escape plan. Besides, it was impossible when she was so heavily pregnant. There was no possibility of collecting and storing food either, and anyway there were no ships in the harbour. Both the *Sirius* and the *Supply* had gone, taking ninety-six male and twenty-five female convicts, as well as twenty-five children, to Norfolk Island in an effort to eke out the rations a little longer. The *Sirius* was then going on to China to try to get desperately needed provisions.

When they set sail from England they had enough food for two years, and now that time was up. Even though the farm at Rose Hill had produced a good harvest of wheat, there was only enough food to last a few more months, with rations cut yet again. Everyone from

Captain Phillip to the lowest criminal was waiting expectantly for a ship to arrive with more food. Daily, people trudged down to Dawes Point, where they could just about see the flag mast on the South Head at the end of the bay. If the flag was struck it would mean a ship was coming, but day after day they were disappointed.

The fear of dying of starvation was very real now. It showed in every convict's face, from the bleakness of their eyes to the hollows in their cheeks, and in the slowness of their movements. With so many of their original number taken away by troops to Norfolk Island, and the countless deaths during the two years, Sydney Cove looked like a ghost town, and empty huts were being allocated to people who had previously shared. With a further cut in rations, no one had the physical strength to work a full day. An order was issued that they need only work until midday; the afternoons could be spent working their own gardens. At last Will was told he could fish without a guard, because there just wasn't the manpower to spare for fishing duties.

Mary had her first labour pains during the early evening of 30 March. She didn't recognize them as labour at first, assuming they were merely hunger cramps. Will was out fishing and it was raining so hard that the ground was a sea of slippery red mud. She put Charlotte to bed and got in herself, but the pains continued, just strong enough to prevent sleep.

All through the night she lay there, staring up into the darkness, listening to the steady dripping of water coming in through the roof. By then she realized the baby was coming, but in her weakened state she felt unable to get up and trudge through the mud and rain to seek help.

For the first time ever, she hoped for death. She was exhausted by the daily struggle to survive, and she felt unable to meet the further demands a new baby would place on her. Even the little cries Charlotte made in her sleep didn't stir her conscience. She hoped that by lying there, ignoring the child struggling to find its way out into the world, it would just fade away and so would she.

But as she closed her eyes and tried to will herself into death's dark valley, her mother's face came into her mind. Mary had tried her best to forget her parents and sister. She had long since given up trying to recall their faces and the sound of their voices or wondering if they ever spoke of her. She had even steeled herself not to think about Cornwall and compare it with here.

Yet there was her mother's face, as clear as if she was standing in the daylight before her. Her grey eyes were full of concern, her mouth slightly pursed as if in disapproval, wisps of grey hair escaping from her linen cap. Her expression was one Mary remembered very well, the one she'd always worn when berating Mary for unfeminine behaviour. Mary remembered then that her mother had always been strong, she'd never shown her anxiety to Mary and Dolly when their father's ship didn't return when expected. Somehow she always managed to put food on the table and keep the fire burning.

It seemed to Mary that her mother was trying to send her a message that she must fight for life, for her children's sake.

With great difficulty she got out of her bed, fumbled in the dark for a piece of sacking to put around her shoulders, and went out into the rain.

The nearest hut was only twenty yards away, but the pains were too fierce to stand up. On her hands and knees, Mary crawled through the mud in agony to get help.

The first dawn light was just coming through the open door of the hut as Mary's baby finally fought his way out, in the none too certain hands of Anne Tomkin.

'It's a boy!' Anne exclaimed with more weariness than jubilation, as she held the baby closer to the door to examine him. 'And he looks healthy enough.'

This was borne out by a lusty, angry scream. It was Mary who had to tell Anne to wrap her son in a piece of cloth, to tie the cord and cut it. Anne had no children herself and her husband Wilfred who had gone for more experienced help hadn't arrived back.

Yet as Mary took her baby in her arms, she forgot the pain, the hunger and even her blood- and mud-caked body. God had given her the boy she wanted, He had spared her life, and that had to mean there was hope for better times.

'I'll call him Emmanuel,' she said softly to herself.

Chapter eight

'He's a beauty,' Will said reverently as he cradled his son in his arms. He'd only just got back from fishing all night, and despite being wet, cold and exhausted he was thrilled to find Mary had borne him a son. 'And he's brought us luck! I've got a fine big mullet for us.'

When Mary shot him an anxious glance, Will grinned. 'It's fair do's. They gave it to me because of the babby. I reckon things will get better for us now.'

Mary relaxed again and smiled. Will had always been affectionate towards Charlotte right from her early days, but he was almost incandescent with pleasure now as he looked down at his own baby. 'Do you like the name Emmanuel?' she asked.

'It's a real good name,' he said, looking tenderly first at his son and then at Mary. 'A hopeful one, and I'll make sure he learns to write it too.'

That day was a golden one for Mary. The rain stopped, the sun came out and Will carried her down to the sea to wash her. There had been many sweet moments between them in the past, but never this degree of tenderness and care. He made her comfortable in a makeshift bed beneath a gum tree by the hut, tucked Emmanuel into Charlotte's old crib, then cooked the mullet over the fire with a couple of potatoes he'd managed to get from somewhere. Later he took Charlotte for a walk to tell Surgeon White about the new baby, leaving Mary to sleep.

She didn't sleep, despite the comfort of the food inside her. Will wasn't the kind of man who spoke of love, but his actions had told her how he felt. There had been times during her pregnancy when she had felt guilty she was trapping him, but that feeling had gone now she had seen his delight in having his own child. They were a complete family now, and whatever life had in store for them, they would cope with it together.

Tench came to visit later that afternoon.

'I heard your baby was born,' he said, looking down at Mary cuddling Emmanuel under the tree. 'I thank God you are both safe and well.'

'Isn't he the bonniest babby you ever saw?' Will asked as he dandled Charlotte on his knee. 'I never saw a more lusty one.'

Tench laughed and leaned down to stroke the child's head. 'He favours you, Will. The same fair hair and strong body. Mind you take good care of him.'

'Me too,' Charlotte said indignantly. They all laughed, for she'd clearly picked up the idea today that her place might be about to be usurped.

'I'll always take care of you,' Will said, picking her up and throwing her into the air. 'You're my little princess.'

'Don't place too much importance on the rumours that Will is going to run out on you when his time is up,' Tench said to Mary after Will had wandered off to boast to a few more friends about his son. 'I don't believe he's brave enough to ever leave you.'

Mary wasn't surprised that Tench had heard the rumours. People stopped at nothing to pass on information here. She wondered what he would think of her if he knew the baby was her secret plan to hold on to Will.

'I don't listen to what people say,' she said stoutly, for she felt so happy today that nothing else seemed to matter.

'You can apply for land of your own when Will's free,' Tench said.

'What would we do with land?' Mary replied with a smile. 'We aren't farmers. Will's only happy fishing.'

'Then he could build his own boat and start his own fishing business. Maybe you could open the first fishmonger's in New South Wales!'

'Maybe,' she replied. She wished she could believe as Tench did that one day there would be a real town here. He seemed to think that once the present problems were solved, the country would attract free settlers, to farm and trade, just as America had. 'And maybe a ship will arrive tomorrow with animals, ploughs, seed, fruit trees, food for us all, medicine and material to make new clothes,' she added with more than a touch of sarcasm.

'The ships will come soon,' he said, as he always did, but this time there was a lack of conviction in his voice. 'I really can't believe England would leave us to perish here.'

*

Emmanuel was baptized a few days later on 4 April, under the same big tree where Mary and Will had been married. As usual on such occasions, everyone was present.

Mary had considered herself poorly dressed for her wedding, but that grey dress had long since fallen apart with wear and become napkins for Charlotte. Its replacement, an issued 'slop', a shapeless sack of a dress in coarse cotton, was almost as worn out. One of the more kindly Marines' wives had given her a red ribbon for her hair, and a piece of flannelette to make a gown for Emmanuel – but for that he would have been wrapped in a piece of rag.

As Mary looked around at the rest of the congregation she saw how much they had all diminished since arriving here. They had in the main been healthy then, eyes bright with excitement and mischief; there was exuberance and hope, even when they were complaining vigorously. Their voices were strong, they argued, fought and laughed, pushing and shoving each other like impatient children. Mary remembered how she had once thought she would never learn so many names.

But it was easy to name every single one now. Death had claimed so many, and the recent removal of scores more to Norfolk Island meant there were perhaps fewer than 150 remaining. Only the number of children and babies had increased, but they were a sorry sight, nothing but huge mournful eyes set in pale, bony faces, legs and arms like little sticks, most sucking their fingers with hunger.

There were no bright eyes anywhere now, not even

among the officers. No pushing and shoving or loud voices, just apathetic, gaunt faces, aged radically by the sun and malnutrition. Laughter was a rare sound too, for those who still managed to get their hands on drink no longer wanted merriment, only oblivion. Even the bright colours of clothes were absent, for the finery some had sported that first day had long since turned to grey rags.

Mary thought they had all become like this savage land. As dull and arid as the scrubby bush, with its grey-green gums, as stunted and hopeless as the vegetables they had struggled to grow.

She would have liked to have put the blame on the officers, but even they were thinner and worn-looking too. As for the Marines, she felt even sorrier for them and their wives and families, for they had the same rations as the prisoners, their uniforms were in rags, and they were dying just as fast.

Watkin Tench went out to Dawes Point early the following morning to check the flag pole out on the South Head. He hadn't slept well, for the christening of Emmanuel Bryant the previous day had unsettled him deeply. While it was good to see Mary and Will's joy in their little son, a bright spot in an otherwise desperately grim period, if the child didn't survive, Mary was going to be devastated.

Tench wished he didn't care so much for her. He had told himself a thousand times that he only felt a bond of friendship with her, but the truth of the matter was that each time he saw her his feelings for her grew stronger.

His heart quickened at the sight of her. He felt helpless in the face of her great need for food and decent clothes. She was proud, she didn't beg for favours, and made light of the deprivation she suffered. Indeed, she made the best of the little she had.

He had even hoped Will's flogging would harden him in the way it had other men, that he would become a real trouble-maker and Mary would lose her loyalty to him. But instead of prising them apart it seemed to have had the reverse effect, baby Emmanuel being part of it.

If only he could stop weaving such futile day-dreams about taking Mary home with him when his term of office was up. If he were to tell anyone his thoughts of finding a little cottage for them somewhere well away from Plymouth, and telling his friends and family back home that she was the widow of a Marine serving here, they would laugh at him.

But that was what he dwelt on. He imagined Mary blossoming again with good food, lying in his arms each night in a feather bed. When he got to that point of his fantasy he would find himself aroused, imagining himself kissing those small breasts he'd so often glimpsed as she suckled Charlotte.

Tench broke off abruptly from this reverie when he saw the flag had been struck on the flag pole. This signified a ship was either anchored in the cove, or had been spotted out at sea.

In great excitement he ran to the observatory where an astronomical telescope had been erected and hastily trained it on the flag pole. He could see only one man strolling by the pole and to his intense disappointment he knew it couldn't be a ship from England, or there would be more frantic activity. It had to be the *Sirius* returning from Norfolk before making her trip to China.

He ran all the way back to find Captain Phillip to report it, and when the Governor said he would take his boat out to meet the ship, Tench begged to be allowed to accompany him, for at least it was a diversion from the normal routine and thinking about Mary.

They were about half-way to the Heads when they saw the longboat from the *Supply* being rowed towards them. Tench recognized Captain Ball making frantic gestures with his hands and his heart sank.

'Sir,' he said, turning to Captain Phillip, 'prepare yourself for bad news!'

Will came haring along the beach to where Mary was washing some clothes. She looked up from her task anxiously at the sound of his pounding feet. 'What is it?' she yelled, hoping against hope it was news of a ship carrying provisions.

'The *Sirius* has been shipwrecked,' he shouted back.

It was some time before Will regained enough breath to explain what he'd heard down at the harbour. The *Sirius* had just lowered its boats loaded with provisions in Sydney Bay at Norfolk Island, when the ship drifted on to sunken rocks. Captain Hunter tried to avert a disaster by dropping the anchor, but he was too late. Before the anchor chain had tightened, she struck the coral reef that ran parallel to the shore. As the sea tore into the holds, the crew cut away the masts to lighten the ship, so she might float free, but by then there was little hope of this.

'They sent out lines to get the men ashore,' Will gasped out. 'Worked till it was too dark to see any more, so I heard. Next morning they got the rest off.'

Mary was deeply shocked. Losing the *Sirius* was a mortal wound to the colony. How would they get provisions from China now?

'Is everyone safe?' she asked. Some of the women and children who had been sent there were people she'd come to care for.

Will nodded. 'Thank God for that small mercy.' His face broke into a smile then. 'Some of the convicts were sent out to the ship to get the remaining animals off. They found some grog, so they lit fires and settled down for a party.'

'Oh, Will,' Mary sighed. 'That's not funny!'

'We have to laugh otherwise we'd go under,' he retorted indignantly. 'And there's another funny story too. Lieutenant Clark got knocked off the raft by a convict falling in. The convict couldn't swim so Clark rescued him and brought him safely to shore. Then Clark beat him with a stick for jeopardizing his safety.'

Mary giggled. That to her mind was typical of Lieutenant Ralph Clark, whom she had never liked. He was a mean-spirited hypocrite who had spent most of the first year here calling all the female prisoners whores, and boring Tench and the other officers to death with tales of his wonderful wife Betsy back home. But then he'd had the nerve to take a lag wife, after all he'd said about the convict women! He was even absurd enough to name the child borne of that union Betsy, after his beloved wife. He'd been sent off to Norfolk Island to take control and as far as Mary was concerned, the harder he found it the better.

'But what will happen to us now?' she asked Will. 'The *Sirius* was our only chance of getting more supplies.'

Will frowned. 'Phillip has called a special meeting of all the officers for six o'clock.'

Mary knew from Tench that Phillip wasn't in the habit of confiding in anyone. He maintained his aloofness at all costs, so he must be extremely worried to call his men in.

'There's going to be even harder times ahead, that's for sure,' Mary sighed dejectedly. 'But let's try and look on the bright side, Will. If a ship doesn't come from England soon, Phillip will be even more dependent on your fishing. It's time you insisted on a portion of the catch for yourself again. Your skill will be the only thing which will keep everyone alive here.'

Captain Phillip was indeed a very worried man as he stood before his assembled officers at six o'clock. For so long he had lived in hope of a ship coming from England to solve the colony's problems, but now he had to face the reality that he had to take other drastic measures or be a witness to wholesale death through starvation.

'A further cut in rations will be necessary,' he began, his voice trembling slightly because he knew that a daily ration of two and a half pounds of flour, two pounds of very old pork, a pint of dried peas and a pound of inedible rice, divided between seven people, just wasn't enough to sustain life. 'We must supplement this with more fish and meat if we aren't to perish. My plan is to requisition all private boats for fishing and to form hunting parties.'

The officers looked at one another in consternation, knowing they were expected to volunteer their services. With the exception of Tench, they all considered supervising such expeditions unpleasant, for they did not like working with the convicts.

'Are you suggesting, sir, that some of the convicts are to be given arms?' one of the more senior officers asked, a look of horror on his florid face.

'Yes,' Phillip said wearily. 'Some of them are good marksmen. I believe if we show trust in them, they will respond with a real effort for the common good.'

He moved on to say he had no choice but to send the *Supply* off to Batavia, in the Dutch East Indies. Captain Ball would charter another ship there to bring back supplies. Philip King, the previous Governor of Norfolk Island, would also leave on the ship to take despatches and Captain Phillip's account of the state of the colony back to England.

The officers were even more concerned at this for the *Supply* was a little ship of only 170 tons, and for her to sail alone in unknown waters would be dangerous. Furthermore, if she was lost at sea they would have no vessel left here to take supplies to the settlement in Norfolk Island.

A murmur of dissent went round, but Phillip silenced it with a stern look.

'We have no choice,' he said bluntly. 'We have no supplies to take to Norfolk Island anyway, and to leave a ship in the harbour waiting for help from England which might never come would be catastrophic. I ask you all to give me your support.'

Fear reigned over the colony after the *Supply* sailed out of the harbour in April. The officers feared for the little ship's safety, and became aggressive. The troops dreaded an attack from the natives now firepower was so low. And the convicts were terrified of everything.

Before the *Supply* left a rumour circulated that the officers and troops were going to sail off in her, leaving the convicts to fend for themselves. They all knew they wouldn't last long alone.

Despite the best marksmen being sent out hunting, all they shot was three very small kangaroos. With all the extra boats and men, and the absolute necessity of catching more fish, the catches improved for a while, but then they began to dwindle again. The officers took back their small boats, and in sheer desperation Captain Phillip allowed Will to use his own cutter.

Mary was never one to allow an opportunity to go by without attempting to make use of it.

'This could be our big chance,' she urged Will one night as they lay in bed. 'With the use of that boat we could make our escape.'

'Don't be foolish,' Will said wearily. He was so weak

with hunger and tired from the strain of trying to bring enough food back for everyone that he wasn't inclined to listen to his wife's wild ideas.

'I don't mean now,' she said, sitting up beside him and leaning over to kiss him. 'We can't do it without instruments, charts or a store of food. But what you can do is win the Governor's confidence. Take the boat out further and further each time, but always come back. He's trusting you now, think how much more trust he'll have in you if you seem to be playing the game his way!'

'I can't see the point,' Will said irritably. 'Even if I did get him to trust me well enough so I wasn't watched, I wouldn't even know which was the best direction to go in to find a port.'

'Tench was telling me about the Dutch East Indies the other day. There's a busy port called Kupang,' Mary said. 'He said it was over the sea at the top end of this place.'

Will made a sort of guffaw. 'Over the sea at the top end of this place!' he scoffed. 'What kind of directions are those? Does he know how many leagues it is? Has anyone sailed to it afore? Don't talk daft, girl!'

Mary slumped back down, angry that he was mocking her. 'I don't know yet, but I'll find out,' she said with grim determination. 'We have to escape, Will. If we don't, Emmanuel and Charlotte will die.'

'No, Mary,' he said, turning his back on her dismissively. 'They won't, food will come, you'll see.'

'Maybe it will,' she said, but she ran one finger down the deep scars from the flogging on his back. 'Perhaps the children will even be lucky enough to survive all the outbreaks of fever, to avoid being bitten by a snake, and they won't be corrupted by the other convicts. But let's hope neither of us lives long enough to see Emmanuel tied to the triangle to be flogged.'

She felt Will stiffen under her fingers. She knew he still had nightmares about the flogging.

'I'd kill anyone who tried to do that to him,' he said.

'You'll be too weak by then,' she said gently. 'Old before your time with the struggle to survive. So will I be. That's why we have to go soon, while we're still capable of protecting the children.'

He sighed deeply. 'I'll think about it,' he said.

'And while you're thinking about it, do what I said and win the Governor's trust,' Mary said. 'Once we have that, we're half-way there.'

Mary lay awake long after Will had fallen asleep. She watched and listened constantly, whereas Will went around with his eyes and ears closed. He might think there were adequate provisions for many months yet in the stores, but she knew better. When the officers dined with the Governor now, they had to take their own bread, and the fare at Government House was little better than her own. One evening they'd dined on dog!

Just a few days ago an elderly convict had died while getting his rations in the store, and when Surgeon White examined his body he found his stomach to be completely empty. The only reason Mary still had some fight left in her, and milk in her breasts for Emmanuel, was because of fish Will brought home from the day's catch, and the grubs and berries the natives had introduced her to.

Bennelong had finally made his escape from the settlement, once the food and rum he had become used to grew short. Gardens, even the Governor's own, had been constantly plundered for vegetables, despite the severe flogging that resulted if the culprit was caught. It wasn't only convicts that did it, a seaman from the *Supply* was caught, and one of the Marines. Will had been compelled to dig a hole under their hut to keep their own meagre rations safe. He'd made it like the ones smugglers used back in Cornwall, lined with wood, and a false floor laid down on it.

Yet Mary thrived and still managed to feed her family because she refused to give way to utter despair as some were doing. As she told Will, it was just a case of hanging on, being helpful and pleasant to the officers so that when ships did arrive, as they surely must, she and Will would be in positions of trust. That way they could make opportunities to get the things they needed.

The days crept on, the misery of hunger growing more acute with each one. The weather turned very cold too, the wind eerily rustling the paper-dry leaves of the gums, and all public work ground to a halt because there was no one fit enough to do it any longer.

The convicts merely shuffled around now, every gaunt face illustrating the nature of real starvation. At night Mary often heard small children wailing pitifully from hunger. It was the worst sound she'd ever heard.

Will had appeared to heed Mary's advice, for he made himself increasingly popular with the officers and troops by his diligence in fishing. For this he was rewarded with a share of the catch, and being allowed to pick his own helpers. James Martin, Jamie Cox and Sam Bird, his most trusted friends, often went with him, and although there were usually a couple of Marines along too, this wasn't always the case. Will fished the waters beyond the Heads frequently, sometimes going several miles out to sea. He also struck up friendships with some of the natives as they fished from their canoes. Often it was they who directed him to large shoals.

Will sometimes saw Bennelong as he sailed down the harbour. He would paddle out in his canoe and occasionally climb aboard the cutter for a chat. Mary was sure that if she and Will managed to get their hands on some spirits, he could easily be bribed into helping them escape.

Just when it looked as if all hope of rescue was gone, in the afternoon of 3 June the flag was struck on South Head. As the cry went up that a ship was coming, pandemonium broke out. Men downed tools and cheered, women came hobbling out of their huts and hugged one another.

Watkin Tench, along with Surgeon White and Captain Phillip, took his boat and went off down the harbour. All three of them were as excited and emotional as the rest of the settlement, despite the discomfort of heavy rain and a stiff wind. As they drew closer to the Heads and saw the big ship coming in flying English colours,

Phillip transferred on to a fishing boat to go back, leaving Tench and White to go and collect welcome news from home.

'Look at that magical word on her stern,' White said, pointing to the painted sign that read 'London'. 'I had begun to doubt I would ever see such a thing again.'

The ship was the *Lady Juliana*, and because of the strong winds she was forced to anchor in Spring Cove just inside North Head, but Tench and White went alongside and called out a welcome to the ship's officers.

'You can't know how welcome you are,' Tench called out. 'We feared we'd never get the provisions we need so desperately. Can you tell us what you are carrying so we can take the good news back to the settlement?'

'Two hundred and twenty-five women felons, whores every one of them,' came the shouted reply from one of the officers.

Tench laughed, he thought it was a joke. But his laughter stopped abruptly when a group of tow-haired women suddenly appeared on deck, shouting obscenities.

'You have provisions too?' White yelled, aware that Tench was too stunned to resume any further questions. 'And the medicine we need?'

'Seventy-five barrels of flour,' the ship's officer called back. 'That's all. We set sail with the *Guardian*, she carried the stores, but she got holed by an iceberg.'

By nightfall all the convicts were in despair.

Captain Phillip had returned to the harbour with a beam on his face, confirming to them that it was exactly as the fishermen had reported, a big English ship, anchored at Spring Cove.

The convicts waited, expecting Lieutenant Tench and Surgeon White to arrive back an hour or two later looking happier still. Many of their number hastily ate the last of their rations, in the belief that by the following day they would be given more than they usually ate in a week.

But Tench and White came back grim-faced and silent, going straight up to Government House without a word to anyone. When one of the men who had been on the cutter reported that there were over 200 women on the new ship and no provisions, they were not believed. Some laughed, assuming it had to be a joke. Yet as they watched other officers speeding up to Government House, and no sounds of revelry wafting out, they slowly realized that it had to be true.

The male convicts were far too weak with hunger to be excited by a huge number of new women descending on them. Their reaction was only fear that their rations would be cut even more drastically. But to most of the women it was a calamity. Bad though it was to be forced to share rations with strangers, the prospect of new women stealing their men away was even worse.

A relationship with someone, whether you were legally married or not, eased the misery of life in the colony. In most cases the partnerships were a compromise, especially for the women. Back home few of them would have chosen the mate they had here. But choice was limited, plain girls were grateful for being wanted, the prettier girls felt safer with a protector, and where a baby was a result of the arrangement, it gave some purpose to their life.

Mary was more nervous than most when she heard the news of the *Juliana* and its cargo of women. She knew it wasn't her beauty or her cleverness that had kept Will with her for two years. He had stayed with her purely because there was a shortage of women, and by the time he'd got to know the prettier ones better, he found most had serious flaws in their characters.

Death, and men being moved to Norfolk Island, had decimated their numbers. There weren't more than seventy men left here now, and a great many of those were physical wrecks. Among 200 new women who had been cooped up on a ship for months, there were almost certainly going to be dozens who would set their sights on Will.

Chapter nine

Every single woman in the settlement turned out to see the women from the *Juliana* being rowed ashore. Apart from the weather, it was almost like a re-enactment of their first day here, for they could hear the same kind of excited laughter and the ribald remarks they'd made themselves. But whereas they had arrived in early February, which in this upside-down country meant summer with blazing sunshine, so hot that many of them ran into the sea to cool down, the new arrivals were experiencing winter. The sky was grey, a keen wind was blowing, making the sea choppy, and it was very cold.

There should have been sisterly concern for the new women. After all, they had been through a long, gruelling voyage, and now they were about to enter hell. Yet just the way they looked, even from a distance, was enough to make the old-timers forget any kindly thoughts and band together in antipathy and resentment. The new arrivals' clothes were vivid colours, many wore hats trimmed with flowers and feathers, they were plump and healthy, and they looked for all the world like a troupe of actresses, not convicts.

Mary clutched Emmanuel closer to her breast in fear.

Her first exposure to the convicts from the other transport ships in the fleet was printed indelibly on her mind.
They had all seemed so much tougher than her, conniving
and ruthless too. Time and the hardships here had made
all the survivors equal now, but she was afraid these new
women would alter everything.

'Lots of ladies,' Charlotte said, looking up at her mother
with undisguised glee. 'Pretty ladies.'

At her child's innocent words Mary felt a pang of
shame. They were, after all, just women like herself. All
of them had known chains and the horrors of prison and
had been wrenched from their families and friends. She
didn't want Charlotte to grow up in a climate of bitterness
and hate. She decided she must put aside her fear and
jealousy and welcome the newcomers.

'I thought we might have had a few fights on our hands,'
Surgeon White said to Tench over dinner at White's
house the following evening. 'But thanks to the actions
of Mary Bryant the new women appear to be settling
in well.'

The two men had become friends on the *Charlotte*,
despite a twenty-year age gap. Their interests and family
backgrounds were similar, and though the surgeon was
more concerned with the general health of the colony,
and Tench with the challenge of making it a success,
they were both intensely fascinated by this new, as yet
unexplored land. They had gone on several exploratory
trips into the bush together, and shared the same curiosity
about its natives. Both of them also had compassion

for the convicts, something few of the other officers felt.

By candlelight, White's dining room would pass for being much like any country doctor's back home in England, with its whitewashed walls, snowy table-cloth, plain, serviceable china, laden bookshelves and a couple of treasured landscapes on the walls. By daylight, however, the crudeness of the building showed. The walls were wattle and daub, and in heavy rain holes often appeared. The floor beneath a rug was uneven boards. But whatever its shortcomings, it was a haven of civilization for White and his dinner guests.

While Charles White often regretted his decision to come out here with the fleet, it was mainly because of the lack of medical equipment and medicine rather than the absence of comforts. A widower for over ten years, he had grown used to the bachelor life, and he had two convict women, Anne and Maria, who cooked and kept house for him. He also had little Nunburry, the native boy he'd adopted, to take care of, and some very good friends. Tonight his mood was mellow. He had managed to acquire a bottle of brandy, and he and Tench had dined on a first-class sea bass, with some carrots and potatoes from White's own garden. It was truly miraculous that the vegetables hadn't been stolen, but perhaps by showing Anne and Maria a little kindness, and giving them some extra food, he had gained their loyalty.

'Mary's a good woman,' Tench agreed. 'I daresay she remembered how hard it was for her to adjust when she first arrived here. If only all the women had her practical nature and generosity of spirit!'

He had been surprised and touched to see Mary helping with the allocation of huts for the new arrivals. She seemed to be making a real effort to make the new women feel welcome. He wished her attitude was a general one; already there had been reports of clothing and other personal possessions being stolen.

'There's a fair few trouble-makers among the new ones,' White sighed, remembering the two women he'd separated for fighting and the profanities they'd screamed at him. 'According to the reports, they carried on their whoring with the sailors all the way here. A great number of them are with child. But they are healthy at least, save for the pox of course.'

Tench smiled. White was always ranting about the scourge of venereal diseases. They were rife here of course, but Tench couldn't believe as White did that the whole future of this new land was at risk because of it.

'At least the *Juliana* brought news,' Tench said cheerfully. 'I am amazed to hear of the revolution in France. When I was in Paris I confess to being appalled by the excesses of the aristocracy. And good news too that King George has recovered from his madness. What do you know of this sickness he suffered?'

'Very little. I'm just an old saw-bones,' White shrugged. 'But I am glad Farmer George is well again. As glad as I was to find the *Juliana* has enough rations for two years for her convicts.'

Tench smiled. That news had been the very best, a huge relief for everyone. It was just a shame they hadn't been told immediately, then there would have been less hostility towards the new arrivals. Now everyone was hoping that the *Justinian* from Falmouth, which was apparently fully loaded with stores and equipment, would arrive before the next huge influx of convicts.

But personally Tench was most grateful for the letters from home that were brought out by the ship. He felt he had stood up remarkably well to all the discomforts and deprivations of the settlement, but the sense of isolation from his friends and family had almost broken him at times. Indeed, if he was truthful, there had been times in the past two years when he feared he would never live to see them again.

'Let's drink a toast to the light at the end of a very dark tunnel,' he suggested.

White filled their glasses. 'Light to banish the darkness,' he said, and chuckled. 'Though with another three transports, and a thousand convicts on their way, we'll need a great deal of light to banish that darkness.'

Mary and Will stood together at the harbour, quaking as they looked out across the bay to the *Neptune* and the *Scarborough*. They could see the longboats being lowered to bring the convicts ashore. But the terrible stench coming from the ships was enough for them to know that what they were about to see was going to be utterly appalling.

It had been bad enough on the previous day, helping the sick from the *Surprise* to the hospital. Many of those convicts were so frail that they were unable to walk, having lain in their own vomit and excreta for most of the voyage. But today was going to be even worse.

The *Justinian* had arrived on 20 June, bringing joy to everyone in the settlement as she carried ample provisions and much-needed equipment, along with animals. She had left England some time after the *Surprise*, *Neptune* and *Scarborough*, the three transport ships carrying another 1,000 convicts. But she had overtaken them and made the voyage in only five months. Full rations were issued once again, and working hours put back to normal. The *Justinian* left again as soon as her cargo was unloaded, to take provisions to Norfolk Island.

On the 23rd the flag was struck again, but it was two days before the ship which had been signalled sailed into the bay. This was the *Surprise*, carrying 218 male convicts and a detachment of the newly formed New South Wales Corps.

It was shocking to hear that there had been forty-two deaths during the voyage, and another hundred were sick. And when the Reverend Johnson went aboard, he reported back that the convicts were lying almost naked in the holds, too sick to move or help themselves.

Mary and Will, along with many other convicts, had come forward willingly to help, but the sights and smells were so awful that many of the volunteers turned tail and ran. Few of the women helpers could stop themselves from crying openly. It was patently obvious that these new arrivals had been half starved and kept below decks for almost the entire voyage. Many of them would never recover.

They had barely got those men washed, fed and under blankets, before the other two ships arrived. The Reverend Johnson went aboard the *Scarborough*, but was advised by the captain not to go below decks. The terrible stench coming from the holds was enough to deter him, and he didn't even attempt to board the *Neptune*.

Tents had hurriedly been erected in front of the hospital, and there was food, water, clothes and medicine in readiness. The night before, as Mary tried to sleep, the smell from the ships at anchor made her stomach heave. It was a hundred times worse than anything she'd experienced on the *Dunkirk*. Although her heart went out to the poor souls in their suffering, she had felt she couldn't possibly help again today.

But by dawn, the anger she felt at men putting profit before human life made her strong again. According to conversations she'd overheard between officers, transportation had been put out to private tenders. As the government offered £17 7s 6d a head for rations, the less the convicts were given to eat, the more food the ships' owners could sell off once they arrived here. If convicts died en route, this made it even more lucrative.

Mary heard one officer comparing the transport owners unfavourably with the slave traders. As he pointed out, at least the traders were motivated to keep the slaves fit and healthy, for the better the condition they were in, the more they could be sold for. There was no such incentive even to keep convicts alive.

'They say Captain Trail of the *Neptune* kept them all chained together,' Will said in a subdued, shocked voice. 'When one of the number died, the prisoners kept quiet about it to get the man's rations. Imagine being so desperate for extra food that you'd lie next to a decomposing body!'

Mary didn't answer him, for she knew from personal experience that she would probably do absolutely anything, however repulsive, to keep herself alive. Now she had two children to care for, her survival instinct was even stronger.

The loading of the longboats began. They watched the first few people climb slowly and hesitantly down the rope ladder, and even from the shore they could see how difficult it was for them. But they were the lucky ones; before long the sailors and troops were practically hurling people into the boats, as if they were sacks of goods, because they weren't capable of walking, let alone climbing.

As the boat rowed in closer, a gasp went up, for the people were like skeletons. There was no eager expectancy on their faces, and they lolled as if close to death – indeed, one was dead on arrival. Two more were to take their last breath as they lay where they'd been placed on the wharf.

'I can't believe what I'm seeing,' Will said, the horror in his eyes matching his cracking voice. 'God save us from men that would let this happen.'

'They aren't men,' Mary said in a loud, clear voice, feeling she could strangle those responsible with her own bare hands. 'They're beasts.'

Her anger fuelled her, stopped her considering the risk of infection to herself or even caring about the smell any more. The convicts were almost naked, their bodies covered with sores, wriggling maggots and faeces. She bent over one man to try to get him to drink some water, and he tried to cover his exposed penis because she was a woman.

'I've seen plenty of those before,' she said gently, touched that even in such a terrible state and close to death, he could still concern himself with propriety. 'You're safe now, there's food and drink, water to wash, but you've got to fight to get better. Don't you dare give up on me!'

'Your name?' he asked, his cracked lips splitting open with the effort to speak.

'Mary,' she said, wiping his face with a wet rag, 'Mary Bryant. And yours?'

'Sam Broome,' he whispered hoarsely. 'God bless you, Mary.'

The sights grew worse as the day progressed, men with dysentery so bad that the fluids ran out of their bodies where they lay. Surgeon White said they were all suffering from scurvy too and ordered men to go out into the bush and pick quantities of the 'acid berries' he'd found had anti-scorbutic properties.

It seemed 267 people had perished before even reaching Port Jackson, and many others had died since. In fact the bodies of those who died after coming through the Heads were thrown overboard. Of the survivors, 486 were desperately sick, and most of them were not expected to recover. Mary heard as she helped one woman with a tiny infant that she hadn't even had her shackles removed for the child's birth. She was to be told that again several more times during the day.

Later that evening in the drawing room of Government House, Captain Phillip sat with Captain William Hill of the *Juliana*, and raged about the obscenity he'd seen that day.

'I have spoken to the captains of the *Neptune* and the *Scarborough*,' William Hill said. 'In my opinion they should be hanged.'

William Hill was considered a hard man, but he had made sure the women convicts on his ship were well cared for. Some of their number had been old and feeble when they embarked, and he'd had a handful of deaths, but the rest of the women were probably better fed than they'd ever been in their whole lives. In Hill's opinion it would have been far more humane for the courts back in England to have sent all these people to the gallows than to allow blackguards like Captain Trail of the *Neptune* to profit by their slow and painful deaths.

'I understand there was a question of the prisoners on the *Scarborough* plotting to take over the ship,' Phillip said, his small face purple with anger. 'That would necessitate putting the ring-leaders in chains. But the conditions on the *Neptune* beggar belief. The ship should never have been considered seaworthy, she took on water constantly. The prisoners were actually up to their waists in water for part of the voyage. No fumigation of their quarters, none of them brought up on deck for exercise and fresh air.'

'I shall voice all this when I return to England,' William Hill said forcefully, banging his fist on the table. 'In my opinion these men are murderers, far worse species than you have in this colony.'

Arthur Phillip went over to the window. Below, the town was quiet, fires burning like little beacons in the darkness. He thought of all those lying in the hospital and the tents in front of it, and wondered how many more would be dead by dawn.

He was close to complete exhaustion. He had taken the position as Captain of the Fleet and then as Governor General because he believed he could make this penal colony a success. He had hoped that he could convert his criminal charges into men and women who would grasp the opportunities open to them and make something of themselves.

Sadly, he seemed to have failed. He knew now that the offer of free land at the end of their sentences would only be taken up by a few. Most were too lazy and incompetent to farm. The survivors of the Second Fleet would be prejudiced against the colony from the outset, and who could really blame them?

He was staring into the abyss again. Today he'd heard a Third Fleet was on its way with another 1,000 convicts. Many of his good officers would be returning home then. He'd done his very best, he'd tried to govern with humanity, but even a gardener couldn't hope to grow something of lasting beauty without basic equipment, good seed and fertile conditions.

'You seem troubled, Arthur,' William said from behind him. 'Today's events are no reflection on you.'

Phillip turned to Hill and pulled himself up erect. 'I think they are a reflection on all of us,' he said wearily. 'On those who stand by and watch the guilty go unpunished, just as much as the guilty themselves.'

'You're very quiet this evening, Mary,' Will said. It was Christmas Day, and he supposed she was brooding on Cornwall, and imagining her family sitting around the fire with a roast goose in their bellies. Lately he'd often heard her telling Charlotte about Fowey and her relatives there. As time went on she seemed to think about them more, rather than less.

'It's too hot to talk,' she said, but smiled at him and affectionately reached out from her stool to pat his thigh. 'It's a wonder the little 'uns can sleep.'

It had been fearfully hot for weeks now, the animals and poultry had taken to lying down in any shade or water they could find. Will considered himself lucky to be off fishing every day, at least out in the bay there was always a breeze.

'I thought maybe you were thinking of home,' he said.

'About how to get home,' she corrected him, and grinned. 'I think I know how to get the stuff we need.'

Will rolled his eyes with impatience. She never let up about escape. Even when she didn't talk about it, he knew she was thinking about it. He'd never known a woman as dogged as Mary.

Will was happy enough in the colony, though he would never admit that to anyone, least of all Mary. While they were all starving, he would gladly have gone, but the colony had got back on its feet since the Second Fleet arrived.

The help he and Mary had given the sick convicts had been noted by the officers, and as the convicts got better, they too were grateful for the kindness they'd been shown. They had nothing to reward him with except their admiration and loyalty of course, but that was enough for Will. It made him feel important.

He had the freedom to come and go as he liked within the settlement. He did a job he loved. He could treat Captain Phillip's cutter as his own. He could get practically anything he wanted in exchange for fish. He even had a fair stash of money too, for the crews of the Second Fleet were all sick of salted pork and were glad to pay him for fish. But above all he enjoyed his status here: men looked up to him, women lusted after him. He had it all.

'So where are you going to get it?' he said wearily.

'Captain Smith,' she said.

Will was so surprised he nearly fell off his stool. Captain Detmer Smith, a Dutchman, had only been here a few days. He was the owner of a snow, the *Waaksamheyd*, that Captain Ball of the *Supply* had chartered while in Batavia. Smith had sailed in on 17 December with provisions for the colony, after an appalling voyage in which sixteen of his Malay crew had died of fever.

There was some sort of wangle with regard to the provisions going on between Captain Phillip and Smith, and it appeared that none of the officers in the colony liked the Dutchman. Will did, however. Smith had none of the stuffiness of the English captains, he was warm, open and friendly.

'Are you mad?' Will asked Mary.

'No, just devious,' Mary replied. 'Detmer likes you and me. And I shall make sure he likes us even more before I talk him into parting with charts and a sextant.'

'He'll never do that,' Will scoffed.

'Why not?' Mary retorted. 'He's being treated shabbily by all the officers, he's lonely and far from home. He's not English, so why should he mind helping a couple of English convicts escape?'

Will always slapped Mary's ideas down as a matter of principle. Women weren't supposed to be the clever ones. Yet deep down he knew her mind was sharper than his. She'd once asked him to teach her to read and write, and he said he couldn't, not without books. She never asked him again, and somehow he knew that was because she'd seen through him. He didn't want a wife who could read and write. It would diminish him.

But then Mary could see through most people. She watched and listened, she took in things Will would never notice. She might even be right about Detmer Smith.

Will made love to Mary that night, and took great care to please her, for he really wanted her to forget about escape. His sentence would be up in March, and though he often told other men he would be on the first ship home, that wasn't what he wanted at all.

He only got nostalgic for Cornwall when he was drinking. He would remember the good parts, the soft climate, the moors and the woodland, the laughter in the tavern, the camaraderie among the fishermen.

But sober, he remembered it wasn't quite like that. Without a fishing boat of your own, you were dependent on the man who had one, hauling nets all night in freezing conditions for a shilling or so. He'd been hungry there too, and no place looked pretty to a man with an empty belly.

At least it was warm here, even in the winter. He might have got cold and wet many times when the weather was bad, but it wasn't the kind of cold that got right into your bones so it almost paralysed you.

It was said that men would be offered free land here when their time was up. Land was of no use to him, what he wanted was his own fishing business. If he could sell his catches to the store he'd soon be a rich man. Then he could build a fine house for Mary and the children. In time, Emmanuel would come into the business with him.

'Was that good?' Will whispered when he'd done. He was soaked with sweat, so hot that it was almost torture to hold Mary's equally hot body in his arms.

'Wonderful,' she murmured against his chest. 'But it's too hot. Let's run down to the water for a dip!'

She didn't even wait for him to agree, but wriggled out of his arms, took his hand and pulled him out of bed.

Then with a little giggle she ran out of the hut and down to the water.

Will smiled. One of the things he liked best about Mary was her spontaneity. She got an idea and she wanted to put it into action right away, not think about it first. Maybe that was what had got her into trouble in the first place, but he wouldn't change that part of her.

She was passionate too, something he had never expected of her, for she looked so chaste and shy. She was always eager for love-making, responding quickly to just a kiss or a cuddle. Time after time she'd taken his mind right off hunger with her sensual touches, the way she wanted to please him.

The moon was bright, catching on her girlish, slender body as she dived into the sea as gracefully as a porpoise. Few other women here could swim, or men for that matter; they walked in up to their waists looking fearful, as if they expected the sea to swallow them up. Will found that daring quality about Mary as sexy as well-rounded breasts or silky skin.

She waved, beckoning him to join her, and Will ran eagerly down the beach. They swam together a little way, then Mary turned on her back and floated, her hair like strands of seaweed around her face.

'We've never done it in the sea,' she said, and giggled softly.

'We might drown if we try this far out,' Will retorted, but he reached out for her, treading water and holding her afloat as he sucked at her nipple.

'First one back to the shallows gets to be on top,' she

said, flipping herself over and making off to the shore.

For once Will didn't try to beat her, he liked her being on top, and watching her face as she came.

'I don't think my John Thomas is all that eager,' he said as he swam over to where she sat in just a foot or two of water. He thought she had never looked so pretty as she did tonight, her wet curls glistening on her bare shoulders. He knelt and showed her his penis, which had shrunk in the cold water so it looked like an old man's.

'I have ways of reviving him,' she said with a grin like a whorehouse madam's. 'Would you like me to show you, sir?'

Will loved it when she played the whore. It made him feel powerful and lusty. He assumed when she reached out for his penis that she was just going to stroke it, but to his shock and delight, she wriggled closer in the water and took it into her mouth.

Will had heard from other men of high-priced whores doing such a thing, but he'd never bedded a woman who would do it. As Mary's warm mouth closed over him he gasped, for it was the sweetest sensation he'd ever known. He was erect immediately, and he was terrified she would stop, but she didn't. Instead, she held on to one of his buttocks, cradling his balls with the other hand, and moving her lips and tongue up and down the length of him. He could barely keep his balance on his knees, and when he looked down and saw himself disappearing into her eager mouth, her naked breasts undulating against his thighs, he almost toppled over.

It was the best thing he'd ever known. All at once he

was no longer in a penal colony, a man stripped of all decency and pride, but transported to a moonlit tropical island, where he was a rich gentleman. He imagined himself in a ruffled silk shirt and velvet knee-breeches with silver buckles, and Mary as an exotic beauty wearing nothing but a garland of flowers, his willing slave.

'That's so good,' he moaned, catching hold of her head and bringing her even closer.

'How good?' she asked, breaking away from him for a moment and looking up at him with an impish grin.

'The best in the world,' he sighed. 'Don't stop now.'

'I haven't told you the price yet,' she said.

'Whatever it is I'll pay it.' Will's voice was cracking with passion now.

'Escape is the price,' she murmured. 'Are you willing to pay it?'

Will was willing to promise her anything. 'Yes,' he groaned. 'Just do it some more.'

Mary smiled to herself as she continued. She had him now. Will might make himself out to be tougher and braver than he really was, but she'd found he always kept promises. She was very grateful to Sadie from the *Lady Juliana* for passing on her secret weapon to get men to obey her. The funny thing was, Mary had expected to find it repulsive but it wasn't, in fact she liked doing it.

Chapter ten

As Will lowered the sack of rice into the hiding place under the hut floor, he thought he must be in love. Why else would he be going along with this madness of Mary's, when in another month he'd be a free man?

He sat back on his haunches for a moment after he'd put the false floor back in place. Anxious as he was about the plan, he couldn't help but smile. Whether or not he was a free man, it would be sweet revenge for all the injustices and humiliations to sail out of the harbour in the Captain's cutter, taking not just Mary and the children, but his friends too.

The Dutch East Indies sounded a fine place to Will, a tropical paradise where a man could live like a king. Of course it was a huge distance, mostly uncharted, and daunting that no one apart from Captain Cook had ever sailed there from here. But in a strange way the danger made the voyage even more attractive to him, the kind legends were made of. Will wanted to be talked of in awed tones even after his death.

It was mid-February, and Will knew they must leave by the end of March or risk running into violent autumn gales. But there was still so much to do, including asking Detmer Smith for assistance.

Mary was with Detmer now, delivering back his clean washing, and no doubt she was charming him for all she was worth. Will didn't mind her doing that, it was necessary, but he didn't like the way she was trying to take complete control of the plan.

She had insisted he shouldn't ask his friends to join them until the last minute. She had to know what hell it was not to be able to confide in them, he wanted a man to talk to about it, not just a woman. Mary said one of them might forget himself when he'd been drinking and start talking. They all had women and Mary's reasoning was that these women might peach if they knew they were going to be left behind. So all Will could do for now was sit it out, get the stores together, and work on Detmer and Bennelong.

Will still often saw Bennelong when he was out fishing. He was naked again, and proudly showed Will new scars he'd acquired in fights. He remembered quite a bit of the English he'd learned while in captivity, and with that, and signs, Will found he could communicate with him quite adequately.

Back last November Bennelong had returned to the settlement, wearing the clothes he'd originally been given by Captain Phillip. This appeared to be a sign that he was willing to be an interpreter, as long as no one tried to chain him up again, and so the Captain gave him a hut to live in and food from the stores.

In Will's opinion, Captain Phillip had bitten off more

than he could chew with Bennelong. The man's real interests were fighting and women; all he wanted from the settlement was the drink the newcomers had introduced him to. Already he'd made a nuisance of himself by getting drunk and wild at Government House, and if Phillip thought that by giving him a house he'd become his lackey, he was mistaken.

Will really liked Bennelong, for his childlike enthusiasm, his wide grin and his curiosity about white men. When he came out fishing with Will he'd taught him some of his language and customs.

It was curious that in Bennelong's culture, if someone wanted a woman they usually hit her with a club and carried her off. Remaining faithful to just one woman seemed absurd to them, yet Bennelong revered Mary. His face lit up when he saw her, he was very anxious to please her, and Will was fairly certain that if Bennelong ever saw him with another woman, he would fight him.

Mary had been right in surmising that many of the natives knew a great deal about navigating the waters round here. They might only have the flimsiest canoes, but the skilful way they manoeuvred them and the speeds they reached were incredible. Bennelong had also shown Will ways of finding water, and which plants made good eating. Will had no doubt he would be only too happy to swim out to the cutter at night and tow her to the shore for their party to get aboard. He had no real loyalty to any of the officers, but he had to Mary and Will.

Although he knew he could count on Bennelong, Detmer was going to be more tricky.

Will and the Dutchman had a great deal in common. They were both big and blue-eyed, with fair hair; both were gregarious men who made friends easily. They were also both, for different reasons, out on a limb.

Since the settlement got back to full rations, many of the original convicts seemed to have forgotten that Will was the one who had saved their lives with his fish. As for the new arrivals, many of them were jealous of his freedom to come and go as he pleased, and often made sarcastic comments about him being the officers' 'boy'.

Detmer was isolated because he hadn't played by the rules with Captain Phillip. There was short weight on the stores he'd brought in, which made the officers distrust him, and now he was driving a very hard bargain with the charter of his ship. Phillip desperately needed it to send some of his men back to England, and Detmer was being foxy. As a result, he was ostracized by the officers, and sharp little Mary, always quick to take advantage of an opportunity, took it.

At first it was a few smiles, a little conciliatory chat, an offer to do his laundry, and finally to share supper with her and Will at their hut. Will didn't object to Detmer coming when he was there; he was good company, and he always brought a bottle of rum with him. But Will was aware that people were beginning to talk about Mary chatting to Detmer on the wharf and sometimes going out to his ship.

Only today someone had suggested she was 'making up' to the man. Will was jealous by nature and he didn't like the idea of his wife alone in any man's company. Yet he knew Mary was far more likely to get Detmer to agree to help them than he was, so he supposed he would have to turn a blind eye as to how she accomplished it.

Will got up from the floor and went out of the hut. Mary was just coming along, with Emmanuel in her arms and Charlotte skipping beside her.

Will thought they made a pretty picture, Mary with her black curls all around her face, Emmanuel chubby and fair-haired in her arms, and Charlotte, a tiny version of her mother, kicking up the sand with her bare feet. The *Lady Juliana* had brought cloth from England. Mary had managed to talk Tench into getting her a length and she'd made a dress for herself and things for the children. Will knew that by his mother's standards back home, Mary's blue striped dress was crudely made, but after seeing her and so many other women just in rags for the last two years, he thought she looked very fetching.

'You were a long time,' he said reprovingly.

'We got talking,' she said, and nodded pointedly in Charlotte's direction, her way of saying that what she had to report mustn't be in front of the child.

Mary heated up some water on the fire and made them a cup of sweet tea, then sat down to nurse Emmanuel. As soon as Charlotte had wandered off a little way, she beckoned Will to come nearer.

'I've asked Detmer to help us,' she whispered.

'You told him our plan?' Will was shocked that she'd done this without him being there.

'The time was right,' she said with a shrug. 'He'd had a row with Phillip again, and I knew it was the moment.'

'What did he say?' Will got a chill down his spine when he thought what would happen to him if Detmer peached.

Mary didn't answer for a moment. The truth was that Detmer's first reaction had been to laugh at the plan. He also said he couldn't see why Will wanted to risk his and his family's lives when he had everything set up here. Mary had to plead with him, explain how she was afraid Will would abandon her when his time was up. She even implied that she was willing to do anything for Detmer in exchange for his help.

His expression was imprinted on her mind. Lips set in a cynical straight line, yet laughter in his eyes. He was seated on a coil of rope in the bows of his ship while she was standing at the rail, half turned away from him because she wasn't quite brave enough to look him in the eye. He was wearing a clean white shirt and tan-coloured breeches that clung to his body like a second skin, his long fair hair blowing in the breeze.

He was similar to Will in looks, sharing the same colouring, height and size, though he was probably as much as ten years older. But Detmer had a polished look which Will could never hope to emulate. His skin was a golden-brown, his hair silky, and his teeth were still very good, white and even. His heavily accented English was attractive too – whatever he said he sounded as if he was trying to woo her.

'Come on, tell me,' Will exclaimed. 'Charlotte will be back in a moment and we can't speak of it in front of her.' Charlotte was very talkative now at three and she was inclined to repeat things she'd overheard.

'He said he would help us,' Mary said. The truth of it was that Detmer had asked, 'How far are you prepared to go to gain my assistance?'

'Why should he want to help us?' Will's eyes narrowed with suspicion.

Mary shrugged. 'Because he likes us. Because he wants to get back at Captain Phillip. Because I was persuasive. Take your pick.'

'Did you tell him what we need?'

Mary leaned closer to Emmanuel so Will wouldn't see her blushing. She had been shameless, just as she'd been with Lieutenant Graham on the *Dunkirk*. But what made it worse in her mind was that she actually wanted Detmer, and if she hadn't had the two children with her, she might very well have let him have his way with her, then and there.

'Yes, I told him, and he'll sell us a sextant and a compass,' she said. 'And he'll throw in a couple of old muskets, some ammunition and a water cask. You can agree a price with him for those.'

'What about a chart?'

'That too, he's going to look it out. He'll need to talk that over with you.'

'So I have got some role in this then?' Will said sarcastically.

Mary wanted to slap him for always wanting to be the big man. If she'd sat back and let him try to organize this escape, he'd be in irons by now because he couldn't keep his mouth shut. Even Detmer, who had only known Will for a relatively short time, had been worried about his reputation for having a loose tongue. But she had to hide her irritation. Everything depended on keeping Will sweet.

'You have the biggest role,' she said, reaching out to stroke his face in a display of affection. 'You are the navigator. Detmer says only a good one like you could manage to sail through the reefs without holing the boat.'

Will was appeased at that. 'I'll whip one of the new seine nets tonight,' he said. 'They won't miss it.'

Mary looked to see where Charlotte was, and, satisfied she was out of earshot, making mud pies, she continued, 'We ought to decide now who we're going to ask to go with us.'

'James Martin, Jamie Cox and Samuel Bird, of course,' Will said. 'They're my mates, been with them right from the *Dunkirk*.'

Mary nodded. She had expected Will would want them. She wasn't too pleased about Samuel Bird, he was such a gloomy man, but then she hadn't tried very hard to get to know him, put off by his red hair and pale eyelashes. 'Yes, but we did think William Moreton would be a good choice too, he knows about navigation.'

Will wrinkled his nose. 'I don't like him.'

Mary didn't like the dark, bull-like man either. Like Will, he was a big-head, full of his own importance. But he could navigate, he was strong and able to keep his mouth shut.

'We need another navigator,' she said firmly. 'You can't do it all alone.'

'Very well, him too, and maybe Wilf Owens and Pat Reilly.'

'Wilf Owens is a fool,' Mary said dismissively. 'And Pat Reilly can't keep his mouth shut.'

Will looked hurt. Wilf and Pat often came out fishing with him and he liked drinking with them.

'So who do you think then?' he snapped at her.

'Sam Broome, Nathaniel Lilly and Bill Allen,' she replied.

'We can't take that many,' Will exclaimed in horror. 'Besides, they aren't our mates, they're all from the Second Fleet. We hardly know them.'

'We'll need that many when we have to row,' she insisted. 'Besides, the boat's big enough. And they can all handle it. What does it matter if you haven't known them long? They are all trustworthy and capable.'

Will didn't mind the idea of Nat and Bill. Nat was another young kid like Jamie, who hung on his every word. He looked like a cherub with his fair hair and big eyes and Will liked having him around.

They called Bill the Iron Man. When he was flogged for theft from the stores, he never cried out once, and walked away at the end of it without even wincing. Compared to most of the men here he was a real criminal, convicted of a serious assault and robbery. Common sense said he was a good choice, they'd need more tough men if they had any trouble with natives.

'Yeah, Bill and Nat can come,' he nodded. 'But why Sam Broome?' he asked, looking at Mary with suspicion. He thought the man a rum sort of cove, he kept himself to himself, didn't like drink, and he was as skinny as a rake.

Mary had taken a liking to Sam from the day she gave him water as he lay close to death on the wharf. She had visited him in the hospital tents until he was well enough to be moved to a hut, and they had become friends. She liked his gentlemanly ways and his reserve, and it was flattering that he obviously adored her.

While no one would describe Sam as handsome – he was too thin and his sandy hair was disappearing fast – he had a strong face, and there was determination in his tawny-coloured eyes. He was also practical, a good carpenter, and steady. Mary needed him as her safety net if Will failed her.

She wished she didn't have these qualms about Will. In many ways he was the very best of husbands. But she had to be realistic, consider every possibility. If they were to reach a safe haven, and Mary was absolutely determined that they would, she couldn't guarantee that the success wouldn't go to Will's head. He liked the drink and it made him belligerent. She had to have some sort of backup plan for that eventuality; she didn't intend to risk her own life and those of her two children for a life that might turn out worse than anything she'd endured so far. She knew Sam Broome would step into the breach if need be.

'Sam has skills we might need,' she said firmly. 'He's a carpenter, remember. He's also a calm, steady man who will get on well with everyone else.'

Will made a kind of snort, implying he didn't agree, but he said nothing further.

Over the following days, Will asked each of the

chosen men to the hut to put his plan to them singly. For now, he wasn't telling any of them who else was in on it. Each one of them was wildly enthusiastic, grateful to be included, and made promises to bring things for the stores. Mary sat back while Will talked his way through it, never interrupting once. It wasn't until each man was about to leave the hut that she gave them her warning.

'You must swear that you won't breathe a word of this to anyone,' she insisted fiercely. 'Not your best friend, your woman, no one. For if you do and our plan is discovered, I swear I'll kill you.'

Bill Allen and William Moreton thought that it was crazy of Will to take a woman and two small children along on such a potentially hazardous escape bid, but even though they were both the kind who normally spoke up when they didn't agree with anything, neither of them dared to with Mary sitting there. When they heard the passion in her voice and saw the chilling determination in her grey eyes, they soon realized that she was no sleeping partner. Without her spelling it out, they knew this was her idea, her plan, and she meant exactly what she said.

Towards the end of February the secret store under the floor of the hut was full of provisions. Two old muskets, ammunition, a grappling hook, various tools, cooking pots, a water cask and resin to caulk the water should the boat spring a leak were hidden in various places around the settlement. The plan was to make their escape after the *Waaksamheyd* had departed for England; that way there would be no other vessel left in the harbour capable of giving chase or informing anyone else that convicts had escaped.

Bennelong had readily agreed to swim out to the cutter on the chosen night and bring it in to the shore for them. There was only one thing left to do now, and that was to collect the compass and sextant from Detmer and pay him the money Will had agreed.

Will hadn't had much problem getting his hands on money. He'd had some saved since he got here and there'd been nothing to spend it on. The rest he'd raised the same way he got the salt pork, rice and flour, by selling fish. A great many of the Marines were only too happy to buy fish, for like Will they had nothing else to spend their money on. They exchanged it for drink mostly, and the officers who ended up with the fish didn't ask questions.

But Detmer insisted it must be Mary who paid over the money and collected the goods, saying it was much less risky. Maybe concealing the money in clean washing and collecting some more dirty clothes with the sextant and compass tucked inside was a sound idea. But Will didn't like the way it looked to the others – he was in charge of this escape, not Mary. He was afraid that before long the other men might start thinking it was all her idea.

Will was brooding about this when he went off fishing one afternoon. Only the previous evening he'd wanted all the men to come to their hut and talk about the escape together. Mary would have none of it. She claimed that such a large gathering would be noticed, then they'd be watched more closely. She ruled that they must only ever continue to meet up in threes or fours.

Even James Martin, Will's closest friend, agreed with Mary. It made Will sick that James would take her part rather than his.

Will was on the cutter, with six other men ordered to help him that day, and about to cast off, when Bennelong came along the wharf. He had his sister and her two children with him, along with Charlotte who often played with them. When Bennelong made signs that he wanted them all to go out on the boat, Will's first thought was to refuse. He didn't like having so many people aboard, and anyway he was in no mood for company. But he knew it was a good idea for Charlotte to get used to the boat, and besides, Bennelong might take offence if he refused him, and then withdraw his promise to help in the escape. He really had no choice but to agree.

It was a pleasant day, much cooler than of late, and Will's bad mood left him once they were out in the bay. When Bennelong excitedly pointed out a quantity of seabirds hovering close to the west side of the bay, Will knew he was saying there was a large shoal of fish there.

Bennelong proved to be right, and it wasn't long before they pulled in the seine and found it full of fish. It was the best haul they'd had in some weeks.

Will was delighted, he kept thumping Bennelong on the back and telling him what a good fellow he was.

'Good fellow,' Bennelong repeated with a wide grin

which showed off his perfect teeth. 'You get good fellow rum?'

'I'll drink some with you,' Will laughed, and made signs to suggest they had a party. With such a good catch he'd be able to keep back a big quantity for himself, and he was in the right mood for getting drunk.

They were sailing back towards the wharf, the bottom of the boat full of wriggling fish, still laughing and congratulating each other on their good fortune, when suddenly a stiff wind came up, catching Will off his guard. The boat gathered speed, heading straight for some rocks, and Will couldn't go about fast enough. There was a crunch, the hooks holding the sails snapped, tipping the boat up, and all at once water poured in.

If there hadn't been so many people on the boat, Will could have dealt with it, but two of the convict men, both inexperienced, panicked, and suddenly the boat keeled right over and everyone fell out.

Will's first thought was for Charlotte as he hit the water, but John, one of the crew, already had her in his arms. She was screaming at the shock, but seemed unhurt. Bennelong's sister had both her two children too, clinging to her back, and with just a shout to her brother, she began to swim back to the shore with them.

'I'll take Charlotte,' John yelled. 'You get the men.'

Bennelong stayed long enough to help Will with the other five men, only two of whom could swim, then he too made off for the shore. As Will helped the floundering non-swimmers catch hold of the capsized boat, he swore to himself. He had lost the entire catch, he knew Captain

Phillip was going to be very angry, and even worse, it probably meant their hope to escape in the next couple of weeks was scuppered.

As Will stayed with the boat, the other men coughing and spluttering, Bennelong reached the shore and called to some other natives. Within a few minutes they were dragging their canoes down the beach to come to the rescue. Some came straight out to the boat to take the crew to safety, others began collecting up the oars and other equipment thrown out of the cutter, and another couple of men came out with ropes, which Will secured to the hull, and they towed the boat in to the wharf.

When Will got back to the hut with Charlotte much later, he found Mary had already heard the news. He expected her to rage at him, and was ready to give as good as he got, but to his irritation she seemed more concerned about Charlotte.

She took the child from his arms and wrapped her in a blanket. 'There, there,' she said as Charlotte began crying again. 'You'll be all right once you are warm again. I'll have to teach you to swim, won't I?'

'That's right! Comfort her,' Will spat at her. 'Don't think about me! I could get flogged again. As for the hope of escape, that's gone.'

Even as he said this, Will knew he was being completely unreasonable. But to have all his hopes dashed when they were so very close to leaving was too much.

His clothes had dried quickly in the wind but he felt chilled to the bone. He knew too that many of the people who resented his freedom would take great delight in his misfortune.

'Don't be such a fool,' Mary retorted, giving him a contemptuous look. 'Why should they flog you? It was an accident.'

Her sharp words seemed to suggest to Will that she wasn't bothered about him in any way. All the resentment which had been building up in him for some time flared up and spilled over, and he lashed out, slapping her hard across the face, knocking both her and Charlotte, who was sitting on her lap, to the floor.

'You cold-hearted bitch,' he yelled at her. 'You don't care about anything but yourself.'

Charlotte was screaming, and Mary quickly picked her up again and got to her feet. She didn't attempt to run out of the hut, but faced Will defiantly with Charlotte in her arms.

'I'm going to put that slap down to shock,' she said haughtily. 'But should you think of hitting me ever again, don't think I'll be so understanding a second time.'

Will had never hit a woman before, and the moment he lashed out he felt ashamed. But he wasn't going to apologize, not when she couldn't behave like a real woman and cry. Instead he turned on his heels and walked out of the hut.

Will came back much later, so drunk that he lurched through the door and fell flat on the floor. Mary had been lying in the dark, awake, but she didn't get up to help him. She suspected he hadn't come back of his own free will, but because his body had a natural homing instinct.

She wondered how he had got the drink, and what secrets he'd revealed under the influence of it.

She couldn't sleep, she felt too wretched. Will didn't seem to have considered that when she first heard the boat had capsized, she thought Charlotte had been drowned. She didn't know John had grabbed her for at least an hour after the event. After going through that kind of agony, a foiled escape meant little.

Yet once she knew Charlotte was safe, the hideousness of this place seemed even more pronounced. While she was waiting up on the wharf, she'd looked around her and seen it for what it really was – a shanty town, built by the sweat of men who had been dehumanized. Everything about it was ugly, from the crudeness of the buildings, the flogging triangle, the bleak, already overcrowded cemetery, to the people trapped here. There was an all-pervading stench about it, a combination of bodily wastes and rotten food. An atmosphere of hopelessness and oppression.

She could not bring her children up here. How could she fight against the squalor, the degradation, the utter despair of it? How could she teach children it was wrong to steal, when it was the only way to survive here? Or that fornication was a sin, when for most of those here it was the only small comfort they had? Nearly all the children were bastards, many of the mothers couldn't even say with any certainty who had sired their child. In years to come these offspring might even unwittingly commit incest.

All Mary's senses were offended by this place. She

was appalled at seeing drunkenness, debauchery, laziness, disease and utter stupidity. Daily, her ears were bombarded with the most vile language and sounds of human misery. The smells nauseated her. Even touch, that most personal of the senses, was distorted here. Wood was jagged and full of splinters, what looked like soft grass was as sharp as needles, her own skin and Will's was hard and rough, it itched from insect bites and often erupted in boils.

How she longed for all those things which were part of everyday life back in Fowey! To smell fresh bread baking, the lavender, roses and pinks in the tiny garden. To see strawberries, apples and plums still glistening with dew. A jug of cold milk, putting on a clean petticoat still fragrant from drying outside. To see her feet pink and soft after washing. To lie on the billowy softness of a feather mattress and watch the curtains fluttering in the breeze.

Only her children gave her a sense of all she'd left behind. Their skin was still silky, their voices soft and melodious to her ears, their breath as sweet as spring water. Apart from their rags, they were no different in nature to children born to the nobility. But just as she couldn't expect them to retain their baby looks, she couldn't hope to shield them from being corrupted either. Soon they would witness the floggings, the rutting behind bushes and the drunkenness, and they would consider that normal. Without something of beauty or worth to show them, how would they ever know the difference between good and evil?

They were innocent of any crime, yet by being born to a convict they became convicts too. And unless she got them away from here, that stigma would be attached to their children, and their children's children. She couldn't let that happen.

The following morning Mary got the children up, fed Emmanuel and made Charlotte some fried bread for breakfast, without waking Will. He was still lying on the floor where he'd fallen the previous night, and the hut stank of rum.

She heard the drum for work sound while she was on her way to collect dirty washing from the officers' houses. Although she wondered whether the loss of the cutter would mean that Will would be expected to report for work like the other men, she certainly wasn't prepared to go back and wake him.

She had a bundle of washing slung over her shoulder, Emmanuel balanced on her hip, and Charlotte skipping ahead of her, when she heard Tench call out her name. She hadn't seen him, even at a distance, in weeks, for his work at Rose Hill kept him there. He was coming out of Surgeon White's house, and she guessed he'd stayed the night there.

'How is Charlotte?' he asked as he came nearer. 'I heard she was in the boat yesterday?'

'She's forgotten it already,' Mary said. 'But it gave me a terrible fright before I heard she was safe.'

'And Will, how is he?' he asked.

'Sleeping it off,' she said, leaving Tench to guess

whether she meant the shock of the accident or drink. 'Or he was when I left.'

'The repairs will be started today,' Tench said, looking over towards the wharf. 'He should be there.'

'Repairs?' Mary's heart leaped.

Tench smiled, reaching out to stroke Emmanuel's cheek. 'Of course. Captain Phillip wants it back in use as soon as possible.'

'Is he angry with Will?' Mary asked.

'Why should he be?' Tench frowned. 'Captain Hunter saw the whole thing and reported back. It could have happened to anyone, after all it happened to Hunter himself on the *Sirius* at Norfolk Island. Phillip is also very heartened by the way Bennelong and his native friends helped out in the rescue.'

'Will is expecting to be flogged.' Mary half smiled.

'I'll go and see him then,' Tench said. 'He has nothing to fear if he throws himself into repairing the boat.'

Mary walked part of the way with Tench, and they talked about Bennelong, and how he'd helped out once before when Captain Phillip was speared by one of the natives.

'It's my hope that in years to come all our people will embrace the natives wholeheartedly,' Tench said.

Mary normally agreed with his views, but today, somewhat jaded by her own fears and despair, she couldn't help thinking he was being naive and even ridiculous.

'They won't,' she said. 'My guess is that there will come a time when the government will want to wipe out all the natives because they don't fit in with their plans for this place.'

Tench looked appalled. 'Oh, Mary, no!'

'That's what they do to anyone who has different values to themselves,' she said defiantly. 'The rich and powerful got that way by trampling on the less able. Even when us convicts have served our time, do you really think our past will be forgotten? My guess is there'll always be a two-tiered society here. Convicts, natives and ex-convicts at the bottom, people like your sort at the top.'

'I don't know what you mean by "your sort",' he said indignantly. 'All men are born equal. It is individual choice whether they rise or fall.'

'It's a damn sight easier to rise if you are educated, with a rich family to steer you,' she snapped. 'But that's not my point. Us convicts are no better than slaves to your sort. The more they send here, the more attractive this country will become to the moneyed classes back in England. I expect in time they'll come here to grab land, and who will work it?' She paused, waiting for him to give her a straight answer. But he said nothing, only looked hurt.

'Us convicts,' she said triumphantly. 'That's who! Don't deny it won't happen, sir, you know it will. Some people might feel badly about capturing a black man and forcing him to work for nothing. But no one at all cares if a bunch of convicted criminals are worked to death.'

Tench was staggered. In all the time he'd known Mary she'd never before shown such bitterness. 'I thought you were quite happy here with Will and your children,' he said weakly. Yet even as he said this he realized he was making the assumption that most of the officers made: that convicts had no finer feelings.

'Happy!' she laughed mirthlessly. 'How can I be happy when Charlotte cries with hunger? When I am afraid for her and Emmanuel's future? They have done nothing wrong, yet they are sentenced to life imprisonment too.'

'I'm so sorry, Mary.' Tench's voice shook, and his eyes swam. 'I wish —'

'Wishes don't come true,' she said, cutting him short. 'Prayers aren't answered, not for women like me. I have to make my own luck.'

Tench stood for a while as Mary went on down to the shore to wash the clothes. He felt impotent, for he knew deep in his heart that every word she'd said was true. When the *Scarborough*, *Surprise* and *Neptune* got back to England, who would care about the number of felons who died on the way out to New South Wales? Or all those who had died here from the First Fleet? None, he suspected. Yet there would be thousands waiting eagerly to hear the reports on what this place was like, with a view to grabbing land here. Maybe most would be put off by the hardships involved, but opportunists would think of the free labour and be prepared to take a gamble. Just as they'd done in America.

Tench watched as Mary sat Emmanuel down on the ground beside Charlotte, then knelt by the water to begin the washing. He was reminded of the first time he spoke to her on the *Dunkirk*, when she was incensed by the filthy conditions in the hold.

She was truly remarkable. She had struggled bravely to make the best of her lot in life ever since that day. Plenty of other young and sparky women like her had just given up. Her friend Sarah was a drunken slattern now, as indeed were most of the surviving women from the *Charlotte*. Seven had died, and God only knew whether some of those might have lived if there'd been a ray of hope that conditions would improve here.

He felt deeply for all of them, but suddenly to hear and see Mary's bitterness, when she had once been so optimistic, was unbearable.

Why couldn't he find the courage to tell her how he felt about her? Put aside all those lofty plans for his future, and urge her to leave Will and come to him? Other officers like Ralph Clark had taken lag wives, and Clark had a wife at home waiting for him, whom he professed to love. It wouldn't be so difficult. Will's time was nearly up, he'd go happily on the next ship without looking back.

But much as Tench wanted Mary, he knew he couldn't do it. He was too bound by convention to take a woman and her children from another man. It wouldn't be right not to give her the security of marriage. Nor could he bear to see her slighted by his friends and family, as they surely would if they knew her history.

Besides, he could be fooling himself that she felt as he did. She had never said anything to suggest she felt anything more than friendship towards him.

271

He looked at her slight figure bent over the water, and there was determination in every inch of her body. She would find some way to help herself. Somehow he knew she wasn't destined to be anyone's slave.

Chapter eleven

1791

'You have the money?' Detmer asked in his heavily accented English.

Mary nodded and held out a bundle of clean washing. 'It's in a handkerchief,' she whispered. She lightly touched the bundle he was carrying. 'Are they in there?'

It was 26 March, Detmer was due to set sail back for England in two days' time with Captain Hunter and his crew from the wrecked *Sirius*.

Mid-morning on the wharf was busy and noisy. Detmer's seamen were rolling along barrels of fresh water for loading, Marines patrolled, male convicts building a new shed hammered and sawed, and a gaggle of women convicts returning from cleaning duties in the officers' houses were shouting to one another. There were many children too, dirty, semi-naked little urchins boldly climbing on the many packing cases for loading. From time to time someone would shout and order them off, and they'd disappear like rats down a culvert, only to appear again within minutes.

The cutter had been repaired, just as Tench said it would

be. As it turned out, the accident had been fortuitous, for now the boat was in far better shape than it had been previously.

'Yes, they are in there. A sextant and compass. I wouldn't cheat you, Mary,' Detmer said, his smile slightly reproving. 'Will you come out to the ship for a farewell drink?'

'You know I daren't,' she said, glancing around her. She was very aware that Detmer's ship was being watched closely, for there had been stowaways on the *Scarborough* when it left Sydney Cove. They were discovered before the ship got to the Heads and were immediately put ashore. But since then all the troops and officers had been far more watchful. She could see a couple of officers coming down from Government House, and knew it would be advisable to get away from the wharf and suspicion as quickly as possible.

'I wish I could do more for you,' Detmer said with a sigh. 'Had I met you anywhere else in the world, I believe there would have been a different outcome.'

Mary blushed and lowered her eyes. She never knew how to take Detmer and his often very personal remarks. Some days she felt certain he did have strong feelings for her – why else would he risk so much to help her and Will? Yet at other times she felt she was just a pawn in his game to upset Captain Phillip.

'Look at me, Mary,' he said, his voice soft and insistent.

She looked into his clear blue eyes and felt that all too familiar tug of desire for him. He looked even more handsome than usual today – his fair hair had been

274

trimmed, he had shaved and his white shirt was spotless. Even his long boots were highly polished, and she wondered if all that was for her.

It was extraordinary that once again she should be attracted to a man so far above her. For two months now Detmer had invaded her thoughts and dreams in the same manner that Tench always had. But whereas Tench would always have a special place in her heart, and she intuitively knew that his feelings mirrored hers, with Detmer it was purely physical.

He came across to her as a man who had never been answerable to anyone. She felt he had salt water in his veins and was happiest out at sea battling against the elements. He was as deep as the ocean, and perhaps just as dangerous.

'That's better,' he said, and smiled. 'I will not be able to see you again before I leave. You must return this washing to one of the crew.'

Mary nodded, not trusting herself to speak. Whatever his motives for helping her, he had been entirely honourable. No blackmailing her into his bed – he had treated her as a lady, not a convict. She would be forever in his debt.

'I am so afraid for you, and your children,' he said, lowering his voice to a whisper. 'I hope to God you make it.'

'If determination counts for anything, we will,' she said, then hesitated. She so much wanted to convey the depth of her gratitude to him, yet she knew if she attempted it she might start to cry. 'Bless you, Detmer,' she managed to add.

'And may God bless you,' he said softly. 'I won't forget you. I'll make inquiries to discover how you fared.'

They exchanged the parcels, and his hand covered hers for a second. 'I must go now,' she said, taking a step back away from him. 'I'll return the washing tomorrow.'

At two in the afternoon of the 28th, Mary and Will stood on the shore together silently watching the *Waaksamheyd* sail down the bay towards the Heads. Seabirds flew in its wake, and they could hear the wind in her sails.

Up on the wharf almost the entire settlement was watching her departure, Mary could hear their cheers and shouted farewells in the distance. Captain Phillip would be among them, and for the first time Mary felt a pang of sympathy for the man.

He must almost certainly wish he was sailing home with Captain Hunter. They had been friends, and had been through a great deal together. In many ways Phillip was as much a prisoner as Mary was, chained to this desperate place by a sense of honour and commitment. Now that her escape was so close she could see clearly that he was in fact a good man. He had been humane, fair and dignified at all times, mostly under the most impossible conditions. She could even find it in her heart to wish him well.

'Just seven hours and we'll be on our way,' Will said with a faint tremor in his voice.

Mary knew he was thinking of what would happen if they were caught. They might very well be hanged; they'd certainly be flogged and put back into irons too. However good their plan was, however careful they'd been, there was always a chance that someone with a grudge had got wind of it, and would give them away.

Mary slipped her hand into Will's and squeezed it. She was scared too, not for herself but her children, for she knew only too well that she was taking a gamble with their lives.

Yet she had to take that gamble. If they stayed here the chances were that the next epidemic or the next cut in rations would carry them off, just as it had so many other children. It was surely better to take their chances with the sea. At least if they drowned, they would all go together. A quick, clean death.

'The cutter is in fine shape now,' Will said, as if to reassure himself. 'Even the weather is on our side.'

Mary looked up at the sky. It was cloudy, and unless it suddenly cleared it would obscure the moon tonight. The breeze was very light, but that hardly mattered as they would be letting the tide carry them out of the bay – oars would make too much noise and sails would be too conspicuous.

'We're going to do it,' she said firmly. 'I know we are.'

It was dark by six, and in the next couple of hours, the men arrived one by one and left silently, each with a sack of goods to be taken further down the shore to the agreed departure point.

Emmanuel and Charlotte were both sound asleep in bed. Mary had no fears that Emmanuel would wake when she picked him up, but Charlotte was a different story. She had been tiresome all day, whining and throwing tantrums. Clearly she had sensed that something was going on, and if she woke to find herself in a boat, she might start screaming.

Mary's mouth was dry with fright as she saw the last sack taken from the secret store under the floor and she was left alone with the sleeping children. Sam Broome would be back soon to help her with them. She would carry Charlotte, he would take Emmanuel, for Will would be waiting for Bennelong to bring in the boat.

She knelt down by the bed and offered up a last-minute prayer for their safety, but her attention wandered to all that this little hut had meant to her in the last three years.

It had been a haven, the one place where she felt an element of peace and safety. She had found joy in love-making with Will, there had been the happiness of Emmanuel's birth, and so many different milestones in Charlotte's development, from her first steps to her first words. Now they were leaving it for the unknown.

'Mary!'

She jumped at the sound of Sam's whisper, and turned to see him in the doorway. 'I'm sorry,' he said.

She realized he was embarrassed at interrupting her prayers.

'It's all right,' she whispered as she got up from her knees. 'Have you see Bennelong yet?'

Sam came right into the hut and looked down at the sleeping children. In the light from the flickering candle his lean face had an almost skeletal quality. He was not a handsome, confident man like Will, but the tender way he looked at the sleeping children touched Mary.

'Will thought he saw him swimming out to the cutter,' he said. 'I couldn't make out anything though, it's too dark, but he said you were to come now.'

Mary lifted up Emmanuel, wrapped him more securely in his blanket, then passed him to Sam. Picking up a sling she'd made from some canvas, she tucked it round the sleeping baby. She tied one set of straps around Sam's waist and the other two were put over his shoulders, crossed at his back and then secured in the front.

'It will leave your hands free,' she said by way of an explanation, afraid he might be irritated at her treating him like a nursemaid.

He gave her a faint grin. 'I'm scared. Are you?' he whispered.

Mary shook her head. Her stomach was churning, she was breaking out in a cold sweat, and the greater part of her wished she'd never dreamed up this plan. But she wasn't going to admit to any of that.

'We will do it, Sam,' she said with more bravado than conviction, and turned back to the bed for Charlotte.

As she lifted the child up into her arms, Charlotte muttered in her sleep, but her head drooped down on her mother's shoulder and she didn't wake. Sam picked up the blanket and tucked it round the child, then smiled at Mary. 'Ready?'

'Almost,' Mary said, and leaning down to the little table picked up a cloth bag.

'What's that?' Sam whispered as the bag rustled.

'Sweet tea leaves,' Mary said, and smiled. 'I have to take the one thing that we liked about this place, don't I?'

They stole silently from the hut, pausing every now and then to check no one was about. Further back towards the town they could see the faint glow from dying fires, but the only sounds were the usual night ones of a sentry's boots up on the quay, snoring from huts, the odd muted cough and the water lapping on the beach. Charlotte stirred in her mother's arms, but Mary wrapped the blanket round her tighter to keep out the cool air, and walked faster to keep up with Sam.

Once Mary's eyes had grown used to the dark, she could just make out the cutter coming towards the shore and Bennelong swimming before it, invisible except for a flash of white teeth every now and then.

She knew that if anyone had discovered their plan, it would be in the next few minutes that they would be stopped. Her ears ached with the strain of listening for running feet, every muscle was taut, and she expected to hear a musket fire with every step. When Will stepped out of the bushes in front of her she nearly jumped out of her skin. It was so eerie: the dark beach, the eight men all standing as still as statues, and the bundles lying like so many boulders. No one said a word, everyone watching as the cutter came closer and closer in.

Will waded out a little way, then swam almost as silently as Bennelong to help him bring the boat in closer. It glided in, just a few feet away, and James Martin waded into the water, climbed into the boat and signalled for the others to bring out the bundles.

Mary's nerves were now at almost breaking point, for every small sound seemed magnified. She rocked Charlotte gently, willing her not to wake, and wished the men could be a little quicker with their loading.

'I'll take her now,' William Moreton whispered to Mary, holding out his arms. 'You go and get in.'

It was the moment Mary had been dreading most, for the child was bound to wake if she was moved from her arms. Yet she knew she couldn't hold her and climb into the boat too. But William took Charlotte as gently as if she were his own child, and nodded to Mary to go.

Hitching her dress up high, Mary waded out silently, then taking a seat she held out her arms for Charlotte again. William Moreton handed her over, then got in. Next came Sam Broome, with Emmanuel, seating himself beside Mary.

Bennelong was grinning, his teeth and eyeballs flashing like white lights as he held the boat steady for the other men to get in with the muskets wrapped in oil cloth. Will sat at the tiller, Nat Lilly and Jamie Cox on either side of him, Bill Allen was the last. Bennelong gave the boat a hefty shove, and they were off.

Bennelong swam with them for some distance, pushing the boat until it caught in the current and began to drift slowly down the bay. Then he broke away, waved his hands in farewell and disappeared into the darkness as silently as a fish.

It was some time before Mary realized she had been holding her breath.

It seemed like many tortuous hours before they finally saw the Heads looming up ahead, like twin black mountains, although in reality it couldn't have been more than three. Everyone remained absolutely silent, for if they were spotted or heard by the lookout he would raise the alarm and shots would be fired.

All at once the water became choppier, they felt the current surging, dragging the heavily laden boat towards the gap between the Heads, and Will was wrestling with the tiller to get them safely through. Charlotte woke, sat straight up on Mary's lap and looked around her in astonishment.

'Hoist the sail,' Will whispered. 'Freedom is ours!'

The sail billowed out, the wind caught it, and all at once they were speeding along, the moon suddenly coming out from behind thick cloud as if to join them in their celebration. James Martin, always the most voluble of the men, gave a low rumble of a laugh, and was quickly joined by the others.

'We're free,' Will said in a shaky voice, as if he could hardly believe it. 'By God, we're free!'

Mary couldn't speak, only smile. She turned her head to look back, but could see nothing but the black rocks and the passageway they'd come through.

She felt no sadness at leaving, it wasn't in her nature to have regrets. Ahead was all that counted. But she did have a picture in her mind of Tench asleep in his bed, and that gave her a little pang of sorrow.

She had never seen him sleeping, shaving, washing or without his clothes. In her mind he would always be in his red jacket, white breeches and long, highly polished boots, striding along the quay. She would remember his soft brown eyes too, and the way his hand felt when he touched hers. All those many little kindnesses.

If she had a regret it was only that she hadn't said goodbye, told him just once that she cared for him. But such thoughts were foolish, because he wouldn't have been able to be party to an escape.

She glanced back once more, sending a silent message to him on the wind, knowing she would never see him again. Then she turned back and made a loud whoop of delight at their freedom.

While she had no idea if they could make it all the way to Kupang, it was enough that the plan to get out of the harbour had worked. She looked around at the eight jubilant male faces, and knew that in her own way she'd won a victory. She might not be able to read and write, or navigate like Will could, and perhaps none of the men would ever acknowledge her part in the escape, but she knew the truth, and come what may, she intended to see they found safety and permanent freedom.

She pressed her lips into Charlotte's forehead, aware that in the weeks ahead she would have to be constantly on guard over her children.

'Haven't you got anything to say about my ingenious plan, Mary?' Will shouted out.

For a brief second she considered pointing out the plan was hardly his. But as her father had often said, 'A battle is won by strategy, not by superior force.'

'Well done, Will,' she said, and smiled at him with affection. 'You are a clever, brave man.'

Chapter twelve

After two days at sea, Mary found herself feeling exactly the way she had on the cart from Exeter to the *Dunkirk*. Just like then, she had started out with so much enthusiasm, then came the aching all over from sitting in the same position for so long. At night she was chilled to the marrow, by day the sun and wind made her face raw. Yet on the trip to Devonport she hadn't had children to placate, amuse and control too. While Emmanuel at least stayed in one place, mostly on her lap, Charlotte kept trying to move around.

Mary had fallen asleep for a couple of hours at a time, once the children were sleeping, but she kept waking with a start, afraid that whoever was at the tiller had dropped off too, and that they were drifting on to rocks.

Yet despite the discomfort, she certainly hadn't found herself wishing she was back in Sydney Cove. The weather was good, with steady north to north-east winds driving them along, and all the men were still in high spirits, discussing endlessly how different people back in the settlement would have reacted to their escape.

'Cap'n Phillip will be wild with fury, to be sure,' James Martin said gleefully.

'I hope Sarah wasn't too sore at me when she found my note,' Jamie Cox said with a touch of sadness.

'You did well not to give in to temptation and tell her before we left,' Mary said soothingly. She knew Jamie was very fond of Sarah Young, and it must have been hard for him to leave her behind.

Although Mary thought she had known all the men quite well before they left the settlement, she had soon discovered they all had aspects to their personalities she hadn't been aware of before. James Martin, the ugly Irishman, had always been amusing, a funny man who could tell a great story, but something of a rake, chasing women and drink, and always ready for a fight. Yet she had found him to be unexpectedly fatherly, often taking Charlotte or Emmanuel into his arms to give her a break.

Red-haired, freckle-faced Samuel Bird had seemed to her a very morose man, and she had never really understood why Will thought so much of him. Yet now they were free he was laughing as much as anyone else and though he didn't say much, he listened to the others and responded.

Bill Allen and Nat Lilly were the ones she knew least, and they were complete opposites. Bill was stocky and bald-headed, with a pug nose that looked as if it had been pummelled with fists. In fact he looked every inch the 'Iron Man' of his nickname. Nat, with his cherubic face, big eyes and long blond hair, wasn't tough at all, in fact Mary had considered him a bit of a nancy boy. But he fitted in with any group of men he was set to work with, and everyone liked him. He was also very loyal to Will.

Both Nat and Bill had been in better health than any of the other men who arrived with the Second Fleet, and Mary had never discovered why. In Nat's case it was probably better not to ask.

It was this ability to survive which had made Mary pick both men for the escape. Yet now she saw they were both surprisingly sensitive. On the very first morning they had fixed up an awning to protect the children from the sun, and took charge of doling out the food fairly.

William Moreton was undoubtedly one of the more intelligent prisoners. He was also unattractive, with a large domed forehead, bulging eyes and a tight, narrow mouth. Sadly, he wasn't improving with knowing; he was very argumentative, and Mary was a little afraid he was going to put someone's back up before long.

Even Jamie Cox and Sam Broome, both quiet, thoughtful men who had appeared to be content to be led by the nose by the others, had asserted themselves a little. At one point Jamie had been brave enough to tell Will to stop bragging, and Sam Broome had told James Martin to mind his language because of Mary and Charlotte. Mary had no doubt that in the next few weeks she would find out even more surprising things about everyone.

Now and then the men would talk dreamily about what they would do when they got back to England. They all knew that it would be foolhardy to attempt going to their home towns, for fear of being re-arrested. London was the favourite destination, there they would be inconspicuous, and with a new name they could start all over again.

Mary couldn't bring herself to think that far ahead, it

seemed like tempting Fate to her. The reality of it was that they had no money, their clothes were in rags, and they'd need a tremendous amount of luck to avoid turning back to crime.

Yet despite her qualms sometimes she couldn't help but lapse into a little day-dream in which she found herself walking up the cobbled street from Fowey harbour holding her children by their hands. She imagined standing at the open door and seeing her mother inside the house, bent over the cooking pot on the fire. She would turn her head, see them and almost faint with surprise and delight. It was of course an unrealistic and fanciful day-dream, but it helped Mary's aching back and warmed her very bones.

The weather turned on the third day, with rain and a stronger blustery wind, and Will became concerned at the boat being rather overloaded. 'We must find somewhere to land until it passes,' he said.

A little later William Moreton, who was up in the bows, suddenly bellowed out that he could see what looked like a good spot.

Everyone looked to where he was pointing and saw a small cove with a pebble beach. Will went in closer to check for rocks under the water, and as there were none, agreed it was ideal.

'Let's hope there's a tavern,' James exclaimed.

That made everyone laugh, even William Moreton who hadn't appeared to have been amused by James's sense of humour up till now.

Will brought the boat in as close to the beach as he could, then James swam ashore with a rope to pull her into the shallows.

'Natives have been here,' James said, once they were all safely on the beach. He pointed to the charred remains of a fire and a great many fish bones.

'Well, they aren't here now,' Will said, scanning the cove carefully. 'Besides, I know enough of their words to tell them we mean no harm.'

The rain stopped, the sun came out again, and Mary chased Charlotte along the beach, laughing at the sheer joy of a night on dry land. There was a stream of fresh water from which they refilled their water cask and washed their salt-encrusted faces, and Mary found a plant that looked like cabbage. While Will, Bill and James took the seine net to fish, William lit a fire, Samuel Bird and Nat collected wood, and Sam Broome and Jamie Cox made a crude shelter under the trees.

The fishing was good, the men came back with a quantity of grey mullet, and along with some of the rice they'd brought with them, and the cabbage leaves, it was quite a feast.

'But for the dire lack of beer and some buxom wenches, I could be happy here,' James said, as he lay back on the beach after the meal.

Mary giggled. She hadn't always approved of James in the past, but she was growing to like him more with every hour that passed. His sense of the ridiculous warmed her and he could make time pass so quickly with his stories. She had always thought him a strange-looking man before, with his very bony, lopsided face, large ears and nose, and thick dark eyebrows that met in the middle. Her mother had always said that was a sign that a man was 'born to be hung', and perhaps he was, for he had only escaped it by a hair's-breadth. But his lack of good looks was compensated by his personality. She didn't find it so odd now that many women back at the settlement were after him.

That night they all slept well, huddled together in their shelter, the fire just outside. As Mary lay there, waiting for sleep to overtake her, Will curled against her back and the children tucked in between her and Sam, she felt warm, well fed and really happy. It wasn't just that she was freed from the penal colony, more that something inside her had been set free.

As a child she'd always wished she'd been born a boy, purely so she could go fishing, climb rocks and have adventures. Girls just didn't get opportunities to do anything more than ape their mothers, waiting on the menfolk. She supposed that when she went off to Plymouth that would change, but of course it didn't. All these years since she was first imprisoned, she'd had to yield to men's superiority, just to survive. But here she was with eight men, and she knew in her heart that in the weeks to come they were going to become dependent on her. She already sensed their admiration for her. She saw in their eyes and their manner that they knew she had dreamed up the plan, however loudly Will boasted otherwise. When she'd taken her turn at the tiller, they realized she knew boats almost as well as Will.

But her trump card was her passionate determination to get to Kupang. The men might believe they shared it, but Mary knew they weren't driven by anywhere near such a powerful force as she was. That force was her children, and she would put up with any hardships, brave every peril to keep them alive to find permanent safety. She slid her arm right over both Emmanuel and Charlotte, the warmth from their small bodies comforting her and adding to her determination.

'How long have we been sailing now, Will?' Nat Lilly asked one afternoon, his voice weary and jaded. He no longer looked so cherubic, his once golden hair was matted and dull with salt, and his fair skin was a mass of blisters from the sun and wind. 'It seems like a year.'

Will kept a log, which he assiduously wrote up every couple of days, and but for him none of them would have known what day or even month it was.

'It's well over a month,' Will replied, pulling hard on the oars as there was little wind that day. 'It's the 2nd of April today.'

'So how much more of this coastline can there be?' Nat asked, his full lips curling petulantly as he looked towards the shore. Not an hour since, he had pointed out that it rarely looked any different however far they'd gone in a day.

'Don't ask damn fool questions like that,' Will replied irritably. 'How would I know, it's not charted is it?'

'Well, whoever sailed it before must have known if it was one thousand miles, or five,' Nat said sullenly.

'Daresay they did, but they didn't bother to mention it,' Will said tersely. 'Now, shut up and row faster.'

Mary was at the tiller, Emmanuel on her knee, and Charlotte at her feet, playing with a doll James had made her from a piece of rope. She heard what passed between Nat and Will, just as she'd heard each of the men at other times questioning exactly how far Kupang was. They all needed a rest and she hoped against hope they would find somewhere soon where they could stay for a couple of days.

Since they made their first stop in what they'd called Fortunate Cove, they had stuck to a pattern: a few days' sailing, then a rest for two days when they found somewhere with fresh water. Tension grew all the time while they were on the boat; they got stiff, cold and sharp with one another. But as soon as they got ashore all the bad feeling seemed to vanish.

Will was getting more and more worried about the boat, though, for it was taking on water badly now. William Moreton kept mentioning the monsoons too, he said he thought they were sailing towards one. The boat might have been fine sailing around Sydney Bay, but it wasn't intended for a long voyage packed with so many people.

Late that same afternoon they came to a big bay as fine as Sydney, and everyone immediately became more cheerful.

'We'll have to get the boat out of the water and caulk her seams,' Will said, then looking at Mary he added, 'You can wash everyone's clothes, my girl.'

Mary smarted, but said nothing in reply. She would have washed everyone's clothes anyway, but ordering her to do it was Will's way of admonishing her.

She knew exactly what was wrong with him; he was losing his spirit. The men had stopped praising him for getting them away. Perhaps too he was dwelling on how if he hadn't escaped, his sentence would have been up now. And of course he was worried about the boat's ability to hold together long enough to get them to Kupang.

Mary thought he'd probably be relieved if someone was to suggest they stayed for the rest of the winter months in a bay like this one. But he wouldn't suggest it himself for fear of looking cowardly. Also, he didn't like the way the men acted towards his wife.

It had begun with James getting a splinter from an oar in his hand about a week into the voyage. Mary had dug it out and he kept calling her 'Mother Mary'. Since then, every time someone had something wrong with them, they asked her opinion on it. To Mary, this was what anyone would expect – she was the only woman after all, and she'd picked up quite a lot of basic medical knowledge from Surgeon White, both on the *Charlotte* and in the settlement. But Will seemed to think it was because they had designs on her.

He had also made a fuss about how all of them, save William Moreton and himself, vied to be next to her in the boat, and took charge of Charlotte when she was feeding Emmanuel. Mary knew perfectly well that none of them did this as a prospective lover. It was just brotherly, and maybe sitting next to her as she nursed Emmanuel reminded them of how it had been with their own mothers. Perhaps, too, they were weary of acting tough the way Will did all the time. Talking to her, they could drop their guard for a while. She couldn't understand why Will saw anything more sinister in it.

Bill had confided in her that he'd been a brute to women in the past, but perhaps that was because his father had always hit his mother. Nat had admitted that he had allowed some of the sailors to use him like a woman on his transport ship, for it was the only way of obtaining extra food and getting out of the holds. Sam Bird had told Mary he stole rations from other people's huts when things were really bad, and now he felt terribly ashamed.

She didn't think any the less of the men for telling her these things, even if they were ugly. She felt shared confidences bound them closer together.

Once they were ashore, a shelter erected and a fire lit, Mary put Emmanuel into his sling, tied it around her, and leaving Charlotte playing on the beach where the men were hauling in the boat, she went off to look for things to eat.

She found some more sweet tea leaves, and some of the acid berries Surgeon White had set so much store by, but having failed to find any of the leaves that were like cabbage, she turned back.

All at once she saw a group of natives watching her from beneath a tree. She was momentarily alarmed as she was some distance from the men, but she waved her hand, which the natives back in Sydney had seemed to understand as a friendly gesture, and smiled at them. She sensed they were just baffled by her, not hostile, so she walked back to the men on the beach.

The following day the natives came closer. They crouched further up the beach, watching intently as the men repaired the boat. Mary was doing the washing, and each time she got up to hang a garment over a bush to dry, she smiled at them.

'What are you playing at?' Will suddenly snapped at her. 'Isn't it enough having eight men around you? Or do you want a few of them too?'

'Don't be a fool, Will,' she said wearily. 'I'm only smiling to show we mean them no harm, as well you know.'

Will continued to be sullen with her for the rest of the day, even though they'd caught enough fish to eat well that night and have some over to salt some down for the future. After Mary had put the children down to sleep in the evening, she sat for a short while by the fire. The men were discussing once again how much farther it was, a conversation she didn't join in. Feeling very tired, she got up from the fire to go and relieve herself before settling down to sleep.

It was a beautiful night, with a full moon, and instead of going straight back to the shelter, she sat down on a rock just to enjoy the quiet. Quiet times were something of a rare treat for Mary. Right from the day she was arrested back in Plymouth, there had always been noise and tumult around her. Even in her hut back in Sydney, she rarely got a chance to be entirely alone.

On the boat every single thing she did was in full view of the men. They were polite enough to look the other way when she relieved or washed herself, but they were there, just feet away from her. There was always someone talking, arguing, singing or even snoring. Even her body wasn't her own: Emmanuel was either at her breast, climbing on her or sleeping on her, and Charlotte demanded her attention most of the waking hours. Even the men used her as a cushion to lean against.

Looking up at the stars, with the sea lapping gently at the shore, she could pretend she was back in Cornwall. She lapsed into a day-dream again, imagining herself in a little cottage, the children safely in a real bed upstairs, and Will out fishing. She could see it so clearly – a candle burning, the fire glowing red and little sparks catching on the soot making pictures.

When she and Dolly were small they had always competed to see the best picture in these sparks. Dolly saw things like people going to church, dancers round a maypole, while Mary had always seen fish, animals or birds. She wondered what Dolly would make of the tales she had heard about the strange animal they called the kangaroo here, or those big birds that couldn't fly but ran faster than a man. Then there were all the millions of pretty birds, so exotic and brightly coloured they took her breath away.

'He isn't coming!'

Mary nearly jumped out of her skin at the sound of

Will's angry-sounding voice. She hadn't heard anyone coming towards her.

She got up and turned, and he was striding towards her. 'Who isn't coming?' she asked.

'Sam, of course, as if you didn't know,' he snarled at her. 'I caught him creeping off to meet you, and flattened him.'

'I didn't come out here to meet anyone,' Mary said indignantly. 'Don't you think I get enough of people all around me every day?'

He struck her so quickly that she didn't have time to move or even duck. The punch caught her on the cheek and knocked her backwards down on to the beach.

'You're my woman,' he hissed at her and threw himself down on top of her, pulling up her dress.

It was enough of a shock to be hit by him, but when she realized what he was trying to do, she was horrified and frightened.

'Don't, Will,' she implored him. 'Not like this.'

She tried to fight her way out from under him, but he was too strong and heavy. All at once he was forcing himself inside her, biting at her neck like a savage animal, his fingers digging into her buttocks as if to hurt her more.

When he was done, he got up and walked away, without even an apology.

Mary stayed where she was for a few moments, too stunned to move. Later she walked down to the sea and washed herself. Her eyes were dry but inside she was weeping, for she had never imagined her Will being capable of such a bestial act. Gentle, sweet love-making had been the one thing they'd had between them that made life bearable in the settlement. It eased hunger, physical pain, and the hopelessness of their situation. If he had wanted her tonight, he need only have said, and she'd have joyfully slipped away with him out here.

She knew what he'd done wasn't uncommon, she'd seen plenty of women with split lips and black eyes back in Sydney. She knew from confidences from some of them that they'd never known any other kind of love-making but the rough sort. But their men were in a different class to Will, low types, who would steal food from their own children without a qualm.

Mary heard a faint sound and turned to see Will had come back and was standing a little way up the beach. 'Come on back with me now,' he called out.

He was holding out his hand to her. It was too dark to see the expression on his face, but his stance was uncertain, as if he was ashamed of himself.

'Why, Will?' she said as she walked up to him. She felt no hatred, not even anger, just a huge well of disappointment.

'I don't know,' he said in little more than a whisper. 'I got all fired up about Sam, I suppose.'

Mary said nothing as they walked back to the shelter. She needed time to think this through.

When Mary woke up the following morning, she was alone in the shelter with the children who were still asleep. Will was already working on the boat repairs with William and James. She couldn't see the other men and guessed they'd gone off to try to catch some shellfish.

Gingerly, she felt her cheek. It was puffy and sore, but the skin wasn't broken.

A little later when she was kneeling trying to light a fire, Will came over to her. He just stood by her for a second or two, looking down at her. She ignored him.

'Do you hate me?' he asked eventually.

'Do you expect me to?' she retorted, looking up at him. He looked rough. Of course they all did, what with wind- and sun-burnt skin and little sleep. All the men needed their hair and beards trimmed, but it looked odd on Will who normally took pride in his appearance.

Yet it was more than that. Will's eyes were dull and sunken, Mary could only remember them looking that way once before. That was after the flogging.

He shrugged. 'I don't know.'

'We've been through a lot together,' she said. 'We've got a lot more still to come, and if we don't pull together we won't make it.'

'So you'll forgive me then?' he said, looking a bit puzzled.

'I don't know about forgiveness, you have to earn that,' she said sharply. 'But I'll put it to one side.'

He made a sort of exclamation with his hands. 'What sort of a woman are you? You don't cry, you don't shout. I don't understand you.'

'I understand you,' she retorted. 'And I don't cry or shout because there's nothing to be gained by it.'

She did understand him. She knew he was afraid she

was usurping the position he'd always held, that of leader. Raping her was his way of making her submit to him. But she wasn't going to.

The natives came back again during the afternoon. The men gave them some of the fish they'd caught and they in turn offered a gift of a couple of large crabs.

The following morning the natives came down the beach and helped them relaunch the boat, waving as they left. It was to be the last time they were to encounter friendliness when they put ashore.

The luck which had held for a month suddenly gave out. The weather turned bad, with strong winds and heavy rain, and though they saw many inviting beaches, the surf was too high to chance trying to go in. The boat was still taking in water, and when they eventually found a bay, natives appeared at once, throwing spears to warn them off. In desperation the men fired the muskets over their heads, and the natives ran away, but they were back in larger numbers the following morning, so there was nothing for it but to flee.

A violent storm caught them unprepared. The waves were like huge green mountains, tossing the boat up and down like a toy. Mary kept Emmanuel strapped to her chest, and held Charlotte tightly for fear she would be washed overboard. She doubted that any of them would see the sun rise again.

It was like the worst sailing nightmare which just went on and on. The sky was so black that even day seemed almost as bad as night. Emmanuel and Charlotte screamed with terror, then when exhaustion overcame them they merely quivered, too petrified, cold and wet to sleep.

The fresh water was nearly gone, but they were unable to go ashore for fear of wrecking the boat on rocks beneath the surf. Will anchored offshore and two of the men bravely swam ashore with the cask to fill it, but natives with spears appeared again and they had to retreat quickly.

Over the next couple of days Mary saw that Will was sinking into an apathetic state. He left William Moreton and James to take charge, and sometimes the wind blew them so far away from the shore that they lost sight of it altogether.

'Pull yourself together, Will,' she shouted at him one day. 'We're heading towards the reef and we'll be holed.'

He muttered something about needing speed to beat the monsoon, which sounded crazy to her, so she took the tiller and headed back towards the relative safety of the shore. By now the boat was filling with water, from both above and below the water-line, and they were in real danger of sinking.

Just when it looked as if all was lost, they saw the mouth of a river. Will rallied round then, took over at the tiller and skilfully negotiated the boat through shoals where the water was only five or six feet deep. At last, close to complete exhaustion, they managed to pull the boat up on to the river bank.

There was plenty of fresh water, but they were unable to catch any fish or find anything else to eat.

Yet even with only rice and the last of the salted pork, just to get dry and be able to stretch out and sleep was enough.

The following morning the men set to work to repair the boat again. The resin they'd brought with them was all gone, but resourceful James came up with the idea of using soap instead. They knew they would have to move on quickly to find food, and Mary was very anxious now about Emmanuel and Charlotte who didn't appear to be recovering as the adults had. They seemed listless. Charlotte took only a couple of mouthfuls of rice and fell asleep again. Emmanuel lay in her arms, not even attempting to suckle.

'They'll be all right,' James said comfortingly to her. 'They're just worn out. Let them sleep.'

They had only gone a couple of miles the following morning when the monsoon finally caught up with them. Torrential rain hammered down, the wind stronger than they'd ever known it before. Once again the sea was mountainous, and they lost sight of land altogether as the wind sped them along.

For the first two days and nights Mary concentrated all her efforts on her children, trying to shelter them with a tarpaulin, singing to them and rocking them. But when she saw all the men were losing heart, she knew she had to induce them to fight for their survival.

'We can do it,' she yelled at them. 'It's no good just giving up. At least this wind is carrying us fast, let's lighten the boat by throwing out all the surplus stuff.'

They threw out spare clothing and personal possessions, and when water still poured into the boat, Mary took off her hat and began bailing it out.

'Come on,' she screamed at them. 'Bail, every one of you. Your life depends on it now.'

One by one they joined her, apathetically at first, but as they saw the boat rise in the water, they worked faster. 'That's right,' she yelled. 'Come on, Sam, Jamie and William, do you want to end up as fish food? You can kill yourselves if you've a mind to when we get ashore, but don't let it happen out here just because you're tired.'

For eight days in all they couldn't see land. Still the rain came down, and still Mary shouted at the men. Her arms felt as if they were coming out of their sockets with bailing and her voice was hoarse, but she knew she was winning. Not one of the men would stop while she was bailing, and the boat was speeding along.

They saw the shore again just as night was falling, but the surf was so high they couldn't attempt to go in. Will dropped the anchor and used the grapnel to hold the boat faster overnight, hoping that by morning the wind would have dropped enough for them to get ashore.

In the early hours of the morning, as they tried to get some rest, they heard the ominous sound of the anchor being dragged along the rocks, and all at once the boat was drifting out towards the reef.

'It will be holed and we'll all drown,' Will shouted hysterically above the sound of the roaring wind. 'Oh God, why did I attempt this?'

Mary scrabbled her way to the mast and pulled herself up. She looked down at the cowering, frightened men, and snarled at them. 'It's just water, wind and rain,' she shouted above the wind. 'We've got this far, we're not going to let it beat us. Don't turn lily-livered on me now, pull up that anchor and we sail on.'

Dawn came as they battled against the elements, and as the sky lightened so the wind dropped a little.

'Keep bailing,' Mary yelled, her voice just a croak. 'We'll get ashore, I promise you.'

'Thank God,' James murmured a few hours later as they sailed into a bay ringed with white sand. 'And thank you, Mary, for having the courage to make us battle on.'

Mary smiled weakly. She felt sick with hunger and she was almost frightened to look at Emmanuel and Charlotte under the tarpaulin in case they were dead instead of sleeping. Maybe it was a victory, but right now she felt utterly defeated.

She had no recollection of coming ashore. The last thing she remembered was sailing close to the shoreline and then waking to find herself on soft, warm sand.

She sat up cautiously and looked around her, puzzled because the sun was in the east. She felt her clothes and they were dry, but stiff with salt. Alarmed by the utter silence, she tried to get up, but she was so stiff she could barely move.

As she turned her head she saw the men asleep under the shelter, Charlotte and Emmanuel tucked in between Will and James. There was the remains of a fire with a huge pile of mussel shells close to it, and the water cask was placed under a tree, a deep track in the sand showing how it had been rolled there after being filled.

All at once Mary guessed she must have fallen asleep or even passed out the day before, and the men had let her sleep undisturbed while they found food and water before finally falling asleep themselves.

That little kindness brought tears to her eyes, and gave her the strength to overcome her stiffness, to stand and stretch, then walk slowly over to the water cask. She drank greedily, mug after mug, until her stomach felt bloated, then she gobbled down the cold rice left in the cooking pot. Looking around, she saw it was a beautiful bay they'd come to, white sand, clear blue sea, and lush green vegetation all around.

Her heart seemed to swell up with gratitude, and she dropped to her knees to thank God for their safe deliverance from the storm.

Chapter thirteen

Sam Broome and James Martin stopped in their search for shellfish in the rock pools and sat down wearily.

'Mary's a hard task-master,' James said with a hint of laughter in his voice. 'But she's a grand woman for all that.' His breeches were so ragged now that they were hardly worth wearing, for most of his legs and parts of his buttocks were uncovered. Sam's shirt and breeches were still in one piece but so threadbare that one more dip in the sea would probably see them float away.

Sam looked back along the beach where they could see Mary hanging washing on some bushes to dry. She'd insisted they were to fill the sack with shellfish or not return to the camp. 'Aye, but she's harder on herself than us,' he replied. He knew Mary wouldn't rest all day. When the washing was finished she too would be out looking for anything edible to supplement their provisions.

James nodded in agreement. He found it incredible that Mary could be so calm and controlled after what they'd all been through in the last couple of weeks. Just last night he had woken from the most terrifying nightmare, and been too scared to shut his eyes again. Even Will, who had put to sea many times in the foulest weather

Cornwall could throw at a fisherman, admitted he'd never known anything like as bad. James believed they had looked into the very face of death that night when the anchor broke away from the sea bed, and it wasn't surprising most of the men were reluctant to set sail again.

'We would have all drowned but for Mary,' Sam stated, his voice shaking with emotion. 'Her courage and endurance puts us all to shame.'

James knew this was true, but it would make him feel uncomfortable to agree with Sam.

'Aye, but you were always sweet on her,' he teased instead. 'You'd better keep your thoughts about her to yourself, Sam. Will can be a dangerous man when he's crossed.'

'My thoughts about Mary are pure,' Sam protested. 'But for her I wouldn't have been alive to come on this escape. I was close to death when they dumped me like a sack of rice on the wharf. I saw other women stealing the clothes of those too weak to protest, they passed me by, not even giving me water because I was in rags. But she came to me, God bless her.'

Sam's passionate statement pricked James's conscience. He hadn't cared enough to help with the sick on the Second Fleet and he remembered he'd hidden himself away with a bottle of rum he'd stolen while helping to load goods in the stores. During the next week or so there was a great deal of talk about how hard Mary had worked with the sick, while he'd even been callous enough to tell her it would be better for all of them if they died.

Looking back further, he could recall his reunion with

Will when the men came ashore that first day in Port Jackson. Will had not known that Samuel Bird and James had been sent out on another ship of the fleet, and he was thrilled to meet up with them again. James remembered talking excitedly about sharing a tent with him and other men from the *Dunkirk*, but Will confounded him by saying he intended to marry Mary and built a hut of his own.

James thought the man had taken leave of his senses. He couldn't believe Will would choose to live with one woman and her child when he could be with his old mates and have a different woman every night of the week.

Yet James had come to envy Will before long. The women prisoners were in the main a disappointment, either conniving bitches or pathetic wretches, and there wasn't much fun to be had when a man was constantly hungry.

Mary had proved to be an inspired choice as a wife. She was bright and cheerful, she kept herself and Charlotte clean and decent. And just to look at big Will, who remained fitter and stronger than anyone else, was enough to know she took care of him in every way.

But then, just as he'd been wrong in his initial judgement of Mary, he'd been wrong about Will too.

''Tis not a good thing to idolize anyone,' he said, thinking aloud. 'Oh, I'm not meaning Mary,' he said quickly as he saw Sam's surprised and rather indignant expression. 'I'm talking of Will.' He didn't think he would ever forget how the big man had sat cowering with fear that last night at sea. Or how Mary'd screamed like a banshee to make them all exert themselves. 'You see, right since I first met him on the *Dunkirk*, I surely believed he was indestructible.'

'A man who has to boast about his strength or cleverness isn't sure of it,' Sam said with a self-satisfied smirk. 'And a man who will lay another out just on suspicion he wants his woman is a fool.'

James shrugged. He might be disappointed in his old friend, but he wasn't about to let some Johnny-come-lately slander him. 'Watch what you say,' he warned. 'Will and I go back a long way.'

'I know,' Sam said carefully. 'But you are no fool, James. You know as well as I do we need a strong leader if there is to be any chance of making it to Kupang. I'm not so sure Will is up to that any longer.'

'Surely you aren't thinking a woman with two babbies can be that leader?' James retorted. He admired Mary himself, but it was not in his nature to believe a woman could be tougher and more resilient than himself or any other man.

Sam chuckled. 'Of course not. We'd have mutiny on our hands.'

James had often called Sam 'the Parson' back in Port Jackson, because of his appearance, mild manners and disapproval of drink. But in the past weeks he'd come to see that the man was strong-willed and resourceful. He had an idea that Sam had some sort of plan of his own, and he thought it best to winkle it out now, so he'd know where he stood.

'What if Will suggests we stay here till the bad weather's over?' he asked tentatively. Will had only hinted at this, and if James were to be totally honest, the idea had some real attractions.

Sam half smiled. To him, this bay they'd christened White Bay was paradise. The soft sand, the lush vegetation and the mild weather were all so seductive. 'I'd gladly stay if we had more provisions,' he admitted. 'I'm no more anxious than anyone else to risk drowning again in a storm. But were we to stay, the flour and rice would run out, and there's a chance a ship might come by and haul us back to Sydney.'

'We could fish and hunt,' James retorted. 'As for a ship coming by, how likely is that?'

'Not very,' Sam agreed. 'But the whole point of our escape was to find a new life. The longer we put it off, the weaker we'll all become.'

'You got that from Mary,' James scoffed.

'Maybe, but that doesn't stop it being true. I think we've got to press on.'

'What if Will doesn't agree?' James said.

Sam shrugged. The gesture implied he thought those who wanted to go had a perfect right to take the boat and leave the others stranded.

James got up and began prising mussels off the rocks with a knife. He wasn't shocked that Sam would cheerfully leave Will here, he'd probably do the same if he could gain something by it. To him loyalty was just a concept men embraced when a mob could have more power than an individual. Mostly James looked after number one and to hell with anyone else.

He was also lazy by nature. He had always taken the

easiest path open to him. On the face of it, the easiest one right now appeared to be to stay here. But was it? They wouldn't be risking their lives, not unless some natives came and attacked them, but they'd need to build real shelters or huts, and they had only a few tools. With only one woman among eight men, they'd soon be fighting one another. Besides, he yearned for city life, for noise and bustle, to be able to get drunk, eat what he chose, ride a horse and charm the ladies.

He remembered how in the first year of the settlement, some misguided fools had run off into the bush thinking if they kept going they would get to China. He had laughed aloud at that, but then he was one of only a handful of men who could read and write, and he had a pretty good grasp of the world's geography.

He knew from Detmer Smith that from Kupang he could get a boat to China, or Africa, even South Africa. Those were all places where a lazy, cunning Irishman might find an easy life.

William Moreton wanted to press on, if only to prove he was as good a sailor as Will. Mary most certainly did, and Nat Lilly would side with Sam Broome now because they'd formed a strong allegiance. Bill Allen was likely to want to get to Kupang quickly, which left only Jamie Cox and Samuel Bird likely to side with Will.

James knew there was a lot more to be gained by siding with Mary than with Will. A plucky, resourceful little woman like her could be very useful to him when they made it to Kupang.

*

That same evening the whole party was clustered round the fire, for it had turned cold once darkness fell. William Moreton had brought up the subject of when they should move on. He wanted to leave the very next morning.

'What's to be gained by staying here?' he said forcefully. 'We've had a rest, dried our clothes and mended the boat.'

William irritated everyone. He had no sense of humour, he was pedantic and believed he knew everything. Nat, who had a mischievous streak, often goaded him by asking why, if he was so clever, he'd managed to get himself caught stealing. But he did have some clout with the group because of his navigation skills.

'I say we stay a while longer,' Will said stubbornly. 'The boat can't take another bad storm.'

All the men had had something to say, but Mary had made no comment so far. She was watching their faces and trying to gauge what each one really wanted. Sam Broome, Jamie Cox and Samuel Bird had almost blank expressions, and she guessed this was because they were weighing up the opinions of the more dominant group members. Then they'd side with whoever they trusted most.

James Martin was liked by everyone. He was good in a crisis, his humour had saved the day many times, he did have leadership qualities, but he wasn't the most rational of men.

Bill was also a good leader. He would row far longer than anyone else, chop wood quicker, light a fire almost instantly, and was sympathetic to those weaker than himself. But he was no sailor.

A month ago all the men would have gone along blindly with whatever Will decided, but he'd lost his hold over them since they'd seen him afraid and unsure of what to do.

Mary felt saddened that they were turning away from Will. They were all terrified during the storms, which were more than any human being could cope with, and she didn't think Will should be judged so harshly because he lost his nerve. But for Charlotte and Emmanuel she too would have panicked; the fact that she didn't was only down to a fierce maternal instinct to protect her children at all costs.

Mary was torn two ways herself. While she desperately wanted to press on to Kupang, to find permanent security, a home for her children and a tranquil life free from anxiety, Charlotte and Emmanuel weren't too well. The sea voyage, the cold and the constant soaking had taken a lot out of them. They were gaunt-faced, fearful and thin, and food was going straight through them. They really needed more time to recuperate. But Mary's milk was drying up, the rice they'd brought with them wouldn't last more than another three weeks, and she didn't know if a year-old baby's stomach could cope with a diet of mainly shellfish.

She thought that most of the men shared her conflict, not for the same reasons of course, but because they were scared of running into another bad storm.

'I agree with William,' Sam Broome said. 'We should go on, as fast as possible. There's nothing to be gained by waiting here till the provisions run out.'

Sam had become popular with the others for his calm practicality and his ability to listen, but since the night Will hit him, he had changed. While still measured, he asserted himself more. Mary sensed he had weighed up the other men and found most of them wanting in some way, especially Will. She didn't think Sam hated Will, or would like to see William Moreton become their leader. But she guessed he wanted some re-alignment of power, perhaps with himself as second in command.

'We can hunt and fish here,' Will argued, his face flushed with anger as no one seemed to be considering him their leader any longer. 'Didn't I keep everyone fed back in Sydney?'

The four men who had come on the Second Fleet hadn't experienced the near-starvation rations prior to their arrival, so Will's claim meant little to them. Only Jamie Cox and Samuel Bird nodded to confirm this was true.

'What about you, James?' Sam asked the Irishman. 'Go on, or stay?'

James couldn't bring himself to oppose his old friend openly. 'I'd like a few jugs of ale and some women,' he said with a contrived carefree air. 'And no amount of waiting around here will produce that.'

Some of the men laughed, but Will looked as if James had just stuck a knife in his back.

'That sounds like you want to go on,' Sam said, avoiding looking at Will. 'Anyone else got anything to say?'

Nat Lilly cleared his throat and spat noisily into the

sand. 'We should go on right enough, but go ashore each time the weather turns.'

Jamie Cox kept his eyes down. He was the youngest of them, and he'd told Mary once that he wouldn't have survived the *Dunkirk* without Will's help. He was slightly built and his sharp features which had reminded Mary of a bird at their first meeting were sharper still now. He clearly didn't care whether they left or stayed, as long as he was still with Will.

'Bill, what do you think?' Sam asked.

'Go on,' he growled, glowering at William Moreton as if to warn him not to try to take command.

Samuel Bird still had a blank expression.

'Mary! Where d'you stand?' William asked her.

Mary hadn't expected to be asked and she hesitated, not wanting to oppose her husband. Yet William Moreton had been the most outspoken about the foolishness of taking a woman and her children with them. If he cared what she thought, then she had a duty to voice it.

'I agree with Nat,' she said. 'We should press on, but stop if the weather changes.'

'So we're to listen to a bloody woman now, are we?' Will exploded. 'What does she know.'

Jamie Cox looked up in astonishment. Bill narrowed his eyes, looking daggers at Will. Sam bristled visibly.

'I'd say she knows more than all of us,' James remarked in a languid drawl. 'But for her we'd be fish food now. But let's have no more of this. Put it to a vote.'

William Moreton looked at Will, perhaps expecting

him to make some kind of speech to regain the loyalty of his former followers. But either Will believed he didn't need to do that, or he knew the outcome already, for he folded his arms sullenly.

'All those in favour of going on tomorrow, raise your hand,' William said.

Only Jamie Cox and Will kept theirs down.

'Motion carried,' William said, and smirked with self-importance.

'Don't cry to me if the boat don't make it,' Will said with a shrug. He then turned to Mary with a look of pure malice. 'And don't you blame me, girl, if the babbies die!'

There were times after they left White Bay when Mary was tortured by the memory of Will's words, for there were many more terrific storms which came on so suddenly they had no chance of getting ashore. Each time she saw her children's stricken faces and heard their shrieks of pure terror, she asked herself what had possessed her to gamble with their lives.

Yet the need to protect them gave her the strength to fight back when she saw the men weakening. Jamie, Samuel Bird and Nat were the worst. They were all small men, with much less muscle than the others, and they couldn't swim either, which made them even more frightened. In turn she praised, implored, bullied and goaded them. She swore at them from her position at the tiller, screamed that they were to bail and keep bailing if they didn't want to die.

But just when she was beginning to think, as the men

clearly were, that it was just a matter of time before death claimed them all, they came into calmer waters. On their left was the shore, to their right a huge reef, and the sea between was calm as a mill-pond.

'Thank the Lord,' William Moreton shouted in an unexpected display of emotion. 'I really thought we were done for.'

Yet even this new calm sea wasn't without hazards, for there were dozens of tiny islands and coral atolls to run aground on. They went ashore on one of the islands, only to find no fresh water, but they cooked up some rice with the remaining water, and when the tide went out set out across the rocks to look for more.

To their astonishment they saw dozens of giant turtles going up on the shore to lay their eggs. The men quickly killed some of them, and as the tide came back in, they hauled them back to their island.

That night they dined well on the first fresh meat they'd eaten since setting out from Sydney. As they fell asleep with full bellies for once, they were rewarded further by the sound of rain filling the upturned shells they'd hopefully left out.

In the days that followed, as James and Will caulked up the boat again with soap, the others caught more turtles and smoked the meat over the fire to take with them.

Bill had done a lot of poaching in his youth, and when he saw a kind of fowl that nested in the ground, he set out to catch them, with Nat as his accomplice. Mary found herself laughing as she watched them, for they certainly made the oddest partnership. Pugnacious, muscular Bill with his bald head glistening in the sun crouched down on the ground making hand signals to pretty boy Nat to drive the birds towards him. But they made a good team, and caught many birds, and Bill taught Nat the art of plucking them too.

Mary found more cabbage leaves, and fruit. She didn't know what it was, but it tasted wonderful, and the children, who were both in a poor, listless condition, began to revive.

After six days' rest they took off again, stopping every now and then to search for more turtles. They didn't find any, but there was shellfish and plenty of fresh water.

Everyone had long ago stopped asking Will when they would come to the end of this gigantic land mass. Where they would make for in England was a subject of the past too. They were all suffering from apathy now, not really expecting ever to find any kind of real civilization. When they saw the Straits ahead, as marked on Will's chart, they looked at each other questioningly, then as it slowly dawned on them that they were actually there, they began to laugh hysterically.

Once through the Straits, they found the gulf beyond was dotted with small islands, and they knew they must go ashore to refill the water cask before the last leg of the journey across the open sea. But as they tried to land on one of them, a group of natives watching them from canoes brandished spears and began paddling out to them.

The men were forced to fire their muskets to warn

them off, but then to their consternation they saw the natives pick up bows and fire arrows at them. Mary blanched as several of these eighteen-inch arrows with a barbed point landed right in their boat, and the men had no choice but to row like mad to get clear of them.

These natives were bigger and blacker than any they'd met before, and they came roaring after them in their canoes. But just as it looked as though they would catch them, enough wind came up to fill the sails and they escaped, all very shaken.

'We have to get water before we go across the gulf,' Will said later. 'It's some five hundred miles at least, and even with a full cask we'll still have to ration it.'

He was obviously right, and Mary was glad to see him taking charge again.

The following day they took a chance and moored at an island, despite a sizable village close by. They filled the water cask and left hastily, then returned to an uninhabited island to spend the night.

The following morning, elated by their success the previous day, they decided to go back for more water and to look for some fruit and cabbage leaves too.

The village looked as peaceful as it had the previous day, but as they sailed closer into shore, all at once two huge war canoes, with thirty to forty warriors on each, came hurtling out of nowhere, making straight for them. They had never seen boats like this before: they were sturdily made, with banks of paddles, sails made of some kind of matting, and a platform which was clearly for fighting.

Will swung the boat around. 'Row like buggery,' he yelled to the men, and quickly pulled up the mainsail.

Mary's heart was in her mouth and she hardly dared to breathe. The natives' faces and bodies were painted with a white pattern, they were chanting something, and she had no doubt it was their intention to kill every one of the intruding white men. They were so close now that she could smell their sweat and see the hatred in their faces. Even worse, there were more canoes coming out to join them.

Will showed them all then what a first-class sailor he was. He tacked back and forth to catch the wind, and once he'd got it, the boat sped forward just in the nick of time before the natives were in range to fire more arrows.

'We'll go straight across the Gulf now,' he shouted. 'Hold on to your hats. We're leaving this Godforsaken country for good!'

The natives followed them for some miles, until they knew they couldn't outstrip the cutter. As they finally turned to go back to land, Will cheered loudly. 'We've beaten the bastards,' he yelled, his smile as wide as the stretch of water in front of them.

Mary joined the men in complimenting Will on his expertise. She was proud of him, not just for his skill, but because she saw he had his old spirit back.

'You did so well,' she said, moving to sit beside him at the tiller.

'Couldn't have done better yourself?' he said, raising one salt-encrusted eyebrow.

'None of us could,' she said truthfully, and kissed his cheek.

'We'll be a bit light on water and food,' he said warningly.

'Then we must ration it,' she said. 'Have you any idea how far it is now?'

He shook his head. 'It's all uncharted now. You'd better start praying, my girl.'

Three weeks later, in the middle of the night, Mary gazed up at the stars and prayed. The many prayers she'd offered up previously, that they should find land soon, had not been answered. Now she was begging God to let her children die before she did, so at least she could hold them to the end.

Emmanuel was in her arms, Charlotte was lying with her head in her mother's lap. They were so thin and weak that they could no longer cry. They just lay there with their dull eyes constantly fixed on her. Mary had thought she was familiar with every kind of suffering, but knowing that she was responsible for her children's slow and terrible death was new and far worse.

The last of the food had gone several days before, and the water ran out at noon the previous day, when Emmanuel and Charlotte were given the last drops. No one had spoken today, for they had all lapsed into a kind of torpor, their eyes fixed on the horizon. They weren't even scanning it for land any longer, just avoiding looking at one another, for the sight of how weak they all were was too distressing.

Everyone but Mary and Will was asleep now. William Moreton sprawled against the empty water cask, Sam Broome and Nat Lilly were curled up like a couple of dogs in the bows, the others lay sagging against each other. Nat and Samuel Bird had suffered the worst from sunburn because of their fair skin, and their faces looked monstrous – red, swollen and blistered. Bill too had his share of sunburn on his bald head, but for the last few days he'd wrapped a piece of rag round it like a turban.

Will was hunched up at the tiller, but when Mary glanced at him she saw a stranger. He appeared to have shrunk, his once fleshy face now skeletal, and his eyes and mouth appearing much too large. It was just as well the wind was favourable, as it had been since they left the Gulf, for no one would have had the strength to lift the oars, much less row with them.

Mary wondered how the stars and moon could still shine so brightly at such a time. They twinkled in the calm, dark water like candles in a shrine. It seemed to her they were telling her to let the children go and spare them any further suffering.

She lifted Emmanuel higher into her arms. He weighed so little now, and she remembered how heavy he had been when they set out all those weeks before. He was all eyes now, for as his flesh disappeared, they had become more prominent. He didn't even turn his head towards her breast the way he used to, as if he'd finally accepted there was no food there now.

'I'm so sorry,' she whispered, kissing his little bony

forehead. She wished they could have survived to see him walk, to hear him talk, to know that he would become as strong as his father when he was fully grown. It wasn't fair that his short life should have been such a hard one. But as she turned her body slightly on the seat, intending to lower him into the water, she felt his fingers curl round one of hers.

It seemed to Mary he was making a silent plea to stay with her until the end. She clutched him tighter, bent her face to his little head and cried inwardly at her own cowardice.

'Mary!'

She woke with a start, to find Will tugging at her dress.

The first rays of light were coming into the sky, and her first thought was that Will was expecting a storm and she must get bowls ready to catch the rain to drink.

'Mary, are my eyes deceiving me, or is that land?' he asked hoarsely.

Mary looked. It did look like land, a darker, wavy shape on the horizon.

A wild excitement ran through her. 'Can we both be deceived at once?' she asked. 'It looks like land to me too.'

She moved along the seat, still holding the children, to be closer to him, and clutched hold of his hand.

'Oh, Will,' she whispered. 'Can it be true?'

They held hands for at least an hour, watching and hoping against hope it wasn't some kind of cruel joke of nature. But the dark shape remained constant, growing closer with each minute, until finally they were convinced it was in reality trees.

'Well, my girl,' Will said, beaming at her, 'I got you there. Today's the 5th of June 1791, and I've got to write in the log that I sighted land. It's sixty-seven days since we left Sydney, and I thank God for our deliverance.'

'Shall I wake the others?' she asked. 'Or let them sleep on?'

'Bloody well wake them,' he said, his once powerful voice a mere husky croak, a tear running down his whiskered cheek. 'God knows it's something worth waking for.'

Chapter fourteen

It was late that same afternoon when Will sailed the cutter into a harbour. None of them knew or even cared if it was Kupang. It had buildings and people, which meant food and water, that was enough.

They were all in a pitiful state. Their clothes were ragged, their skin and hair stiff with salt, their skin peeling from long exposure to the elements. They sagged in their seats, too weak and exhausted even to smile at the prospect of salvation.

Mary's tongue was swollen from thirst and she barely had the strength to hold Emmanuel in her arms, but when she saw the throng of people gathered on the wharf looking curiously at the unkempt occupants of the cutter, her mind sharpened again.

'Whatever happens, remember to stick to the story,' she hissed at the men. 'If we let the truth slip we'll be sent back there.'

She didn't think this could be Kupang, as Detmer had said it was owned by the Dutch. She couldn't see anyone white, they were all brown- or yellow-skinned, but at least they bore no resemblance to the savage natives back in New South Wales.

'Water!' William Moreton called out. 'Water!'

His cry, whether actually understood or not, had a galvanizing effect on the bystanders. One man came forward with a hooked pole and guided the boat into a berth. A small, half-naked brown man leaped down on to the boat, taking the rope and throwing it back to his companions on the wharf. Then, miraculously, a wooden bucket of water was passed down.

All the men lunged at the bucket, rocking the boat furiously. But Will filled a mug and passed it to Mary. She let Charlotte have the first drink, and she glugged it down so fast that much of it ran down her chest. Emmanuel was almost unconscious, so Mary had to coax him by dipping her fingers in the water and getting him to suck them until he rallied enough to drink. Finally Mary got some, and nothing in her whole life had ever felt so good as the sensation of cool water running over her parched, swollen tongue and throat.

Although she couldn't understand a word of what the crowd were saying, she sensed by their frantic gesticulating and the tone of their shrill voices that they were in total sympathy with her, her children and the men. She tried to stand but she was so weak she fell back, and from then on everything became disjointed and hazy. She sensed rather than felt arms lifting her. It seemed to her she was laid down on solid ground, and then more water was given to her. Something pungent-smelling was thrust close to her face. She could hear a babble of voices around her, then she was lifted again, to be put down on something softer, and she could no longer see the sky above.

326

'Charlotte, Emmanuel,' she called out in panic.

A brown-faced woman was leaning over her, wiping her face with a cool, damp cloth. She spoke in a foreign tongue, yet whatever the words meant they were as soothing and kindly as the cloth, and Mary felt that at last she was safe enough to sleep.

She woke some time later to find herself lying on a mat, Emmanuel on one side of her, Charlotte on the other. A candle was burning on a low table, and she raised herself slightly to see a woman with glossy dark hair and brown skin asleep on another mat across the room.

Although the candle shed little light, Mary sensed by the peaceful way the children slept that they had been fed and washed. The room appeared to be a hut, larger than the one she and Will had lived in back in Sydney Cove, but similar. Tears of gratitude welled up in her eyes. A stranger had taken them in and cared for them, and she wished she knew this woman's language to be able to thank her.

The following days were something like being lost in a fog, which now and then cleared enough for Mary to know she was being fed drinks and soft, mushy food. Through the fog she heard voices and dogs barking; she smelled food cooking and sometimes she even thought she heard Charlotte laughing. But she couldn't quite manage to open her eyes and look around her.

She was finally brought out of it by Will. She heard his voice and that of James Martin.

'She must get better,' she heard Will say. 'Wanjon wants to see her.'

'She's just worn out,' James said. 'There's no hurry, he'll wait.'

Mary had no desire to see or talk to anyone, she was happy in her little twilight world where no pain and anxiety could touch her. But Will's voice struck a chord somewhere inside her, reminding her that she had responsibilities.

'Will?' she muttered, trying to focus her eyes and see him.

'That's my girl,' he exclaimed, and knelt down beside the mat and took her hand in both of his. 'You've been scaring us all. We thought you were lost to us.'

His hands were rough and callused, but the tenderness in them touched something deep inside her. 'Charlotte, Emmanuel, are they dead?' she asked.

'Would I be sitting here grinning at you if they were?' he replied.

She saw his grin then, the same cheeky one which had made her smile on the *Dunkirk*, but it was a minute or two before she realized what was different about him.

'Your beard,' she exclaimed. 'It's gone!'

He rubbed his bare chin. 'A change was in order,' he said.

He looked much younger without it, and although his face was very bony and gaunt, he looked much better. His eyes had regained the sparkle she had noted so often in the early days, and apart from flaking skin, he looked none the worse for their ordeal.

'Where are we?' she asked.

'In Kupang, where else? Aren't I the wonder boy getting you here?'

Mary smiled weakly, for his bragging assured her she wasn't dreaming. 'Where are the children, and the others?'

'All close by, nothing to worry about,' he said. 'Emmanuel's still weak, but he's getting better by the day. You're the one that had us in a spin.'

Mary sat up gingerly. She looked down at herself and found she was wearing a kind of shirt, long, loose-fitting and striped.

'How long have I been here?' she asked in bewilderment.

'Ten days now. You've been waking and taking food, then going off again. But you've got to take notice now. The Dutch Governor, Wanjon, wants to see you.'

Will and James helped her up and took her outside. Mary stared around her in utter surprise. Although she hadn't consciously formed any picture of the surroundings beyond the walls of the hut, she'd assumed by the amount of noise that she was in a town. In fact it was just a group of round huts, the roofs made of broad leaves. They were encircled by tall trees and thick bushes, like nothing she'd ever seen before. Around a dozen or so small, naked, brown-skinned children were playing together, and a few chickens, a couple of tethered goats and a group of old people sitting together completed the picture of a peaceful village.

'That's jungle,' James said, pointing to the trees. 'Through there,' he pointed to a well-trodden track, 'is the beach, as pretty as a picture.'

'I thought there was a town.' Mary frowned in

bewilderment. She vaguely remembered warehouses and brick-built houses at the wharf. Lots of people, hustle and bustle.

'There is, back there.' Will waved his hand vaguely. 'You and the children were brought here after you passed out.'

Will helped Mary to sit down on a log, and then, sitting with her, he and James explained what had happened. After being given some food and drink and a night's rest, they were taken to see the Dutch Governor, Timotheus Wanjon. They told him the story they had rehearsed while at sea, that their whaling ship had been wrecked back in the reef, and they'd taken to the cutter and sailed here.

'He swallowed it,' Will grinned. 'Like I told you, being first mate of a whaler, I could have my wife and kids with me. I told him I thought the captain and the rest of the crew were in the other boat and maybe they'll turn up too before long. I told them my name was Broad, wouldn't do to use Bryant in case they get to hear of the escape from Sydney.'

James then went on to say that Wanjon, who seemed an understanding, decent sort of cove, had agreed they needed clothing, food and accommodation, and as Will was a merchant sailor he could sign for whatever he needed and all bills would be passed on to the English government for payment.

'This place is heaven on earth,' Will chortled with unconcealed glee. 'Everything a man could want is here for the taking.'

For some odd reason that remark made Mary feel a

moment of disquiet. She asked Will to get the children and bring them to her, and the moment he'd gone she turned to James.

His beard was shaven too, but apart from that he looked exactly as he always had, skinny, wild-eyed and mischievous.

'I hope Will has been behaving,' she said.

'He's very full of himself,' James admitted. 'Especially when he's got the drink in him.'

'He's been getting drunk?'

'So would any red-blooded man who'd expected to die,' James replied.

He had said just what she expected, yet she sensed a faint note of sarcasm in his voice.

'Has he been bragging?'

James shrugged. 'Only to us. We humour him mostly. We all know who really got us here.'

Mary blushed, knowing he meant her. 'He did get us here,' she said staunchly. 'Maybe I bullied him, but it was his knowledge and skill that did it.'

'The loyal little wife to the end,' James said, giving her a wolf-like grin. 'Will's a lucky man.'

The moment Mary saw her children and held them in her arms again, she began to recover. Charlotte was just like any other four-year-old again, lively, inquisitive, full of mischief and prattling away about anything and everything. As the native women found her utterly beguiling she led a charmed life, being constantly fed with titbits, played with and petted. Although still very thin, she had colour in her cheeks again, brightness in her eyes, even her hair was beginning to thicken and shine. She seemed to have forgotten what she'd so recently come through.

Emmanuel took much longer to recover. His stomach could only cope with the blandest of food, and he slept erratically. Before they left Sydney he had been taking a few hesitant steps, but this was arrested by being on the boat, and he still preferred just to sit rather than try to crawl or pull himself up on anything. But he was a very happy baby, smiling broadly at anyone who made a fuss of him, and everyone adored him because of his blond hair and blue eyes.

As for the other men, they had all recovered. Nat and Samuel Bird still had scars from sunburn, and Jamie had been weakened further by dysentery, but was now on the mend. Bill and William Moreton looked particularly well, for their darker skins had turned a rich brown, making them look almost like the natives. They were happy too, working in the dock, loading and unloading ships by day, coming back to the peaceful village by night where the native women would giggle flirtatiously as they cooked for them.

It seemed to Mary that God had not only answered her prayers and got them all here safely, but was showering her with extra blessings. The climate in Kupang was perfect, hot but not overpoweringly so, there was an abundance of food, and its people were happy and generous. It was so beautiful too, with the white sandy beaches, crystal-blue sea and lush green jungle.

Yet over and above the kindness and comfort they enjoyed now was the admiration and respect shown to Mary. Word had got around that it was she who had provided the men with the will to make it here, and everyone, from Wanjon right down to the poorest of the natives, had taken her and her children to their hearts. She had never known admiration before. As a girl in Fowey she had been constantly rebuked for being unfeminine. When she went to Plymouth she was laughed at for being so unworldly. Then, after her arrest, she was treated with utter contempt and cruelty. Even when Will became something of a hero in Sydney, she was vilified as being in some way unworthy of him.

All at once she was a person in her own right, considered brave, steadfast and intelligent. When the Assistant Governor's wife gave her some new clothes, she was even told she looked beautiful by several men. Mary couldn't put into words what it meant to put on a pretty pink dress, to wear a petticoat soft as thistledown beneath it. She might have lost her peachy bloom of youth through the sun and wind, she might be as skinny as a stray dog, but she no longer looked like a felon or a beggar.

She felt feminine now, somehow worldly-wise and special. These good people who smiled at her with such warmth didn't know she had been in chains, or forced to barter her body just to stay alive. And she could forget that too, for she had saved her children from a life of hunger and degradation. Her plan to escape from New South Wales had worked, without loss of life. She had achieved what most people would consider impossible.

To Mary, Kupang was everything she'd ever dreamed of and more. The busy port had much in common with Plymouth, in as much as ships came in from every quarter of the globe. Because it was a major trading centre for the Dutch East India Company, it also had a rich and diverse brew of every nationality and religion. Up on the hills were grand houses where rich merchants' wives sat gossiping in beautiful exotic gardens. There were elegant townhouses where Mary saw dusky maids with almond eyes and snowy-white aprons polishing the door knockers and sweeping the steps. And while it was true that there were far more of the crudest of shacks for the workers than grand places, and disreputable boarding-houses, brothels and bars frequented by the sailors, it all gave the place more colour and vibrancy.

She would remind herself when she saw the many beggars here that at least they weren't cold and wet like their counterparts back in England. They could sit in the sunshine smiling at those who dropped alms into their bowls, they could sleep on the beach in comparative comfort, and fruit grew in abundance, free for the picking.

Mary had fallen in love with Kupang for giving her and her children back their health, for the kindness she'd received. She wanted nothing more than to stay here forever, to live the simple native life, fishing, collecting honey, swimming and bringing up happy, healthy children. She felt drunk on the aroma of sandalwood, which wafted through the village on the lightest of breezes. It clung to her clothes and skin, and she heard it was the island's main export. She felt she and Will had a future here, and they could live happily forever.

'Pssst!'

Mary was just putting Emmanuel down to sleep in the hut she and Will had been given to live in, and she jumped at the hiss from the doorway. She turned to see James Martin beckoning to her. 'I'll be with you in a minute,' she said, assuming his reluctance to come inside was from propriety. 'Has Will sent you with a message?'

Will had been absent a great deal in the past three or four weeks. He usually claimed this was through work in the port, but she knew perfectly well he was in a bar somewhere getting drunk. She just hoped James hadn't come to tell her that he'd signed on a ship and left her. That was what he'd threatened to do several times.

'No. But come outside.'

Mary bent to kiss Emmanuel, and after tucking a blanket around him she joined James outside. Her smile froze when she saw James's expression. He looked haunted.

'What's wrong?' she asked.

'Everything,' James snapped, and taking her arm pulled her away from the hut towards the jungle surrounding the village. 'A group of English sailors came into port just now in open boats,' he whispered. 'They were ship-wrecked back in those Straits we came through.'

'So?' she exclaimed.

James rubbed his hands over his face distractedly.

'Don't you see? As soon as they are taken to Wanjon,

he's going to assume they are the rest of the crew from our supposed wreck. Bloody Will, he could never tell a story without adding some embroidery.'

Mary winced. She had been cross with Will when she heard he hadn't stuck to the exact story they'd planned while out at sea. He should have said that the whaler sank and they were the only survivors. That way it would all have been cut and dried. But once Will had Wanjon's sympathy he couldn't stop embellishing the story and added there were other survivors in another boat. Why he said this Mary didn't know, but as a result Wanjon would be duty-bound at least to make inquiries about the missing men.

Mary's heart skipped a beat. James was right, this was likely to be their undoing.

'Have they come from Port Jackson?' she asked.

'No. From Tahiti in a ship called the *Pandora*. Captain Edwards, the master of the ship, had been out searching for the mutineers from the *Bounty*. He's still got ten he captured. The rest went down with the *Pandora*.'

Mary gasped. They had all heard about the mutiny on the *Bounty* from Detmer Smith back in Sydney, and they were even more intrigued when they arrived here in Kupang to discover that coincidentally this was where Captain Bligh and eighteen of his men landed two years earlier, having been cast adrift in an open boat by the mutineers.

While Mary had no way of knowing whether Captain Bligh deserved his plight or not, one thing she did know was that if the English Navy had sent out another ship to bring the mutineers in, the captain wasn't going to be a soft touch like Wanjon.

'We'll be called in for questioning,' she said, her stomach turning over. 'Oh God, James! What are we going to do? It's easy enough to fool someone who doesn't speak much English, but it won't be so easy with an English sea captain.'

James half smiled. One of the things he liked most about Mary was how quick she was to grasp things. 'If we just stick to our story, we might be all right. Four months is far too short a time for the news of our escape to have reached England, and I doubt this Captain Edwards could have heard it anywhere else.'

Mary thought for a moment. If James did the talking, she was pretty certain he could convince anyone they were the crew of a whaler. But an English captain would want to know where the ship came from, the name of its owner and a great deal more information than they could plausibly invent. Then there was Will!

'What if Will gets drunk and starts bragging?' she asked.

'That's what I really came to talk about,' James said, putting his hand on her arm. 'Mary, you've got to take him in hand, make him stay away from the bars, and the port too, until these men sail off.'

'And how am I going to do that?' she asked.

'You're a clever woman,' he smiled. 'You'll find a way.'

After James had gone to round up the other men and warn them of the danger they were in, Mary called

Charlotte, who had been playing with some other children, and put her to bed with Emmanuel.

It was growing dark now, and she sat with the children until Charlotte fell asleep. As she looked down at their peaceful little faces, tears trickled down her cheeks. She had put them through so much, taken them almost to the jaws of death, and now there was a further threat to their safety.

Was she jinxed? Had some evil spell been cast over her at birth that meant her whole life would be an endless round of suffering and anguish? She had reconciled herself to the fact that Will might leave her. She didn't want him to, for despite his faults she cared deeply for him, but she knew she could cope with that. She had also realized that she was unlikely ever to get back to England, with or without Will. But that didn't seem to matter either. The only really important thing to her was to keep her children safe, happy, healthy and well fed. Until now she had believed she could do that here, with or without Will, for she knew that the other men, particularly Sam Broome and James Martin, held her in high regard.

It was strange, considering she wasn't a real beauty, that she had some kind of inexplicable power over men: Lieutenant Graham, Tench, Detmer Smith, and Will too, though he fought against it. Was it likely to work on this Captain Edwards, or even Wanjon?

She went outside later and sat down on a low stool by the door. It was dark now and very quiet, just a few people sitting by their fires, talking in low voices. A crescent moon hung above the palm trees, and Mary could hear waves breaking on the shore in the distance. It was paradise here, and until James had told her this disturbing news, she would have been only too happy to stay for ever.

Should she go now and try to find Will? She glanced back at the hut and decided against that. It was too late to ask someone to keep an ear out for her children, and if Will was drunk he would only be abusive.

She wondered if he had a woman in the port, as he often didn't come home at all. Now she came to think of it, he hadn't made love to her once since they arrived here. Was that because she had been sick? Because he was afraid she might get pregnant again, or just because he felt he wasn't the big man now she was the one who was admired and respected?

Mary had never been above using sex as a lure to get Will to fall in with her plans before, but she wished she had some other option now. Why should she have to appease him just to get him to listen to her? Surely any decent man faced with a potentially dangerous situation for his wife, children and friends would happily stay sober, lie low and keep quiet until it had gone away?

It was some hours later that Mary heard him stumbling down the path into the village. She knew by the unsteadiness of his feet that he was very drunk, and it would be wiser to wait until morning to tackle him. He fell into the hut, crashing down on to the floor, not even making it to the sleeping mat, and was out cold within seconds.

Birds singing and squawking woke Mary up. It was barely dawn, but just light enough to see that Will was stretched out on his back, a few feet from her. He stank of sweat and rum, and his shirt and breeches were filthy, perhaps, as he so often claimed, from unloading a ship.

Swallowing her revulsion, she moved nearer to him and snuggled into his chest, unbuttoning his shirt and running her fingers over his chest.

'Get off,' he growled. 'Can't a man sleep in peace?'

'Take your clothes off and come on to the mat with me,' she whispered, kissing his chest and moving her hand down to the buttons on his breeches.

'Leave me alone, woman,' he snapped, pushing her away harshly. 'If I wanted that I could get it in the port.'

'So this is just a place to sleep, is it?' Mary retorted angrily. 'If you don't come back here to see me and the children, bugger off for good.'

Even as she said it she knew it was a mistake. He leaped up and kicked out at her, sending her flying back to where Charlotte and Emmanuel lay asleep.

'You're a she-devil,' he yelled. 'My luck ran out when I got stuck with you. What you want is a lap-dog. But I'll never be one. I'm off on the next ship to be free of you.'

His boot had caught her in the ribs and it hurt badly, but it was the venom in his voice which hurt more.

'Shut up and listen to me,' she insisted. 'There's some English naval men arrived in open boats. Didn't James find you last night to warn you?'

She saw a flicker of something flash across his face, and knew James had found him, but Will had probably been too drunk to take in what he'd said.

'We're all in danger,' she went on, her voice cracking

with fear. 'This is no time for being spiteful. We've got to plan what we're going to say. You've got to stop drinking and keep your head clear.'

For a moment she thought he was going to calm down, but instead an angry red flush swept across his face. He had put on weight in the two months they'd been here, and he looked like a giant as he glowered down at her.

'I'm sick of you telling me what to do,' he snarled. 'You can lead the others round by the nose like prize geldings, but not me. I'm not afraid of some arse of an English officer. No one's going to put me in chains again, especially you.'

He wheeled round and left the hut, taking a swipe at the door post as he left, which trembled from the force. She could hear him muttering as he went off up the path to the port, and her heart sank.

For the next few days Mary lived in acute fear, expecting at any moment to be summoned to Wanjon's house. He had been very kind to her at their only meeting after she had recovered from her sickness. He had praised her for her fortitude, made a fuss of the children, and asked her to come to him if she needed further help at any time. She felt he was the kind of honourable man who, if she had been able to admit the truth about herself in the first place, might very well have protected her now. But men like that weren't likely to feel much sympathy when they felt they had been duped in the first place.

To make matters worse for her, Will continued to stay away. The other men told her he was drinking even more, swaggering around the town as if he was a ship's captain. James Martin, William Moreton and Samuel Bird had all tried to make him see sense and retreat back to the village and keep out of sight as they were doing. But Will would have none of it; he even said that he'd completed his sentence so no one could touch him.

'The bastard doesn't care that he'll bring us all down,' William Moreton admitted to Mary one evening. 'I wish to God we'd left him stranded in White Bay.'

Mary looked at each of the men grouped around her and her heart ached at their fearful expressions. They had become like brothers to her in the weeks at sea, each sharing some personal story with her, whether about their mother, the crime for which they were sentenced, or a girl they loved back home in England. They had behaved like gentlemen to her, and Emmanuel and Charlotte would go to any one of them for comfort as easily as they went to Will. They weren't bad men, just boys who went astray for a while and had surely paid the full price for their crimes. They had been semi-starved, savagely flogged and sent to the other side of the world in terrible hardship.

Mary knew she couldn't just watch and wait while her husband, their so-called friend, acted like a fool and put them all in jeopardy. She had to stop him.

'I'll try to talk to him again,' she said. 'Stay here with the children. I'll go up to the port.'

Mary found Will in the third bar she looked in. He was sprawled on a bench, a half-empty bottle of rum on the table in front of him, and several days' growth of beard on his chin. There were five or six other men near him, yet from Mary's viewpoint, looking through a dusty window, they didn't look like real friends, just drinking companions.

It was the first time she'd been to the port after dark, and her heart was pounding with fright, for she'd already been accosted twice by foreign sailors. She knew that most if not all of the women out on the crowded streets were whores. She was frightened to go into the bar, for she couldn't count on Will protecting her.

Taking a deep breath and tightening her shawl over her shoulders, she walked in and went straight up to Will.

'Please come home, Will,' she begged him. 'Emmanuel's ill.'

She knew he would be angry when he discovered this wasn't so, but it was the only thing she could think of which might make him come with her without an ugly scene.

He looked at her suspiciously, his eyes barely focusing. 'What's wrong with him?'

'He's got a fever,' she said quickly. 'Please come, Will, I'm worried about him.'

There was a titter of laughter from the men he was drinking with. Mary realized they probably didn't speak English and therefore they might think she was a whore offering herself to him. 'Please, Will,' she pleaded. 'Come now.'

His lip curled back disdainfully as he glanced at his

companions and the bottle of rum. Thankfully it seemed his son had a greater value, for he got up unsteadily.

'I'll be back,' he said self-importantly to the other men, and they grinned, showing rotten teeth. One made a crude gesture with his fist.

Out in the noisy, crowded street, Mary sped on ahead so Will couldn't question her, leaving him lumbering along behind. But when they reached the narrow path to the village, Mary had to slow down in the pitch darkness, and it was only then that she became afraid of how he'd react when he found she'd dragged him away from his drink on false pretences.

'He's coming,' she said as she got into the clearing where the men were sitting by the fire waiting for her. Nat's big eyes were even bigger with fear, Jamie was white-faced, and even Bill, the tough one, was chewing on his knuckles. Mary made a kind of hopeless gesture with her hands, hoping that would warn them she hadn't yet had an opportunity to talk to Will, and she didn't expect him to be receptive.

'Will!' James exclaimed as he came staggering out into the clearing. 'Where've you been hiding? We need to talk to you.'

'Not now, Emmanuel's sick,' Will retorted, his face tightening to see them all there.

'He's not sick,' Mary said quietly. 'I said that to get you back here.'

'You did what?' Will said, glowering at her.

'I had to, it was the only way,' she replied, taking a step back from him in case he took a swing at her. 'We're all

344

worried. It isn't just your freedom you're risking, it's all of ours.'

'That's right, Will,' James agreed. 'We're all in this together. Or so we thought.'

Will looked slowly round the group of men, then shrugged. 'I promised to get you away from the camp. I did that, brought you here. Do you expect me to wet-nurse you forever too?'

'None of us need wet-nursing,' Bill growled at him, getting to his feet and clenching his fists. By the light of the fire he looked menacing, but Will didn't appear to notice. 'There's questions being asked about us all around town,' Bill went on. 'You're drawing even more attention to us all by getting drunk and shooting your mouth off. You should be staying here with Mary and your children.'

Will turned to Mary, his face dark with fury. 'You bitch,' he spat out. 'Thought you'd trap me here by getting them all to side with you, did you? Can't you get it into your thick head I'm sick of you? Next boat out I'll be on it.'

Without drawing breath once, Will embarked on a cruel verbal onslaught. That he wasn't legally married to her, that she was a nag, a whore and she brought him down. He claimed he could have sailed off with Detmer Smith but he didn't because he'd promised to get his friends to freedom. 'And I did,' he finally roared out. 'It was me who sailed us here, and you've even robbed me of that by making out you planned the whole thing and kept us all going.'

'I've not said a word about anything,' Mary said

truthfully. She was afraid of Will now, she'd never seen him quite this angry before.

'That's right, she hasn't,' Sam Broome spoke up. 'But we all know the truth about what went on at sea, Will. We couldn't have made it without her. She might not have navigated, but she sure as hell gave us the spirit to keep on. You're a bag of wind, Will. And that wind will get us all hanged.'

Will drew back his fist and punched out at Sam, knocking him to the ground. 'Let's see who's a bag of wind,' he yelled. 'You want her, then take her, you're welcome to the scheming little witch. Like I said, I'm off on the next ship.'

Bill and Sam grabbed Will, both of them desperately trying to hold him fast until James could talk some sense into him. But Will shrugged them off and backed away towards the path to the port.

'Don't come near me,' he roared. 'I'm sick of the lot of you, clinging to my shirt-tails one minute, doing me down the next. I can sail out of here, my skill is in demand. None of you have anything without me.'

He turned and went off up the path, and Bill started off after him. 'Don't,' Mary said, putting a restraining hand on his arm. 'It will only make him more determined.'

'What shall we do?' Jamie Cox asked, his voice trembling.

'Let's hope he does get the next ship out,' Mary said, and went to help Sam up off the ground. 'He's more trouble than he's worth.'

*

It was two days later, soon after dawn, that Mary heard the ominous sound of tramping boots coming towards the village.

She had woken earlier with a strange sense of foreboding, and when she heard the sound she immediately recognized it as soldiers marching. There was no other plausible reason for them to come to the village, it had to be for her and the men.

Her first thought was to grab the children and flee into the jungle, but she quashed this desire immediately, for it would only confirm they had something to hide. So she put on her pink dress, put her feet into the shoes she'd been given and never yet worn, and quickly brushed her hair. Then, picking Emmanuel, still sleeping, up in her arms, she went out to greet the soldiers with what she hoped was an innocent-looking smile on her face.

Chapter fifteen

'There is no point in denying it, Mary.' Wanjon sighed in exasperation. 'I know you escaped from the penal colony, your husband told me.'

At Wanjon's words Mary felt as if she was tumbling into a black, bottomless pit, from which there would never be any way out.

She and the children had been separated from the men as soon as they arrived at the Castle gaol, so they had no opportunity to confer about what they were going to say. They didn't know either whether Will had been arrested too. But Mary found herself being treated gently by the soldiers, the cell she was put in was clean, and she was brought water, bread and some fruit, so that gave her every hope.

Yet as she watched the sun rise through the tiny grilled window overlooking the port, and gradually move directly overhead, without anyone coming to her, her heart began to sink.

'Why have we got to stay here, Mumma?' Charlotte asked. She had accepted the situation patiently so far, but now she was getting restless. 'I don't like it here, I want to go home.'

'We have to stay because a man wants to ask us some questions,' Mary said, distractedly running her fingers through the child's hair. 'Now, be a good girl and let's play with Emmanuel.'

But Mary had no heart to encourage Emmanuel to toddle between the two of them, and tell him what a clever boy he was for walking unaided. She was terribly afraid that this tiny cell, less than four feet wide by six feet long, was going to be their home for the unforeseeable future.

Charlotte looked so pretty now, dark curls framing her small sun-tanned face, her bare arms and legs plump and dimpled. She reminded Mary very much of her sister Dolly, for she had the same pouting lips and turned-up nose. All the care and attention over the last two months, and the company of other children, had given her more confidence; she'd even learned many of the native words.

It seemed to Mary that Charlotte had left babyhood behind and become a little girl now. Only a few days before she had refused to put on the dull grey dress she had been given when they first arrived here, and insisted on wearing a brightly coloured one her mother had made from a length of locally produced material. Mary had wanted to keep it for best, as she did her own pink dress, but Charlotte had made such a fuss that she'd given in.

Clearly Charlotte had forgotten that back in Sydney Cove she had only one dress, so worn, faded and patched it had fallen apart on the boat. Mary was very glad her daughter appeared not to remember the colony, or how they all were when they arrived here, fainting with hunger

349

and thirst, their skin and hair crawling with lice. Mary had managed to blank it out too, but now, faced with the possibility they might be sent back there, it was back in the forefront of her mind again. It was bad enough imagining herself living that way again, but how could Charlotte stand it now that she knew a different kind of life? As for Emmanuel, his little stomach couldn't possibly take a harsh prison diet. He wasn't strong, just the slightest variation in his food brought on sickness again.

Later, when both he and Charlotte had fallen asleep, their heads on her lap as she sat on the floor, Mary stroked Emmanuel's blond hair back from his eyes and choked back her tears. He was almost too pretty to be a boy, with his pure blond hair touching his shoulders, eyes like periwinkles, and translucent fair skin. She had kept him alive by sheer will-power on the boat, but if they had to stay in this gaol, or be sent back to the colony, how could she find that strength again? She knew that back home in Cornwall he'd be one of those babies people called 'a special one'. That meant the child had the look of an angel, and therefore was not long for this world.

Mary could tell from the length of the shadows outside the window that it was about five in the afternoon when the gaoler unlocked the door of her cell. He was swarthy-skinned, with almond eyes, and he said something unintelligible to her, beckoning for her to follow him. Holding Emmanuel in her arms, and taking Charlotte by the hand, she was finally taken to Wanjon.

He was in one of the upper chambers of the Castle, a

gloomy, cool room which presumably was his office for along with a desk there was a lamp and books on shelves, and many personal items, like a painting of a woman who was perhaps his wife, and a snake made of beads adorning a wooden bowl of fruit.

The white jacket Wanjon had been wearing the previous time she met him was slung on the back of his chair, his white shirt was crumpled and he smelled of sweat. Mary had thought him very personable and pleasant at that first meeting, but now he looked tired, hot and irritated. He was small and stout, with jet-black hair slicked down with oil and parted in the middle. She assumed from his name, almond eyes and coffee-coloured skin that he was native to this country, but he must have been well educated, probably in Holland or even England, as he could speak both English and Dutch fluently, along with the local language.

He began to ask her questions about the whaling ship: how many hands there were, the master's name, where the ship was registered, and the last port they'd called into before the ship was wrecked.

Everything except where the ship was registered had been rehearsed by them all back in the cutter. But even as Mary began to spill out that the master was from Rio de Janeiro, his name was Marcia Consuella, there were eighteen hands, and they'd sailed out of Cape Town, she knew none of it would stand up to close scrutiny. When Emmanuel began to cry, she hoped that Wanjon would be irritated enough to give up.

Sadly, the only effect it had was to make him stop

wasting any more time and come out with what he really believed.

'This is all lies, Mary,' he said, getting up and pacing up and down the room, his hands behind his back. 'You were not on a whaler. You have never been on a whaler. You stole the boat back in New South Wales. You are escaped prisoners.'

Mary jogged Emmanuel up and down in her arms as she protested he was badly mistaken. And it was at that point that he informed her Will had told him everything.

It took Mary some time to come to terms with the shock. She had asked the guard earlier if her husband was being held here, and he'd said he wasn't. Of course the guard had only a word or two of English, and her knowledge of his language was about the same, yet he appeared to understand what she asked. Will stood out in Kupang because of his size and blond hair, and Mary was sure that if he was in the Castle, everyone would know. She'd begun to think he might have made good the threat he'd come out with two nights ago and signed on a ship.

'My husband, though it grieves me to admit it, likes to brag,' she said wildly. 'Perhaps he thought that was a more exciting story to tell than the truth.'

'I have seen the log he kept,' Wanjon responded wearily.

It was all Mary could do not to scream when she heard that, for she had begged Will to destroy the log, even before they arrived here.

'This is all somewhat embarrassing for me,' Wanjon went on as he continued to pace around the room. 'You see, but for the arrival of Captain Edwards, I would have put you all on board the very next ship bound for England. But Captain Edwards wanted to know more about you all, so I had to bring in your husband and he told me everything.'

'Will peached on us?' she asked incredulously.

'Peached?' Wanjon frowned. 'What does that mean?'

'Told on us. Turned King's evidence,' Mary said.

'Yes, he told on you,' Wanjon nodded. 'Some men have no loyalty when they think they can save their own skin.'

Mary broke down then, she could no longer hold back her tears. 'Please, sir,' she pleaded with him, 'don't send us back there. Emmanuel still isn't well, Charlotte has only just recovered. They'll die if we have to go back.'

'My dear, this is beyond my jurisdiction,' Wanjon said with a dismissive wave of his hand. 'Your English naval officer, Captain Edwards, is the only one with the authority to decide what is to be done with you.'

He opened the door and gave an order to the guard.

'You will go back to your cell now,' he said, turning back to Mary. 'You will be brought food and water. I am not a cruel man, Mary. You and your children will be treated well during your stay here.'

Wanjon stared out of the window for some time after Mary had been led away and his heart felt heavy. He had accepted the men's story about how they made it here after their ship was wrecked, purely because it was so similar to what had happened to Captain Bligh two years earlier. It didn't even cross his mind that they might have escaped from the penal colony in New South Wales. Who would think a bunch of mere convicts could make a journey of some 3,000 miles in an open boat?

Even Captain Edwards, for all his seamanship, had come to grief in the Torres Straits, but then he was a bull-headed man who thought he knew enough to sail through such dangerous waters at night. The man clearly had no heart, for he had put his fourteen captured mutineers into a box-like structure on the deck, leaving them there in all winds and weathers, their legs and arms shackled. When his ship was going down he refused to let any of the crew unchain them, and it was only thanks to one of the men who ignored the order that ten of them survived.

Wanjon sighed deeply. It grieved him to hand Mary and her companions over to Edwards, for he knew they would suffer sorely at his hands. Mary was an exceptionally courageous woman, and whatever the crime that led her to be transported, she had already paid dearly for it. As for those innocent little children, they had been a hair's-breadth from death when they arrived here in Kupang. What right had any government, be it English, Dutch or any other nationality, to send them somewhere where their early death could be the only outcome?

It was over a week before Mary got to see any of the men. She was told by one of the guards who spoke a little English that they were being kept in one cell, Will included.

Wanjon had been as good as his word to Mary. She'd

received wholesome food for herself and the children and was even brought a sleeping mat, a blanket and water to wash with. Daily, she was taken down to the yard with the children so they could have some fresh air and exercise in the Castle courtyard. Sometimes she even allowed herself to believe the Dutch Governor would intervene and let her go free. For surely a man who could treat her and her children with such kindness would not send her away to be hanged, and leave Charlotte and Emmanuel orphaned?

So when the guard told her she might visit the men in their cell, she couldn't help but think that this was the first step to being released. The English captain hadn't come to see her, perhaps he'd even left Kupang.

The men's cell was much lower down in the Castle than hers, a big, dark, dank room with its slit-like window too high up in the wall to see out. They crowded round her, kissing and hugging the children, asking how she had been treated, and it was a minute or two before she noticed Will had remained sitting on a stool, his back to her.

'Don't you want to see Emmanuel and Charlotte?' she asked.

'He doesn't deserve to see them ever again,' Bill growled. 'He peached on us.'

Mary looked hard at her friends, pleased to see that they all still looked well and their clothes were clean. But their glances towards Will were malevolent. Even Jamie Cox and Samuel Bird, who had followed him blindly for so long, looked as though they hated him.

Mary had had time to consider what Will was supposed to have done, and she'd come to the conclusion that he was unlikely to have gone purposely to Wanjon to inform on them. He would know that he would be counted as guilty as the rest of them, and though he might not be hanged for escaping because his sentence was already up, stealing Captain Phillip's cutter would still warrant a death sentence.

'I really can't believe that of Will,' Mary said, moving closer to him. He still hadn't turned to look at her. 'Tell me. Did you inform on us?'

'They all believe I did,' he said in a low voice. 'So you might as well too.'

Mary caught hold of his chin and jerked him round so she could see him. She gasped. He'd been badly beaten, she assumed by the other men. Both eyes were hidden by purple, swollen flesh, his lip was cut, and his shirt was covered in bloodstains.

'You deserve that for ignoring my warnings to keep out of sight,' she said sharply. 'You're a louse, Will Bryant, a loud-mouthed, full-of-yourself, no-good bastard. But I still can't believe you'd turn us in.'

'I didn't, I swear I didn't,' he said hoarsely. 'I was drunk, some English sailors came in the bar, and we got swapping stories.'

Mary nodded, she could imagine it. The other men had talked about what they'd been through in their open boat after the shipwreck, and Will had to go one better and boast he'd been through worse.

Still she was furious with him – if she'd come face

to face with him the day after they'd been arrested, she would have tried to kill him with her bare hands. But time, and the belief that Wanjon might still intervene on their behalf, had calmed her down enough at least to try to understand why and how Will had got them into this.

'So, when were you brought here?' she asked.

'That same night,' he said weakly. 'I was just leaving the bar and the guards grabbed me. They took me to Wanjon early the next morning. He said you were all on your way here. He'd already got my log of the voyage from the place I was staying in. I couldn't do anything but tell the truth, he'd got me cornered.'

Mary closed her eyes in an effort to calm herself. She felt confused by conflicting emotions. She had always cared a great deal for Will, and it was tragic to see him brought low like this. Although he should have kept his big mouth shut, she also knew none of them would have stood up to close and prolonged questioning. Their story was too full of holes.

But she certainly didn't blame the other men for beating him. Both James and William had said he should destroy the log, and she knew exactly why he hadn't. He saw himself as a hero, and he wanted the whole world to acknowledge him as such. Even if he hadn't blurted it out here when drunk, he would have shouted it out sometime. The log was proof of his incredible feat. He probably hoped he could make money out of it too.

'Why couldn't you be satisfied with what we had?' she

asked bitterly. 'We were safe, Emmanuel was getting better. We were all happy, for God's sake. But you had to have more. Drink, other women –'

'I didn't have other women,' he interrupted her.

Mary gave a hollow laugh. 'I'd bet anything that you were staying with some whore. She'll be the one that handed the log to Wanjon or one of his guards, for a bit more money than you gave her.'

He turned his head away and she knew then that that much was true. It hurt so badly that she felt sick.

'I might not be the prettiest, cleverest woman in the world,' she said brokenly, 'but I was true to you, Will. Even when we were starving back in the camp, you never had to fear I would steal some of your rations, or your money. I made the best of what was there, and I should have killed to keep you and the children safe.'

'I'm sorry,' he whispered.

'Is "sorry" going to help Charlotte and Emmanuel when we are hanged?' she asked, her face contorted with anguish.

'We won't be hanged,' he said.

'We will be if we get sent back to England,' she retorted. 'And if we get sent back to New South Wales we'll be flogged and put in chains again.'

She turned away from him, unable to cope with the picture either of those punishments brought to mind. She would rather have died at sea than live to see the day when her husband would put fame and money before her, their children and his friends.

*

On 5 October, Mary, Charlotte and Emmanuel were brought out of their cell to sail with the men on the Dutch ship *Rembang*. Captain Edwards had chartered this ship to take them, his eighteen crew members from the *Pandora* and the ten remaining captured mutineers to Batavia. Mary had no real idea where this was, all she knew was that it was another island in the Dutch East Indies with a big port. It seemed Captain Edwards planned to get another ship from there to Cape Town, then on to England.

In the two months they had been gaoled in Kupang Castle, Mary had clung to the hope that Wanjon might let her and the children stay here. She knew she had his sympathy for he sometimes let her and the other men out of the prison, always just in pairs, but it meant Mary could go to the village, let the children play on the beach and talk freely with whoever accompanied her.

She was never allowed to go with Will, however, perhaps because Wanjon thought that was too much of a risk. The only time she saw Will was in the Castle yard, and his endless apologies only served to upset her further. He was not the man she'd known so well any more. Being ostracized by the other men, especially James Martin, Jamie Cox and Samuel Bird, once his closest friends, had made him withdrawn and inclined to emotional, often nonsensical outbursts. He would frighten the children by holding them too tightly, and when Charlotte ran away from him or Emmanuel hid behind Mary's skirts, Will would cry like a child. He would tell Mary he had always loved her, and beg her to forgive him. Wearily she would say she had, but in her heart she felt she never could. Often she wished she was able to ignore him as the other men did, but pity for him got the better of her.

They were only told a few days before the *Rembang* was due to sail that they'd be on her. As Mary had found one or two people who spoke some English when she was let out of the Castle, she could only view this with further dismay.

She had learned about Captain Edwards's fearsome reputation. The tale about the *Pandora*'s 'box' where the mutineers were held and four died was common knowledge. It seemed that the *Rembang* had an extra deck. It didn't take much imagination to see that this structure, with no portholes or hatches in it, just small holes along the roof, was yet another 'box'. And that was where Captain Edwards intended to hold her and the men.

She had also been told that Wanjon had asked Captain Edwards to honour the many bills for food, accommodation and clothing Will had signed for. Edwards had refused, and Wanjon told him that he would be given no provisions for the month-long voyage unless he paid up. Mary knew that meant Edwards would have a grudge against them right from the start.

All in all, Mary knew that the trip to Batavia was going to be just like being back on the prison hulk in England, with little food, in darkness, and in chains. She was right on all counts. The extra deck had been divided into three, the front for the escaped convicts, the middle for the crew of the *Pandora*, and the aft for the mutineers. Yet even more frightening than the dark was the 'bilboes', a long pole fixed to the floor, from which sliding shackles were attached to their ankles, rendering them unable to move at all.

Mary took one last look at the port before she was shoved into their new cell. It had rained during the night, and the whole town glistened in the sunshine. She saw women from the village with babies in their arms waving to her from the wharf where stalls were piled high with fruit and vegetables. Fishermen were carrying huge baskets of freshly caught fish, and the young boy she had so often tried to converse with, who trundled a small cart laden with coconuts, called out to her. The smell of sandalwood hung in the air like an aromatic, invisible cloud, and her eyes filled with tears at saying goodbye to the place which had become so precious to her.

'Why is he doing that to you, Mumma?' Charlotte asked as one of the ship's crew fastened the shackles around Mary's ankles. 'How can you walk now?'

Mary couldn't answer, she was too overwhelmed by the impossibility of caring for both her children under these conditions. But Charlotte's questions were halted when the door was slammed shut and bolted, leaving them in pitch darkness. She let out a piercing scream, and falling over the pole in the darkness, she landed in Mary's lap on top of Emmanuel.

'The captain had a cabin for you and the children aft of the ship,' Jamie Cox said from across the darkness of the cell. 'That bastard Edwards said you had to stay in here with us. He wants his pound of flesh because he's disappointed he didn't catch all the mutineers from the *Bounty*.'

'I'll cheerfully swing for him,' James Martin growled, then after a moment's pause spoke to Will. 'Well, you've got your ship at last, big man,' he said jeeringly in the darkness. 'How d'you like your cabin? How does it feel to have yer missus and babbies with you?'

Day by day the agony of that dark cell grew worse. When the sun shone outside, it was so hot they felt they were being cooked alive; when a storm broke out, they were soaked through. They were given only the bare minimum of food and water to keep them alive, and the way they were shackled meant they couldn't even move to relieve themselves. Mary screamed for mercy, if only for Charlotte and Emmanuel, but if anyone on the ship heard her, they ignored her. On the rare occasions the door was opened, she saw for herself that the improvement in her children's health in Kupang had been undone. They sat crying in bewilderment, caked in the filth all around them, and after only a few days Emmanuel went down with fever.

The men hardly spoke. When Mary could see their faces, their eyes were haunted. Nat and Jamie whimpered in their sleep, Bill swore, and James seemed to be constantly awake, his eyes glowing in the dark. Only Sam Broome tried to pretend everything would turn out all right, but Mary knew he was acting that way for the children's benefit.

They ran into a cyclone, and water poured in, threatening to drown them. As the ship pitched and rolled, thunder crashed and lightning momentarily lit up each of their terrified faces. Mary prayed then that the ship would go down and put an end to their suffering.

They heard the crew of the *Bounty* shouting and swearing as they pitched in to help the *Rembang* men. Much later she was to hear that many of the Dutch crew went below decks to play cards while the English struggled to keep the ship off the rocks.

Will caught the fever too, crying out in his delirium for his mother. Mary could do nothing to help him, for she couldn't move and had both the children in her arms. Jamie came out of his anger at his old friend sufficiently to give him sips of water, but the mood of the other men was ugly towards Will.

'Die thinking of what you brought us to,' William Moreton shouted out on several occasions. 'I hope you burn in Hell, you bastard.'

The *Rembang* sailed into Batavia on 7 November. A whole month at sea had seemed more like a year to them. Apart from the foul conditions they were chained up in, which became worse daily, and the hunger and thirst, it was almost like being blindfolded too, for they had been unable to see out. They didn't know whether they had passed other islands, big land masses, or whether they were just sailing on the open sea. They had lost all sense of time and distance too.

Hamilton, the ship's surgeon, came into the hold briefly, holding a handkerchief over his nose against the smell but retching anyway. He barely looked at the men, but ordered that Emmanuel was to be taken to the hospital, and Mary would go with him. The remaining convicts and mutineers were to be moved to a guard ship until such time as a ship bound for England could be found.

'Charlotte must come with me too,' Mary pleaded, fearful for her little girl being imprisoned in another ship without her protection. 'She'll get sick too without me.'

Hamilton was a hard-faced man with a bushy beard. 'She'll get sick in the hospital even faster,' he said. 'They call this place the Golgotha of Europe, and the hospital is a stinking hole. But take her with you if you must.'

Mary didn't understand what he meant then as she had imagined Batavia would be much like Kupang. A month's sea voyage must mean it wasn't so very far away, and she'd heard Batavia was the centre of the Dutch East India Company's operations. But she was soon to discover the difference. The first thing she saw when she was taken up on deck was dead bodies floating in the water, and she vomited over the side.

Kupang was a place Dutch East India Company employees felt fortunate to be posted to. It might be noisy and crowded with people of every nation, but the air was clean and invigorating, the climate perfect. It was also very beautiful just beyond the town, with jungle, mountains and idyllic beaches.

But Batavia sweltered in a hot, steamy atmosphere. The Dutch had built canals through the town, and the stagnant, putrid water bred diseases that killed Europeans like flies. Mary saw that the ship's crew were reluctant to go ashore, a sure sign it wasn't a good place. She overheard one of the English sailors who had been here before claim that even the healthiest ship's crew would be decimated by fever within weeks.

As Mary was led away by two guards, carrying Emmanuel in her arms, with Charlotte trailing along behind, she looked back at her friends on the deck and tears filled her eyes.

They were all gaunt and filthy. The only touch of colour in the group was Samuel Bird's red hair, but even that was muted by dirt. Nat Lilly and Jamie Cox, the two smallest, looked like little boys. Bill Allen was making a show of looking tough, and James Martin was rubbing his eyes with his fists. Sam Broome and William Moreton were supporting each other. Then there was Will standing apart from them all, swaying on his feet with the fever.

Mary's heart sank. They all looked so sick that she felt sure she was never going to see any of them again. But the guards dragged her away, and she felt even more demoralized, for the teeming hordes of small, brown-skinned natives who milled around them were sickly-looking too.

The surgeon's words about Batavia came back to her as she saw crudely constructed shanties instead of fine houses. The sticky heat, the revolting smells and the flies which bombarded her made her feel queasy and terrified for her children.

Her first impression of the two-storey hospital was that the builders had left it only half built. A few windows were shuttered, but the rest were just holes. There was a foul-smelling bonfire smouldering in the yard in front of it, and at least a hundred people were sitting or lying outside. Many of them had filthy, bloodstained bandages around their heads or limbs, flies had settled on those too weak to swat them off, and the sound of their wailing and groaning was terrible to hear. Charlotte clutched her mother's dress, whimpering with fright, but the guards prodded Mary on through the door, which suggested to her that the people outside were in better condition than those within.

The smell inside made Mary recoil in horror. It was utterly evil, so thick she could barely breathe. She knew then that nothing short of a miracle could prevent Emmanuel from dying. Even on the ship he'd given up crying, he just lay in her arms staring up at her. She had kept trying to make him drink, but he couldn't keep anything down. One moment he was so hot she could have fried an egg on his forehead, the next he was shivering violently.

An aging nun with a filthy apron over her white habit came forward. The guards said something to her in Dutch, and she peered at Emmanuel, making a tutting sound with her tongue, and indicated that Mary was to follow her.

As they passed several rooms, Mary saw that each held thirty or forty adult patients lying on mats, but she was led into a room at the far end of the hospital where there were only babies and small children being nursed by their mothers.

The nun left after pointing out where the spare mats,

washing bowls and buckets were kept. There was no explanation as to where the water was, whether a doctor was coming, or where food came from.

Mary put two mats in a corner, laid Emmanuel down and sat Charlotte beside him, telling her not to move. Then she picked up a bucket and asked the nearest woman in sign language where she could get water.

As night fell Mary lay down with the children. She had got water from a well outside to wash all the ship's filth off them, and found a grimy kitchen from which she could get a daily meal of rice. Anything else had either to be bought from a formidable-looking native woman who presided in the kitchen, or brought in from outside.

She heard the familiar sound of rats scuttling around the room, even above the moans and cries of the mortally sick, and put her arms protectively around Charlotte and Emmanuel. Her last thoughts before she fell asleep from exhaustion were to wonder how you got food and water if you were a patient without friends or relatives, and if a doctor ever came near the hospital.

She found the answer to her questions in the next day or two by observing and communicating in sign language with the other mothers. A doctor visited occasionally but saw only those with money to pay him. A handful of Dutch nuns did what they could, but faced with the huge numbers of sick people, it was like trying to empty a lake with a thimble.

It was soon apparent to Mary that this was more of a pest house than a hospital. People were sent there in an attempt to contain infection. Those outside in the courtyard were suffering from injuries rather than disease, and often had to wait up to a week to be examined. Most of the inmates died without ever being spoken to, let alone examined, and very few made a recovery. The children's room was kept reasonably clean by the mothers, but a glance into the adult ones revealed a horrifying sight. Vomit and excreta lay on the rough wood floors, walls were splattered with blood and pus. The cries, screams and delirium of the patients were ignored.

Mary sold her pink dress on her third day there, to buy soup and milk for Emmanuel, and to have some meat and vegetables in the rice for herself and Charlotte. She thought about running away, for it would be easy enough to slip out and mingle with the crowds outside. But she couldn't bring herself to subject Emmanuel to being carried about in the hot sun, and at least in here it was cooler, with a plentiful supply of water. She had to make his last days as comfortable as possible.

Her isolation was the worst aspect of the hospital. There were as many nationalities as there were in Kupang, but no one she had met so far spoke English. There was no one to turn to for help. Dying children were a fact of life here, it seemed, and even Emmanuel's ethereal appearance extracted no sympathy. She bathed him with water to cool him down, wrapped him in blankets when he shivered, squeezed water into his mouth drop by drop, but each day he grew weaker.

She desperately wanted to share her anxiety for him with someone. She was terrified to think of what would become of Charlotte if she caught the fever herself. It was no place for a healthy child to be either – daily, Charlotte was subjected to sights that would make even an adult turn pale. It wasn't fair that she had to spend every day surrounded by desperately sick children. In many ways it was worse for her than being on the ship – at least there she'd had the men to tell her stories and sing to her.

Sometimes Mary thought she might go mad with the noise, smells, heat and filth. She wondered too what she'd do when the money from selling her pink dress ran out. All she could do was blame Will, and vow to herself that when she got out of here she'd kill him.

Towards the end of November, one of the nuns who spoke a few words of English told her Will had been brought into the hospital too. Even if Mary had wanted to see him, she couldn't, for Emmanuel was far too sick. She had begun bribing one of the other mothers to get the rice and water for her because she didn't dare leave his side.

On 1 December, Emmanuel died in Mary's arms. She was rocking him and singing him a lullaby, when he just stopped breathing.

'What's wrong, Mumma?' Charlotte whispered, as she saw tears coursing down her mother's face.

'He's gone,' was all Mary could say brokenly. 'Gone to live with the angels.'

She had expected it. She had believed she was prepared. Day by day she had seen his flesh shrink until he looked like a little wizened monkey, yet even in his sickness, his small fingers had felt for hers. Now suddenly those fingers were motionless and cold, and she wanted to scream out her pain.

He hadn't even survived to see his second birthday, yet in the short time he'd lived, he'd given her so much joy and hope. It wasn't right that his whole life had been overshadowed by suffering, and that he should have died here in such an ugly, dirty place.

His body was taken from her by one of the nuns, to join others who had died that day, in a communal grave. Mary expected they'd come back for her when the service was due to start. But there was no service, a nun told her later. Too many people died here for that.

The following day, Mary sent Charlotte out into the yard, telling her to stay there till she came back. She was full of rage, and she wanted to find Will to tell him she held him responsible for his only son's death, before she had to go back to the guard ship.

She found him in a room at the far end of the hospital. The smell coming from it was so evil that she had to cover her nose and mouth when she looked in. There were at least fifty men inside, far more than in any other room she'd seen. They were squashed up together so tightly that they were lying in one another's vomit and faeces. The groaning and retching was so awful that she was about to turn away when she spotted Will. He was the only one not lying down.

He was almost skeletal, sitting huddled up in a corner wearing nothing but a pair of breeches. His fair hair and beard were matted with filth, his once bright blue eyes pale and red-rimmed with fever. He was twenty-nine, but he looked like a very old man.

Mary had told herself she would laugh if he was dying, she would speed his end by berating him for what he'd done to her. Yet as she stared at him, she wondered why it was she didn't feel appeased by finding him in such obvious misery.

A memory shot into her mind of him carrying her down to the sea to wash her after Emmanuel was born. He'd been so gentle and loving with her, making her forget she was a convict. That day, and on many more besides, she'd felt equal to any honoured wife and mother back home.

It had become very easy for her to believe Will was all bad. She had made herself forget that he had saved her from rape, married her to protect her, and that his skill and hard work at fishing had kept her from starvation. He had often given Charlotte part of his supper, pretending he wasn't hungry. She had been proud to be his wife, and despite Will saying he was going to get a ship home when his sentence was up, he didn't.

All at once she knew she must nurse him. Maybe she wouldn't be able to forgive him entirely, but for all that they had been to each other in the past, he deserved better than to die like a dog without one kind word.

Mary picked her way gingerly through the filth and bodies to his corner.

'It's me, Will,' she said softly as she reached his side.

She was appalled that such a big, strong man could end up like this. It reminded her of the way the convicts on the Second Fleet had been when they got them off the *Scarborough*.

'Mary!' he said weakly, trying to lift his head. 'Is it really you?'

'Yes, it really is me, Will,' she said, bending towards him. 'I've come to take care of you. First I'll get you some water, then I'll get you into a room which isn't quite so dirty and crowded.'

He caught hold of her hand. 'Emmanuel! How is he?'

She was touched that his first thought was for their son.

'He died yesterday,' she said abruptly.

'Oh no,' he groaned, squeezing her hand tighter. 'I am to blame.'

Part of her wanted to agree, to ease her own pain with spite, but the greater part of her felt soothed by having someone to share her grief with.

'No,' she whispered. 'It was the cruelty of that Captain Edwards, this stinking place, and bad luck.'

He opened his eyes wider and tears ran down his cheeks. 'You can say that after the way I treated you?'

Mary didn't trust herself to answer that question. 'I'll get some water,' was all she said.

'Charlotte! Where is she?' he asked, looking stricken.

'She's fine. I told her to wait outside while I came to see you.'

'Thank God for that,' he said, crossing himself.

She got Will drinking water, helped him into a cleaner room, then washed him all over. It was horrifying to see

372

his once big, strong body so emaciated, and she browbeat one of the nuns into giving her a clean shirt for him so that at least he still could have some dignity.

Mary knew he was going to die; since being in this place for three weeks she'd learned the signs. But she told him he would get better, stroked his forehead until he fell asleep and then crept away to get Charlotte.

As she went out into the backyard by the well, she paused for a moment, suddenly aware that this was a perfect time to escape, before Emmanuel's death was reported and Captain Edwards sent guards for her. She could sell her good boots, buy some provisions, then take off into the jungle with Charlotte. She had made friends with the natives in Kupang, and she could do the same here. Maybe in a few months, with a false name and a plausible story, she could get on a ship out of here.

Mary took a few steps towards Charlotte who was sitting on the ground making mud pies in the damp earth around the well. She was dirty, thin and pale-faced and moved lethargically. She hadn't been that way in Kupang, and it hurt Mary to see what the prison regime on the ship had done to her. It was another very good reason to run for it now while they still could.

'Did you see the man?' Charlotte asked, looking up.

That question caught Mary short. All she had said to the child when she told her to stay out here was that 'she had to see a man'. If Charlotte had known who the man was, she would have wanted to see him too. She had been asking, sometimes several times each day, when they were going to see Dada again.

Will had always treated Charlotte as if she were his own daughter. When Emmanuel was born he'd made no distinction between the two children. Even when they had rows, he never once used Charlotte's parentage as a weapon. Will loved Charlotte, and that was evident today when, sick as he was, he wanted to know she was safe.

So how could Mary run out on this man and leave him to die alone?

She lowered the bucket down into the well, filled it and pulled it back up.

'Let me wash you,' she said, pulling a rag out of her pocket. 'We're going to see Dada.'

The heat seemed to increase with every day, and Will became weaker and weaker. Mary sold her boots to buy food for the three of them, but he never managed more than a couple of spoonfuls before falling asleep again.

When he was awake he would lie there looking at Mary, just the way Emmanuel had. He found it too much of an effort to talk, but he would smile when Mary told him stories about her old neighbours in Fowey, of smuggling yarns she'd heard from her father, and described the harbour and the people who worked there.

Every day, at least two people in the room died, and their places were quickly filled again. When Will was asleep, Mary would wash the others and give them water. It made no difference to her whether they were natives, Chinese or Dutch, they all had that same pitiful, childlike expression in their eyes, and at least when they took their last breath they weren't alone.

The nuns looked at Mary as if they thought her mad. Yet sometimes they brought Charlotte an egg or some fruit, which seemed to indicate they also had some sympathy for the English convict woman who was risking her own health staying in such a hell-hole to nurse her husband.

'Is it Christmas yet?' Will croaked out one evening just as the light was fading.

'Three more days,' Mary said.

'Ma always used to make a plum pudding,' he said.

Mary smiled, for she could visualize her own mother stirring ingredients in a big basin at the kitchen table.

'And mine,' she said.

'Ma used to tell us all to make a wish as we stirred it,' Will said in little more than a whisper. 'If I had one now I'd wish that I told you I married you because I loved you.'

Tears prickled at Mary's eyes and she wished she could believe him.

'I'm telling you the truth,' he said. His eyes were red-rimmed and sunken with the fever and he looked old and haggard, nothing like that big, handsome man she'd married. 'I fell for you on the *Dunkirk*. Even if all the beauties in England were lined up for me to choose from, I'd still have picked you.'

Mary's tears began to fall faster. If this was true, why couldn't he have told her before?

'I'm such a fool,' he sighed, as if knowing what she was

375

thinking. 'I thought if I told you, you wouldn't value me. That's why I used to say I was getting a ship home too. I wanted you to say you couldn't live without me.'

'Oh, Will,' she sighed, and took his hand and kissed it. She knew it was true now, Will wouldn't dare go to his death with a lie on his conscience.

He drifted off into unconsciousness again then, clearly the effort of talking was too much. Mary lay down beside him and held his hand for some time, thinking over what he'd said.

When she was a young girl, she'd always imagined this thing people called love hit you like a ripe apple falling on your head. Her wild desire for Tench confirmed this idea. Yet was that really love? Wasn't it more likely that she only felt that way about Tench because he was kind and interested in her at a time when she desperately needed something lovely to take her mind off reality? Would she have continued to feel such passion for him if they'd been able to live together forever?

The circumstances that led up to her marrying Will were hardly romantic. Yet despite her belief it was purely a marriage of convenience, there was passionate love-making, a warm and comfortable relationship, they could talk about anything together, they laughed a great deal. They were friends.

She thought most intelligent people would define that as love.

The first rays of daylight were slanting through the window when Mary felt Will tossing and turning. She touched his forehead and found he was burning hot again, yet shivering at the same time.

'I'm here,' she whispered, sitting up and reaching for the cloth and the bucket of water to cool him down.

'I'm so sorry about what I did,' he gasped out.

'It doesn't matter any more,' she whispered back, laying the cooling cloth on his brow and stroking back his hair. 'I've forgiven you.'

All at once she realized she had. Like love, it had crept up on her unnoticed.

'Keep Charlotte safe,' he managed to get out with great difficulty.

She knew then that this was the end.

'I married you because I loved you,' she said, and kissed his hot, cracked lips. 'I still love you, and I don't want to live without you.'

She didn't know if he heard the words he'd always wanted to hear, for he slipped into unconsciousness again. She stayed beside him holding him, her head so close to his heart that she felt it when it stopped beating an hour or two later.

Chapter sixteen

It was nearly four months after Emmanuel and Will died in Batavia that the *Horssen*, a Dutch ship, sailed into Cape Town with Mary and Charlotte aboard.

'I think that's the ship that's going to take us home, Mary,' Jim Cartwright said over his shoulder while pointing towards the harbour. 'Come and look! The sight of one of His Majesty's ships will cheer you.'

Mary smiled weakly. Jim was one of the crew from the wrecked *Pandora*. In the last few weeks of the voyage from Batavia, when both she and Charlotte came down with the fever, he had taken it upon himself to try to cheer her. Sometimes it was with different fruits or nuts, but more often it was with jokes or chat. Mary was very grateful for his kindness, but because of her fears for her daughter, she often found it difficult to respond.

Leaving Charlotte lying on a mat on the deck, Mary went over to the rail to look. It was cheering to see Cape Town again, for she had good memories of Charlotte's christening here. Of course she had hope then, to be a pioneer in New South Wales had seemed more of a huge adventure than a punishment.

But the thirst for adventure was long gone. All

she hoped for now was that Charlotte would recover, and to be treated kindly on the last leg of the voyage home.

Yet despite her jaundiced views, she couldn't help but feel some emotion at seeing an English ship. The *Gorgon* was graceful, its deck scrubbed almost white, rope neatly coiled and brass gleaming in the sunshine. She reminded Mary of similar ships she had admired in Plymouth – foreign vessels never seemed to be so spruce and polished. With Table Mountain as its backdrop, she couldn't imagine a prettier sight. Yet however lovely the *Gorgon* looked, the chances were she would have to endure hardships aboard just as great as those she'd experienced on the way here.

She did see Will buried, and heard a prayer said over him, even if it was a communal grave and the prayer in Dutch, so she couldn't understand it. But just as she was putting her few remaining possessions together and thinking of escape again, the guards appeared. They chained her, right there in the hospital, and took her and Charlotte to the guard ship where the other men were being held.

Mary's grief at Emmanuel's death, which she supposed she'd contained while she nursed Will, erupted as soon as she was locked up again. James and the other men were distraught at the death of Emmanuel, but they had no such sympathy for Will. To be imprisoned with them again, in stifling conditions, for almost a month, with water rationed to only a couple of pints a day and hearing them constantly blaming Will for their predicament, was too much to bear. She got so low that she even wished for death.

She rallied a little when she heard that she and Charlotte were to go on the *Horssen* to Cape Town, along with the crew of the *Pandora*. James and the other men, along with Captain Edwards and the mutineers from the *Bounty*, were to go on the *Hoornwey*. Despite the strong bonds she had with her friends, she was relieved that she and Charlotte would at least be alone together, away from the men's bitterness.

But fever had slunk aboard the ships, along with the provisions for the journey, and it showed no distinction between prisoners, officers, their wives and children, or crew. Almost daily Mary heard that yet another man, woman or child had gone down with it. It wasn't long before both she and Charlotte became ill too.

Fortunately for Mary, the captain of the *Horssen* was humane, and brave enough to defy Captain Edwards's orders that all prisoners were to be shackled and kept below for the entire voyage. When he was told that Mary and Charlotte were sick, he had Mary released from her chains so she could take care of her child.

It was only then, touched by this act of kindness, that Mary began to worry about how her friends were faring on their ship. All of them had looked appalling back in the guard ship and it was some wonder, after being kept below for weeks in fetid conditions, that they hadn't already succumbed to the fever. She knew Captain Edwards wouldn't show any of them mercy, and she was desperately afraid that not all of their number would survive to see Cape Town.

'You'll be going home with your mates,' Jim said cheerfully. 'So buck up now, and let's see that pretty smile.'

Mary wondered what this pint-sized sailor with red hair had between his ears, for however kindly he was, he appeared not to see the gravity of her situation. Charlotte was very sick with fever, and they were going home to England for Mary to be hanged and Charlotte orphaned. Could he really believe she ought to see the last leg of the journey as some kind of party?

'Are you always so jolly?' she asked, hoping he wouldn't note the sarcasm in her tone.

'Jolly Jim, that's what me mam used to call me,' he laughed, clearly taking it as a compliment. 'Now, you'd better get your things together 'cos I reckon we'll be going aboard the *Gorgon* very soon.'

It could have taken less than a second for Mary to gather together her few belongings. But she spun it out, examining each and every item, even though they had no value. A blue cotton dress, given to her in Kupang. The length of brightly coloured cotton from which she had intended to make another dress for Charlotte, but instead used to wrap Emmanuel in when he was in hospital. She held it to her face, hoping it still smelled of him, but that was gone now, just as he was, and the colours were faded from the many times she'd washed it. A string of blue wooden beads given to her by James Martin in Kupang. A lock of Emmanuel's blond hair, tucked into a folded piece of brown paper. The blanket Watkin Tench had given her here in Cape Town, for Charlotte.

It had been white and fluffy then, now it was brown with age, so threadbare it resembled a cobweb, but just holding it brought back many memories of both her babies. There were a couple of pretty shells, picked up on the beach in Kupang, and finally the bag holding sweet tea leaves.

She didn't really know why she'd held on to them all this time. They were the last of those she'd picked back in the colony. They were brown and crackly now, and she doubted they had any flavour left. But she couldn't throw them away, they too held good memories. She could see herself sitting by the fire with Will outside their hut, sipping at the hot tea as they planned their future. That tea had kept hunger at bay, it had warmed them when they were cold, comforted them when everything looked black.

She would put on the blue dress, for even if it was ragged, it was clean. She'd worn it all the time at the hospital in Batavia. She wished she still had the pink dress and the smart boots, or even her shawl and sun bonnet, as they would have made her feel a whole lot better going aboard the new ship. But if she hadn't sold them, they might not be alive now.

Charlotte had even fewer possessions, just a little shift and her colourful dress, now faded to just a blur of pastels, the stitching coming apart on the seams. She had stopped complaining about wearing the plain grey one back in the hospital. Now Mary came to think of it, she hadn't complained about anything since then — not the lack of food and water, or even when she was taken sick.

Mary glanced down at her. She was lying on the bench where they slept, curled up like a small dog, using her two hands as a pillow. Her face was pale and drawn, she was pitifully thin, and her eyes looked haunted.

'It will be better on the new ship,' Mary said, smoothing back her dark curls from her face. 'You'll get well again.'

Charlotte merely sighed. It was the sound of disbelief, and it hurt Mary more than a sharp retort.

Jim Cartwright was right about which ship they were going home on, but wrong that they would go to it immediately. They sat at anchor for over two weeks. The crew went ashore, but Mary was kept aboard. She wasn't put in chains again, but she was locked back in the hold with Charlotte, and even refused a couple of hours a day on deck for fresh air and exercise.

Daily, Charlotte became weaker, burning up with fever, and all Mary could do was bathe her, try to get her to drink, and curse a system which would allow an innocent child to suffer such cruelty.

Carrying Charlotte, who was barely conscious, Mary staggered up the gang-plank of the *Gorgon*, too weak even to respond to the sound of English voices.

Jim had told her the *Gorgon* had come from Port Jackson, and that the whole ship was filled with plants, shrubs, animal skins and even a couple of captured kangaroos.

He'd been impatient to see these wonders for himself. But Mary was more intent on being reunited with her fellow deserters, as they were now labelled, than concerning herself with whether there would be anyone else on board that she knew.

She was dizzy with fever and the heat. Shouting, thumping, squeaking and banging bombarded her ears, and her limbs ached intolerably. The glare of the sunshine on the water hurt her eyes, and the smells of spice, fish and human sweat made her feel nauseous.

The dizziness suddenly grew far worse as she stepped off the gang-plank on to the deck, which was crowded with people and boxes. Her legs felt as if they were made of rubber and, afraid she would drop Charlotte, she stopped, leaned against a packing case and closed her eyes for a moment to gain her equilibrium. Then she heard someone calling her name.

The voice was so familiar, but in her befuddled state she couldn't place it. She opened her eyes, but everything was a blur.

'Are you sick, Mary?' she heard the voice say as if from a great way off. 'Let me take Charlotte.'

She could only suppose she fainted, for the next thing she knew she was lying down on the deck and someone was dabbing at her forehead with a wet cloth.

'Charlotte!' she called out in alarm, trying to sit up.

'She's being taken care of,' a man said. 'Drink this.'

The drink was rum, and the man offering it to her had to be a sailor, judging by his white ducks and shirt. He had curly fair hair and a sun-blistered face. Mary was in a patch of shade now, and her vision seemed to have returned to normal.

'Who was that who spoke to me and took Charlotte?' she asked.

'That 'ud be Cap'n Tench,' the man said.

'Tench!' she exclaimed. 'Watkin Tench?'

'That's right, me lovely,' he said with a broad grin. 'And I take it you're the one he's been fretting about since we got told you was to sail 'ome with us?'

Mary lay on a bunk, Charlotte asleep beside her. She was bewildered, unable to make up her mind if she was really in a cabin, complete with open porthole, or if she was dreaming.

The cabin certainly looked real enough, very small with just the bunk, a kind of washstand, and a couple of hooks on the wall for clothes. Her bundle was on the washstand, beside it a pitcher of water. Through the porthole she could see barnacle-covered timbers, which had to be the sides of the wharf.

If it was a dream it was a lovely one, for she seemed to think the sailor who gave her rum had said Watkin Tench was on this ship.

She certainly hadn't dreamed about the rum, she could still taste it in her mouth. But maybe she'd drunk it too fast, for the events after that weren't clear at all. Could Tench have been one of the two men she'd heard talking by her? She was sure that one of them said, 'She's been through enough. I want her put in a cabin with her child. That way at least they'll stand a chance.'

Mary lifted herself up a little to look at Charlotte. Her breathing was laboured, her skin felt hot and dry and she was so thin every bone in her small body stood out. It didn't look to Mary as if she stood a chance. She had the same look Emmanuel had towards the end, and Mary had become all too familiar with the signs of approaching death during her time at the Batavia hospital to believe it was mere coincidence.

A rapping on the door woke Mary later. 'Come in,' she said weakly, surprised that anyone would treat an escaped convict with such deference.

The door opened, and there was Watkin Tench, looking exactly the way she remembered, slender, lean-faced, his dark eyes full of concern. Tears filled her eyes. So it hadn't been a dream! He had come back into her life to rescue her.

'Mary!' he exclaimed, and moved closer to her, leaving the door open. 'You cannot imagine my shock to hear you were travelling home on this ship. It is the most extraordinary coincidence.'

To Mary it was far more than coincidence. Only God could have worked this miracle.

'I thought I was dreaming when I heard your voice,' she admitted. 'Then I found myself in this cabin.'

'You have Captain Parker to thank for that,' Tench said. 'He is a good man, and when he heard the circumstances and saw how ill both you and Charlotte were, he gave the order. The surgeon will be along to see you both soon, and much as I want to know everything that has happened since we last saw each other, you must rest.'

'Do you know that Emmanuel and Will died?' she asked.

He nodded gravely. 'I am so sorry, Mary. I wish I had the right words to comfort you in your loss.'

The sincerity in his voice made her cry. In the past he had comforted her in so many different ways, for so many different reasons, and to find he was close by again when she needed a friend so badly was almost too much to bear.

'You were always such a good friend,' she said through her tears. 'And here you are again.'

'I missed you a great deal after you'd gone from Sydney Cove,' he said. 'It just wasn't the same place without you. You can't imagine the rumpus you caused.'

Mary tried to control herself and wiped away her tears. 'James, William and the others, are they here too?' she asked.

'James Martin, Bill Allen, Nat Lilly and Sam Broome are,' he said.

The hesitancy in his voice alerted her that something was wrong. 'And the other three?' she asked.

He looked away for a moment, as if afraid to admit the truth.

'They're dead, aren't they?' She slumped back on to her pillow in utter dejection. 'Was it the fever?'

He nodded. 'William Moreton and Samuel Bird died soon after leaving Batavia,' he said, reaching out to touch her arm in sympathy. 'Jamie Cox jumped overboard in

387

the Straits of Sunda. Maybe he was trying to escape, but it's more likely he was maddened by the fever.'

Mary looked at Tench in horror. 'Oh no,' she croaked out, 'not Jamie!'

Jamie had become like a member of her family, he'd shared so much with her and Will. On the *Dunkirk* and then the *Charlotte* and in Sydney Cove he'd been Will's shadow. He had always seemed more of a boy than a man, even when he shared a hut with Sarah. He had a sweet innocence about him that set him apart from the other male prisoners. It was horrible to think of him ending his life in such a way.

'The other four are in poor shape,' Tench went on, 'but I believe they will soon recover. James told me everything about the escape, and that they all owe their lives to you. They send good wishes to you and Charlotte. They hope once we sail they'll be able to see you both.'

Mary turned her head towards Charlotte who lay asleep in the crook of her arm. 'I don't think she'll live to see them, let alone England,' she whispered.

Tench didn't reply, and when she turned her face to look at him, she saw tears in his eyes.

'Fate has treated you extraordinarily harshly,' he said in a low voice, 'and you have been so very brave. A line should be drawn now. You have suffered enough.'

'Did I hear right?' she asked. 'Did that sailor call you Captain Tench?'

He touched her face gently. 'How like you, Mary, to think of someone else at such a bad time for you. Yes, I'm Captain Tench now. I'm just glad my higher rank gets me a few more privileges, like this cabin for you.'

And with that he left suddenly, and Mary hugged Charlotte tighter and cried. Would Tench ask why they escaped? Or would he understand?

She had left New South Wales with eight healthy men and two children. Maybe she hadn't known some of the men very well then, and some she'd grown to like more than others. Yet they'd become a family, they had pulled together and made it to Kupang. But now there were only four left: cherubic Nat, funny James, stalwart Sam and pugnacious Bill. Half their number gone. And one of the children. Now Charlotte was mortally ill too, and the remainder would be hanged.

She had prided herself on being the mastermind behind the escape. In fact she'd led them all to their deaths.

The *Gorgon* sailed out of Cape Town on 5 April. Mary had her porthole open, and heard the shouted farewells from the wharf, but she was once again bathing Charlotte with cool water and didn't even look out. Her only interest was in making her daughter well again.

As the ship got underway, Mary found herself treated with the utmost kindness. Food and water were brought to her, the ship's surgeon visited her each day, and she was allowed up on deck at any time.

There were many familiar faces aboard other than Tench's, for they were all people who had been in the penal colony and were now returning home after their term of duty was up. Among them was Lieutenant Ralph Clark, the hypocritical man who had spoken to the convict women as though they were dirt under his feet, yet took up with one himself, and there were dozens of Marines with their wives and families.

Mary was far too despondent to talk to any of these people and ask how old friends like Sarah and Bessie had fared after she left. She could see a kind of irony in her situation. Had she become a lag wife to Tench or any of the officers, instead of marrying Will, she would have been left behind when they sailed. A widow here, or a widow there, whichever road she'd taken would have ended the same.

Mary doubted Ralph Clark had any sympathy with her – when she ran into him on deck he pointedly looked the other way – but everyone else was kind. Captain Parker's wife visited her once, bringing her a green and white striped dress, and a night-shirt for Charlotte. She was cool, but then Mary didn't expect a woman of her status to be friendly. It was enough that she'd overcome her fear of the fever to bring clothes.

Mary was gradually recovering her own health, feeling a little better each day, but Charlotte continued to sink. Some days she would swallow a little soup or mashed-up fruit, and stay awake long enough for Mary to sing to her or tell her some stories, but at other times she was delirious and unable even to sip water.

It became hotter and hotter in the next couple of weeks, and Mary was told by the surgeon that other children belonging to the Marines were sick. By Mary's twenty-seventh birthday at the end of April, five children had died and were buried at sea.

Tench came whenever he could, and his deep concern for Charlotte was very touching. He often brought messages from James Martin and the other three men, who were just as anxious about her.

'Kiss her for me,' Tench said, reading from one of James's notes. 'Tell her all her uncles are waiting to see her.'

'Are they well?' Mary asked. Half of her wanted to see her friends, but the other half was afraid in case they started on about Will again. But as she didn't like to leave Charlotte even for a minute or two she had the perfect excuse.

'Much recovered,' Tench said with a smile. 'Eating like pigs. James teases and flirts with the ladies. He is as much of a success with them as he was with the women back in Sydney. He is also talking about writing his memoirs, which should make interesting reading. Bill plays cards with the crew, Sam and Nat are always dozing.'

Mary smiled. It was good to hear they were being treated well too. She was also very glad they were able to put aside what lay ahead for them in England, if only for a few weeks.

During the night of 5 May, Charlotte finally gave up her long struggle and died in her mother's arms.

Mary continued to hold and rock her small body for over an hour, sobbing out her anguish. She wound her fingers into the dark curls so much like her own, and looked back at all the milestones in her short life. Her birth on the *Charlotte*, her christening, first teeth and wobbly steps. But it was the time in Kupang Mary lingered most on, for there Charlotte had been truly happy, well fed for once, as free as any other child, and adored by everyone who met her.

At least now she wouldn't have to suffer the loss of her mother when she was hanged, or be subjected to the miseries of an orphanage or workhouse. She would join her little brother in heaven.

Yet even though Mary could claim a dozen good reasons why she ought to be glad her daughter died at sea, her heart felt smashed into a thousand pieces. Everything Mary had done had been for her. Charlotte gave her reason to go on, and without her there was nothing.

Charlotte's body was committed to the deep that afternoon with almost the entire ship's company, the passengers and the other convicts looking on.

It was Sunday, and raining, and Mary stood bare-headed and stony-faced as Captain Parker led the prayers. She had sewn Charlotte's body into the piece of sackcloth herself, and cried the last of her tears over it. She was empty now, nothing left, and she couldn't understand why her own heart kept on beating so stubbornly.

Even as the small package slipped over the side, she didn't cry out or turn to James or Sam for comfort. She wanted to join her daughter in a watery grave. Yet she knew if she tried to run forward and throw herself in, someone would try to stop her, and failure would make her feel even lower.

*

Agnes Tippet, one of the Marines' wives, watched Mary walk away from the service, and turned to the women next to her. 'She didn't care one bit,' she said in shocked tones. 'No tears, nothing. I've never seen anyone bury a child with such a hard face.'

Watkin Tench heard Agnes' remark. 'Be quiet, you foolish woman,' he snapped at her, incensed. 'You have no real idea what she's been through, or how she feels inside. Count yourself lucky your children are well, and don't make judgements on another.'

As Tench strode away, he could hear the women whispering among themselves and he choked back tears of sadness and frustration.

He knew Mary so well. She would not burden anyone with her grief, least of all him. He had seen the desolation on the faces of James, Sam, Nat and Bill, and he knew it wasn't only for the little girl they'd all come to love and look upon as their own, but for her mother as well. Mary had saved their lives, been a friend, sister and mother to each of them, and they all knew this latest tragedy had broken the last of her spirit.

Back in Sydney a year earlier, their escape had been a huge shock to Tench. He had believed he knew Mary and Will well enough to guess if they were hatching something like this up, yet he hadn't had the faintest suspicion.

He didn't have much faith that they would make it to the Dutch East Indies, for by all accounts it was a long and dangerous voyage. Yet he understood why they felt they had to attempt it, and greatly admired their courage.

He had missed Mary so much. Hardly a day passed

without him thinking about her. He offered up prayers for her safety, and a small part of him believed she must have survived, because he was sure he'd feel it if she were dead.

Even as he packed up his belongings to leave Sydney Cove, Mary was still on his mind. He could see her small, eager face in his mind's eye, the way her eyes used to light up when he called at her hut. He could still see her slender but shapely legs as she tucked her dress up to wade into the sea and help with the seine net, and her dark curly hair tumbling about her face as she washed clothes. Yet it wasn't the physical things about her he missed the most, it was her inquiring mind, her dry sense of humour and her stoicism.

Even if he had known she'd survived, he would never have considered he might run into her again. When Captain Parker told him in Cape Town that they would be taking deserters from Port Jackson back to England for trial, then named them, Tench was utterly astounded, almost disbelieving.

It seemed to him then that his fate and Mary's were linked. That God in his infinite wisdom had always intended them for each other. This belief grew even stronger when he talked to the surviving men and learned of the voyage, and how Will and Emmanuel had died in Batavia. He was of course distressed to think that Mary had lost her husband and her little son, but according to the other men Will had betrayed them all, and he hadn't got to know Emmanuel as well as he had Charlotte.

Then Mary came aboard, so weak that she collapsed,

and sweet little Charlotte, the child so many of his men believed was his, was mortally ill. Under the circumstances it wasn't appropriate to tell Mary what was in his heart. All he could do was make sure she and Charlotte got whatever they needed to recover, and that he was around when she needed a friend.

Yet it had become even less appropriate to tell her how he felt since Charlotte's death. She had survived the hulks, the long voyage to New South Wales, and four years of near-starvation in the penal colony. She'd had the audacity to plan a fantastic escape plot, and by sheer force of will got to the planned destination. Then she was betrayed by her own husband and found herself once again a prisoner, facing execution back in England.

Tench knew in his heart that it wasn't any of these things, terrible as they were, which had broken her. He had no doubt that if her children had survived she would have plotted yet another daring escape, and carried it out. But those children were her Achilles' heel. Once Emmanuel became sick she had to nurse him. Likewise with Charlotte. Now they were both gone, freedom was worthless. Mary would go to the gallows without fear. Death was the only escape she wanted now.

'You can't give up on her,' he muttered to himself. 'You've got to find a way to put some fight back in her.'

Several days later Tench came upon James Martin and Sam Broome on deck. They were sitting leaning back against a locker, to all intents and purposes just enjoying the sun and fresh air. They were both painfully thin, the horrors they'd endured still showing in their eyes, and they looked much older than they had back in New South Wales. But though they seemed relaxed, Tench picked up some animosity between them. Guessing it had something to do with Mary, he stopped to talk to them.

After some general conversation about there being little room on the deck because of the boxes of plants and shrubs from New South Wales, and whether or not the two kangaroos would survive in a colder climate, Tench mentioned Mary.

'Have you seen her on deck today?' he asked.

'She was up here for a while,' Sam said. 'She don't seem to want to be with us now.'

There was a note of real despondency rather than complaint in his voice, and Tench guessed he was in love with her. He knew it had been Mary who nursed Sam back to health when he came in on the Second Fleet, and probably any man would love a woman for that. Tench liked Sam, he was calm, good-hearted and a talented carpenter, and Tench couldn't help thinking that perhaps he would have made a better husband for Mary than Will, if he'd been on the First Fleet.

'She doesn't want to be with anyone,' Tench said soothingly. 'That's the way grief takes some people.'

'Or they only want to be with people who'll be useful to them,' James said with a slight smirk, looking pointedly at Tench.

'She isn't like that,' Sam said, his face flushing with anger.

All at once Tench saw the problem between James and

Sam. James was assuming Mary was as calculating as himself.

Tench hadn't ever really liked the wily Irishman that much. He was amusing and intelligent, but as cunning as a fox. 'Sam's right, Mary isn't like that,' he said firmly. 'You should know better, James.'

'I'm not blaming her for it,' James shrugged, his ugly face taking on a slightly remorseful expression. 'If there was anyone around who I thought could save me from the long drop, I'd lick their arse if that's what it took.'

Later, alone in his cabin, Tench found himself thinking about what James had said. The man was wrong about Mary of course, she wasn't talking to anyone, not for sympathy or any other reason. She was a prisoner inside herself right now.

But James had made a good point too. Mary could do with someone influential on her side. Tench was prepared to go to any lengths himself for her, but he was just a Marine, recently promoted to Captain, and he hadn't got an ounce of influence back in England.

He went through a mental list of everyone he knew, but none of them were in any better position to help her than himself.

Turning to his journal as he always did when he was troubled, he flicked back over the pages, reading parts of it at random. The penal colony in New South Wales was history in the making, and he had wanted to produce a work which in years to come would be a valuable source of information about the colony's first years. It wasn't ever intended to be a personal account of his own part in it, but a broader view.

Overall he considered he had done that rather well. Maybe when he retired from the Marines he'd take to writing articles for newspapers on the subject. And then suddenly, a thought came into his mind like a thunderbolt. That was it! A way to get influential help for Mary. He'd write a full account about her to the newspapers in England!

Despite his usual calm and controlled manner, he felt very excited. He couldn't write under his own name of course, there was bound to be some kind of law against a serving officer divulging information. But no one would guess it was him if he wrote the Bryants' escape story in a florid and sensational manner. Newspapers the length and breadth of England would devour such a story. Men would love the daring of it, women would weep for Mary losing her husband and children. Surely no one with a heart would want to see her hanged after going through so much pain already?

Tench's smile spread from one ear to the other. It could work. He had to make it work.

Mary sat in a sheltered nook at the stern of the ship, looking out at the fast-approaching coast of England with a mixture of pleasure and trepidation. It was a beautiful June day, warm, sunny and with just enough wind to send the ship scudding along at a good speed. Perfect sailing weather, and she could recall so many other days just like it, out in a boat with her father.

She had thought about her parents and Dolly so much over the years. Had they found out what happened to her? If they hadn't, maybe they thought she had forsaken them for high life in London. Or even supposed she had died! Whatever they knew, or believed, it was going to distress them terribly if they discovered that she was awaiting trial in London's Newgate prison.

She hadn't understood at nineteen what it was to be a mother. Mothers were people who nagged, wanted you to be ladylike, to cook and sew as well as they did, and to marry a respectable man so they could be smug and pat themselves on the back for bringing their daughters up well. They didn't want their daughters to have fun or adventure, because they didn't have any themselves.

Mary knew better now. All any woman wanted for her child was for it to be safe and happy. All that nagging was only an attempt to prevent harm. A way of showing love.

She wished there was a way of letting her mother know she understood that now. She also wished she could reassure her that death by hanging didn't frighten her. It was what she wanted, to rid herself of the terrible burden of guilt for her children's deaths.

Everyone on this ship had been so kind to her, but it would have been better if someone had called her a murderess, for that was what she knew she was. At the time she planned the escape she thought it was preferable to risk her children drowning at sea, a clean and quick death, than to watch them die slowly of hunger or disease in the colony. She still stood by that. Yet despite all her efforts they had in the end suffered a far worse fate than could ever have befallen them back in New South Wales. And she was to blame for putting them in that position.

A shadow falling on her made her look up. It was Tench.

'So thoughtful,' he said with a smile. 'Will you share them with me?'

Mary couldn't tell him she was thinking about her children, so she played safe. 'I was thinking about my mother.'

'Would you like me to write to her for you?' he asked, squatting down in front of her.

Mary shook her head. 'She can't read, she'd have to take it to someone else.'

'Maybe I could call on her at some time then,' he suggested.

'I can't put that burden on you,' she said, imagining how her mother would view a gentleman like Tench. She would be embarrassed to have him call at her humble home, so she'd be curt with him, as if she didn't care about Mary. Then she'd weep for days after he'd gone.

'I just hope I get tried and hanged quickly and no one will know about it. That's the kindest thing for everyone concerned.'

'Not for me it isn't,' he said, looking horrified. 'I believe there will be public sympathy for you and I hope you'll be set free.'

Mary gave a tight little laugh. 'That's foolish. You know perfectly well I'll be hanged or sent back. I just hope it's hanging.'

Tench didn't make any reply for a few moments. He

had been on an emotional see-saw with Mary for so long, sometimes he didn't know for certain how he really felt. She looked pretty today in her green and white dress, her hair neatly tied back with a white ribbon, her cheeks pink from the sun and wind. She had regained a little weight since Charlotte's death, and she looked a world away from the waif in rags he'd known back in Sydney Cove.

But her grey eyes looked dead now, no sparkle, no fire. Even her voice was muted. He couldn't bear it.

'It's difficult to find anything further to discuss after hanging has been brought up,' he said, afraid he might make a fool of himself and cry.

'Maybe it's because there isn't anything more to say,' she replied. 'We've had an odd sort of friendship, haven't we? It was always an uneven one, you with the world in front of you, me with nothing.'

'I never saw it like that,' he said sadly and with just a touch of indignation.

'Neither did I, once.' She sighed. 'But then I'm better at seeing things as they really are now.'

Tench felt helpless. He remembered her audacity back on the *Dunkirk*. He'd been fully aware she was always looking for an opportunity, whether that was escape, work on deck, extra food or clothing. It was that ingenuity and daring that initially attracted him to her. He couldn't believe she'd lost it all. But maybe if he told her how he really felt about her, some of it might return.

'I don't think you are that good at seeing everything,' he began cautiously. 'My feelings for you in particular.'

She looked at him inquiringly and it gave him heart.

'I love you, Mary, I always have,' he blurted out. 'I wish I had told you so long ago, and never let you marry Will.'

Mary just stared at him. Not disbelieving, nor scornful. She simply looked at him as if she was seeing right down into his soul.

'It's true,' Tench insisted. 'I want to find a way to get you released so you can share your life with me.'

She remained silent for another couple of moments, and Tench held his breath, waiting for her reply.

'I'm not for you, Watkin,' she said at last, her voice soft but firm, and her use of his Christian name sounded odd. 'You want me to have hope.'

'Of course I want you to have hope. For a future together, marriage, and a real home,' he said passionately.

She smiled wearily. His dark eyes had all the fire in them she once dreamed of, but it was too late now. 'I have hope for you,' she said. 'I hope you'll have a long and distinguished career, and a wife suitable for your station who loves you with all her heart.'

'But don't you see that it was Fate who brought us together again?' he said fiercely, catching hold of her hand and pressing it. 'We're meant to be together, I know it.'

'I think Fate brought us together only to give me a little comfort in seeing a dear face once again,' she said, putting her hand on his cheek. 'You have been the very best of friends.'

'But is that all?' he asked, his face full of hurt and disappointment.

Mary thought for a moment. She wasn't sure whether telling him the truth would hurt him more, or comfort him. Yet her mother would have said the truth is always best.

'It was you I wanted, right back on the *Dunkirk*,' she said with a sigh. 'Charlotte should have been your child. I carried that loving with me right through the voyage to New South Wales, even through my marriage. If you had said you wanted me as your lag wife, I believe I would have left Will for you.'

'Well then,' he said triumphantly. 'There's nothing to stand in our way now.'

Mary shook her head slowly. 'There is, Watkin. I'm not the same person any more,' she said almost wistfully. 'I have a thousand ugly pictures in my head. I'm all used up.'

'I don't understand.' He shook his head, dark eyes boring into her. 'If you were set free all that would go.'

'Some of it maybe,' she said, tears forming in her eyes because she wished what she was telling him wasn't the truth. 'But you love the old Mary, and that isn't what you'd get.'

'I don't understand,' he implored her, clutching her hand and lifting it to his lips.

'The Mary you loved was a scheming little minx,' she said with a half smile. 'She cared only for survival, she made things happen. But too much happened in the end. Things you can't even imagine. The old Mary died back in Batavia. All you see now is an empty shell.'

Tench looked into her eyes, saw the bleakness there and instinctively knew she truly believed what she said. 'Let me kiss you,' he whispered, not caring if anyone was watching them because he was sure it would change her mind.

Mary nodded. It seemed fitting to her that she should end this with the one thing she had so often dreamed of.

He slid his arms around her and drew her to him, his heart aching with the need to bring back the mischievous and audacious girl who had captured his heart and held it for so many years. Her lips were soft and yielding, but disappointingly her kiss was one of farewell. Tender, clinging, yet without passion, just a goodbye. He knew then there was nothing more he could do or say which would persuade her.

He cupped her face in his hands. 'I'll do my best for you,' he said fiercely. 'I'll write and come to visit you.'

'No, Watkin,' she said firmly. 'I don't want you to. You've been one of the best people in my life, I have a hundred bright memories of you in my head. If I'm to be hung they will sustain me. Let it be at that. Find someone from your own class who can bring you happiness.'

Of all the many traits of Mary's personality Tench had come to know and admire over the past years, her resolution was the most powerful. He knew it was that which had kept her alive and helped her make the best of what was thrown at her.

He knew she was resolved now. Even if by some miracle he could sweep her away from Newgate and the gallows, she would not allow him to sully his family name or his career by marrying her. Tench knew he had never known anyone so heroic and unselfish.

He stood up and moved to the ship's rail. He wanted

to find a persuasive counter-argument, yet knew there wasn't one. 'We're nearly at Portsmouth,' he said eventually, looking towards the shore. 'I have to leave the ship there while you go on to London.'

He couldn't stand the thought of it. He knew that very soon she would be put back in chains, just the way she was when he first met her.

'God go with you,' she said from behind him, her voice shaking. 'You are destined for greatness, Watkin. And I'll always count myself fortunate to have had you as a friend.'

Chapter seventeen

Late in the afternoon on a fine, sunny day at the end of June, Mary shuffled dejectedly along behind the Newgate gaoler, her four friends behind her. They had been processed and now they were being led along a narrow, dark stone passageway into the prison itself, to be locked up until their trial.

Mary's ankles were raw and bleeding from the chains that had been put back on her earlier in the month when the *Gorgon* docked at Portsmouth. They had remained on for the last part of the voyage to the London docks. She was also hungry, for she hadn't eaten anything since dawn when she, James, Bill, Nat and Sam left the ship, shackled together to wait to be escorted to Newgate prison.

Mary had felt very much as she had when she left the prison in Kupang to be transferred to the ship which would take them to Batavia. The difference was that the voices around them were now English ones, and more poignantly, four of the men and the two children were missing.

They hardly spoke as they waited on the busy wharf for the prison cart to arrive. They just sat in a row against a wall, clutching their small bags of belongings on their laps, each wrapped in their own private thoughts. Mary could understand why people passing through the wharf looked at them so curiously, for they must have been a strange sight. Chained convicts were usually ragged, dirty and malnourished, whereas they were clean and healthy. The men had all been issued with canvas breeches and shirts, and Mary was wearing the green and white dress given to her by the captain's wife. Muscular Bill with his bald head and prize-fighter's features might look like a dangerous man, but Nat, with his angelic face, blue eyes and blond hair shining in the sunshine, had more in common with a page or a choir boy. As for James and Sam, they gave the impression of being two impoverished, scrawny aristocrats. James looked arrogantly down his long nose at anyone who glanced his way, and Sam was in a world of his own, tawny eyes fixed on the distant horizon.

There was nothing to say to one another. No comment on the hurly-burly of the wharf, where piles of goods were being loaded and unloaded into ships. They didn't react to casks of wine and spirits being rolled over the cobblestones, nor to the shouts of porters and dockers, nor even to half a dozen horses being led nervously on to a ship.

The long voyage from Cape Town had restored their health, and the horrors of past imprisonments had begun to fade. But as they waited to be taken to Newgate, which by reputation was the hardest and cruellest prison in the whole of England, all of them were struggling to control their fear.

The cart didn't arrive until mid-afternoon, and it was only once they were in it, trundling slowly away from the frantic activity on the wharf, that Bill broke the silence.

'I'd forgotten what horse shit smelled like,' he exclaimed, as their cart joined a throng of others carrying goods along a narrow road between tall, grimy warehouses.

'It smells like Dublin,' James retorted, giving an exaggerated loud sniff. 'Do you think if we asked the driver nicely he'd take us to an ale house?'

Mary half smiled at their show of bravado. She knew they were every bit as scared as she was. She had finally made it to London, the place she'd dreamed of since she was a child, but it wasn't in her dream to see it from the back of a prison cart, or to die there, dangling on a rope.

Yet despite the knowledge that Newgate lay at the end of the cart ride, all five of them found much to distract them on the way there. The streets, whether wide and elegant or narrow and dingy, teemed with people from all walks of life. Ladies in silk gowns and fancy hats, on the arms of gentlemen in wigs and frock coats, strolled nonchalantly past blind beggars, drunken slatterns and bare-footed street urchins. It was pandemonium, carts and carriages charging along at breakneck speeds, strident-voiced street vendors offering everything from fly-blown meat pies to posies of flowers. There were organ grinders and men playing tin whistles and fiddles. She saw market porters carrying huge tottering piles of baskets on their heads, a fresh-faced dairy maid with pails of milk supported on a yoke across her shoulders, and a bow-legged man with his hands clenching live, fluttering chickens by their claws.

The shops were as diverse as the kinds of people who passed by them. One sold nothing but silverware, the next displayed great pink hams, pheasants and rabbits laid out on white marble slabs. A milliner's selling hats that could surely only be worn by royalty, and then in complete contrast a shop with mountains of secondhand boots and shoes.

Mary could hardly believe that women could go out on the streets wearing such low-cut gowns, displaying their breasts for the whole world to gawp at. Yet they appeared to be ladies of quality, for all had a soberly dressed maid or footman with them. In Plymouth only a whore would show so much naked flesh.

The clamour, dirt and evil smells ought to have shattered Mary's long-held illusions that it was the city of miracles. But until she saw Newgate, some hours after they'd left the docks, she was still clinging to them, expecting that any moment she would be rescued.

But no rescue came. The bony horses even picked up a little speed at the sight of Newgate's forbidding grey stone walls, relieved perhaps that they could now shed their heavy load.

Suddenly all those stories Mary had heard back in Sydney Cove of public hangings at Tyburn Tree, where huge crowds gathered to watch as if it was a sideshow in a fair, took on a new and horrific meaning.

As the gates opened to let the cart enter, the smell hit them. It wasn't just the familiar stench of human waste, more the certain knowledge that this really was the absolute bottom of the barrel of life.

Even James, who had joked and chatted most of the way from the docks, was silenced as the cart trundled into a small, cobbled, tunnel-like area with more heavy doors beyond. The two burly gaolers who had opened the outer gates closed and locked them behind the cart, then, picking up a cudgel each, stood by as the cart driver unlocked and pulled out the chains that had secured the prisoners together.

Mary was terrified as they were shoved into a small room off the yard. She remembered other women telling her back in Sydney Cove how the gaolers here would knock you out even for asking a question and body searches were just an excuse to humiliate prisoners. She was dreading the moment, too, when she would be separated from the men.

But there was no search, perhaps because they'd come directly from a Royal Navy ship. The only questions asked were for their names, which were duly marked down in a ledger, and after a brief wait, they were led down the passageway to another door.

There Mary glanced behind her at the men. She expected that this would be the point when they were separated. She wanted to say something, but the prospect of awaiting trial apart from them was so daunting that she was robbed of speech.

The gaoler opened the door, and the unexpected waft of warm air and sunshine beyond made Mary gasp. But if it wasn't enough of a surprise to find herself stepping out into an open courtyard, the sight that met her was so totally astounding that she stopped in her tracks.

'Holy Mother of God!' James exclaimed behind her.

It might be a yard within the prison walls, but the scene within it was more like a carnival than a place of punishment. At least a hundred people were milling around enjoying themselves. The noise of drunken revelry was as loud as in any of the taverns they'd passed on the way here.

Mary rubbed her eyes, thinking it was some kind of hallucination. It couldn't be prison, she could see no chains, no evidence of starvation, many of the crowd were even in fine clothes, men in wigs strutting around like gentlemen, women in what, to Mary at least, looked like ball gowns, bedecked with jewellery. One woman in turquoise satin, surrounded by men in velvet and brocade jackets, was actually fanning herself with a feathered fan as if she was at a private soirée.

Where were the poor wretches in chains they'd expected? The diseased, hollow-eyed old whores in rags, the pathetic young girls who had been led astray, and the scarred brutes who'd finally got their just deserts? These people cavorting, drinking and chatting certainly weren't being punished.

'Move along now,' the gaoler said impatiently, prodding her with his cudgel. 'It ain't like you never was in a prison afore.'

'I've never been in one like this before,' Mary retorted, glancing back at the men to see their reaction. But they looked as staggered and unbelieving as she.

Drink obviously played a major part in the festivities. They could see people coming out of a door carrying brimming tankards. There were even a few women dancing a jig accompanied by a man with a black patch over one eye, playing a fiddle.

Noise came from every quarter. Mary looked up at the grey prison building and saw many people craning their heads out of small barred windows and shouting to those below or either side of them.

As the gaoler urged them forward, suddenly a hush fell on the crowd, all eyes turning to Mary and her group.

'It's them!' someone shouted. 'Give 'em a cheer!'

As wild and frantic cheering went up, Mary suddenly felt like a bride who had turned up at the wrong wedding. She saw no reason why anyone would want to cheer them. It had to be a case of mistaken identity.

The crowd were coming towards them with shouts of welcome, broad grins, and hands outstretched to greet them.

'It's a pleasure to welcome you to Newgate.' A man in a stained black frock coat bowed and doffed a battered top hat. 'There's plenty of us know we're bound for Botany Bay, it gives us heart to hear of your escape.'

'They've found out what we done,' Sam said incredulously, holding on to Mary's arm as if he thought she'd faint with shock. 'God's teeth! I never thought we'd be famous.'

Clearly fame didn't preclude locking them up, for they weren't given a chance to speak to anyone, ask how they knew about them, or anything else. The gaoler pushed them on up a couple of flights of winding stone stairs and into a cell, slamming and locking the door behind them.

Temporarily stunned by what they'd seen out in the yard, and the welcome they'd had from the other prisoners, no one spoke for some minutes. The five of them just stood there, speechless.

Mary pulled herself together first. The cell was very small, the straw was dirty, and the only light came from a small slit window, too high up to see out. But compared with the conditions on the *Rembang* and in the hospital in Batavia, it was quite decent. To Mary, the best thing of all was that they were all together, and they weren't sharing it with anyone else.

'This is better than I expected,' she said, breaking the silence first. 'But I'd like to know why those people in the yard aren't chained.'

'I can tell you that, me darlin',' James said with a grin. 'It's money. Didn't you ever listen to any of those back in Port Jackson who'd been in here?'

'I listened, but I couldn't understand them,' Mary said, recalling how the Londoners with their flash lingo had sounded as if they came from a foreign land. By the time she'd learned enough of it to understand, they had moved on from talking about their old prisons to their plight in the new one.

'Well, they said you had to pay for what they call "easements",' James said with a shrug. 'They had it in Dublin too. You slip the gaoler something and off come your chains. You can get food brought from outside too.'

Mary nodded. She remembered now that that had also been the case with food and drink back in Exeter.

'I expect if you've got enough money, or at least something to sell, you can have a room on your own and a servant to bring you food and drink,' James said with a hollow laugh. 'But as we haven't got anything, this is all we can expect.'

The men slumped dejectedly down on the floor. Nat fell asleep almost immediately, and Mary was reminded of the women on the *Dunkirk*. Some of them managed to sleep almost round the clock, it was their way of escaping from the cruel reality of prison.

Mary sat down, arranged her chains so they didn't dig into her, and hunched her knees up under her dress. Leaning back against the wall, she considered her friends' plight.

Her own meant nothing to her, she wanted death to rid herself of the mental torment she felt. She might have regained her physical health on the voyage home, but she couldn't recover from the crushing guilt at taking her two children on such a hazardous journey and causing their deaths. Real hell to her was being sent back to New South Wales, and she would escape from it by jumping overboard at the first opportunity.

But the men hadn't become reconciled to the certainty of hanging. James had some kind of blind faith he was safe, for his original sentence was up now. Sam believed that if he showed enough remorse they would let him off.

Bill and Nat tried to blank out the possibility by sleeping or talking about something else.

Yet seeing London today had sparked something inside Mary. It hadn't made her want to live again, or lessened her grief, but it had brought the men's predicament sharply into focus for her.

None of them were bad men, and they'd already suffered so much. Mary couldn't hope to save them from hanging, but if she could just think of some way to get those 'easements', that might make their last few weeks a great deal more bearable.

She thought about it for over an hour, and then smiled as she came up with a solution.

'What've you got to smirk about?' James asked curiously, moving nearer and squatting down in front of her.

'I've had an idea,' she said.

'If it involves ropes and files, forget it,' he grinned. 'I did an inventory of our belongings before we left the *Gorgon*. We haven't even got a knife between us.'

'I'm glad you've still got your sense of humour,' she said, patting his bony face affectionately. 'That might come in handy for my idea. You see, I've been thinking. If we are famous, maybe we can wring some money out of it.'

Nat continued to sleep, looking like a sweet child in the dim light. But Bill and Sam sat up. James only raised his eyebrows questioningly.

'Will thought he'd make money from our story, that's why he hung on to his log,' Mary explained. 'We've still

415

got all the stories in our heads. So why don't we sell them?'

'To who?' he said sarcastically.

'To anyone who cares to hear them,' she said, feeling a little of her old self coming back now she had a challenge again.

No opportunity presented itself to Mary before it was dark, but the following morning, when she heard the gaoler coming along the row of cells to unlock them so they could empty the night bucket, she was ready.

She brushed the straw off her dress and ran her fingers through her hair as the key turned in the lock.

'Come on, get that bucket emptied,' the gaoler shouted, far more loudly than was necessary. He looked the way Mary remembered the gaolers back in Exeter, fat and unhealthy, with shifty eyes and rotten teeth.

'How much for having the chains struck off?' she asked.

He sucked his rotten teeth, eying her up speculatively. 'That depends.'

'Depends on what?'

'Whether I want to or not,' he replied, and cackled with laughter.

Mary took hold of the front of his greasy shirt menacingly. 'You'd better want to,' she hissed at him. 'We've fought with cannibals and killed animals with our bare hands, and we're going to hang for daring to escape from New South Wales. So we won't think twice about slitting your throat. Now, do you want to be our friend or our enemy?'

His eyes rolled back in his head in alarm. Mary couldn't see the men behind her, but she had to hope they were doing as she'd ordered and looking fierce.

'W-w-what's in it for me?' he stuttered.

'That depends on how you go about it,' she said. She let go of him and smiled sweetly. 'I want you to put the word about that we're ready to receive visitors. They'll have to pay of course. Enough for the shackles to come off, for food, drink and hot water to wash with.'

It was a gamble. Mary had no real idea if anyone in the prison or outsiders visiting it had enough interest in them to pay for the privilege of meeting them.

'I don't know,' he said, still looking scared. 'Did you say cannibals?'

'I did, they had metal-tipped arrows this long,' she said, holding her arms out wide.

'I'll see,' he said, and moved back as if to lock the door.

Mary grabbed the night bucket. 'Empty this before you go,' she said, and thrust it at him. 'Rinse it out before you bring it back,' she added, 'I don't like the smell.'

He walked away with it as meekly as a child ordered to go and buy bread, and Mary turned to the men and giggled. 'I think we've got a deal,' she said.

By noon the shackles were off, they were eating mutton pies, and had a large flagon of small beer between them. The gaoler, whom they now knew as Spinks, was as resourceful as he was greedy, and they had already received two groups of four people, all desperate to meet the escapees and hear about the cannibals.

James was the story-teller and he did it well, embellishing the true story about the native warriors who chased them in a war canoe, to hand-to-hand fighting on land.

'In their village they had dozens of human skulls on poles,' James lied cheerfully. 'We saw piles of human bones. They wore the teeth as necklaces and used human skin to cover their shields.'

After the second group left, Mary and the men dissolved into laughter.

'Well, they could've been cannibals,' James said indignantly. 'I mean, we didn't stay around for long enough to find out, did we?'

Mary thought how good the sound of laughter was, which she hadn't heard since they were captured in Kupang. Even on the *Gorgon* they'd been very subdued. Yet she couldn't help feeling just a twinge of sadness that Will wasn't still with them. He would've loved an opportunity to tell such tales, and he would probably have made it even more exciting than James had done.

'You are a wonder, Mary,' Sam said a little later, as he licked his fingers clean of the meat pie. 'None of us could have thought up such a cunning plan. When James got to that bit about you hitting one of the cannibals over the head with an oar, I almost believed you'd really done it. I reckon you'd think of something to save us even if they were just putting us in the cooking pot.'

Mary smiled. It was good to have the men's admiration again. And even better to see them lifted out of their gloom. 'We mustn't go too far with the stories,' she warned them. 'We want sympathy, not people calling us liars.'

It was on the following day that they discovered how the other prisoners had found out about them. A forger by the name of Harry Hawkins came to see them. Like many others in Newgate, he expected to be transported. He was a slimy character, small and thin, with a beak-like nose and strangely unkempt long hair for a man who dressed well.

'I read about you in the *London Chronicle*,' he said, and proceeded to prove it by fishing a dog-eared cutting from his pocket.

All of them had assumed the news about them had merely passed by word of mouth, that was the usual way in prisons. It was a shock to find someone had written about them in a newspaper.

James read it aloud, then passed it back. 'It's not completely accurate. It was the Governor's boat we stole, not Captain Smith's,' he said airily.

Mary was astounded that James could be so blasé about such a florid and admiring account of their escape.

'Who wrote it?' she asked. She hadn't for one moment expected anyone in England to be sympathetic to them.

'It don't say,' James replied, looking at it again. 'But whoever it was, he knows a lot. He might have got it wrong about who owned the cutter. But everything else is right.'

The five friends had no further chance then to discuss where all this information came from, because Harry Hawkins wanted to talk about his plight. It was clear that what he wanted from them was inside information about officials in Botany Bay.

It amused Mary somewhat that this man, and everyone else waiting for transportation, still thought the settlement was in Botany Bay. Apparently no one here knew that place had been rejected by Captain Phillip. In fact it seemed that very little information had yet reached England about the colony. Mary suspected most of it had been withheld purposely as the government wouldn't want to publicize their terrible mistakes. That made the situation even better for her and her friends.

'It isn't like this place,' she said with a wry smile. 'You can't buy a better hut or bigger rations, the only way you can advance yourself is by having a skill they need.'

Hawkins looked disappointed. 'But you must've had some inside help, or slipped someone a back-hander!' he retorted.

'We didn't,' James said indignantly. 'It was all down to Mary charming the Dutch sea captain for the navigational instruments and charts.'

Hawkins gave her a disbelieving look and Mary blushed. She supposed he couldn't imagine a plain and worn-looking woman being able to charm anyone.

'The captain was lonely,' she said by way of an explanation. 'Me and my husband used to talk to him. He would come and have supper with us sometimes.'

'So he'll be the one who paid for you to have this cell?' Hawkins asked with a touch of sarcasm.

Mary and her cellmates looked askance at each other.

'Paid for this cell?' James exclaimed. 'No one paid for it.'

'Someone did, before you even got here,' Hawkins said, looking a bit uncomfortable. 'You'd have been put on the common side otherwise.'

An hour later, when Hawkins left, Mary turned to her friends. 'Who could have paid for it?' she asked them.

Hawkins had been happy to explain the prison system to them. Everyone, unless someone had intervened on their behalf prior to their arrival, got put in with the common criminals, hence the name 'common side'. These cells were filthy, stuffed to capacity and hotbeds of infection. The prisoners were at the mercy of the insane and the dangerous, and you'd be lucky to wake to find you still had your boots on your feet. Young women and boys were certain to be raped on their first night, and rarely by only one person.

Hawkins then went on to explain that as long as a prisoner had some money or goods to sell they could buy their way into somewhere cleaner and safer, and get the extras they'd already discovered for themselves. The merriment in the courtyard was proof of all this; the people they'd seen were either wealthy or had rich and influential friends. But once a prisoner had run out of money, it was back to the common side for him or her.

Hawkins had cited a highwayman who had his own feather bed brought in, hot water for a bath brought up to him each morning, his shirt laundered, meals with fine wine, and during the afternoons he was visited by his mistress. He was eventually hanged, but as Hawkins pointed out, bribes couldn't get you out of everything.

'Do any of you know *anyone* in London?' Mary asked the men in bewilderment. None of them had any idea who their mysterious benefactor could be.

'I used to know a few people,' James replied. 'But not the kind who'd even buy me a pint of ale, let alone a decent cell.'

'Maybe it was someone who felt sorry for us after reading that in the *Chronicle*?' Sam suggested.

'That would be it,' Bill said, stroking his beard thoughtfully. 'There was a man murdered in Berkshire when I was a boy, he left a wife and five children, and when people heard the story they sent money for them.'

'That's fair enough. But who told the story about us in the first place?' James asked, looking puzzled. 'That paper was four or five days old. We were still on the ship in the English Channel. How could they have got the story?'

'Someone must have talked when the ship docked at Portsmouth,' Sam said, and his face broke into a wide grin. 'Captain Edwards left then, and he would have informed the authorities about us. A big number of people left the ship there too, anyone of them could've talked to a newspaper.'

All at once Mary realized the story could only have come from Watkin Tench. Captain Edwards had no sympathy with them or the mutineers he'd caught, so any information from him would have cast them in a very bad light. As for any of the other officers who went ashore at Portsmouth, their accounts wouldn't have been so accurate.

Tench would also know about corruption in prisons

from his time on the *Dunkirk*, and how to go about fixing a cell for them in Newgate.

Instantly Mary decided to say nothing to the others. She was a little surprised they hadn't considered Tench, but then none of them had been as closely involved with him as she had. To tell them what she thought now would only raise questions she didn't want to answer. Besides, if Tench had done it in secret, he wanted it to stay that way – it might put his career at risk if it got out. Better that they continued to think it was a benevolent stranger.

'Luck's smiling on us again,' James chortled gleefully, not even noticing Mary had made no comment about it all. 'Maybe if the money keeps rolling in we'll end up like that highwayman, sleeping in feather beds.'

'Bless you, Watkin,' Mary thought, and she had to turn away from the others so they didn't see the tears of gratitude in her eyes.

In the days that followed they had many visitors to their cell. Some wanted to hear only of their escape, but more were facing transportation themselves and wanted to know what to expect.

Mary felt a little guilty that they were taking money from these people. It was bad enough for them to face parting from their loved ones, without compounding their misery by telling them of the dreaded flogging triangle, of hunger and unremitting heat. But as James said, it was better for them to spend some of their money on preparation for what lay in store for them than to drink it away, and she supposed he was right.

The first time they were allowed out into the prison yard, Mary felt she was entering a select party. People greeted them with genuine warmth, offering drink from the tap-room, advice and friendship. James and the three other men accepted this with alacrity, especially the overtures from women prisoners. But Mary hung back.

While it felt good to be admired, rather than scorned or pitied, her emotions were too raw to want to talk and laugh with strangers, however well-meaning. All she wanted was to sit quietly in the sun, but this was denied her, for everyone wanted something of her.

Some were after details of the escape, others asked her about their friends and relatives who had been transported, some women even wanted to know her experiences in childbirth. Then there were men either trying to court her or making lewd suggestions.

Within a few hours Mary had seen and heard enough. She didn't want to be a performer in this circus, or even part of the audience.

She had never before considered her feelings about the criminal world which she'd belonged to for so many years. Whether on the prison hulk, on the ship or in the penal colony, she was just another convict serving her time, doing whatever was needed to survive. As such she was loyal to her fellow prisoners, covering up, aiding and abetting sometimes in thefts from the stores and other wrong-doing, because that was the code by which they all lived.

But losing both her children had opened her mind wider.

She had never really been sorry she stole that woman's bonnet in Plymouth. She was sorry she was caught, angry with herself for being so reckless. But she'd never put herself in that woman's shoes and imagined how it was for her to be struck and robbed.

Now, when she thought about it, Mary felt deeply ashamed. She wasn't actually starving at the time, she didn't need the bonnet. She could look back on good people she'd known in her childhood, like Martha Dingwell in the baker's who gave the unsold bread at the end of the day to those unable to buy any, or Charlie Allsop, the gravedigger, who would do little unpaid jobs for the bereaved, his way of showing his sympathy. These two, and others like them, had little enough themselves, and there were those who had sneered at them. But Mary could see now that the Marthas and Charlies of this world enriched life. Criminals only made it frightening and ugly, contaminating everything with their selfish lust for money and goods they hadn't worked for.

As she looked around the prison yard, all she could see was people who cared for nothing but themselves. They had no remorse about lying, cheating, stealing or killing. The fact that they had money to bribe their way out here to boast drunkenly about their crimes proved that.

These were, she thought, without doubt some of London's worst villains and thugs, hard-bitten whores and the most cunning of thieves. Whether from wealthy backgrounds or the gutter, they all used that flash lingo, the underworld language she'd become so familiar with in the colony. She could also sense a dangerous undercurrent flowing around in the yard – jealousy, sexual frustration, pent-up violence and unsettled old scores, simmering as people drank.

Mary was no prude. She knew drink was a powerful remedy for alleviating misery and fear. But however desperate she felt, she knew she would never sell herself for a glass or two of gin, and allow the sexual act to take place in full public view. That was what some women were doing, and with their own children looking on.

She had averted her eyes several times during the afternoon as men rutted like beasts with women so drunk they were almost unconscious, but it appeared some of them had a taste for children too. An elderly woman, who came and sat by Mary for a while, told her that some of the men bribed the gaolers to bring them a constant fresh supply of children from the common side. She had cackled with laughter, and Mary might not have believed it, but later she saw a burly man fondling a ragged little girl of no more than six.

Mary's heart ached at the number of young girls in the yard. They reminded her of herself at the same age – the same fresh complexions, that same curious mix of innocence and courage. They were too busy flirting with the more gentlemanly prisoners to talk to her. Perhaps they thought the elegantly dressed fops would take them with them when they bribed their way out of Newgate.

Mary knew better. The girls would have lost their innocence after a week or two in here, and their courage would fail them on the transportation ships. A few years out in Sydney and they'd look like her. A bag of bones, all hope and spirit gone.

They had all been in Newgate for over a week when Spinks came to the cell and told Mary a gentleman wanted to see her.

Mary had struck up a wary kind of friendship with Spinks. She couldn't really like him, he was too wily, always on the lookout for a way to bleed money out of the prisoners. Yet when he'd found out about her children dying he'd shown real sympathy. He often came along when she was alone, sometimes bringing her a mug of tea or a piece of fruit, and for these there was no charge, he just wanted to chat for a while. Perhaps he was as lonely as she was.

Spinks found her alone more often than not, for after seeing a stabbing on her second visit to the yard, she had decided the gloomy cell was a better place to be. She was alone that day too, for the men were all down in the yard.

'Who is this gentleman?' she asked. Spinks called all men with money 'gentlemen'.

'By the name of Boswell,' he replied with a smug grin. ''E said 'e's a lawyer.'

'You mean he's from outside Newgate?'

'Well, we don't get many lawyers staying in 'ere,' Spinks retorted, and laughed at his little joke. 'Now, do yer want ter see 'im or not? Makes no difference to me.'

Mary sighed. She didn't feel like talking to anyone, but someone from outside might distract her from her melancholy. 'Bring him up,' she said wearily.

'That's my girl,' Spinks said affectionately. 'Now, why don't you comb that pretty 'air of yours while I'm gone? Look, I've brought you a ribbon fer it too.'

He pulled a red satin ribbon from his pocket, thrust it into her hand and was gone. A lump came up in Mary's throat as she ran it between her fingers, remembering her father. He always brought her and Dolly ribbon when he came back from sea. She'd been such a tomboy then, and she never really appreciated it. But she did appreciate this one; she needed something bright and feminine to cheer her.

'Good afternoon, Mrs Bryant!'

Mary spun round at the sound of the melodious voice. She was so engrossed in tying the ribbon at the nape of her neck that she hadn't heard the man coming along the landing.

Spinks was right for once, this one was a gentleman. Perhaps fifty or so, very stout with a red-tinged face, of middling height and wearing very fine clothes – a dark green three-cornered hat trimmed with gold braid, and a coat made of fine brocade. He was also out of breath and wheezing from the stairs.

'I'm known as Mary Broad now,' she said sharply, glancing down at his spotless white stockings and shoes with fancy buckles. 'Why have you come to see me?'

'I want to help you, my dear,' he said, and held out his hand. 'Boswell's the name, James Boswell. I am a lawyer, though better known for my book on Dr Samuel Johnson, my dear departed friend.'

428

Mary recognized his accent as being Scottish, for there had been a couple of officers in Port Jackson who spoke just the same. But the part about his book on his dead friend meant nothing to her. She was more impressed by his gold watch-chain and extravagant silk waistcoat. She thought even the King couldn't be dressed so well.

She shook his hand, and was astounded by any man having one so soft. It felt like a piece of warm dough. 'I'm beyond help,' she said. 'But it's kind of you to offer me some when I am unable to even offer you a chair.'

He smiled, and she noticed his eyes were large and almost luminous dark pools. As he wore a wig, she couldn't see what colour his hair was, but she guessed by his bushy eyebrows it had once been as dark as hers.

'I don't believe you are beyond help,' Boswell said stoutly. 'I wish to defend you. So I would suggest you tell me your story. All I know is the extraordinary tale I read in the *Chronicle*.'

Chapter eighteen

James Boswell strode away from Newgate prison, his feathers ruffled because Mary hadn't fallen at his feet and seen him as her saviour. It hadn't for one moment occurred to him that she wouldn't welcome his offer of help.

'Damn her,' he muttered. 'A heroine she may be, but she's clearly lacking a brain.'

A dear friend had once claimed years ago that 'Bozzie' was addicted to lost causes. He was referring to his passion for whores in that instance, but it was a well-known fact that Boswell was extraordinarily sympathetic to anyone he considered was being treated unjustly. He had often defended poor people without charge, and took on cases that no one else would.

In truth, nothing excited him more than a case everyone said he couldn't win, or a woman who was hell-bent on self-destruction. And Mary Broad was both rolled into one.

What all his worthy friends who poked fun at him didn't really appreciate was that he felt he had a great deal in common with his clients and his whores. He knew what it was to be forced into an unwanted career; he was often misunderstood, he made errors of judgement, and he was reckless.

His father, Lord Auchinleck, a judge in the Supreme Courts in Scotland, had insisted his son become a lawyer, despite his desire to join the Guards. As soon as he'd finished school, Boswell ran away to London and became a Roman Catholic, which appalled his dour Presbyterian family. Indeed, he flirted briefly with the idea of becoming a monk too. But a Catholic couldn't become an Army officer or a barrister, nor even inherit his father's estate, so he soon abandoned Catholicism and reluctantly went along with his father's wishes and entered the Inns of Court. But this wasn't a real change of heart, it was more so he could stay in London and use his allowance to cut a dash in society.

Boswell himself would concede that he was a poor student. He spent more time in the theatre, at the races, and drinking and picking up women than he did at his studies. His father also expected him to make an advantageous marriage, but Boswell disappointed him there too by marrying his cousin Margaret, who had no money of her own. But he married for love, and that to him was far more important than money.

Then his friendship with Samuel Johnson was misunderstood. People claimed he was worming his way into the great man's affections for self-advancement. They said Boswell was a snob, a social climber, a womanizer, a drunk and a hypochondriac.

It was true that he liked women and wine. He couldn't resist a pretty chambermaid or whore, but surely that was only the sign of a zest for life? What his critics failed to see and understand was that he spent the greater part of his life planning, compiling and collecting material for his work, *The Life of Samuel Johnson*. To do it justice he had to enter into the circles that Johnson moved in, to watch, listen, and see through Johnson's eyes. He enjoyed it of course, and maybe he did make use of some of the contacts he made. But he never used Johnson's friendship for self-advancement; he loved the man, and wanted the whole world to share his wisdom, intelligence and humour.

In his heart, Boswell knew he had produced a brilliant biography of his friend, and he was sure that in years to come his name would be up there with other great literary figures. Even if he wasn't getting the kind of rapturous praise and adulation that he felt he was due, he had made a considerable amount of money from his book. He had an elegant home just off Oxford Street, and fine clothes. He ate and drank well, had a great many friends, and his beloved children were a great comfort to him. All in all, he supposed that should be enough for any man.

Yet he still had a yen to do something sensational before putting down his pen and hanging up his wig and gown. He was fifty-two, widowed, no longer in the best of health, and time was running out for him. He wanted to be remembered as 'the Greatest Biographer of All Time', but it would give him immense satisfaction to confound those who considered him a mediocre lawyer too. To win one big, dramatic case was all he wanted; to be looked back on as a man who was the champion of the weak and oppressed.

Boswell smiled to himself, aware that he was being somewhat egotistical. It was absurd really that he felt so strongly about the case of Mary Broad, for until this very morning he had known nothing of her and her companions' plight. To be strictly truthful, something his father had been a stickler for, he had never before even considered the welfare of the felons sentenced to transportation.

In his view transportation was both humane and practical, for it removed criminals to a place where they could do no more harm to society. A far better solution than hanging. When he was a young man he had watched the public execution of a highwayman and a young thief called Hannah Diego, and the horror of it had never left him.

Yet there he was that morning, drinking a leisurely cup of coffee at home and reading the newspaper, merely passing some time before visiting his publishers to see how his book was selling, when he happened to come across an account of the escape from Botany Bay.

It was the quote from Mary herself which captured his interest. 'I'd sooner be hanged than sent back there.'

Clearly Botany Bay wasn't quite the tropical paradise which the newspapers had led most people to believe. Boswell had to read on.

He was shaken that Mary, eight men and two small children had sailed some 3,000 miles in an open boat. Even more disturbing was that four of the men had died after capture. But it was the loss of the two children which really plucked at his heart. As a man who adored his children, and felt blessed that they were all close to him, he couldn't imagine anything more tragic than to lose even one of them. This poor woman had lost everything, her husband and her children, and now she was likely to lose her life too.

In his mind's eye he again saw Hannah Diego struggling as she was dragged to the hangman's noose. He could smell her fear, hear the ghoulish roars from the watching crowd, and remembered the nightmares he'd suffered for so long after that day.

He felt a surge of sickness and anger. He couldn't stand by and let Mary Broad share that fate. It was barbaric. She had suffered enough.

Boswell was also curious about the character of the woman. She surely had immense courage and determination to lead those men to freedom, such strength to survive fever and starvation. He wanted to know more, to meet and talk to her. With that he suddenly put down the paper, called for his coat and hat, and set out for Newgate.

In his imagination, Boswell had pictured Mary Broad as a big woman, strong and lusty, just like his favourite whores. It was something of a surprise to find her small, thin and softly spoken. She looked old beyond her years too, weighed down with grief, her grey eyes already showing a resignation to death.

She told him her story very simply, as if she was weary of recounting it yet again. There was no attempt at trying to gain his sympathy, no shocking details of hardship, deprivation or cruelty. The only time tears sprang to her eyes was when she spoke of Charlotte's burial at sea. Even those she brushed away quickly, and went on to say that she was treated with kindness on the *Gorgon*.

Boswell found himself immensely touched, sensing all the horror Mary had left out. He had been in Newgate many times before, so he had come prepared for lies, exaggerations and distortions of the truth. Like most of his contemporaries, he believed in a criminal class, a stratum of people who were pre-ordained to undermine a decent society. They could be identified easily by their brutish manner, their idleness and their lack of principles. Down in the prison yard he'd seen so many of them, strutting around as if in a private and very select club.

Mary certainly wasn't one of them. She had more in common with the debtors, who sat disconsolately in small groups, bitterly ashamed of the events which had brought them into prison, all hope and spirit gone.

Yet the shiny red ribbon in Mary's dark hair, which was a little incongruous when her dress was so shabby and stained, suggested that the indomitable spirit which had kept her alive through so much hardship was still there, even if subdued for now. She'd asked boldly if he was prepared to defend her four friends too. When he'd stated that he felt it was only her cause he could fight, she'd turned away as if the interview was over.

'Then I cannot accept your help,' she'd said finally. 'We are all in this together, they are my friends, and I will not abandon them.'

It was inconceivable to Boswell that anyone in such desperate straits would put friendship before her own life. He pleaded with her, explained that he could win her case as public sympathy would be on her side because of her children. What he also thought, but couldn't admit, was that he saw her trial as a kind of showcase for his talents. He wanted it to be emotionally charged, he saw himself making a dramatic and heart-rending closing speech. But if he had to defend the four men too, all of whom were probably dubious characters, the sympathy he'd built up for Mary would be very much diluted.

'I have nothing left now but those four friends,' she said simply. 'We have been through hell together, and they are like brothers to me. I'll take my chances with them.'

'Do you think they would do the same for you?' he asked her. 'I think not, Mary, each one of them would do anything to save his own skin, regardless of what happened to you.'

'Maybe,' she sighed. 'There was a time when my own survival counted for more than anything else on this earth. But that's in the past. I don't value it very highly any more.'

James was impressed by her sense of honour, but he supposed she'd lost her common sense along with her spirit.

'Just how are you going to restore her spirit, Bozzie?' he asked himself, tipping his hat to a pretty maid walking with an elderly chaperone.

He paused and turned to look back at the girl, noting her tiny waist, the pert bow on the bustle of her pink gown and her bonnet trimmed with daisies. Veronica and Euphemia, his two older daughters, had many such gowns and bonnets, and nothing cheered them more than new ones. Perhaps Mary would begin to hope again with something pretty to wear?

The air in the small cell in Newgate was tense, the four men staring at Mary with cold, suspicious eyes.

'Don't look at me that way,' she said indignantly. 'The only reason I didn't tell you of his visit was because he can't help us.'

The men had come back to the cell late in the afternoon and they were all very drunk. Had they been sober she would probably have told them about the visit from Mr Boswell, but while they slept off the drink she came to the conclusion that there was nothing to be gained from such a disclosure. Mr Boswell only wanted to help her, not them, and if she told them that they'd only be hurt.

Unfortunately she hadn't realized that a visitor from outside would attract so much attention and speculation among both prisoners and gaolers. By the time the men sobered up and went back to the tap-room, it seemed the whole prison was talking about the lawyer gentleman who'd called on her.

'What scheme are you cooking up?' James burst out, his lean face flushed with anger.

'There is no scheme,' Mary retorted. 'Spinks brought

him here, he was curious about us all, but not interested enough to defend us.'

'You let a lawyer come and go without getting me?' James roared at her. 'I could have made him interested.'

Mary shrugged. 'When you were drunk? He would have been even less inclined to help us.'

'I can hold my drink, talk anyone round, drunk or sober,' James snarled. 'I'll wager you didn't even try to persuade him. You might welcome a rope around your neck, but none of us do.'

Mary looked appealingly towards the other three. 'Surely you know I'd do anything in my power to help you? Has cheap gin rotted your minds?'

They all looked a trifle sheepish.

'But James is right, you should have come and got us,' Bill said mulishly. 'He's the one who is good with words. You just don't care any more.'

'I might not care about myself, but I care about you,' Mary retorted heatedly. 'And if you want to know, I think you are becoming like everyone else in this place, drinking yourselves stupid and fucking anything that moves.'

'Is this man coming back again?' Nat asked hopefully.

'I doubt it,' she said curtly. 'There's nothing he can do for us.'

They heard Spinks coming down the passage, locking the cell doors for the night. Mary retreated over to her corner of the cell and lay down, hoping that the fast-fading light would put an end to the bitterness. James and Bill carried on talking for some time in low voices. Mary didn't even attempt to listen for she was bone-tired and dejected.

Mr Boswell had been such a nice man. Apart from Tench, no other man had ever shown such a keen interest in her. Maybe she ought to have tried a bit harder to persuade him to help all of them? What if she'd pleaded tearfully, clung to him, or even offered herself to him?

'No man would want you, not the way you look now,' she thought to herself. She knew without even seeing herself in a looking-glass that she was no prize. Exposure to hot sun and wind and a poor diet had made her prematurely old; she had no curves, no softness about her. Even Sam, who she knew had had romantic feelings about her in the past, seemed to have lost them since their capture in Kupang.

She could hear a woman screaming in the distance. It sounded like the agony of childbirth and it made Mary's stomach contract in sympathy. It seemed so strange to hear that after all the terrible things she'd seen in the past years, the hurts and humiliations, she still felt others' pain. She ought to be entirely numb by now, unconcerned whether a newborn baby would survive. But she did still care; each time she passed the doorway to the common side of the prison, she felt guilty that those poor wretches were starving, filthy and sick, while she was able to go outside, eat, drink and sleep in a decent cell.

The screaming stopped suddenly. Mary wondered if that was because the mother had finally delivered, or had died. Perhaps for her sake she should hope it was the latter, for the woman's troubles would surely only increase if she lived.

Three days passed, and slowly the men returned to their old easy manner towards Mary. On the fourth day they were taken to the court to be brought before the magistrate, Mr Nicholas Bond.

All five of them had become very nervous as soon as their chains were put back on. Then, as the prison cart rumbled through the crowded, noisy streets, nervousness turned to terror at what lay ahead. Nat's blue eyes were wide with fear, Bill clenched his fists so hard his knuckles were white, Sam appeared to be muttering a prayer. Even James was silenced for once, and when the cart was suddenly surrounded by a horde of people, all shouting at them, he clutched at Mary's hand.

All at once Mary realized this wasn't a mob baying for their blood, quite the reverse. Their shouts were 'Bravo', 'Good luck' and 'God go with you'.

Someone threw a sprig of white heather into the cart. Mary picked it up and smiled. 'They are on our side,' she gasped.

They had all got used to their notoriety in Newgate, but it hadn't occurred to them that their story would be of interest to ordinary people too. Clearly it was, and had touched their hearts too, for so many to have made their way towards the court to show their solidarity with Mary and her four friends.

*

As they were led up to the dock, they saw that the gloomy and dusty courtroom was packed to capacity with spectators. Among them Mary glimpsed James Boswell.

'Mr Boswell's here,' she whispered to James, assuming he and the others would start on at her again if she said nothing. 'The fat man in the fancy jacket.'

James looked, half smiled at the man and passed on the whispered message to the others.

The magistrate, who had a thin face and spectacles perched on the end of a very sharp nose, questioned them one by one, and seemed remarkably attentive to their replies. This in itself was a further surprise, for all five of them had experienced complete indifference from their judges during the trials which led to their transportation. And they all knew people who were shoved through the courts and sentenced without any real evidence or witnesses being produced.

When it came to Mary's turn, the magistrate was far more than just attentive, he was clearly truly interested and committed to getting a real picture of the events. Nervous as she was, she looked right at him and spoke in a clear voice. The only time her voice cracked was when she was questioned about the deaths of her children.

'It was all my idea to escape,' she admitted. 'I planned it and got hold of the charts and navigational equipment. I bullied my husband Will into going along with it, and made him persuade the others to join us.'

She sensed the men looking sideways at her. Clearly they were surprised she should put herself forward as the instigator.

'How long were you planning this escape before you actually left the colony?' the magistrate asked, peering at her intently.

'It was in my mind to escape almost from my first day there,' she said. 'But it was when my husband was flogged for nothing more than keeping back a couple of fish he'd caught that I became determined we should go. We were starving, people were dying all around us, yet my Will, the only man who was supplying any food, got a hundred lashes. It wasn't right.'

His questions went on and on, and Mary answered them all truthfully. Finally the magistrate asked her if she had repented of the crime that sent her to New South Wales.

'Indeed I have, sir,' she replied. 'Not a day went by out there when I didn't regret it.'

A murmur of approval at her words rippled round the courtroom.

'But tell me, why did you choose to risk your two small children's lives on such a long and perilous journey in uncharted seas?' he asked.

'The perils were every bit as great in the colony,' she said resolutely. 'I believed it was better for us all to die together in the sea than to die slowly one by one of starvation or some terrible disease.'

The murmur of approval from the spectators became a roar. When the noise had died down, the magistrate announced that he was not ready yet to commit them to trial and so they would be returned to the prison and brought before him again for further examination in a week's time.

As the five were led away, they were bombarded with more shouts of sympathy. They were put into a cell beneath the court to await their return to Newgate.

'Can you believe that crowd?' James said gleefully, his eyes dancing the way they used to back in Kupang. 'They are all on our side. Surely we won't hang now?'

Mary said nothing. To her, spending a great many more years in prison was a far worse prospect than hanging.

'You were wonderful,' Sam said to her, grinning from ear to ear. 'But you shouldn't have taken all the blame.'

Mary shrugged. 'It was all true, I did bully Will and got him to involve you.'

'You're a brave woman and no mistake,' Bill said in a shaky voice. 'I'm sorry we thought badly of you the other day.'

Before Mary could reply, she suddenly heard the unmistakable sound of Mr Boswell's voice. He was at the end of the stone passageway, demanding to be let in to see her. Mary's heart sank. If he made another offer to defend her in front of the men they would think her a liar.

All at once he was there in front of the grid, resplendent in a dark blue jacket and embroidered waistcoat, his round red face wreathed in smiles.

'Mary, my dear, you gave such a good account of yourself,' he boomed out joyfully. 'The crowd took you to their hearts. Within days people everywhere will read the newspapers' report on today's events, and everyone in England will be behind you.'

'Not just me, I hope,' she managed to say, hoping he'd have the sense to realize her predicament with the men. 'We are all in it together, and you haven't yet met my friends.'

'Of course, of course. They felt for you all up there,' he said, then held out a box containing a considerable sum of money. 'There was a collection for you to help with expenses while you are in Newgate. I am overjoyed for you all.'

James introduced himself and the other men. 'Does this mean you are prepared to defend us now?' he asked, taking the box from Boswell's hand.

'Now that the public has joined Mary in twisting my arm, I have reconsidered and think I can defend you men too, that is, if Mary is prepared to reconsider.' Boswell beamed, looking to each of the men's faces and apparently not seeing Mary's frantic gestures from behind them.'I hope you appreciate your loyal friend! And now we must talk about the next stage. I believe there is no possibility of the death penalty now, just prison. But I'm determined to get you all a pardon.'

He didn't wait to see how they took this news, but carried on, 'I'll be there for all of you next week, and meanwhile I'm going to see Henry Dundas, the Home Secretary. He's a dear friend of mine.'

The moment Boswell had gone, James let out a whoop of joy and jingled the box of money. 'He knows the Home Secretary,' he gloated. 'And people made a collection for us. We're going to be set free!'

Sam looked at Mary reflectively, making her blush. 'He offered to defend you alone and you turned him down, didn't you?' he asked in an awed voice.

The other three men frowned, not understanding. Nat asked Sam what he was talking about.

'Don't you see?' Sam shook his head at their stupidity. 'That lawyer wasn't here by chance. He came to see Mary again. The reason she didn't tell us about his visit the other day was because he only wanted to defend her. She turned him down because of us!'

'You did that?' Nat said, his blue eyes wide with incredulity.

'Holy Mother of God,' James exclaimed. 'And we laid into you!'

Mary blushed furiously. 'It doesn't matter now,' she murmured.

'It does matter, Mary,' Sam said, putting his arm around her. 'That crowd up there collected the money for us because of what you said in the dock. I'm sure that's why the lawyer changed his mind about us too. Once again you've saved our lives.'

Mary couldn't sleep at all that night for her mind was whirling with 'what ifs'. What if they stayed in prison for months or even years until the public lost interest in their fate? They would never get a pardon then. What if Boswell was just a braggart like Will and didn't really know the Home Secretary? What if she did get pardoned? Where would she go, and how would she live?

If the public's imagination was fired up about her plight

as Mr Boswell said, then her family would be bound to hear of it. Her mother would surely die of shame to know her daughter's name was in the newspapers. Mary couldn't help but be amused to think of her worrying about that, after all she'd been through. But her mother's feelings were still very important to her. And she badly wanted to see her and the rest of her family.

At the second hearing in the magistrates' court, the five returned escapees were told officially that they would not be hanged. They were to receive an indeterminate sentence without a trial. To the men this was good enough; they had fame and enough money to be comfortable in Newgate, which after some of the other prisons they'd been in was paradise. It would of course be wonderful if Boswell got them pardoned, but they weren't counting on it.

But Mary couldn't see it the same way. She wanted to be hanged or to be freed, no half measures. She could wait for freedom, but she needed to know exactly how long it would take before she could walk on grass again, swim in the sea, smell flowers and cook her own meals. She couldn't spend her days in a gin-soaked stupor, the time-honoured way of Newgate.

Boswell was right in saying everyone in England would hear about them. The story had spread far and wide. But Mary took no pleasure from her fame. Each day people came to the prison to meet her. A few were from organizations who were firmly against transportation, others were journalists, but in the main they were just curious people, wanting to look at the woman who was in the news as if she was a freak in a side show.

Mary couldn't refuse to meet any of these people. She knew she and the men were dependent on public opinion to get a pardon. But it was painful to keep on telling and retelling the story, and have people raking up things she would rather forget.

James loved it all, especially the grand ladies who kept returning to visit him. Mary knew they didn't really care about his plight. Visiting Newgate was a diversion from their otherwise dull lives; it was exciting to go somewhere so dirty and dangerous. James turned on his Irish charm and he flirted with them, telling them shocking things they could repeat in whispers to less daring friends over afternoon tea. In return they brought him food, new clothes and books. He had also made a start on writing an account of their escape which he hoped he could sell for enough money to go back to Ireland and breed horses.

As for Nat, Bill and Sam, they felt important for the first time in their lives. They too had women admirers, and as each day passed they seemed to need Mary less.

Then there was Mr Boswell. Mary liked him – he was clever, entertaining and very kind – but she didn't know what he wanted of her.

James Martin had made it his business to find out everything about the man, and some of it was a little frightening. While he was a famous and much admired writer, and mixed with the aristocracy, he was also a rake who drank heavily and consorted with whores. He might be a good and loving father to his children, but it was said he neglected his wife, to the extent that he hadn't gone home to Scotland when she was dying. He wasn't even considered a very good lawyer.

Mary thought he was similar to Will in character. He gave the impression of great capability, of intelligence and daring, just as Will did. Of course Mr Boswell was much older, well-educated and a gentleman, but if she could strip him of his years, his book learning and fine clothes, he and Will had a great deal in common. He talked of friends in high places, but were they really friends or just passing acquaintances? He boasted, too, of cases he'd won in courts, and of his success with women, and how he was a descendant of Robert the Bruce.

But Mary could smell drink on him, whatever time of day he visited her, and the redness of his complexion was a sure sign he over-indulged in it. Drink had been Will's weakness too, and she couldn't forget the part it had played in their downfall.

Yet during Boswell's visits Mary believed in him totally. It was so easy to, for his melodious voice with just a hint of a Scots accent was easy on the ear. He painted a new world for her of dinner parties, ladies' gowns and country houses. He made her laugh with his vivid descriptions of people he knew. Yet for all that showiness his kindness was apparent too. He hated injustice, he had real understanding of weakness, especially in women. He loved children, he wanted a fairer society, and schools for the poor.

While he was with her, the room felt warm and full

of light, his conversation stimulated her, she felt hopeful. But the moment he'd gone, the shadows came back. What did he really want with her? Somehow she couldn't quite believe that he was doing so much just out of kindness. He had to have a motive, people always did.

Early in August, just over a month after they'd arrived in Newgate, he came to see her, this time in a small room downstairs in the prison which was furnished with a table and chairs.

'Dear me, it is *so* hot today,' he began, wheezing from the exertion of his long walk to the prison in the hot sun and wiping his brow with a handkerchief. 'I am off on holiday tomorrow. To Cornwall, my dear, but I have put things in hand on your behalf and it is my belief we shall have good news on my return.'

He launched into an explanation about a letter to Henry Dundas, to which he still hadn't received a reply. It seemed to Mary that his earlier claims at what a good friend this man was were probably exaggerated.

But then Boswell put the brown parcel he was carrying down on the table. 'Something for you, my dear. It isn't new, but I hope it will cheer you.'

Mary opened it, and gasped in surprise to find it was a dress, probably a cast-off from one of his daughters, she thought. It was pale blue and the low neckline was trimmed with white lace.

'It's lovely,' she said, blushing with embarrassment. It was in fact the kind of dress any woman would dream about, but it was surely intended for a lady of quality taking afternoon tea or a walk in a park, not for a prisoner in Newgate who had lice in her hair. 'Thank you so much, Mr Boswell, but I'm not sure it's suitable for me.'

'My friends call me Bozzie,' he said reprovingly. 'I consider you a friend. And of course it's suitable for you, you are still a young woman, and with freedom ahead of you. I shall enjoy seeing you wear it.'

'Will I really be freed?' she said, putting the dress to one side and sitting down. 'And if I am, what will I do?'

'I am certain you will walk free,' he said firmly. 'And I am your friend, so I shall make arrangements for somewhere for you to stay. It will give me great pleasure to be able to show you London properly.'

'I couldn't expect you to do that, sir,' she said, a little alarmed. 'I'd be more than happy to get a job as a housemaid or seamstress.'

He put one of his soft podgy hands over hers. 'You will need a little pampering before you can work,' he said, looking into her eyes. 'You are skin and bone, you need feeding up, a tonic to purge your blood. You will also have to learn London ways.'

Mary had a sudden, sharp picture of Lieutenant Graham. Did Mr Boswell believe he was going to take her as a mistress?

While she knew that if he did get her pardoned her gratitude would compel her to go along with it, the thought revolted her. He was fat, his breath smelled of drink, and she didn't think she could even bear to kiss him, let alone lie with him.

'I must make my own way in the world,' she said after a second's thought. 'I am so grateful to you, Bozzie, but if I do leave here, I shan't lean on you.'

He laughed, and tickled her under the chin. 'Smile for me, Mary. You are a pretty woman when that doleful expression vanishes. Do not be too hasty, for London is a harsh place without a friend.'

He changed the subject then, much to Mary's relief, and spoke of his planned holiday to Cornwall.

Just the mention of Cornwall was enough to evoke vivid mental pictures of home for Mary. It was just about seven years since she'd boarded the boat for Plymouth, and Dolly's words, '*You could travel the whole world and never find a place as pretty as Fowey*', came back to her.

She had travelled the world now, and it was true, she had never seen anywhere so pretty. If she shut her eyes she could see the sea sparkling under the summer sun, smell the seaweed, hear the gulls.

'I've never been to Truro, Falmouth or Land's End,' she said, when Boswell told her these were places he intended to visit.

'No!' he said in surprise. 'Really?'

'You will understand why when you visit them,' she said, and smiled because despite his age he had a very boyish enthusiasm for life. 'They might not be far away in miles from Fowey, but the roads are bad, little more than tracks.'

'There have been riots in Truro,' he said with a sigh. 'The Army had to be called to quell them. But then there have been riots everywhere since you've been away.

England has been affected by the revolution in France, I suspect, so much dissatisfaction and unrest.'

Mary knew Boswell read a great many newspapers. One of the things she liked best about his visits was the chance to talk about what was going on outside the prison walls. She might have her four friends for company, but their conversation was very limited. She was tired of discussing their escape, and the people they knew back in New South Wales, and she had even less interest in discussing the other prisoners here.

'I wish I could read,' she said regretfully. 'I am very ignorant of world affairs.'

He put his hand on hers again. 'Mary, you can learn to read if you wish for that. But do not say you are ignorant, for you have a greater intelligence and wisdom than many people I know who consider themselves clever.'

He got up then. 'I must go now. Try not to fret, and be sure you will be on my mind all the time I am in Cornwall.'

He kissed her on the cheek. 'Wear the dress, Mary, it might make you remember the days before your young life turned sour.'

Mary did wear the dress, a great deal. And Boswell was right, it did make her remember her girlhood. She thought of running to meet Thomas Coogan in Plymouth, the way he used to catch her in his arms and spin her round, and the heady delights of kissing him.

There were no looking-glasses in Newgate, but she could tell by the way men looked at her in the dress that she wasn't as worn and plain as she had previously thought. Knowing that helped her; she found herself thinking of freedom more and more, and despairing sometimes that it would never come.

Chapter nineteen

'What ails you, Mary?' Boswell asked, reaching across the table in the Newgate visiting room to take her hand. 'You've hardly said a word to me today!'

Mary had been imprisoned for seven months now, and it was a bitterly cold February day. She was wearing a man's great-coat, one of two that had been given to James Martin by his lady admirers. She had thick woollen stockings, and mittens on her hands, but she was still so cold she felt she might just die from it. But it wasn't only the cold which was making her so morose, she had lost heart.

'Will we ever get pardoned?' she asked in a small voice. 'Tell me now if it isn't going to happen, Bozzie. I can't go on waiting and hoping like this.'

Each time Boswell came to see her he told her how busy he'd been on her and her friends' behalf. He said he was making a nuisance of himself to everyone, browbeating Henry Dundas and anyone else who was influential. But as the months crawled by, Mary couldn't help but suspect Boswell's promises were empty ones.

'It is seven years now since you were first arrested,' Boswell said gently. 'You have borne that with such fortitude. Surely you can be patient for just a little longer? Or is it that you've lost faith in me?'

Mary didn't want to admit that was the case, for she was very aware of how little she knew of the world outside the prison gates, or of lawyers, judges and Home Secretaries. Boswell tended to talk to her as an equal, telling her about famous people he'd met, parties he'd been to, the theatre or concerts, assuming she knew who or what he was talking about. But how could she? She was an illiterate country girl. The closest she'd come to a concert was seeing a marching band in Plymouth. Not once in her life had she sat down to dinner at a table laid with silver knives, forks and crystal glasses.

When Boswell spoke of Lord Falmouth, Evan Nepean and Henry Dundas, people he was seeing on her behalf, they were just names. She didn't know who or what these people were. For all she knew he could be inventing them to make himself sound busy.

Her father used to have a saying: 'In the kingdom of the blind, the one-eyed man is King.' She had only come to understand what was meant by that when she was in Port Jackson. There she was smarter than most of the other prisoners, many of the Marines, and indeed some of the officers too. She had come to believe she was astute about people and capable of coping with almost anything.

But London and Newgate were a very different kettle of fish to Port Jackson. Everyone was sharp here, they might not have any more book-learning than she, but they were cunning. All of them, convicts, gaolers or visitors from outside the prison walls, had far more breadth of knowledge and experience than she did.

She might have been to the bottom of the world and back, but since arriving in Newgate, she had seen how limited her own abilities really were. She could catch a fish, gut it and cook it. She could sail a boat, help build a hut too, but there wasn't much else. She had pinned all her hopes on Boswell because he was clever and educated, but maybe she'd been foolish to do that.

'I think it's myself I've lost faith in,' she said with a sigh.

'That is very understandable,' he said, his dark eyes softening with sympathy. 'Newgate tries to destroy all that comes in through its doors. But you must fight against it, Mary. Look around at the women who sell themselves for a glass of gin, the men who would steal a man's boots while he sleeps, and remind yourself you are not one of them. You, because of your courage and forbearance, have captured the hearts of a nation. Each day people ask me how you are, they press money into my hands for you.'

'They do?' Mary said in surprise, and then her eyes narrowed. 'So where is it?'

Boswell chuckled. 'I'm keeping it safe for the time when you will need it. It wouldn't be wise for you to have it here, but I jot every penny down, and when you are released it will go towards lodgings, clothes, food and transportation to wherever you wish to go.'

She nodded, taking heart that he had said 'when' rather than 'if'. 'Can you tell me how many more weeks before I know for sure?'

Boswell shook his head. 'I can't, Mary. I'm doing everything I can to force the hands of those with the power to get you released. I can do no more.'

After Boswell had left, Mary went to the tap-room in search of the men. Despite her aversion to the place, she was loath to wait alone in the cell for their return.

As always, the fumes of cheap spirit, tobacco and human odours almost knocked her back as she opened the door. The room was small, a cellar-like place with grey stone walls which felt cold and wet to the touch. It was lit by a smoking lantern and the only furniture was a couple of rickety benches. Fresh air only came in via the door, but the regular drinkers appeared to have adapted to the smog-like conditions.

It wasn't as crowded as it normally was, perhaps because gaol fever was raging on the common side. But there were still around sixteen men and four women, two of whom Mary thought might be recent arrivals as she hadn't seen them before. One of them, gaudily dressed in a purple and blue striped dress, was perched on a man's knee, letting him fondle her breasts as she swigged at a bottle.

As always when she had occasion to come in here, Mary's stomach churned. It wasn't that she disapproved of people drinking here or anywhere else – drink was just as valid a way of coping with being in prison as prayer was. But the tap-room seemed to bring out the very worst in people. They boasted, they whined, they tore other people's characters to shreds. Sexual fumbling, often with a running commentary from the perpetrator, was a regular occurrence. She had come in here once to see a man push a woman off his lap, having just completed the sex act, and another man grabbed her and used her too, while people applauded him.

Plots against unpopular prisoners were hatched in here as well, and as jealousy was usually the reason behind most of the vicious attacks in Newgate, Mary often feared for herself and her friends.

'Mary, my little darlin'!' James exclaimed as he saw her in the doorway. 'Come and have a drink with us!'

James had undergone a quite dramatic change since their arrival in Newgate. The notoriety, his ability to read and write, and his natural charm had set him apart from the other prisoners almost immediately. But his image had been further enhanced by the stream of ladies who came to visit him. In smart new clothes, clean-shaven and with his hair neatly trimmed, he now had the persona of a member of the Irish aristocracy. He could never be called a handsome man, with his big forehead and nose, but he wore the new clothes with style, and his humour and warmth were very attractive.

Mary's heart sank when she saw his face flushed by drink and the way he staggered as he moved towards her, but far worse than the drunkenness was the company he was keeping. Amos Keating and Jack Sneed were real scum, as ugly in their appearance as they were in their hearts. The pair of them had bludgeoned a wealthy old widow to death when she caught them robbing her house. Even now, awaiting their execution, they showed absolutely no remorse, they even bragged about it. Nat, Bill and Sam weren't in the room, and Mary suspected they'd left because they didn't wish to mix with the likes of Amos and Jack.

'I just wanted to talk to you, James,' she said, backing away. 'But it will keep.'

'Too high and mighty to drink with us?' Amos, the smaller of the two men, leered at her, showing his rotting teeth.

Mary hesitated. It wasn't in her nature just to walk away silently from such a remark. But her hesitation was her undoing, for Jack, Amos's accomplice, a six-foot brute with a face like raw liver, was across the room in two strides and caught hold of her round her waist.

'I like 'em 'igh and mighty,' he said. 'They've always got the tightest cunts.'

He lifted Mary up, holding her in a vice-like grip, and tried to kiss her. Mary slapped out at his face, but he only laughed.

'That's right, you fight me,' he roared out in delight. 'I don't like me women too willin'.'

Mary struggled, but he was holding her too tightly to let her get free and, spurred on by strongly voiced encouragement from the other drinkers, he wasn't going to relinquish her.

'Let me go,' she shouted, pummelling him with her fists. 'James, help me!'

Mary saw him lurch forward, but Amos caught him around the neck to hold him back, and she knew in that instant that she was in real danger.

The majority of men in Newgate, whether prisoners or gaolers, believed all the women were theirs for the taking. Mary had always considered herself reasonably safe because of her elevated status as an escapee and her four male friends who stayed close to her. But Jack and Amos clearly weren't in awe of her, and believed she was easy game.

'A woman who lets herself be shared by four men shouldn't mind someone new having a turn,' Jack hissed in her ear, before flinging her down to the floor. He unbuckled his belt and leaped on top of her, the sour smell of his filthy clothes making her gag.

Mary screamed to James again, and she caught a fleeting glimpse of him as the other drinkers closed round to watch what Jack was going to do. James's face looked stricken, but she guessed he was still being held back by Amos and could do nothing.

Mary fought Jack, pulling his hair and scratching his face, but he caught her two hands with one of his, while the other groped frantically under her clothes. He was hampered a little by her heavy great-coat, and she was wriggling like an eel.

'Get off me, you filthy bastard,' Mary yelled, spitting into his face. She tried desperately to get a grip on the floor with the heels of her boots in an attempt to force his body off her, but the surface was too slimy. She continued to scream at the top of her lungs, but that only seemed to inflame Jack more, along with all the other men watching. Desperately, she remembered that screams in Newgate were too commonplace for anyone to come to her rescue.

She could feel the sudden charge in the air as the onlookers grew excited, and if Jack got his way with her, she had no doubt other men would follow him. But she wasn't going to succumb to rape after all she'd been through. She'd sooner die.

She fought him with every vestige of strength, getting her hands free again to claw his eyes with her nails, and pulling at his greasy hair until a handful came away in her hand. As he tried to suppress her with a kiss, she bit his lip hard.

'You little hell-cat,' he exclaimed, almost in admiration, pausing for a second to wipe blood from his mouth.

Mary took the opportunity to buck under him, and managed to get a few inches away to her left. But Jack was too quick; he grabbed her tightly again, pinning both her body and her right arm down, and pulled off his belt with his left hand.

'No, you bastard!' she heard James yell out, and perhaps he tried to get closer to help, though Mary couldn't see. But if he did, he didn't succeed, and Jack was clearly intending either to beat her into submission with the belt, or use it to tie her hands.

In a way the sight of the onlookers was even worse than what Jack was planning to do to her. The light from the lantern was dim, but she could still see the malicious glee on their faces clearly enough. Her terror grew into fury at their depravity and made her all the more determined not to give them the kind of entertainment they wanted.

Mary had always been observant, and over the last

seven years this had become even more finely honed out of necessity. She had noticed empty bottles lying on the floor when she'd been here before. It was too dark to see if there were any there today, but she stretched out her free arm and swept it quickly across the floor until she felt one.

Jack had now got his breeches unfastened, and his penis stood out like a purple-tipped barber's pole. He lunged towards her again, his belt in his hand, and she guessed his intention was to choke her into submission and silence.

She screamed again to divert him, squeezing her legs together so he would be forced to let go of one end of the belt to prise them apart. He faltered, not quite knowing which end of her to attack first. Mary seized the opportunity to tap the bottle sharply against the floor, leaving a broken jagged edge, then with one swift movement she thrust it into his neck, just below his ear, with as much force as she could muster.

Jack let out a bellow of pain, jerking up on to his knees, his hands going to his neck. Mary leaped up off the floor and stood with her hands on her hips, panting from the exertion, looking contemptuously down at her attacker.

The tap-room fell silent. Jack was still on his knees, blood spurting out between his fingers. His eyes were rolling fearfully, and he was making a horrible gurgling noise in his throat.

'Let that be a lesson to you,' Mary said between her teeth, and kicked out at him so he keeled over.

She turned to the rest of the crowd, the broken bottle still in her hand. They moved back a step or two, assuming by her bared teeth that she was going to attack them too. For a moment she wanted to, but they reminded her of the rats in the hospital in Batavia. Like them, these people all had sharp features and a furtive manner. They preyed on the weak too. They were despicable and beneath her contempt.

'If any one of you even thinks of touching me again, I'll kill you,' she snarled at them. 'Now, get help for him. And James, you come with me.'

The other three men were not back in the cell, even though it was nearly dark now. James, who had been apologizing profusely all the way up the stairs, slumped down on to the straw, drew his knees up to his chin and lowered his head on to them.

'You look as if you think I'm going to hit you,' Mary said sharply. 'Perhaps I should, for keeping company like that.'

'What if he dies, Mary?' James bleated out, his face chalk-white in the gloom.

'Do you think anyone will care?' she exclaimed as she lit a candle. 'He's a murderer and due to be hanged. But he won't die from what I did, it was only a flesh wound. If it keeps you out of the tap-room for a week or two, I won't have done it for nothing.'

James was silent for some time. Mary sat down and leaned her back against the wall. She felt very cold and shaky now, aware it was rather more luck than strength or superior intelligence that had enabled her to overpower Jack.

'Do you hate me?' James asked after a little while, his voice quavery and weak. Mary thought the shock had sobered him up.

'Now, why should I hate you?' she retorted. 'It wasn't you that tried to rape me.'

'I should have found a way to stop him. I let you down.'

'All men let me down,' Mary said, and suddenly she was crying. She hadn't once resorted to tears since they'd arrived in Newgate. She had told herself that after losing her children, nothing could make her cry. But once again she had been forced to fight for herself, and it seemed to her that her entire life had been one long fight, which she was now too tired to continue.

'Don't, Mary,' James said, and quickly moved across the floor to comfort her. 'I can't bear to see you cry.'

'Why?' she asked bitterly, tears running down her cheeks. 'Are you afraid if I crumple there'll be no hope for any of you?'

She had replied without thinking, but all at once she saw it was true. She had had people leaning on her, sapping her strength, right from the days back in the *Dunkirk*. She remembered setting up camp in Port Jackson, with everyone asking her how to do this, how to do that. They wanted her to listen to their problems, enlisted her help in everything from nursing a sick child to pleading with the officers for a blanket or a cooking pot. It never let up, right through the escape and afterwards.

But who did she have to lean on when things were

bad? Mary was forced to keep a grip on herself because she knew she couldn't count on anyone.

'We would flounder without you, that's for sure,' James said ruefully, as if he'd read her thoughts. 'But you do know how much me and the others love you?'

'I don't know that I believe men can love,' she sobbed. 'When men can use the very same act when they say they love a woman, as they do to show her how much they despise or hate her, I can't believe they have hearts.'

James put his arms tightly around her and rocked her against his chest. 'That's a very cynical thought, Mary. I've done a lot of things I'm ashamed of, but I've never taken a woman by force. And a man can love a woman with no thought of lying with her. Me, Nat, Bill and Sam, we all feel that way about you, you're like a sister to us.'

'But where are you every day if you care so much?' she burst out. 'I'm in here alone for hours on end. You leave me to see Mr Boswell, it's me that bargains for the food from Spinks, gets our washing done. What do any of you do but drink?'

'We leave you to see Boswell because we know it's you he wants to see,' James said indignantly. 'You get better deals from Spinks too because he likes you. And if we leave you alone it's because we thought that was what you wanted.'

'Is that so?' she retorted.

'You certainly know it's right about Boswell and Spinks,' James replied defensively. 'Was it something Boswell said that made you come to the tap-room for me?'

Mary thought for a moment. She had all but forgotten what had passed between her and Boswell. 'I think I was just upset because he had no news of our pardon,' she said, wiping away her tears with the back of her hand. 'I'm beginning to think there will never be one.'

'Then maybe it's time I wrote to the newspapers,' James said. 'A little reminder we are all still here, it might prompt some action.'

Mary was aware that the men weren't as desperate as she was to be freed. They wanted it of course, but they had grown used to Newgate, and as long as money came to them for drink and food, they were content. But in Mary's opinion James was living in a fool's paradise. He'd had ambitions when they first got here, of writing a book and going home to Ireland to breed horses, but all he did now was drink the time away. He didn't seem to realize that none of the women who found him so fascinating now would want to know him or help him once he was released. He had to start thinking about that day, now.

She sat up and caught hold of his face between her two hands. 'Listen to me, James,' she insisted. 'You've got to stop going into the tap-room. The people you meet in there aren't doing you any good. Please spend your time writing your book, reading, anything other than drinking, or when we do get out you'll get yourself in trouble again and you'll end up back here.'

'Don't preach, Mary,' he said, shrugging her away. 'I know all that.'

'Do you?' she asked. 'Then you are a great deal cleverer

than me. You see, I've thought about it constantly, and I still don't know how I'm going to live. I ask myself, what can a woman do to make an honest living when she can't read or write? I wonder what right-minded person would want a convicted felon working in their fine house.'

'There's always someone,' he said blithely.

Mary raised one eyebrow questioningly. 'Oh really? You believe that the stink of prison will disappear the moment I walk out the gate? That there'll be a kindly person waiting for me, ready to take me to their house and run the risk I might run off with their family silver?'

James winced. He never liked it when Mary reminded them all that they were convicted thieves. 'Mr Boswell will help you. Besides, some fine fella will come along and marry you, maybe you'll have children again too.'

Mary gave a harsh little laugh. 'I look like an old crow, James, what man would want to marry me?'

'I would,' he said, taking her hand and squeezing it. 'Sam too. You are beautiful, Mary, you are strong, brave, good and honest. Any man with half an eye would be joyful to have you.'

It was on the tip of Mary's tongue to point out that if she chose to marry either of them, her problems would be doubled rather than solved. But she realized James had intended it as a compliment, and it would be churlish to demean it. 'You could charm most of the women in London speaking like that,' she said with a watery smile. 'But not me, James, I know you too well.'

467

'But you don't know yourself very well,' he said, leaning over to kiss her cheek. 'Believe me, you are a prize, Mary. Worth far more than you know.'

James Boswell stood warming his backside by the fire in his drawing room, a glass of brandy in his hand. It was past seven in the evening and he felt drained, both mentally and physically.

It was a week since he'd seen Mary, and her despair had made him redouble his efforts for her. Since ten this morning he'd been calling on his most influential friends and acquaintances to secure their involvement. While most had heard him out and had even shown enough sympathy to give him a donation for her fund, not one had been sufficiently moved by her plight to offer their time or expertise to get her freed.

He moved over to his armchair and sat down heavily. As he leaned back in the chair and sipped his brandy reflectively, he had yet another sharp mental picture of Mary. Her large grey eyes which reminded him of stormy seas. That mane of thick dark curly hair, the pert little nose and lips that so easily curved into a warm smile. She was too thin and sallow-skinned to be a beauty, hard times had left their mark and the elements had aged her prematurely, yet there was something indefinably arresting about her.

They had had so many meetings, both alone and with the four men. Boswell knew the escape story inside out now, the individual character of each of those involved, including the ones who had lost their lives after the capture. He had learned to tune in to what lay behind Mary's words, for she always simplified a tale, usually leaving out her own crucial part in it. She had said what day in December Emmanuel had died in the Batavia hospital, and also mentioned how Will arrived at the hospital before then. Only a chance remark later, about when she rejoined the other men in the guard ship, made him see that she had stayed on at the hospital with Will until he died.

Boswell knew how the other men felt about Will, and why. Mary too felt he had betrayed them all. When he asked why she stayed with him until his death, she shrugged. 'I wouldn't leave anyone to die alone without some comfort,' she said.

To Boswell, that was the core of Mary's character. She didn't see such action as noble or generous, to her it was basic humanity. Most women who had just lost their baby would want the father to suffer even if he was only partially responsible. Mary could certainly have used that valuable time to escape with Charlotte, but she didn't. She stayed and cared for Will.

It hadn't been easy to really understand Mary. She was adept at changing the subject, making light of incidents and giving others credit when it ought to have gone to her. But Boswell was tenacious and also had a very good memory, and by fitting things the men had told him about Mary with what she had said herself, the truth emerged.

Her courage, endurance and intelligence were all remarkable. There was something decidedly masculine about the way she showed so little emotion under stress, yet she was very feminine in other ways. She was passionate in her anxiety about babies born in prisons, and the lack of care for the mothers. She would admire Boswell's fancy waistcoats, tears had welled up in her eyes when he brought her a posy of snowdrops, and she showed real concern when he arrived out of breath. He had noted her tenderness towards her friends, and the way she kept herself and their cell clean and tidy. In Newgate, that was almost unheard of.

It was well below freezing outside, but Boswell's drawing room was warm from the blazing fire, and very comfortable. Shutters and heavy brocade curtains kept out the draughts, his armchair supported him perfectly. He had only to ring the bell and his housekeeper would bring him anything he wanted – a plate of ham or cheese, a bottle of port, or even a blanket to put round his knees. She would warm his bed with a hot brick before he got into it and his night-shirt would be hung by the fire to warm too. In the morning he was woken with a tray of tea, the fire would already be lit, and hot water ready for his morning wash.

Tonight in Newgate it would be bitingly cold, and he could hardly bear to think of Mary trying to sleep huddled on straw. Yet she never complained about the conditions, in fact she showed gratitude that she had been spared the common side of the prison. It was only when she recalled her native Cornwall that he saw a hunger in her eyes for fresh air, the majesty of the pounding sea and the wildness of the moors.

His own trip to Cornwall had made sense of some of

Mary's traits. While he had in the main found it a wet and cheerless place, with worse poverty in some areas than London, when the sun came out and he had seen the spectacular scenery, he had felt humbled.

The way the tiny fishing villages had insinuated themselves into the shelter of the cliffs spoke reams about its natives' tenacity. They fished, went down mines and farmed. However poor they were, the Cornish didn't kow-tow to the wealthy landowners. James had a sense all the time he was there that the common folk had the heart and the courage to rise up and take back what was rightfully theirs, if they so chose. Mary was Cornish through and through, sturdy and wild as a moorland pony, as tenacious as the limpets in rock pools, and often as deep as its pit shafts.

But last week he'd thought she was sinking, that she was unable to take much more of everything she'd endured so stoically. He was afraid that her low state would make her vulnerable to infection, and she'd have no strength left to fight it.

Perhaps he had initially looked for glory by defending her, but he certainly cared nothing for that now. He wanted so much to lead her from that dreadful place, to watch her blossom with good food, pretty clothes and freedom.

A friend had teased him recently by asking if there weren't enough whores in London to satisfy him, without rescuing a convict. Once he would have laughed off such a remark, and in the past his ultimate aim would have been to bed the woman once she was free. But Mary had touched something deep inside him that had nothing to do with lust. It stung that his friends didn't see this.

Mary, he believed, was his chance to redeem himself for past carelessness with women. He had truly loved his wife Margaret, but he had neglected her and been unfaithful many times. All those scores of whores, serving maids and often innocent young women he'd bedded! He wasn't guilty of callousness, for many of them had engaged his heart. But he had been like a butterfly, sipping nectar here and there, moving on as soon as the sweetness faded.

He wasn't going to lose interest in Mary, though – for once in his life he intended to see this through, whatever the cost to him. His aim went beyond getting her and her friends pardoned, he was going to help Mary on to a secure and prosperous life as well.

He swallowed the last of his brandy and reached out for the decanter to pour himself some more. He couldn't have picked a worse time to plead for Mary. For the past three years, the whole country had been in a state of unrest. The poor had good reason to feel bitter, the Enclosures Act forced many of them off the land into the cities, and craftsmen were finding that their skills were no longer needed as new manufacturing processes came in. They voiced their discontent in huge riots, and with men like Thomas Paine inciting rebellion with his belief that the monarchy should be abolished and the working classes rise to take control, the government was running scared.

Rioters were being arrested, charged and transported

before they had a chance to infect others with their inflammatory views, and although Henry Dundas had originally agreed that the five returned transportees should be pardoned, quite recently, when James asked him to fulfil his promise, he had denied making it and accused him of having a vivid imagination.

Boswell had gone to Evan Nepean, the Under Secretary of State. This man had been responsible for organizing the First Fleet of transport ships, and it was said he had been appalled to hear so many convicts died on the ships of the Second Fleet. There was no doubt that Nepean did care in general about the welfare of convicts, but he took the view that the government had already been lenient in not hanging these five, and saw no reason why they should be pardoned.

James felt a little ashamed now that he'd allowed Mary to believe Henry Dundas was an old and close friend. Their only connection was that they'd been at school together but they hadn't even liked each other. He would contact him yet again tomorrow, though, and write to Lord Falmouth too.

'I cannot, will not give up,' James muttered to himself. 'Right must triumph if I remain persistent.'

As James dozed later that evening in front of his warm fire, Mary was lying awake in the dark, her face wet with tears. She was so cold she could no longer feel her toes or even shiver, and every bone in her body ached.

She could hear someone wailing in the distance. It was a cry not of pain but of sheer hopelessness, and the sound echoed her own feelings. She was so weary of fighting that once again death looked desirable. She could no longer remember why survival had once been so important to her. What was there to live for?

Chapter twenty

'What's the date today, James?' Mary asked, turning on the crate she was standing on to see out of the cell window. She couldn't see anything more than the roof of the part of the prison opposite and the sky beyond, but it was infinitely better to look at the clouds and birds than at the cell walls.

James was sitting on the floor writing. He stopped at her question and looked up. 'The second of May,' he replied. 'Any special reason you want to know?'

It was mid-morning and they were all in the cell, Sam whittling an animal from a piece of wood. Nat busy sewing a patch on his breeches, Bill laboriously plaiting straw into fancy shapes. He called them 'corn dollies', and said that in the Berkshire village where he grew up they were considered fertility symbols. James had more than once joked that if there was a sudden increase in births in the prison, Bill would be responsible.

Since the attack on Mary in the tap-room, they all spent much less time there. Jack had survived his wound, but he was hanged for his crimes just a couple of weeks later. Since then Mary had found herself treated with extreme caution by the existing prisoners. But there were new arrivals every day, and many of them were even more dangerous than Jack, so the men had taken Mary's advice and kept out of the way.

They had all become adept at finding ways to fill the daylight hours. Mary was knitting a shawl, they played cards, they visited other prisoners in their cells, on fine days they went out into the yard. They also reminisced a great deal about New South Wales and their escape, as James was finally writing his book about it. When they did visit the tap-room it was only for a couple of hours in the evening.

'The second of May!' Mary exclaimed. 'Then it was my birthday two days ago, and we've been here nearly eleven months.' Her birthday meant little to her other than it came the day before May Day, which had always been special in Cornwall. No one had even mentioned that in here, so perhaps Londoners didn't celebrate it.

'It seems we've been here a whole lifetime, and they say it's bad manners to ask a lady's age,' James said with an impudent grin.

'You're older than me,' she retorted, and jumped down from the crate to sit on it.

'I have difficulty keeping track of years now,' Bill said thoughtfully, scratching his bald head. 'I'm not sure if I'm thirty-two or -three.'

'I'm still the youngest at twenty-five,' Nat chipped in.

Mary was loath to admit she was now twenty-eight. It seemed so very old. But then she felt old, and she'd been in Newgate for so long that almost everyone she'd met when she first came here had been hanged, died of fever, or been taken away for transportation.

'Someone's coming,' Sam said, looking up from his whittling.

He was right, they could all hear brisk footsteps coming along the passageway. It wasn't Spinks, who had a kind of shuffle, and the other prisoners walked slowly. Mary had found that odd at first, until she discovered herself doing it. What was the point of rushing anywhere when you had a long, empty day to fill?

The footsteps stopped outside their cell, and the door was pushed open. It was one of the guards from the gate, a tall, broad-shouldered man with a pock-marked face. They had seen him on their arrival here, and when they had been taken to court.

'Mary Broad!' he said, looking to her. 'You are wanted below.'

Mary exchanged a puzzled glance with the men. Normally when a visitor arrived for one of them, Spinks came to tell them.

'Maybe it's the King,' James said, and laughed at his joke.

Mary picked up her shawl and followed the guard down the stairs, across the outside yard and into the small office she had come through on her arrival.

'Mr Boswell!' she exclaimed when she saw him waiting there. He looked even grander than usual in a dark red jacket trimmed with black braid, and he had a cockade of red feathers in his three-cornered hat. 'I had expected something bad. Why didn't the guard tell me it was you?'

'Because this is an official visit,' he said, glancing at the guard, then suddenly his face broke into a joyful smile and he pulled a sheet of paper from behind his back. 'This, my dear, is your pardon!'

Mary was too stunned to respond. She blinked, caught hold of the edge of the desk for support and just stared back at Boswell.

'Well, say something,' he laughed. 'Or won't you believe it till I read it to you?'

He cleared his throat, made a sweeping bow as if about to deliver a proclamation to royalty, then held up the sheet of paper.

'*Whereas Mary Bryant, alias Broad, now a prisoner in Newgate,*' he read aloud, and paused to smile.

'Go on,' she whispered, afraid she might faint with shock.

'*Stands charged with escaping from the persons having legal custody of her before the expiration of the term which she had been ordered to be transported, and whereas some favourable circumstances have been humbly presented unto us on her behalf, inducing us to grant our Grace and Mercy on her and to grant her our free pardon for her said crime.*'

Boswell went on reading and finished up by telling Mary that the letter was signed by Henry Dundas at His Majesty's command. But she could barely take it in: the only two words which really meant anything to her were 'free pardon'.

'Oh, Bozzie,' she gasped as he finished. 'You did it! I'm free?'

'Yes, you are, my dear,' he beamed. 'As from this very

moment. You can walk out through the gates right now with me. You have spent your last night in Newgate.'

She rushed to hug him, kissing both his cheeks.

'You are a wonderful, wonderful man,' she said joyfully. 'How can I ever thank you enough?'

Boswell's face was always so red it was hard to tell if he was blushing, but he caught hold of her two hands and squeezed them hard, and there was an emotional tear in his eye. Mary had never kissed or attempted to hug him before, and he had expected her to take the news with her customary coolness. To see her so moved by joy was enough thanks for him.

'You can thank me by getting your things quickly and then we'll go off to celebrate,' he said.

Mary took two steps towards the door, then stopped sharply and turned to him again. Her smile had gone, replaced by a look of extreme anxiety.

'What about the men?' she said in little more than a whisper. 'Are they pardoned too?'

This was the moment Boswell had been dreading.

'Not yet,' he said carefully, afraid she might not want to leave without them. 'But they will get one in due course. I am promised that.'

She hesitated.

'Mary, they will be freed,' he insisted. 'I am sure they will be glad for you. You can do more for them on the outside than by sticking here with them.'

She left then, but walked away slowly, her head bent as if in thought.

*

Mary blurted out her news from the cell door, and began to cry when she got to the part that the pardon was only for her, and they'd have to wait a little longer. She thought they would be angry, hurt and resentful, and covered her face in expectation of a volley of verbal abuse.

James was stunned, but as he saw her gesture he felt ashamed that she anticipated jealousy at her good fortune. She deserved her freedom more than any of them, for her losses had been so much greater.

'That's all right with us, ain't it, boys?' he said, giving them a warning glance not to say anything mean-spirited.

'But I wanted us all to go together,' Mary said, tears running down her cheeks. 'How can I leave without you?'

As one, the four of them leaped to their feet, each man moved by her unswerving loyalty to them.

'Don't be a numbskull,' James said. 'We always expected you to go first, so bugger off and enjoy it.'

'You deserve it more than any of us,' Sam said, his warm smile softening his gaunt features. Nat patted her affectionately on the shoulder, while Bill gave a whoop of delight and punched the air.

Mary wiped away her tears, touched that they could be so joyful for her and hide their own disappointment. 'We've been together for so long I don't know if I can manage without you,' she said.

'Get away,' Sam said, waving her to the door in an exaggerated gesture. 'We'll be glad to be rid of your nagging.'

'We'll turn the cell into a midden, we'll drink all day, and we'll invite whores up here,' Bill growled, but his lips were trembling.

'I'll take your blanket,' Nat chirped up. 'It's thicker than mine.'

Mary looked at their faces with tear-filled eyes. Four brave smiles, four warm hearts, each one so very dear to her for a thousand or more different reasons. They had seen one another at their best and their worst. They had fought, laughed and cried together. Now she had to leave, and learn to live without them.

'Don't get drunk or fight, and James, you finish your book,' she said weakly, falling back on motherly advice because she knew that if she tried to tell them how much she loved them she would break down. 'I'll be back to see you, and we'll all celebrate together when you get your pardon too.'

She slipped off her old dress and put on the blue one Boswell had given her, then, tipping the straw out of the linen sack which she'd brought from the *Gorgon* and had been using as a pillow, she put her few belongings into it.

James came up behind her and fastened the buttons at the back of her dress, then turned her round to tuck a stray curl behind her ear. 'God bless you, Mary,' he said, his voice cracking with emotion. He kissed her cheek, then held her close. 'It'll surely be a lucky man who gets you.'

Wordlessly, Mary broke away from James to kiss and hug the other three, lingering just a little longer with Sam.

'Don't go wrong again,' she whispered to him. 'And find a woman worthy of you.'

She paused at the door, taking one last look at them. She could remember how disreputable and ugly she'd thought James was when she saw him marching off to work with Will from the *Dunkirk*. He was the last link with that stinking hulk, yet through his ability to charm ladies, he looked more like a gentleman now than a convict.

Nat had seemed suspect when she first met him. She had noted the shine on his hair, the smooth flesh on his bones, and guessed how the pretty boy had survived the *Neptune*. It saddened her to think she had judged him for that. It was no different to what she did with Lieutenant Graham.

Sam hadn't had the looks to trade his way to comfort on the *Scarborough*. He'd been close to death when she gave him water on the quay. He'd fought to live, just as he'd fought the elements with her to get them to safety.

As for Bill, she'd been impressed by his toughness when he walked away from his flogging, but she hadn't actually liked him until after they'd escaped. But time had proved there was a kind and decent man under that rough exterior.

She couldn't even claim that any of them had burst into her life like a fire cracker. They were just four seemingly unremarkable men who through desperation had become like her brothers. Every aspect of their characters was etched in her heart, she would hold each dear face in her mind forever.

'I love you all,' she said softly, her eyes filling with tears again. 'Please don't any of you break the law again, I want you to be honest and happy.'

She fled then, tears streaming down her face.

'I have found rooms for you in Little Titchfield Street,' Boswell said as he settled her into a hansom cab. He had noted her tearstained face, and guessed she was upset at parting from her friends. But he felt the separation could only be a good thing. He wasn't entirely convinced that the men would become honest and hardworking on their release, and he wanted no bad influences around Mary now she was free.

'Now, I have money for you,' he said, taking a notebook from his pocket to show her. 'Over forty pounds, a princely sum. I shall pay for your lodgings from it, and you will need clothes too. But for now you must just enjoy your freedom.'

The sadness at leaving her friends behind was eased by the excitement of freedom and seeing London. Boswell pointed out that the view of it she'd seen before when brought from the docks to Newgate was a rather squalid part of the city, and she was now going to a respectable area.

Mary could only stare in silent wonderment. It was a bright, sunny spring day, and the streets were crowded, forcing the cab driver to slow the horses to a mere walk. The iron-rimmed wheels on heavily laden carts, cabs and carriages made a racket on the uneven road surface. Sedan chairmen nimbly bypassed the many piles of horse dung, and wove in and out of the heavier traffic.

Ladies out shopping were wearing gowns and pretty bonnets in every colour of the rainbow, men in frock coats and hats like Boswell's hurried as if on urgent business. Street traders yelled out their wares in strident voices. There were thin little flower girls with baskets of primroses, small boys selling newspapers, and burly tradesmen unloading goods from carts or carrying everything from ladders to pieces of furniture.

But it was the buildings which took most of Mary's attention. Whether private houses, banks or other places of business, they were all so grand. Marble steps, pillars, stone carving such as she'd only ever seen on churches before, so many different designs, pushed up together as if the builders had been short of space, yet each one striving to outshine everything around it. Some places looked very old, half-timbered buildings that leaned out precariously into the streets. Then there were elegant new ones, three or four storeys high, with splendid long arched windows.

There were many smart carriages too. Some had dashing scarlet wheels, on others the graceful horses wore feather plumes, some even had footmen resplendent in gold and red livery.

Boswell pointed out things he thought might interest her – men carrying sides of meat coming from Smithfield market, the Inns of Court where he had studied to be a lawyer, Lincoln's Inn Fields, and many fine houses belonging to people he knew. He told her about the Great Fire of London, and how the city was rebuilt afterwards.

'Look!' Mary interrupted him as he was talking about a coffee house where he used to meet Dr Johnson. She pointed at a woman pushing what could only be called a baby carriage, for a small child was sitting inside the splendid large-wheeled vehicle, waving its little hands in excitement. Mary had never seen anything like it before. 'Are folk so rich here in London they wheel their children around?'

Boswell chuckled. He thought it was so like a woman to be more interested in a child in a wheeled conveyance than hearing about his great friend. He supposed, too, that when a person couldn't read or write, they wouldn't understand why anyone would bother to write a dictionary, or even need to use one.

'I see nursemaids wheeling their charges around the London parks so often that I don't find the carriages remarkable,' he said. 'But I suspect it's not only the cost of them which deters most mothers, they are a little unwieldy.'

'But it's a good idea,' Mary said. 'Especially if you had two or three little ones.'

'I daresay ordinary women with several children would like water coming into their houses in pipes, even more than baby carriages,' he said. 'That would save so much drudgery for them. Some of the rich people have rooms just for bathing in, and the dirty water is disposed of easily by opening a sluice.'

Mary looked at him in disbelief. 'They do?'

'Oh yes,' Boswell said. 'Whole terraces of houses have been built with water brought in by elm pipes, and drains to take away the waste. Maybe one day when these conveniences spread throughout the city our streets will be pleasanter places to walk.'

Mary began to laugh, for just ahead of them she saw a maid tipping the contents of a pail out of a second-storey window.

'I've been unlucky enough to be drenched that way dozens of times,' Boswell said ruefully. 'I think proper drains are something that the government ought to see as a priority.'

'I didn't think London would smell as bad as Plymouth,' Mary said, wrinkling her nose. 'But it does.'

'What can we expect with all these horses?' Boswell remarked, waving his hand to indicate at least thirty of them within their view. 'On a wet day the cart and carriage wheels splash their muck up all over you. They have tried to stop cattle being driven through the city, but to no avail.'

'At least London people seem to be mainly plump and well,' Mary said.

Boswell sighed. 'This is a respectable part of the city,' he said. 'There are other parts like St Giles which tell a very different story. But I'm not going to show you poverty and squalor, you've had quite enough exposure to that.'

The lodgings Boswell took Mary to in Little Titchfield Street were in a narrow but tall house in a terrace, with a gleaming brass knocker on the door and the whitest steps Mary had ever seen. She had a moment's panic as Boswell paid off the driver, for surely he didn't think someone like her should stay in such a place?

But the apple-cheeked woman with a lace-trimmed cap who opened the door and was introduced by Boswell as Mrs Wilkes didn't seem shocked or surprised by Mary's appearance.

'Come in, my dear,' she said. 'Mr Boswell has told me all about you, and I'm sure we'll get along famously.'

Without stopping to draw breath, she commented on the fine weather, and told Mary that she provided breakfast and supper, was happy to do her laundry, and that she must think of her rooms here as home.

'I have water heating for your bath,' she went on, though dropping her voice as if this was a delicate matter. 'Mr Boswell said that would be what you wanted. I only ask that you carry it up yourself because the stairs are too much for me.'

Mary could do no more than nod, for the closest she'd ever come to such startling comfort and splendour was peering through windows of the grander houses in Plymouth. From the narrow hall with its polished wood floor, she could see a thick fringed carpet, upholstered chairs and a shiny wood table with dozens of small ornaments. Yet the way Mrs Wilkes kept looking at Boswell, as if seeking his approval, suggested he was accustomed to even greater things. Mary felt weak with shock, terribly aware that she must stink of Newgate and had undoubtedly brought many of its smallest inmates with her.

'I will leave you to settle in now under Mrs Wilkes's

tender care,' Boswell said, and took hold of Mary's hand to pat it. 'You need another woman now, and some rest and quiet. I shall return at six-thirty to take you out to supper.'

A couple of hours later Mary lay on her bed, too thrilled to sleep even though she was tired.

She had two rooms at the top of the house. The one overlooking the street was a living room, with a table and chairs and two wooden armchairs, one of which rocked.

Her bedroom at the back contained an iron bed, a closet for clothes and a washstand. Compared with what she'd seen downstairs, the rooms were simply furnished, with similar items to those she remembered from home in Fowey. But after so many years of hardship and terrible discomfort it was like a palace, and almost everything she looked at made her want to cry.

She had gladly lugged up the pails of hot water, laughed aloud as she stripped off her clothes and climbed into the tin bath. She couldn't remember when she last had hot water to wash with, let alone submerge herself in. Nor could she remember when she last had a door she could shut others out with. As she scrubbed off the prison smell from her skin and hair, she felt reborn.

Mrs Wilkes was comfortingly blunt, once they were alone.

'I think it's best I burn all your clothes,' she said. 'Mr Boswell brought some things round for you last night, his daughter's I think. And in a day or two we'll go out and buy others. You'll find everything you need in the closet. But you make sure you wash that hair properly.'

Afternoon sunshine streamed in through the bedroom window, and as Mary sat up on the bed to look at her reflection in the looking-glass above the washstand, she was astounded to see that her hair shone the way it had when she was a girl. Mrs Wilkes had brought her up some fresh water with a little vinegar in it, as a rinse. She claimed it would make her hair shine, though Mary suspected it was really to kill off any remaining lice. But whatever the reason, it had performed a miracle, and her hair had never felt so soft or looked so pretty.

It would have been good to have found her face prettier than she imagined, but sadly that wasn't so. Her complexion was grey and coarse, there were lines around her eyes, and her cheeks were hollow. But Mrs Wilkes had made her swallow a huge spoonful of malt, and she insisted that with fresh air, good food and plenty of sleep, in a week or two Mary wouldn't know herself.

Yet happiness was already bringing a little colour to her cheeks, she thought. She'd had to enlist Mrs Wilkes's help not only to lace up the stays, but to take her advice in which order she had to put on all the undergarments. The dainty soft chemise which smelled of lavender and reached to her knees went on first, the low neckline drawn up over her breasts with a ribbon. Then came the petticoat trimmed with lace, and a skirt of blue cotton before the stays. Mrs Wilkes had to show her how the front pointed part of the stays went over the skirt, with small tabs fixed inside the waist. Finally the blue and white dress which had panniers over her hips went on almost like a coat, leaving the stays, chemise and much of her small breasts on view.

'That's the fashion in London, my dear,' Mrs Wilkes assured her when she saw Mary's bewildered and anxious expression. 'At least they've done away with those ridiculous hooped skirts I had to wear when I was your age. Now, let me help you with your hair, you can't wear it all wild like a gypsy.'

Mary put her hand on the bedcover and smiled with delight. It was a simple woven material the colour of oatmeal, but to her it could have been silk. Would Mrs Wilkes realize that she hadn't slept in a bed with sheets and real pillows since she left home for Plymouth eight years ago? Even there they'd been a rare luxury for ordinary people, and Uncle Peter had brought them home for her mother from one of his trips abroad. Would Mrs Wilkes understand, too, how strange it was for her to be in a room with furniture, when she had sat on either a dirt floor or a stone one covered in straw for so many years?

Mary didn't think even Boswell would fully appreciate how miraculous, strange and even frightening everything would be to her for a while. How could he? She hadn't even realized it herself until he brought her here.

'Who is this gorgeous creature?' Boswell joked when he arrived back to take her out for supper. 'Surely there is some mistake, madam? Your name cannot be Mary Broad!'

'It is indeed, sir,' Mary giggled. 'London water, it seems, has magical powers.'

She knew her transformation wasn't merely the result of a bath and new clothes but the spirit of freedom. She had stayed in the lodging-house all afternoon, but the thought that she could, if she wished, walk out of the front door and mingle with the crowds in the streets was like a tonic. To lie on the soft bed, knowing the airy, fresh-smelling room was just for her was so thrilling that she felt she could stay there forever and never be bored.

But Mrs Wilkes had fixed up her hair with some combs and a little lace cap, and she was wearing blue stockings and a pair of shoes with gilt buckles. Now she must go out and test her newfound freedom.

'I don't think I can do this,' Mary said in panic as Boswell helped her down from the cab in a busy street full of shops.

'You can't eat supper?' he exclaimed.

'Not in there,' she said, looking at the sparkling windows of the supper rooms he was intending to take her into. She could see a lady and gentleman sitting at a table by the window. The lady wore a pearl necklace and she was elegantly sipping wine from a glass. Mary thought that to go in there would be like bursting into Captain Phillip's house uninvited when he had other officers for dinner.

'Why on earth not?' Boswell laughed.

'It's too grand,' she blurted out. 'I'll make a fool of myself and embarrass you.'

'No, you won't,' he insisted firmly, and tucking her hand through his arm he led her purposively towards the door. 'All you have to do is smile, and copy what I do. I promise you there's nothing to it.'

Boswell may have thought there was nothing to walking into a place like that, with every single face turning to look at you, but to Mary it was more terrifying than a storm at sea. She realized by the curious stares, the smiles and nods at Boswell and the buzz of muted conversation that they all knew who she was.

Mary felt herself growing hotter and hotter. Her face felt as if it was on fire, for even though the other people didn't continue to stare at her once she was sitting down, she guessed they were watching her out of the corner of their eyes and talking about her.

Boswell was studying the bill of fare and commenting on various dishes he'd eaten here before. He didn't seem to be aware how uncomfortable she felt. 'What would you like to eat, my dear?' he asked. 'The beef pudding is very good here, but so is the rabbit and the duck.'

Mary had been ravenous before they left Mrs Wilkes's house, but that had gone now and she felt sick instead. Her stays were digging into her and the new shoes were too tight. Yet after all the years of living with constant hunger she couldn't possibly refuse a meal.

'You choose for me,' she whispered.

She tried to remind herself that she had been out to supper before, back in Plymouth with Thomas Coogan.

It hadn't been such a smart place as this, there weren't white tablecloths, but she hadn't disgraced herself there, so she wouldn't here. That was over nine years ago, though, and since then she'd become accustomed to gobbling down anything that came her way, whether it was ship's rations slopped into a bowl, or whatever she'd managed to cook in one pot. Choice had never come into it.

The whole idea of sitting at a table to eat was alien to her now. When she looked at the silver cutlery she blanched because a spoon and a knife were all she was used to, and she'd often had to eat with her hands.

'I expect everything feels a little strange to you,' Boswell said solicitously as he filled her glass with wine, 'but you'll soon get used to it. Now, drink up and enjoy your first night of freedom.'

Mary couldn't enjoy it, however. She was more on edge than she had been on her first night in the hospital in Batavia. There it was rats she was watching out for, now it was for people watching her.

The supper arrived, and it looked and smelled wonderful, but it seemed that every time she managed to get a mouthful of food on to her fork, the way Boswell ate, someone would come up to the table to slap him on the back and compliment him on his outstanding success in getting Mary pardoned.

They meant to be kind, their smiles were warm, and they wished her a long and happy life. But she was tongue-tied, and all she could do was force a smile and murmur her thanks.

'You can't blame them for wanting to meet "the girl from Botany Bay",' Boswell said, after it had happened several times. 'Everyone in London is talking about you.'

Mary couldn't bring herself to complain. She thought he had a right to take pride in what he'd achieved, and to bask in his friends' admiration. So she pretended she was every bit as happy as he was, and kept it to herself that she wanted to go home.

When they finally left, Mary was a little unsteady on her feet. She had drunk far more than she'd eaten, but she felt she'd managed to get through the evening without letting Boswell down.

'Goodnight, my dear,' he said, as Mrs Wilkes opened the door to them. 'Sleep well and savour your newfound freedom. I'll call on you tomorrow.'

Mary could hardly wait for Mrs Wilkes to light her a candle to see her way up the stairs to her room. Yet as soon as she'd shut the door, she felt afraid. For nearly a year she'd shared a cell with four men, often cursing them for their snoring or coughing at night. But now this sweet-smelling room with the comfortable bed seemed so eerie by candlelight and too big for her to sleep in all alone.

'Don't be foolish,' she told herself. 'Surely you wouldn't rather be back in Newgate than here?'

Chapter twenty-one

A month after Mary's release from Newgate, she was strolling with Boswell one afternoon in the sunshine of St James's Park.

Visiting London's parks had become one of Mary's greatest pleasures. It was so good to get away from the noise and dirt of the city's streets and see grass, trees and flowers. Many had enclosures with deer in them and there were sheep and cows too. She found it amusing that the cows in St James's were led back to Whitehall in the afternoons to be milked, and you could buy a glass of milk for a penny.

During the week the gentry used the parks to meet friends and be seen in their most fashionable clothes. They didn't appear on Sundays, however, as that was the day the common people came in their hordes. Staymakers, milliners and shop girls had a chance to enjoy their day off and perhaps meet a handsome young clerk, or even a dashing soldier.

St James's Park was Mary's firm favourite, as the only riders or carriages allowed to use it were from the Royal Households. There were ducks, swans and geese on the lake and the flowerbeds were a riot of colour.

'I think I should find some employment now,' Mary said thoughtfully as she and Boswell stopped to watch some children feeding the ducks with stale bread. 'That money won't last forever.'

He patted her hand tucked into his arm. 'No, it won't, my dear, but it will last for a good bit longer yet, and you have to decide what you want to do, and where you want to go first.'

Mary was tempted to argue with Boswell, maybe even to tell him she wasn't entirely happy about her increasing dependence on him. But in the light of everything he'd done for her, that seemed ungracious.

It seemed absurd to Mary now that she had been so afraid when she was first released. Now she woke up each morning and gave thanks to God for His mercy and for sending James Boswell to her. But for the first week there had been many times when she'd almost wished herself back in Newgate.

It was wonderful of course to feel clean, to be free, to have a comfortable bed and good food to eat. Yet freedom was terrifying too, especially when Boswell drove her headlong into it, as he had at that first supper, making no allowances for her lack of knowledge of the world he lived in.

Boswell's friends were all gentry, and when he took her to visit some of them in their homes, she felt she would rather be left below stairs with their servants than be studied as if she were some curious specimen brought from overseas.

There was guilt too. Many nights she'd lain awake in her comfortable bed and all she could think of was Emmanuel and Charlotte. It didn't seem right that she was living so well now, when their short lives had been so wretched. Even now, a month later, she couldn't get away from that thought, it cropped up again and again whatever she was doing. She would go over every part of their lives, looking for something she'd done, or hadn't done, which had caused their deaths. And it always came back to the same thing. If she had stayed in Port Jackson, they might have survived.

These thoughts didn't only come when she was alone. She could be riding in a cab with Boswell and see a mother and child together, and she would feel a stab of pain. When she saw little girls of Charlotte's age in rags, out on the streets, she felt a surge of anger at a society which cared so little for its youngest members.

She also missed James, Sam, Nat and Bill desperately, not only for their company and the shared memories, but for the position she held in their group. She was the leader, the one whose intelligence, practicality and knowledge were valued. Outside Newgate she was an oddity, and people talked down to her as if she was dim-witted.

As the days went by she gradually adjusted. She accepted she would have to learn how to fit in with normal people again, that she would have to learn to make small-talk, and to live within the boundaries expected of women.

She found the courage to cross busy roads, weaving in

and out of the carriages. She learned how to use a fork by practising at home and to put her hair up the way Mrs Wilkes taught her. She even mastered lacing up her stays by herself.

Mrs Wilkes was such a kind, good woman, old enough at over forty to be motherly, but still young enough to understand just how inadequate and overawed Mary felt sometimes. She admitted she sometimes found Mr Boswell a little too bumptious for her taste, but she put that down to his breeding and fame as a writer. She would make a cup of tea, invite Mary to sit with her in the kitchen and get her to talk about anything that worried her.

Mrs Wilkes explained anything Mary was embarrassed to ask Boswell about. She understood why Mary didn't want to be put on show to his friends, and suggested ways in which Mary could make this clear to him. But above all she knew how strange it was for Mary to suddenly find herself out of her real station in life.

'Don't allow it to swamp you,' she advised. 'Learn as much as you can by watching and listening. Enjoy your fame without wondering how long it will last. After what you've been through, you deserve it. But above all, Mary, hold on to your courage, that's what makes you so fascinating.'

When Mrs Wilkes wasn't offering tea and advice, she dosed Mary up with malt, made her drink lemon juice for a clearer complexion, and took her shopping for new clothes. Even though Boswell believed he alone was teaching Mary how to be what he called 'a middling sort', a big step up from the poor but respectable roots of her childhood, in truth it was Mrs Wilkes who taught her most.

Yet along with the painful and bewildering moments there were many more joyful, happy ones. Mary had been to the Tower of London and seen the lions there, she'd visited St Paul's and the Monument and seen the royal palaces, and had been by river to Greenwich. She loved the parks, the busy shops in the Strand, the markets, and just looking at all the fine houses. Mostly Boswell took her to see the sights, but she loved exploring on her own too. He might need a cab because he was getting older, but she liked to walk, to stop and gaze at people, street scenes and buildings.

Now, a month after her release, she could probably fool some people into believing she'd always lived this way. She saw poor people every day, sweeping streets, selling flowers and begging on street corners, and she was very aware that this comfortable life she'd landed in more by luck than her own initiative wasn't secure. She knew she had to find some way of making it so.

She was far too astute to think that a few pretty clothes would land her in a good position. People wanted their housemaids young. They wanted real cooks, capable of coping with large dinner parties, not someone who had gained their experience throwing anything vaguely edible into one pot over an open fire. Housekeepers had to know everything, from how to care for linen and silver to keeping accounts. Mary knew none of that, and she had no references either. The more she looked around, the more she saw there were few work opportunities for any woman.

Even Mrs Wilkes, whom Mary had thought of as gentry, had no choice but to run a boarding-house. She had been widowed ten years earlier, and when the little money she was left with ran out, she'd got a position as a companion housekeeper for an old gentleman at that same house in Little Titchfield Street. When he died, leaving his money to his nephew, Mrs Wilkes inherited the contents of the rented house. Taking in lodgers was the only way she could manage to stay in the home she'd come to love.

Mrs Wilkes's answer to Mary's problems was marriage. She had hinted that Boswell might make the ideal husband. He was after all a widower, very fond of her, and a man of means.

There had been brief moments when Mary toyed with the idea. She liked Boswell very much, he was kind, entertaining and generous. Sadly, however, she knew she could never go willingly to his bed. He was getting old and fat and his teeth were rotten. He was also a very clever man, with children he thought the world of, so he certainly wasn't going to risk their disapproval for an ex-convict who hadn't already proved her love and passion for him.

'I think I would like to live by the sea again,' Mary said as they walked over the little bridge across the lake. London was exciting, but she often found herself longing for the serenity of the moors, the fresh wind from the sea and a calmer life.

'Then perhaps we should make contact with your family,' Boswell said. 'You will remember I met the Reverend John Baron of Lostwithiel while I was in Cornwall. A good man!'

Mary nodded. Boswell had mentioned this man, but as she had only been to Lostwithiel twice in her life, she didn't know him.

'He would call on your mother and father if I asked him to,' Boswell said. 'Shall I write to him? He was very sympathetic to you.'

'I'm afraid they would show him the door,' Mary said dolefully. She remembered only too well her mother's loudly held views on those who broke the law. Mary thought she must be thoroughly shamed by her daughter's notoriety. She wasn't going to like a man of the cloth pleading with her to forgive and forget. In fact it would probably set her even further against Mary.

'It's worth a try,' Boswell said.

'No,' Mary said firmly. 'It's up to me to throw myself on their mercy, it's cowardly to get someone else to act on my behalf. I'll go when the men are pardoned.'

Visiting the men in Newgate was one thing Boswell had refused to let her do. He said it was because of the danger of infectious diseases, but she guessed it had more to do with keeping her away from any harmful influences. As he had been so good to her, she felt she couldn't disobey him, so she had to make do with passing messages through him.

'That might not be for some time yet, Mary,' Boswell warned her. 'You know I am doing my best for them, but the law drags its feet, especially in summer.'

'Then I'll wait,' she said.

He smiled and squeezed her arm. 'Good, there's so much more of London still to show you. And don't worry about money. You still have more than enough.'

The remainder of June, July and the first two weeks of August were an exceptionally happy time for Mary. People's curiosity in her had waned, and she found herself far more comfortable in her new life. She helped Mrs Wilkes as much as she could, going shopping with her and often doing the washing and preparing the supper.

Yet every now and then a strange kind of melancholy came over her. She would think of Will, Tench and Jamie Cox, and all those she'd liked but left behind in Port Jackson. She would dwell on little moments she'd shared with them, and often found herself crying. It irritated her that people in England neither knew nor cared how grim or badly run the colony was. Yet conversely she often wanted to tell people that New South Wales was beautiful and intriguing. And she wondered why she could still think so after all that had happened.

She would be caught short, too, by the extreme contrasts in her new life to the old one. One day Mrs Wilkes asked her to throw away some meat which was going bad. Mary had to fight with herself not to eat it, for the thought of wasting food after experiencing starvation was terrible. It seemed ridiculous to her, too, that as a lady she was expected to be weak, helpless and squeamish, when she had collected and eaten grubs, hacked up turtle meat and been the driving force behind a 3,000-mile voyage in an open boat. A lady shouldn't mention bodily functions either, and certainly not in mixed company. But she had coped quite well with having to perform hers in the company of eight men, and after living with them in such close proximity for so long, there were no mysteries about men left for her to discover.

But as time passed Mary found herself looking back far less. While her children were always in her mind, she found other memories were fading, and she was living in the present again. The weather was good, and Boswell continued to call on her frequently, taking her out to the parks, on river trips, and to the countryside surrounding London.

One day in August, he took her out in a cab to the village of Chelsea. He appeared to be very much amused by poems about them which were being widely circulated around the town. It seemed the writers believed they were lovers, and in one of the poems they met their deaths on the gallows together.

'Perhaps I should marry you, my dear,' Boswell said jokingly. 'It would confound all those poetic simpletons.'

'I think your daughters might find that a little distressing,' Mary said with a smile. 'I am not the stepmother of any girl's dreams.'

'Your heart is still with Captain Tench?' Boswell said, raising one eyebrow quizzically.

Mary had often mentioned Watkin Tench, but had

never given Boswell any indication of how she had felt about the man. Even her four friends in Newgate knew nothing of that. So she was amazed to hear him say this. 'I don't have a heart,' she said flippantly.

'Untrue,' he retorted, but he laughed all the same. 'I found out he paid for your cell, Mary. You see, he stopped paying when you were pardoned, and the men had to make new arrangements.'

Mary had met her equal in quick wits with Boswell. Like her, very little passed him by. 'So! We were friends, he helped me, that doesn't mean I was in love with him.'

'I think it means he was in love with you,' Boswell said sagely. 'Marines aren't known for their largesse as a rule. But he strikes me as a gutless wonder for not coming to London to claim you if he knows you are free. He's on HMS *Alexander* now, part of the Channel Fleet.'

Mary's heart quickened at this news. She'd always imagined Tench had sailed off to some faraway place again.

'Aha,' Boswell chortled. 'I see a faint blush. Now, would that be because he's still close to England?'

Mary decided there was no point in trying to pretend any longer.

'I did have strong feelings for him, and he for me,' she said with a shrug. 'But it could never be. And he's not a gutless wonder. I insisted that he wasn't to try and contact me.'

During her time in Newgate Mary had tried not to hope Tench might turn up to see her. And in the prison it was easy to see he belonged to a different world.

However, now she was free, looking for all the world like a respectable widow, she couldn't help but drift into little day-dreams of him coming up to London to claim her and whisking her off to a country cottage. At times she even believed she'd changed so much that she could become the perfect wife for an officer.

'You are right. It couldn't be,' Boswell agreed, disappointing Mary somewhat. 'I've had my share of falling for unsuitable ladies, and it brings nothing but grief on both sides.' He took her hand and squeezed it in sympathy. 'Grief is something we should all try to avoid. Whatever our age or circumstance.'

Although on the face of it his remarks were only about her relationship with Watkin Tench, Mary had a feeling Boswell meant more. The earlier mention of marriage had been a joke, but she had a feeling he was also trying to sound her out to see if she expected him to propose to her. She thought it would be wise to make it clear that wasn't her aim.

'Well, tell me, O Wise One!' she joked. 'What sort of a man is likely to make me happy?'

Boswell pondered on this gravely for a moment or two. 'A sea-going one, I'd say,' he said eventually. 'A well-set-up mariner. Perhaps a widower, who would be less likely to feel aggrieved that you have a past. Not more than thirty-five. Young enough to want a family.'

'You wouldn't happen to know him already?' she asked laughingly, for he spoke as if he knew the very man.

'No, my dear, sadly I don't,' he chuckled. 'I'm just a romantic old fool who would like to see a happy ending for you. But to my mind, one of the best things about life is that one never knows what is around the next corner.'

Chapter twenty-two

'That wretched man again!' Mrs Wilkes exclaimed in exasperation at the hammering on her front door. 'Only yesterday I tried to tell him he wasn't doing your reputation any good by calling here at all hours. And here he is again, on a Sunday!'

It was 18 August and very hot. Mrs Wilkes and Mary were sitting out in the cool of the backyard with some sewing. They had been talking about Mary's friends still in Newgate. Mary had become a little tearful, afraid that their pardon would never come and that they would begin to believe she had stopped caring for them.

Mrs Wilkes, like Boswell, thought visiting was a bad idea, given the high risk of infection, but she offered to write them a letter for Mary. At the moment they heard the rapping on the door, Mary was thinking of all the things she had to tell them.

Mary smiled at her landlady's outburst, for she knew perfectly well that Mrs Wilkes enjoyed having neighbours gossiping about Boswell calling so often. He was, after all, famous and a gentleman, and noon, whether it was Sunday or not, was a respectable time to call.

'I'll go,' Mary said, getting up. 'Shall I tell him to go away?'

'No, of course not,' Mrs Wilkes said hurriedly. 'You must take him into the parlour and I'll bring you in some tea.'

But Boswell was not alone this time. He had a burly, florid-faced man with him, who in a somewhat loud checked jacket, matching breeches and a very poorly fitting dull brown wig, looked like a tradesman.

'Good day, Mary,' Boswell said, lifting his hat. She thought he looked flustered. 'This is Mr Castel, a glazier by trade, and a native of Fowey. He wishes to give you certain news of your family, and he insisted we came right away to see you.'

Mary looked from one man's face to the other, noting how hot and agitated they both looked. Boswell clearly wasn't happy about this man's insistence on coming to see her, and she guessed he suspected some kind of confidence trick. There had been several occasions previously when people had come to him claiming they knew Mary and asking for her address. So for Boswell to have brought this man to her door, there had to be some kind of credence to his story.

Mary invited them into the parlour and once they were sitting down, she looked hard at the man. 'So you are from Fowey, Mr Castel?' she said. 'I don't know any family of that name.'

'I left many years ago, when you would have been just a little girl,' he said calmly. 'But I know your sister Dolly very well.'

Mary gasped, despite herself. 'You know Dolly? How? Where is she?'

'I have only known her since she came to London,' he said, mopping perspiration from his face with a handkerchief. 'She is in service for Mrs Morgan of Bedford Square. I met her there when I was replacing some glass, and we got to talking about Fowey.'

'Dolly's here in London!' Mary could hardly believe what she was hearing, and even though Boswell was giving her a warning look as if he didn't want her to get too excited, she couldn't help but be.

'It seems Mr Castel wants your permission to write to your family in Fowey and inform them about you,' Boswell butted in, with a very cynical tone in his voice. 'He claims he also knows a relative of yours there, Edward Puckey.'

'Ned!' Again Mary gasped. She and Dolly had been bridesmaids at her cousin Ned's wedding.

'You have a relative called Edward Puckey?' Boswell asked.

Mary nodded. 'My cousin,' she said.

Mr Castel looked at Mary and his frown indicated that he felt aggrieved. 'It seems Mr Boswell doesn't trust me. I knew Ned Puckey when I was a lad, though he's a few years younger than me. It was through that connection that I got to know Dolly so well. All I want now is to see two sisters reunited and pass on news that could be advantageous to you.'

Setting aside Mr Castel's clothing and the ill-fitting wig, which did suggest questionable taste, Mary thought he had an honest face. He looked directly at her, he wasn't licking his lips or fidgeting nervously. He had also retained his Cornish accent.

'What news?' she asked suspiciously, and glanced at Boswell. He was tense, sweating profusely, and his frown suggested he wished to silence this man.

'That your family have come into a fortune.'

Mary laughed out loud and rocked back in her chair. 'I can't believe that, even if I wish to believe you know Dolly,' she said.

'It's true,' he insisted. 'Dolly told me. Your uncle, Peter Broad, died while you were in Botany Bay, and he left a fortune to your family.'

Mary stopped laughing suddenly. Her uncle Peter, her father's brother, was a master mariner, which meant he was hired to take control of a ship, unlike her father who was just an ordinary seaman. She had not known Uncle Peter very well as he was away at sea for very long periods. But whenever he came home she remembered that he always came visiting with presents of food, sweetmeats and other luxuries. It had been Uncle Peter who brought the pink silky material her mother had used to make the dresses she and Dolly wore the day they went swimming naked. It was always said around Fowey that he was rich too, in fact whenever her mother spoke of wanting something out of the ordinary, her father had always said jokingly, 'You'd better bide a while, my dear, until Peter comes home.'

'I don't know what to say,' Mary exclaimed. 'This has come as a shock, Mr Castel.'

'I'm sure it has,' he said. 'But believe me, there is no mischief in my desire to impart this news to you, only to try and bring a family together. You see, Dolly and I are friends. We met some four years ago and she told me she had a sister who had gone off to work in Plymouth and hadn't been seen since. She said her parents still fretted about you, not knowing whether you were alive or dead.'

'They didn't know what happened to me?' Mary wasn't sure whether this pleased or saddened her.

Mr Castel shook his head. 'According to what Dolly told me, your father went looking for you in Plymouth, but without success. Dolly had the idea you'd come to London, and that was mainly why she took a position here, hoping she'd run into you one day. But as the years passed that hope faded. I saw how important you were to her, that first day I met her. The moment she heard my voice and knew I was from Cornwall, she went out of her way to talk to me.'

Mary nodded. That sounded logical to her. For if she met someone with a Cornish accent she knew she'd immediately want to talk to them. 'Did you know then where I was?'

Castel shook his head. 'Indeed not. With a girl like Dolly you wouldn't ever think she could have a sister that might have been transported.'

'Why?' Mary asked.

'Well, she's so . . .' He stopped, clearly unable to find the right words.

'Honest?' Mary decided to help him out. 'You didn't think she could have a sister who was a thief?'

Castel looked embarrassed. 'I didn't mean that,' he said hurriedly. 'Dolly's timid and industrious. I imagined her sister was just like her.'

Mary was sure now that this man knew Dolly. 'Timid and industrious' was a good description of her. Mary had often described her to people as a mouse!

'So why has it taken you so long to come forward?' Mary asked. It was some fourteen months since the news of her arrival in Newgate had been in the newspapers. The pardon, when there had been more news, was over three months ago.

'You can call me slow if you like,' he said, and looked sheepish. 'Because I read all about "the girl from Botany Bay" in the newspapers, even noticed your name was the same as Dolly's sister. But I didn't think for one minute it could be the right Mary Broad.'

'You didn't?' Mary said in some surprise.

He fingered his stiff collar nervously. 'It was too extra-ordinary. No one knowing Dolly would think her sister could be that daring. Besides, Mary Broad is a common enough name and the paper I read didn't say you were from Cornwall.'

'So what finally made you think I might be her sister?' Mary asked curiously.

'A poem,' he said. He looked at Boswell as if hoping for some support, but Boswell didn't offer any.

'A poem?' Mary said. She guessed he meant one of those that Boswell had mentioned, though he'd never read one of them to her.

'They've been sticking them up all over the place since your pardon,' he said awkwardly. 'But I never really read one properly till they put one up by my shop. I can't explain why exactly, but I got this feeling about it which wouldn't go away. I didn't want to show it to Dolly, in case she got upset that her sister might have been transported. Or that the poem suggested you were more than friends with Mr Boswell. So I went round to his house this morning to ask his opinion.'

Mary looked at Boswell questioningly.

'The first thing he asked me was if you were from Fowey,' Boswell said with a despairing kind of shrug. 'I agreed you were, and then he told me of Dolly. I wanted to come alone to see you, but Mr Castel is a persistent man, my dear. Now, my suggestion is that I check out his story, and return to you when I have proof.'

Later that same day, Mary was helping Mrs Wilkes wash the supper things when someone knocked on the front door again. 'I'll wager that's Boswell again,' she said with a worried look. 'Maybe he's found out more about Castel.'

Mary had been anxious all day. She wanted to believe Mr Castel, but as Boswell had seemed so suspicious about his claims, she had tried very hard not to build up her hopes.

She hurried down the hall, removing her apron as she went, but as she opened the door, her knees went weak.

There was Mr Castel again, and by his side was Dolly.

There was no mistaking her sister, she looked just the same as she had nine years ago, when she stood waving goodbye to Mary as she took the boat to Plymouth. She had kept the image of that small upturned nose, and those blue eyes locked inside her all these years. All Mary could do was gasp and cover her face with her hands.

'Mary!' Dolly said softly. 'It really is you! I was so afraid Mr Castel was mistaken.'

All at once Mary was enveloped in her older sister's arms, and they stood on the doorstep rocking each other, both sobbing out all the years of separation.

'Now, will you please come inside?' Mrs Wilkes said firmly from behind them. 'This is all very heart-warming, but I don't wish it to be the talk of the street.'

Once in the parlour, the two women could only hug each other and cry for some minutes. Then they began to laugh hysterically through their tears. Everything was jumbled, half questions only half answered, a nonsensical struggle to bridge the gap of nine years.

Mr Castel had explained to Dolly some of what had happened to Mary, but his version, which had come from newspapers, wasn't accurate. Although Mary tried to give her sister the truth of it, Dolly was clearly too shocked and bewildered to take it all in.

'I look so much older than you now,' Mary said at one point, gazing at her sister with pride.

They had always been alike in as much as they both had dark curly hair like their mother's and the same sturdy build, and were a little taller than most other girls in the village. But Dolly's eyes were blue, not grey like Mary's, and then of course there was Dolly's more pronounced upturned nose.

The differences were in their characters. Dolly had always been the meek, practical, obedient one. For as far back as Mary could remember, she had always looked neat and tidy, her hair braided tightly back off her face, her pinafore spotless. She skirted round mud, avoided brambles, and would sit quietly on the doorstep watching as Mary played rough games with boys and tore and muddied her clothes.

Dolly was still dressed in a sober and neat manner, as befitted her position as a lady's maid. Her blue pin-tucked dress had a high neck with tiny pearl buttons and she wore well-polished black button boots and a small straw hat with just a plain blue ribbon round it. Mary knew her to be thirty, but she looked closer to twenty, her complexion clear and unlined.

'I haven't had the hard times like you,' Dolly said, her eyes awash with tears. 'You are so thin, Mary, I remembered your face being plump and bonny.'

With Mr Castel and Mrs Wilkes looking on, it was impossible for the sisters to talk frankly. Dolly started to ask about the two children, but stopped half-way through. Likewise, Mary wanted to ask so much about her mother and father, and whether Dolly had a sweetheart, but she couldn't in front of Mrs Wilkes and Castel.

Then, in the midst of it, Boswell came back.

Mrs Wilkes opened the door to him, and Mary heard her telling him that Dolly was already here. 'Oh, it's wonderful,' she gushed. 'They've been crying and laughing fit to bust.'

Boswell looked petulant when he came into the room. He had asked Castel this morning to let him arrange the meeting between Mary and Dolly. An hour ago he had gone to Bedford Square to see Dolly, only to find that Castel had already been there, and had brought the young woman here. But faced with Mary's joy, he recovered his natural good humour and apologized to Castel for doubting him. He then turned his considerable charm on Dolly, flattering her with compliments and saying that if he had appeared obstructive it was only because he had to protect Mary.

Mrs Wilkes opened a bottle of port wine to celebrate, and suggested that maybe it would be wise for the two men to leave Mary and Dolly to talk.

'But I promised Mrs Morgan I would escort Dolly home,' Castel said quickly, and from the adoring way he looked at her, it was obvious to everyone that he was sweet on her.

'I can't stay much longer anyway, I'm afraid,' Dolly said, turning to Mary. 'Mrs Morgan expects me home by half past nine. But I can spend my day off on Wednesday with you.'

'Well, perhaps, Dolly, before you have to go, you'd like to tell Mary about the inheritance from your uncle?' Boswell suggested. 'It's impertinent of me to ask, but I think it's something Mary would like cleared up.'

'It's quite true,' Dolly said, clutching at Mary's hand as if afraid that if she let go her younger sister would disappear again. 'Uncle Peter did leave all his money to Father. A considerable sum too. Father got Ned to write to me, explaining it all and urging me to come home as there was no longer a need for me to work.'

'So why didn't you go, Dolly?' Boswell asked. He couldn't quite bring himself to ask crassly how much money there was, especially in front of Castel.

She blushed. 'I like London,' she said, 'and my position. I'm very happy with the Morgans. I didn't want to be an old maid in Fowey.'

'I doubt if you would remain unmarried for long,' Boswell said gallantly.

'Mary would understand,' Dolly said, looking to her sister for support.

'Do you, Mary?' Boswell asked.

'I do,' she said, giving her sister a wry smile. 'All the years I've been away I've always imagined you married with a parcel of children. That was what you wanted as a young girl. But whatever the reason you left, you've made a good life for yourself. To go back would be like burying yourself alive.'

'That's just how it would be,' Dolly agreed earnestly. 'I couldn't change my station in life just because Father had money. We might live in a bigger house, have better clothes and food. But who would I have as friends? My old ones are poor. They would avoid me. The rich people would turn their noses up at me.'

Mary nodded in sympathy. She thought this was very likely. But there was also the question of fortune hunters. Dolly would want a man to love her for herself, not for her money. Mary guessed it could be quite difficult to be certain of a man's real feelings until well after the wedding.

'You don't ever intend to go back?' Boswell asked Dolly. He wondered if there was already a man in her life. Castel clearly had designs on her, but Boswell didn't think the attraction was mutual.

'Maybe in a few years,' she said, then looking at Mary she smiled. 'But I think Mary should go. At least to see our folks. They will be so overjoyed to know she is safe and well.'

Mary asked if she was sure their parents didn't know about what had happened to her.

'They certainly didn't when I heard from Father last year. You see, he mentioned you, and said he hoped it was a husband and children which had prevented you returning from Plymouth.'

Mary thought on this for a moment. It seemed almost laughable that her parents had imagined her just forty miles away in Plymouth, when in fact she had been right round the world. If she were to go home, how on earth was she ever going to be able to explain everything she'd done and seen? It was hard enough to deal with her memories, the contrasts, and the sheer distances she'd covered in her life, herself. She didn't think her mother, who'd never been further than twenty miles from Fowey, could possibly grasp it.

'Might Father have discovered about me since the letter he sent you?' she asked.

'Maybe,' Dolly said with a frown. 'Mr Castel told me there was much about you in the newspapers. But if I didn't hear about it, here in London, why should they, so far away?'

Mary sighed. 'Perhaps it's better that they never know about me, Dolly. It's too shocking.'

'Better to be a little shocked than to go through life

believing their daughter deserted them or is dead,' Dolly insisted.

Boswell left with Castel and Dolly later, and the two sisters arranged that Dolly would come again on her day off. After they'd gone Mary went off to her room, for she very much wanted to be alone.

She sat by the open window, looking out into the darkness. Sounds of carriage wheels, chatter, laughter, babies crying, and the tinkle of a distant piano wafted up to her on the still, warm air as it had on many an evening since she'd been with Mrs Wilkes. It was the sound of family life going on all around her, and until tonight she had always felt terribly alone when she heard it because fate had estranged her from her own.

Sometimes she had even had cynical thoughts about her freedom. She had thought that although she could walk around the town, she was still shackled mentally by guilt, shame and grief. She knew too that she was utterly dependent on Boswell, and that made him another gaoler of sorts. A kindly one, of course, but he decided everything, where she would go, who she would meet, and provided for her too. Until now she hadn't been able to see any way that she could step out of that dependency and into a life that was truly her own.

That chance had come now.

'But are you brave enough to go home?' she murmured to herself. It was one thing to tell it all to Dolly, she was still young, without any hard-held prejudices. Her father would probably be as understanding too, for he had sailed to many different countries, met men from all walks of life.

But her mother was a different story. Her world was a tiny one, bound by the church and her neighbours. Would she be able to open her mind wide enough to accept that Mary had received far more punishment for her original crime than it warranted? Could she forgive and remain resolute in the face of village gossip?

Mary doubted it. Grace Broad had never been a forgiving or tolerant person. As a child Mary had been considered odd because she liked to hang around the fishermen, went swimming, climbed trees and wandered away from home. Her father had laughed and said she ought to have been a boy, but her mother's face had always been dark with disapproval.

Yet Mary could understand why that was now. Becoming a mother herself had made sense of many things which once seemed so odd. A mother's role was to nurture and protect, showing praise and disapproval were merely ways of guiding a child to keep them safe. She had no doubt now that her mother had been frightened by her daughter's wilfulness. Maybe she always feared it would get Mary into serious trouble. And she was right of course.

Mary also doubted that the gossips in Fowey would see heroism in the daring escape, as people in London did. They would brood on the aspects of prison hulks, chains and the shadow of the gallows, whisper that she'd spent much of her time with a gang of men, and that would be interpreted as her being a wanton woman.

A tear trickled down Mary's cheek. She knew she'd been foolhardy and selfish as a young girl, but all that was gone now, and she so wanted to be taken back into her family. She had never been able to speak to anyone about the agony of losing her two children, but perhaps if her mother enfolded her in her arms, she'd be able to tell her. She wanted to tell the whole family the place they had in her heart throughout her imprisonment. Perhaps as an adult she could make amends for all the sadness and worry she'd brought them.

Mary also felt that she needed the familiar peace and loveliness of her own village to cleanse her soul of the ugliness trapped within it. She may have had forgiveness from the King and the government, but that meant little without the forgiveness of her own people.

During the next few days Mary's thoughts became even more confused. The day spent alone with Dolly was one of the best in her whole life, as they talked through everything that had happened to them both in the last nine years.

Dolly had always been held up to Mary as a paragon of feminine virtue. Her skill with the needle, the care she took in cleaning and laundry, her ability to cook tasty meals from almost nothing, and of course her lack of insolence and her sweet nature had all served to make her seem dull company in the youthful Mary's eyes. Yet nine years on, Mary found her older sister had a far more lively mind than she had supposed.

Dolly had used her position as lady's maid to become

acquainted with all aspects of the gentry's way of life. There was little she didn't know, from how to dress a fashionable woman's hair to the running of a large household. But she had picked up a great deal more than domestic skills from her master and mistress. She knew their secrets, their views on everything from religion to politics. Through them she had become educated, and she was no longer an innocent country girl. She might still be timid, in as much as she wouldn't speak out of turn or go out alone at night, but she had had two lovers.

She confided in Mary that one was a younger brother of her master, and it had made her realize that an intelligent woman could control her own destiny. She said she had no intention of marrying a humble footman or even a tradesman like Mr Castel and spending the rest of her life bringing up children in reduced circumstances. She said that if she didn't find a gentleman as a husband within the next few years, she intended to start up her own business, perhaps a bureau for domestic staff.

Dolly said that her father wouldn't reveal the size of the bequest for security reasons. In the letter he'd had written for him, all he would say was that it was enough to live on very comfortably and that if she required a 'nest egg' to advance her own position, she had only to ask.

As Mary listened to Dolly, she had no doubt that her sister could start her own business. Beneath her sweet, calm exterior there was a great deal of determination and good sense. So when Dolly insisted that Mary should go home to Cornwall, she was inclined to believe she was right.

Dolly had foresight and imagination. She said that with just a little capital, Mary could run a boarding-house down in Cornwall. She suggested Truro as many people passed through there, or even Falmouth where she could cater for ships' officers and their families. Another idea was that their parents might be persuaded to buy a small farm, and Mary could grow produce to sell.

'I might even join you in it if London begins to pall for me,' Dolly laughed. 'What you've got to keep in mind, Mary, is that you aren't an ordinary woman, you are brave, strong and sharp-witted. That's more than enough to succeed. If you stay in London, the only positions open to you will be lowly ones, like kitchen maid. You'll hate it. You can't kow-tow to a grumpy cook or a snooty mistress, you've seen too much for that. Be brave once more and go home.'

September came in with glorious weather, and whenever Dolly could get away from her mistress for a few hours, she spent them with Mary. The shared laughter, the pleasure of discovering how much they had in common, eased Mary's grief for her children, and she felt her old optimism and strength returning.

Mr Castel, with Boswell's help, had written to Ned Puckey to ask him to pass on the news of Mary to the Broads. Boswell had written to his friend the Reverend John Baron of Lostwithiel, seeking his help too in making sure Grace and William Broad were willing to receive Mary home.

Yet long before either the Puckeys or the Reverend Baron could have received these letters, one arrived at

Boswell's home from Elizabeth Puckey, Ned's wife. It seemed her family had only heard about Mary when she was pardoned. At that time the story about her transportation and subsequent escape was in a Cornish newspaper. Now they were very anxious to know how and where she was. Elizabeth urged that Mary should come home to her family, who as she put it *'were now in very different circumstances, due to a sizeable inheritance'*. She said Mary would have the warmest of welcomes from all members of the family and that William and Grace Broad were very relieved and happy to know their younger daughter had survived her terrible troubles.

While that letter assured Mary of her family's affection for her, and made her wholeheartedly wish to see them, she was still torn. She liked London, she wanted to stay close to Dolly, Boswell was such a good friend and such stimulating company, and then there was Mrs Wilkes too, of whom she'd grown very fond.

Boswell showed her a life which didn't exist in Cornwall. He took her to the theatre, coffee houses and restaurants. With Dolly she could recapture her girlhood, discuss men, clothes and the many differences in their lives now to the one they were born to.

Mrs Wilkes was a mother–aunt figure. She was wise and kind, knowledgeable and refined too. Mary sensed she wanted her to stay with her, and help her run her boarding-house. This was very appealing to Mary, for she felt safe there, but as Dolly pointed out, she would have to do the rough work, emptying slop pails, carrying hot water, doing laundry and scrubbing floors. Dolly said she should aspire to more than that.

Then there were the men still in Newgate. Mary didn't feel able to leave London while they remained in prison. Soon after she met up with Dolly again, despite advice from both Boswell and Mrs Wilkes, she went to visit them. After living in such comfortable surroundings, she was horrified and appalled by Newgate, and it seemed impossible that she could have borne those terrible conditions for the best part of a year. Whilst she knew Boswell was still battling for her friends, there was no pardon in sight yet.

Sam was so demoralized that he'd applied to enlist in the New South Wales Corps, a body of men who were to take over the role of the Marines and police the new colony. His reason for this change of heart was that he'd come to see England had nothing to offer men like him, and out in New South Wales as a free man he would be given a grant of land.

James was still working on his memoirs. He said Nat and Bill had a different idea every day for what they were going to do when they became free. Mary was terribly afraid that day would never come, but the men insisted it would, that they were happy enough, and that she must get on with her own life and not be held back by thoughts of them.

It was Sam who managed to convince her that she must separate her life from theirs. He walked her to the gates alone and talked to her.

'We will be pardoned,' he insisted. 'But you must not wait for that, Mary. Us four won't stay together when we are released, we've been held together this long by circumstance, not by choice. I want to go back to New South Wales, James talks of Ireland. Bill will go to Berkshire and Nat back home to Essex. We have shared the biggest adventure and the hardest times imaginable, but once free that will be just a memory, nothing more.'

Mary knew he was telling her that they'd only become so close because of adversity, and that was the only thing they had in common. She guessed too that he wanted to distance himself from the others because he was afraid they could become a liability. Deep down inside her she shared that fear, though she wouldn't have voiced it.

'You saved my life on the wharf in Port Jackson,' he said, his voice growing thick with emotion. 'I hope one day I'll be telling my children about you. But go now, and don't come back to visit again. You've done enough for all of us.'

Mary cupped her two hands round his bony face and kissed his lips lightly. 'Good luck, Sam,' she said tenderly, remembering how she'd once seen him as her safety net. She knew now that she didn't need one.

Towards the end of September the glorious weather ended suddenly with a huge storm, uprooting trees in the parks and flooding the streets. It continued to rain even after the gales had abated, and all at once Mary saw for herself the conditions Boswell had described on her release from Newgate.

The streets were treacherous, cloying mud mixed with human and animal refuse, showering anyone rash enough to attempt walking anywhere. Fever sprang up in the poorest districts and Boswell told Mary that the pits where the dead were taken for mass burial were filling rapidly. An evil stench hung in the air constantly, along with a sulphurous fog that swept in each night.

Mary was virtually imprisoned in the house in Little Titchfield Street, and it came to her that unless she left for Cornwall soon, before winter set in, she would be here till the spring. Her parents were getting old, and she would never forgive herself if something happened to either of them before she got there. And then there was the call of Cornwall itself, a siren that sang its beguiling song each night when she closed her eyes, urging her to return to where she belonged.

She would imagine herself standing in the bows of a ship coming into Fowey harbour just as daylight was fading and the autumn sun like a huge fiery ball sinking slowly into the sea.

She could see the small town rising up the hill from the quay. Grey stone cottages clustered together, with glimpses of the cobbled streets between them, where children were hurrying home before dark.

Down on the quay the fishermen would be getting ready for the night's fishing. The landlord of the tavern would be lighting his lamps, and the old men of the town would be hobbling slowly down towards it, raising their caps to any women who might still be abroad.

Mary could almost smell pilchards cooking, she could

hear the slap of the waves against the quayside, the shriek of the seagulls and the wind in the trees above the town. She wanted to fill her lungs with that clean, salty air, to hear those Cornish voices, and submerge herself in the simplicity of village life. She didn't belong in London.

'I think I must get a passage back to Cornwall,' Mary said to Boswell one evening when he'd called to see her.

He didn't say anything for a while, just sat looking quizzically at her. 'Yes, you should,' he said eventually. 'But I don't want you to go.'

'Why?' she asked, thinking perhaps he thought she would have a brighter future in London.

'Because I'll miss you,' he said simply, and to her utmost surprise she saw he had tears in his eyes.

Mary didn't know what to say. Was he implying he was in love with her? If so, what was she supposed to say or do?

'You won't miss me. You can go and visit all those grand friends you've neglected for so long,' she said flippantly.

'I've neglected them because they are all shallow compared to you,' he said, his voice quivering. 'You have given me a purpose in my life, opened up so many new vistas.'

'That is a lovely thing to say,' she said, a little overwhelmed. 'But I have even more to thank you for. You gave me back my life.'

He shook his head a little, looking down at his lap. 'I've been something of a fool for most of mine,' he said in a small voice. 'But I feel honoured that Fate singled me out to help you. Mary, you are the most astounding person I have ever encountered. You have taken what life threw at you with courage and fortitude. I have never heard you utter a word of blame against anyone.'

'There *is* no one to blame,' she said tartly. 'Only me for doing wrong.'

He began to laugh. 'Oh, Mary,' he spluttered, 'that is the absolute essence of you. If the whole world was to share your attitude, it would be a far better place. All my life I have been surrounded by those who seek to blame someone for their misfortune. I too have blamed my father, my mother, my dear departed wife, whores, drink, lack of money and even food for my failings. I wish I were a younger man and could start out on the road through life with you at my side.'

He ran his fingers over her hair affectionately, then, picking up a curl, he took a pair of scissors from Mrs Wilkes's sewing basket on the table beside him and snipped it off.

'A little memento,' he said, tucking it into a small purse he took from his pocket.

'I'll keep all my special memories of you in here,' Mary said, putting her hand over her heart. 'And make sure you get my friends pardoned or I will blame you.'

'It will come soon,' he assured her. 'Henry Dundas has it in hand.'

On the evening of 12 October Mary and Boswell were at Beals Wharf in Southwark where Mary was to board the

Anne and Elizabeth, due to sail to Fowey on the early morning tide.

It was a windy, wet night, and they hurried into a tavern nearby for shelter. When Boswell had called to collect Mary and her box of belongings from Little Titchfield Street, he had brought James, his fifteen-year-old son, to meet her.

Young James Boswell had the same beautiful dark eyes and full lips as his father, but he was taller, slender, graceful and clear-skinned. He was understandably shy, but eager to meet her. He said his father had told him and his sisters her whole story, and that they all wished her well for the future.

James arranged to meet up with his father later that evening, and as the cab rattled along the wet, windy streets towards the Thames, Mary was silent, her mind whirling with misgivings. She wasn't so sure now about returning to Cornwall, and especially about leaving Boswell, her dear friend and saviour. She glanced at him many times during the journey, sorrow welling up unbearably within her. She knew he wasn't in the best of health. His high colour and the stiffness of his limbs suggested to her that infirmity was catching up with him.

She would see Dolly again, maybe Mrs Wilkes too. But she had a feeling that the few remaining hours before she had to board the boat would be her last with Boswell.

In the tavern, Mary removed the heavy dark green wool cloak Mrs Wilkes had given her. She felt almost as indebted to the kind-hearted woman as she was to Boswell, for she had taught Mary so much. No one in this waterside tavern would take her for a whore or a felon. Everything, from the cloak and bonnet to the warm woollen dress and sturdy boots gave a picture of a genteel governess. Yet Mrs Wilkes had not only chosen the clothes because they were warm and serviceable, but because they made her look attractive too. There was a ruffle of cream lace on the high-necked dress, more lace on her petticoat, and her stockings were a fashionable red. Mary had many more clothes in her box too, and she found it hard to equate the pretty woman she saw reflected in a looking-glass, with the same poor wretch who had once worn rags and fetters.

As they drank rum, sitting side by side on a settle by the roaring fire, a tender current flowed between them. Mary wished she could find the right words to tell Boswell how she felt about him. Boswell, unusually silent, kept his hand covering hers on the settle, a gesture that showed he wanted to hold on to her for as long as he could.

The place reminded Mary of the taverns in Fowey and Plymouth, the flag-stone floor wet from men's boots, the air thick with smoke, the smell of wet clothes overpowering. Yet it was snug, a friendly place where sailors swapped stories, found a willing woman and drank their hard-earned money away. To Mary it was fitting that they should spend their last hours somewhere she found so familiar. The following day Boswell would be back where he belonged, dining in elegant places, drinking coffee with his illustrious friends or sitting at his desk writing again, while her boat battled its way through heavy seas to Cornwall.

'I have arranged with the Reverend John Baron in

Lostwithiel to give you an annuity of ten pounds a year,' Boswell blurted out suddenly. He took a five-pound note from his pocketbook and pressed it into her hand. 'This is for the first half year, and you must go to him next April for the next half, and sign your name as I taught you.'

'But Bozzie,' she exclaimed in consternation, 'why? I won't need it, and I know you aren't a rich man.'

Even though Boswell was wealthy in comparison to ordinary working people, Mary had discovered he had spent most of his life lurching from one financial crisis to another. Again and again he had come very close to ruin. It was only luck and good friends that had saved him from it.

'It will give you some security,' he said. He didn't add that it was in case things didn't work out for her in Fowey. Perhaps he was reluctant to point out that was a possibility, but Mary knew that was what he meant.

She thanked him, the lump in her throat making it impossible to say more. She put the bank note into the little reticule Mrs Wilkes had embroidered for her as a leaving present, and drew out a small package tied with a red ribbon.

'This is a keepsake from me,' she said softly, pressing it into his hands. 'It isn't of any value, but it was the only thing which comforted me during the bad times in Port Jackson.'

Boswell looked curiously at her, noting the tears in her eyes, and then opened the package carefully. All it contained was a few dried crumbling leaves.

'That was what we called "sweet tea",' she explained.

'I picked the leaves on my last day there before our escape. I kept those last few back throughout the voyage, through Kupang and Batavia, right home to England and Newgate. I wish I was able to give you a gold watch with your name engraved on the back, but these mean more, however humble. Look at them now and then and remember me.'

Boswell retied the package and put it into his pocket. 'I will keep them forever,' he said, his voice quavering. 'But I do not need them to remember you, Mary, you have a very special place in my heart.'

He picked up her hands and held them to his lips, his dark luminous eyes scanning her face as if imprinting it on his mind.

'I have vowed love to so many women in the past that I hesitate to do so again for fear of trivializing what I feel for you, my dear,' he said. 'But true friendship, the purest kind, is sprung from love. It never dies, never tarnishes. It remains even after death.'

Suddenly a loud cheer interrupted the tender moment and both Mary and Boswell looked up to see the men in the bar greeting another two coming in. One was a small, wiry man of about forty-five, the other tall, fair-haired and perhaps ten years younger.

'The older man is the master of the *Anne and Elizabeth*, by the name of Job Moyes,' Boswell said. 'I met him when I booked your passage. The other is his first mate. I shall invite them over for a bowl of punch. We mustn't spend our remaining time together in sadness.'

*

Job Moyes and his first mate, John Trelawney, greeted Boswell and Mary with great warmth, and it was clear they knew all about her.

'It will be a pleasure to have you aboard, Miss Broad,' Job said, his blue eyes twinkling. 'We know we'll be able to call on your sailing skills if we run into heavy weather.'

John Trelawney looked at Mary with frank admiration. 'You are a great deal smaller and prettier than I expected,' he said. 'I hope you'll tell me of your adventures during our voyage.'

Mary felt a warm glow from his compliment. He was a striking-looking man, with amber-coloured eyes that reminded her of a cat's, high cheek-bones, very white teeth and thick blond hair tied back at the nape of his neck. His voice was easy on the ear too, deep and resonant, with just enough of a Cornish accent to remind her of home.

The bowl of punch arrived at the table, and Boswell raised a toast to Mary's future. As he asked Moyes some questions about his cargo, John was looking at Mary in a way that made her heart flutter.

She had fully believed she was incapable of feeling romantically attracted to any man again, and it seemed preposterous that she should feel it now on the eve of her departure from London.

'What part of Cornwall are you from?' she asked.

'Falmouth,' he said, and smiled, showing his beautiful teeth. 'But I've no one there now, my parents passed on a few years back and my brother has gone to America.'

'So where do you call home?' she asked.

'The *Anne and Elizabeth*,' he chuckled. 'But if I was to settle down in one place, Fowey is where I'd choose.'

'No wife or sweetheart then?' She raised one eyebrow questioningly.

He shook his head. 'I never met a woman who was prepared to accept that the sea was my mistress.'

That phrase jolted something long buried within Mary. She looked at him curiously.

'I stole that line from your uncle,' John said. 'Peter Broad. I sailed under him when I was a lad. He was a good man and taught me all I know.'

Mary gasped. 'You sailed under my uncle?'

John nodded. 'And your father too, Mary. He is another good man, and I'm proud to be taking you home to him.'

'What's that?' Boswell asked, picking up the tail-end of the conversation.

'Just telling Mary I sailed under both her uncle and father, sir,' John said. 'But then you know that.'

'Bozzie,' Mary said reprovingly, 'is that why you were so adamant I had to go on this boat?'

His smile was a mischievous one. 'Would I entrust such a precious cargo to just anyone?' he asked. 'I spoke to several ships' masters before I found Job. I wanted one you would feel at ease with.'

They filled their glasses again and Boswell made the men laugh with a very funny account of what he called 'his Cornish jaunt' the previous year.

Mary was happy just to watch and listen. It was good to see the way Boswell sparkled as he told a tale. He had a gift of being able to describe a scene and the people there so well that the listener entered into it too. She was going to miss him, but her trepidation about going home was gone now. Cornwall was where she belonged.

It was after ten when they finally left the tavern to walk to the boat. John carried Mary's box, walking a little ahead with Moyes, while Mary followed, holding Boswell's arm.

'Leave me here,' she said to him as they got to the boat. 'Don't come aboard, you must go back to meet up with James as you promised.'

The wind had blown itself out and the rain had stopped. For once there was no fog, and the moon and stars were clear and bright, making twinkling lights in the inky river. The sound of water slapping gently against the hull reminded her poignantly of that other desperate voyage, something she hadn't thought of for a very long time.

'Will you be all right?' Boswell asked her, his customary confidence deserting him.

'Of course I will,' she said, kissing him on the cheek. 'The sea holds no terrors for me.'

Boswell caught her by the forearms fiercely, his face suddenly more youthful in the blaze of a lighted torch by the boat. 'If ever you need me, send a message,' he said.

She nodded. 'You take care of yourself, Bozzie,' she said. 'And say goodbye to James, Bill, Nat and Sam. Tell them I'm sorry I couldn't be there to celebrate their freedom.'

Mary heard Moyes or John cough and knew they were waiting for her to go aboard. 'Goodbye, my dear friend,' she said, kissing him again, this time on the lips. 'I shall never forget you. You gave me back my life.'

She left him quickly, not trusting herself not to cry. As she reached the deck she turned and waved just once. He was just standing looking up at her, the silver buttons on his coat and his gold watch-chain glistening in the light from the torch. He raised his three-cornered hat and bowed majestically, then turned and walked away.

'Will you miss London?' John said at her elbow.

Mary turned to look at him and smiled. She had a feeling that his real question was would she miss grand people like Boswell, not the city itself.

'No, I don't think so,' she said truthfully. 'I'm glad I've seen it, but I prefer a simple life, and people I can be myself with.'

Suddenly, she had the oddest feeling of having been here before. Puzzled, she looked around her, but in the darkness she could see little but the gleam of brass and the whiteness of coiled rope.

'What's the matter?' John asked. 'Don't tell me a born sailor like you is disturbed by the movement beneath your feet?'

'No, of course not,' she said, then laughed because John's Cornish burr was enough to jog her memory. The smell of river water, and a man who attracted her, completed the picture from the past.

She was on the deck of the *Dunkirk*, a girl in rags and chains, setting her heart on an officer with a faint Cornish accent.

'Let me show you to your cabin,' John said. 'You'll get cold up here.'

All at once Mary felt completely liberated, far more so

than when she was released from Newgate. She was going to a cabin, not the hold. Tomorrow at dawn they would set sail, she would eat meals with Moyes, John and the other seamen. And she could use a spoon if she wanted to, because no one here would mind. They would drink rum and swap sailing stories, and she would be the men's equal.

She began to laugh as she climbed down the steep steps to the cabins.

John stood at the bottom with her box in his arms and laughed too. 'Are you that happy to be aboard?' he asked, tawny eyes twinkling. 'I'm very happy about it. But we expected you'd have had enough of ships to last a lifetime.'

'I thought I had too,' Mary replied, with laughter still in her voice. 'But this one feels like I'm already home.'

Postscript

I confess that I never looked at these people without pity and astonishment. They had miscarried in a heroic struggle for liberty; after having combated every hardship and conquered every difficulty.

The woman had gone out to Port Jackson in the ship which transported me thither and was distinguished for her good behaviour. I could not but reflect with admiration at the strange combination of circumstances which had brought us together again, to baffle human foresight and confound human speculation.

An extract from Watkin Tench's journal, 1792

Afterthoughts

It was hard for me to leave Mary on the deck of the *Anne and Elizabeth*. I had become so attached to her that I would have loved to have written an entirely fictional account of her falling in love with John Trelawney on the voyage home. I would also have loved to have taken you to view the joyful reunion with her parents in Fowey, and later to go on to a romantic wedding for her and John, then the birth of a couple of healthy, bonny babies.

But Mary's story is a true one, and though I have added my own imagination to her personality, her friends and the many hardships she endured so bravely, I have stayed within the historical facts about her and the other main characters who played major roles. Therefore it would be wrong to misrepresent her life after leaving London.

Sadly, nothing is known of what happened to Mary after returning home to Fowey. We know she did collect her annuity from the Reverend John Baron, and this gentleman also wrote to James Boswell on Mary's behalf to thank him for his kindness, and recorded that she was behaving herself. But there are no records of marriages, births or even deaths that set her firmly in Fowey.

But I think such an intelligent and daring woman would

not have wanted to stay for ever in a place where she was gossiped about. If James Boswell's account of her family's legacy was true, and there is no reason to doubt it, I think she would have moved away, maybe even overseas.

I do believe too that a woman who was liked and admired by all the men close to her would have married again. I certainly hope she found a good man, and had other children.

James Martin, Sam Broome (who was also known as Butcher), Bill Allen and Nat Lilly finally got their pardon in November, soon after Mary left London. They went straight from Newgate to see James Boswell to thank him for his kindness.

Sam did join the New South Wales Corps, and went back to Australia. Nothing is known of the other three. But I like to think that James Martin either returned to Ireland, having made enough profit from his memoirs to breed horses, or went off to America.

As for James Boswell, sadly he died on 17 May 1795. His family cancelled the annuity to Mary, and although he recorded in his diary that he wrote four pages about 'the Girl from Botany Bay', these pages have never been found. But I am sure James rests happily knowing that *The Life of Samuel Johnson* did indeed become known as the very best biography of all time.

Watkin Tench went on to become something of a hero. He was captured in France, and supposedly escaped from the prisoner-of-war camp. He reached the rank of Major-General. I smiled when I discovered he married an Anna Maria Sargent. Sargent was my maiden name, and my father was a Royal Marine. Watkin and Anna Maria had no children of their own, but adopted his sister-in-law's four children when her husband died in the West Indies.

Watkin Tench's journals survived along with those of many other officers who went out to Australia with the First Fleet, and there is no doubt that he was an intelligent, compassionate and fair-minded man.

Mary never divulged who Charlotte's father was, for Lieutenant Spencer Graham was my own invention. Some people think Watkin Tench was responsible, but I doubt that very much, for he would surely have recorded his anguish at seeing Charlotte's burial at sea.

I like to think that the good men on that First Fleet, whether felons, officers or Marines, would be proud and pleased to see what a wonderful country Australia is now.

Who knows, maybe Mary slipped back there under another name and her descendants are still there, as brave and resourceful as she was.

FREE HOTEL
ACCOMMODATION

Enjoy up to three nights' FREE accommodation for two people with over 150 hotels nationwide to choose from. Based on two people sharing & paying for their breakfast & evening meal.

HOW TO CLAIM

Simply cut out the token on the bottom of this page and send it, along with a stamped, self-addressed envelope (SSAE) to Remember Me Free Hotel Offer, MKM House, Manchester, M16 0XX. You will be sent a brochure detailing all the participating hotels and containing your free hotel accommodation voucher within 21 days.

Should you have any queries about how this promotion works, please call our HELPLINE on 0161 877 1113 (lines open Mon – Fri 9am – 5.30pm, calls charged at standard rate.)

FROM THE NO. 1 BESTSELLING AUTHOR

LESLEY PEARSE

Remember Me

FREE HOTEL
ACCOMMODATION

Enjoy up to three nights' FREE accommodation for two people with over 150 hotels nationwide to choose from.

Offer open to UK and ROI residents 18+. Claim by 31.10.04. Offer valid until 31.12.04, Token - cash redemption 0.01p

TERMS AND CONDITIONS:

1. All promotional instructions form part of these terms and conditions.

2. Offer open to UK & ROI residents aged 18+. Tokens must be received by the Closing Date which is 31.10.04.

3. The Promotion address for Tokens is Free Hotel Offer, MKM House, Manchester, M16 OXX.

4. The Free Hotel Accommodation voucher is valid for use until 31.12.04, excluding Bank Holiday weekends, the Christmas and New Year periods and special events (e.g. Valentines Day) unless otherwise specified in the brochure. Other dates may not be available at individual hotels.

5. The voucher entitles two people sharing a twin or double room up to three nights' free accommodation at one of the listed hotels. For each night's stay, one breakfast and one dinner per person will be charged (even if not taken); the room itself is provided free of charge.

6. Offer subject to availability and hotel's individual terms and conditions apply at the duration of your stay. This applies to new bookings only. One voucher per booking. No Group bookings. Not to be used in conjunction with any other voucher or promotion.

7. Voucher holder is responsible for contacting the hotel, stating that the booking is to be made using a MKM free accommodation voucher and confirming the booking in writing. Voucher must be handed in to reception on arrival at the hotel to ensure that the stay is calculated at the special free accommodation offer rate.

8. Prices are per person, per night during high season (unless otherwise stated) and are the minimum spend necessary during this period. Prices may be lower at other times of the year; individual hotels will be able to confirm at time of booking. The hotel management reserve the right to change tariffs without notice.

9. There is no cash alternative to this offer.

10. Original voucher only will be valid.

11. No responsibility can be accepted for tokens which are incomplete, damaged, illegible, lost or delayed in the post or otherwise fail to reach the promotion address given above by the Closing Date.

12. Further terms and conditions of, or any queries regarding this promotion can be obtained by contacting the MKM Marketing & Promotions Ltd Helpline on 0161 877 1113 (lines open Mon-Fri 9am to 5.30 pm, calls charged at standard rate)

13. This promotion is administered by MKM Marketing & Promotions Ltd., MKM House, Warwick Road, Old Trafford, Manchester, M16 OXX on behalf of the Promoter, Penguin Group UK [UK], 80 Strand, London WC2R ORL.